Summer Friends

Books by Holly Chamberlin

LIVING SINGLE

THE SUMMER OF US

BABYLAND

BACK IN THE GAME

THE FRIENDS WE KEEP

TUSCAN HOLIDAY

ONE WEEK IN DECEMBER

THE FAMILY BEACH HOUSE

SUMMER FRIENDS

Published by Kensington Publishing Corporation

Summer Friends

Holly Chamberlin

KENSINGTON BOOKS
www.kensingtonbooks.com

KENSINGTON BOOKS are published by

Kensington Publishing Corp.
119 West 40th Street
New York, NY 10018

All Kensington titles, imprints, and distributed lines are available at special quantity discounts for bulk purchases for sales promotion, premiums, fund-raising, educational, or institutional use.

Special book excerpts or customized printings can also be created to fit specific needs. For details, write or phone the office of the Kensington Special Sales Manager: Kensington Publishing Corp., 119 West 40th Street, New York, NY 10018. Attn. Special Sales Department. Phone: 1-800-221-2647.

Kensington and the K logo Reg. U.S. Pat. & TM Off.

ISBN-13: 978-0-7582-3507-7
ISBN-10: 0-7582-3507-0

First Kensington Trade Paperback Printing: July 2011
10 9 8 7 6 5 4 3 2

Printed in the United States of America

As always, for Stephen.
And this time, also for Ruth.

Acknowledgments

Thanks to John Scognamiglio for his generous supply of patience and support. Thanks also to fellow writer Brenda Buchanan for a much-needed kick start—twice. Welcome to Mitzi. This is in memory of Lucy Sutherland.

It is one of the blessings of old friends that
you can afford to be stupid with them.
—Ralph Waldo Emerson

Prologue

1971

It was late August, the end of summer, at least, the end of summer for nine-year-old Delphine Crandall and almost-nine-year-old Maggie Weldon. Both would be starting the fourth grade in about a week, Delphine at the local public grammar school five miles from her home in Ogunquit, Maine, and Maggie at Blair Academy, a private grammar school in Concord, Massachusetts, where her family lived. It was the end of the summer, but it also felt like the end of the world. It was bad enough having to go back to school, but it was far worse to be parting from each other for what would be a whole ten months. In other words, forever.

The girls were hanging out in the backyard of the Lilac House, the expensive and recently renovated home Maggie's parents had rented for the summer. There was a giant swing set, metal monkey bars, and a slide. Two banana-seated girls' bikes lay on the grass; each had a plastic basket in front and streamers from the ends of the looped handlebars. The new pink bike was Maggie's. The old red bike had once belonged to Delphine's ten-year-old sister, Jackie, but it belonged to her now.

Delphine, who was swinging ever higher, legs pumping furiously, wore a faded red T-shirt that, like her bike, had once belonged to Jackie. Across the front were the words—also now faded—"Red Sox Rule." Her jean shorts had been cut down from full-length jeans that had badly frayed at the knees. Her sneakers, caked in mud from a morning's romp around the edges of the pond in the woods behind her house, had once been white, back when her mother had bought them at a resale shop in Wells. Her hair, which was thick and the brown of glossy chestnuts, hung in a messy braid down her back, fastened near the end by a rubber band that had once held together a bunch of scallions. Her eyes were as dark and luminous as her hair. Her skin was deeply tanned. Since school had let out she had grown an amazing three inches and was now as tall as Jackie, which meant no more hand-me-down pants. Secretly, Delphine hoped she would grow to be really tall someday. But given the fact that both of her parents were well under six feet, she doubted that she would.

Maggie was on the swing next to Delphine. She was too hot to move and was sitting as still as possible. The neck of her pale pink T-shirt was embroidered in darker pink thread. Her white shorts, which she hated but which her mother made her wear, came almost to the knee and, worse, had a crisp pleat right down the middle of each leg. Her sneakers were white, coated only that morning with that liquid paint-like stuff that came in a bottle with a picture of a nurse on the front. The coating was her mother's idea, too. Maggie's hair, which was the color of jonquils, was neatly drawn into a ponytail and held in place by a wooly purple ribbon. Her skin, almost white during the winter, was now a pale gold. Her large, almost navy blue eyes were currently distorted by the thick lenses of a pair of tortoiseshell-framed glasses she had gotten right after school had let out for the summer. She was still embarrassed by them, though her parents and even Mr. and Mrs. Crandall had assured her that she still looked pretty.

Maggie was tall for her age, taller than Delphine, who,

even though she had sprouted, was never going to be a towering Weldon. Maggie's mother bragged about being "model tall" at five feet ten inches, and Maggie's dad was six feet two inches. Peter, her thirteen-year-old brother, was already the tallest kid in his class, though he was terrible at basketball, something Maggie found very funny. She was bad at basketball, too, but it didn't matter for girls to be bad at sports. Not at Maggie's school, at least.

Around her left wrist, each girl wore a macramé bracelet. Earlier in the summer, Dephine's sister had taught them how to make them, and if the bracelets weren't as perfect as the ones Jackie turned out, Maggie and Delphine thought they were beautiful. Delphine's was already dirty and a bit frayed. Maggie's looked as fresh as the day Delphine had given it to her. Still, when it got dirty, which it would, Maggie would not let her mother coat it with that white paint stuff she used on her sneakers. That would be so embarrassing.

"Are you sure these glasses don't make me look like a dork?" Maggie asked for what Delphine thought was the bazillionth time.

Delphine began to slow her swinging. "I'm sure," she said. "Why would I want to be friends with a dork?"

"Ha, ha, very funny. I just hope the kids at school won't laugh at me."

"If anyone laughs at you—which they won't—tell them your best friend in the world will come down from Maine and beat them up." Her feet dragged in the sand below the swing and she came to a stop.

"No!" Maggie looked genuinely shocked. "You wouldn't really beat someone up, would you?"

Delphine grinned. "Try me. I beat up Joey, once."

"Liar. Your brother's, like, huge compared to you."

"Well, I bet I could beat him up. He makes me mad enough."

"Because he's a boy and boys stink," Maggie said emphatically. "And they're stupid."

"Mostly," Delphine said with a shrug. "My dad's okay, though. And your dad is pretty nice."

"Yeah, but my brother is gross."

"Maybe boys get nicer as they get older. Like, really old, like our dads. Well, anyway," Delphine said, "remember you're leaving in like an hour. We have to do a swear about being best friends. We have to do a pinky swear."

"What's that?" Maggie asked.

Delphine laughed. "Come on! Everyone knows what a pinky swear is."

"Well, I don't. We don't do pinky swears in my school."

Delphine rolled her eyes dramatically. It made her feel slightly dizzy. Maybe it was all that swinging. And it was really hot. "Oh, all right," she said. "Stick out your pinky. Now I link my pinky with yours and we swear whatever we're swearing and then we pull our pinkies apart."

The girls linked pinkies and Maggie said, "Me first. I swear I will be your best friend forever and ever."

"Me too," Delphine said.

"No, you have to say all the words."

"Okay. I swear I will be your best friend forever and ever."

"Pinky swear."

The girls pulled their pinkies apart, and Maggie said, "Ow."

Delphine leapt off her swing and stood with her hands on her hips. "So, write to me the minute you get home later, okay?"

"Okay. And you write to me the minute I leave, okay?"

"Okay." Delphine considered. "But I won't have much to say. Maybe I should wait till just before I go to bed tonight. Maybe Joey will do something stupid at dinner. The other night he laughed so hard at something Jackie said milk came out of his nose and all over the table. It was gross. Also kind of funny, though."

"I guess it's okay if you wait."

Delphine suddenly looked doubtful. "You're sure your

parents promised you could come back to Ogunquit next year?"

"Yeah. Mom said Dad already gave the guy who owns the house some money. So it's all set."

"Cool. I'm thirsty. Does your mom still have stuff in the 'fidgerator?"

"Refrigerator," Maggie corrected. "I think so."

Maggie got up from her swing, and with their arms around each other's waists the girls trooped into the Lilac House for lemonade.

1

Where the past exists, the future may flourish.
—Peter Ackroyd

2011

Maggie Weldon Wilkes steered her Lexus IS C 10 convertible around a slow-moving station wagon decorated with three bikes and a canoe. The Lexus had been a present to herself for a very successful bonus season. Retractable hardtop, cruise control, even a backup camera—this particular car was more of an indulgence than a necessity.

She reached for her iPhone on the seat beside her. She knew it was dangerous to text while driving—everybody knew that, especially after Oprah had made a deservedly big deal out of it—but Maggie did it anyway, occasionally. It gave her a bit of a thrill to do something possibly illegal and definitely reckless, though she could barely admit that to herself. Besides, it wasn't like she reached for her phone on a busy New York City street. Like right now, mid-morning on a Friday, there were only a few cars within sight and what was the harm in typing out a brief, abbreviated note to her husband? Nothing. Not much. Except that in spite of wearing bifocal contact lenses she couldn't quite see what she was doing.

"In ME," she managed, the intelligence of habit overcoming the limitations of vision. "How r u?" She put her phone back on the passenger seat and realized that she hadn't actually heard Gregory's voice in days. They had tweeted and texted and e-mailed but not actually spoken, not even on voice mail. This, however, was par for the course with the Wilkeses and not to be taken as a sign of marital distress or discord. Maggie reassured herself on this point with some frequency. She and Gregory were a highly successful career couple whose jobs took them out of each other's sight, not out of each other's minds. Maybe they weren't as close as they once had been, but . . . It was what it was.

So, she was on her way to spend a few weeks in Ogunquit, that "beautiful place by the sea." She had been so happy there, mostly, of course, because of Delphine Crandall, but also because of the sheer beauty of the area. Maggie still remembered the slightly punky smell of the wildflowers that grew in profusion along the road to the Lilac House, the place her parents had rented for all those years. She could hear in her mind the absurdly loud chirping of the teeny peepers in the pond in the woods behind the Crandalls' house. She remembered the softness of the summer evening air. She remembered how she and Delphine and sometimes their siblings would go down to the beach at a superhigh tide, when the water would come all the way up to the parking lot. She remembered being both frightened and excited by the cold Atlantic rushing around her feet. She remembered the swing set behind the Lilac House and the new kittens at Delphine's family's farm. She remembered the joy.

Now, after almost three hours on the road Maggie was finally getting close to her destination. So much had changed since she had last driven this far north. Traffic was definitely worse than it once had been, especially now along Route 1 in Wells. There were just way too many people, period. She didn't recognize half of the restaurants along the road, though she was pleased to see that the rickety old clam shack that Delphine's family had taken them to once a summer was still open. There was a whole new crop of summer cottage developments sprawled on either side of the road. Some of the cottages were unbelievably tiny; it was hard to imagine even a family of three being comfortable in them. Then again, kids could be comfortable anywhere, especially with the beach within sight. Still, Maggie could not imagine herself tolerating such tight quarters, not now, not as a forty-eight-year-old. She had become used to a degree of luxury. A high degree of luxury, in all honesty. Her hair color was professionally maintained at an award-winning salon on Newbury Street. She had a manicure and pedicure once every two weeks. Around her left wrist she wore a Rolex, another gift to herself after a particularly good year at the office. Around her neck, on a white gold chain, she wore a two-carat diamond set in platinum. That was from Gregory, an anniversary gift she thought, or maybe a birthday gift. She couldn't really remember. He had given her so many expensive presents. He was very good about that sort of thing. For their wedding, though he could barely afford them at the time, he had given her diamond stud earrings.

Thinking about those earrings, Maggie realized that the last time she had seen Delphine had been at the wedding, and that was over twenty years ago. Maggie had invited her with a guest, but she had come alone, and had only accepted the invitation after ascertaining that Robert Evans, her former fiancé, wouldn't be there. He had been invited, also with a guest, but would be on an assignment in Thailand. It would have been ridiculous to turn down a major journalistic gig for the sake of a friend's wedding. Besides, Robert and Maggie had really only been friends because of Delphine. Once Delphine had gone back home to Ogunquit after breaking up with Robert, Maggie's friendship with him had steadily waned. She hadn't heard from him in over fifteen years, though she could see his face, hear his name, and read his words all over the media. You'd have to be living in a cave not to be aware of Robert Evans.

Maggie adjusted the air-conditioning a bit and thought of the pale blue velvet box carefully tucked between layers of clothing in her suitcase. Inside the box was an aquamarine pendant on a gold chain. Aquamarine was Delphine's birthstone; her birthday was March 23. The necklace should have been hers. And it would have been if Maggie had asked Delphine to be her maid of honor. But she hadn't. The necklace had been in that pale blue velvet box, in the back of Maggie's lingerie drawer, for close to twenty-four years.

She was crossing into Ogunquit now and traffic was still at a crawl. Every other minute it came to a complete stop for pedestrians crossing the road, many of whom ignored the official crosswalks and dashed out at random. Maggie frowned. She did not care for traffic jams or for pedestrians who didn't follow the rules. Well, she supposed nobody did. As she waited for a family, which included a baby in a stroller and three small children, to organize themselves across the road, her mind wandered.

Delphine Crandall. There had been long periods of Maggie's life in which she hadn't thought about Delphine at all. Like when business school had overwhelmed her, and when she was starting her career, and then when the children had come along. There had been other long periods when she thought of Delphine occasionally, randomly, and without much emotion. Like when her daughters did or said something that reminded her of her own childhood self, or when Robert Evans's face popped up on the TV screen. Once in a very great while Delphine would make an appearance in a dream, and mostly those dreams were somehow disturbing, though Maggie could never remember them clearly when she woke. Some details lingered—something about being forced to leave boxes of books behind, an eviction, someone crying, dirty floors. None of it made any sense.

But in the past two years or so, Maggie had found herself thinking more and more often of her old friend. Specific memories were coming back to her with a vividness that was startling. The time when they were about ten when they had stumbled on a teenage couple kissing behind a shack in Perkins Cove and had run away giggling and shrieking. The time when they were about sixteen and had snuck out one night to go to the only dance club in town, even though their parents had forbidden them. The time in college when Delphine had woken in the middle of the night with a raging fever and Maggie had bundled her into a cab and then to the emergency room. The time when Maggie had thought she was pregnant. She had been too frightened and ashamed to buy an at-home pregnancy kit, so Delphine had bought it for her, and had sat holding her hand while they waited for the result.

And the feelings, too, they were coming back, rather, memories of how it had felt to be so comfortable with someone, so loved and appreciated. She had begun to think of Delphine Crandall with a longing that seemed more than mere nostalgia. It was a longing that finally became too real to ignore.

So back in April, Maggie had made a decision to find her. She had no idea if Delphine was online or if she had married and changed her name, so she sent an old-fashioned, handwritten letter to Delphine in care of her parents. In it Maggie mentioned her job, Gregory's job, her daughters' being in college. She suggested that she come to Ogunquit to visit. August would be a good time for her. She had several weeks of vacation saved up. She would stay in a hotel so as not to burden anyone. She needed a low-key, quiet break from her busy life. She said nothing about the memories or the dreams.

She had waited a month, hoping for a reply, and when no reply came she took the more direct measure of making a telephone call. There was a Delphine Crandall listed in Ogunquit. It was her Delphine Crandall.

She called one night, about eight o'clock, and was surprised to hear a voice groggy with sleep. She asked Delphine if she had gotten her letter. Yes, Delphine had. But she had been terribly busy and hadn't had time to reply. She said she was sorry. Maggie hadn't entirely believed her.

"So," Maggie had said, suddenly nervous, "what do you think about my coming to visit this summer?"

There had been a long beat of silence, one Maggie couldn't attribute to anything other than Delphine's reluctance. Just when Maggie, feeling both embarrassed and annoyed, was about to retract the suggestion of a visit, Delphine had blurted something like, "Yeah. Okay." The moment of retreat had been lost. A reunion was going to happen.

Traffic was crawling again, which was better than sitting still. Maggie felt a tiny flutter of anxiety, which seemed to be growing the closer she came to her destination. There was no doubt about it. Delphine had sounded less than thrilled about this visit. Maybe she had just caught her at a bad time. And then again, Delphine had never been a particularly effusive person. Or had she? Maggie frowned. Memory was a tricky thing, made up of truth, fiction, desire, and a whole lot of dubious detail. She wondered if the Delphine Crandall she would find today would have anything in common with the Delphine Crandall of her memory. The thought was troubling. And it was nonsense to think that someone's character and personality could change so drastically over time that she would be unrecognizable. Nonsense.

There it was, coming up on the right. Maggie turned up into the driveway of Gorges Grant and brought the car to a stop outside the hotel's big front doors. She had chosen to stay here because it offered not only a heated indoor pool and Jacuzzi (both of which she would definitely use), and an outdoor pool and sunning deck (she had brought plenty of high-powered sunblock), but also a fitness center. She never went anywhere without her workout gear. At forty-eight, closing in on forty-nine, she was in the best shape of her life, thanks to a healthy diet and a rigorous exercise regime. For someone who worked as hard as she did—long, tension-filled hours in an office and frequent travel, always a nightmare what with security issues and unexplained delays—being in good physical shape was essential. Which didn't mean she didn't occasionally crave junk food and a nap, rather than an apple and a half hour on the treadmill. Not that her fit and healthy body seemed to attract Gregory's attention these days. Then again, she hadn't exactly been seeking him out for anything other than resetting the digital clock on the oven after a blackout. It was what it was.

Maggie shook her head, turned off the ignition, and got out of the car. It was time to forget, at least for a while, all the troublesome stuff of daily life back in Massachusetts. Stuff like a diminished sex drive and a husband you communicated with mostly in cyberspace. Stuff like children who seemed to forget you existed until they needed money for iPhones and iPads and whatever electronic gadget was going to replace them. It was time to revive an old friendship. At least, it was time to try.

2

Delphine Crandall was out of bed by five o'clock most mornings, which wasn't so hard to do when you were asleep by eight o'clock the night before. Farming was not a job for night owls or late risers. This particular Friday morning she had been awake since four, unable to keep thoughts of Maggie Weldon Wilkes's imminent, and largely unwelcome, arrival out of her head.

With a groan that was not strictly necessary, she got out of bed and made her way to the kitchen for that blessed first cup of coffee. She enjoyed mornings at home, a brief time of peace and quiet before the demands of the day started clamoring. Alone with Melchior, her three-year-old cat, she could scratch and grumble and moan and not feel guilty about it. This morning, Melchior was waiting for her at his empty food bowl, eyes narrowed in annoyance.

"Is it breakfast time?" she asked him unnecessarily. He answered with a deep and affirmative, *Waah*.

Delphine flipped on the coffee machine—she always set it up the night before—and went about getting Melchior's breakfast. Melchior's predecessor had also been a barn cat. Felix had died at the ripe old age of twenty-one. To say that Delphine missed Felix was an understatement. You couldn't share a home with another living being for twenty-one years and not feel bereft upon his death. For months after Felix had passed she was unable to bear the thought of taking in another cat, and then, suddenly, the thought of continuing to live without another cat was intolerable. So she had gone out to the barn, where one of the females, a small calico, had recently given birth to a motley litter, and watched. On Delphine's very first visit, one of the kittens in particular had caught her eye. This one's father had clearly been a Maine coon cat, and an extrabig one at that. Even at a few weeks old, this kitten was larger than his siblings, even a sister who seemed also to have a Maine coon, possibly the same one, as a father.

From the very first the male kitten had disdained—that was Delphine's dramatic take on it—life in the barn with his numerous siblings and cousins and whenever she visited had followed her around more like a dog than a cat, pawing at her ankles and attempting to climb up her leg. Well, the climbing was very catlike, and very painful. So when Melchior—she had already given him this name, one fit for a king—was about two months old she had taken him home, hoping he would like his new, more sophisticated digs, and within hours he had settled in as lord of the house. He barely tolerated people other than Delphine and hated dogs, two traits that probably had come from his mother or some other, more distant relative, not his Maine coon father. When Delphine's sister, Jackie, stopped by with her mixed-breed dog named Bandit, Melchior made a great show of hissing, which only made the good-natured Bandit wag his tail. Also unlike other Maine coons, Melchior had little interest in play, preferring to spend his time eating, sleeping, and watching his surroundings with a careful, critical eye.

Delphine gave Melchior his wet food and refilled his bowls of dry food and water. He dug in ferociously. He was a big boy, pushing twenty pounds. His coat was long, wild, and a riot of black, brown, and white. Long tufts of fur sprouted from the tips of his ears. His ruff alone made him look like a particularly imperious and important courtier or politician from the court of Elizabeth I. Delphine sometimes thought she should have named him Leicester, or Cecil, or Essex, instead. The fact that Melchior hated to be brushed was a bit of a problem. Delphine woke each morning with cat hair in her eyes and cat hair glued to her lips. Every piece of furniture was decorated with clumps of fur. She wouldn't be surprised if, in spite of her vigilant daily cleaning rituals, she herself coughed up a hairball one day.

Coffee mug in hand, Delphine went back upstairs to get washed and dressed. Twenty minutes later, she said good-bye to Melchior, who was now cleaning himself on the couch in the living room. In response, he ostentatiously closed his eyes on her. Delphine locked the front door behind her and skipped down the steps of the porch. Most people she knew, including her parents, didn't lock their doors, but Delphine did. She wasn't really sure why. Maybe it was a habit left over from the years she had spent in Boston.

Delphine climbed into her big old red F-150 pickup truck, with "Crandall Farm" painted on the creaking driver's side door. Well, actually, what was visible on the door now read: "Cranda   Farm." The original outline of the missing letters was just barely visible and Delphine swore that someday she would get around to filling them in with matching black paint. But in Ogunquit and its surrounding towns there really was no need for further identification. Everyone knew the Crandalls.

She steered the truck out onto Larsens Road and before she had gone a mile she passed two new construction sites. Another overblown McMansion, she thought, maybe two of them. There were already too many ostentatious new homes and unattractive house farms in and around Ogunquit. Too much of the area's charm had been suppressed and even erased. And the destruction was still going on. Roads were being cut into once pristine forest to ease the way to the obscenely large houses, and beautiful marshland seemed always to be threatened by some big developer hungry for yet more profit. Change was inevitable, she knew that, but why, she wondered, did it so often have to be ugly? More jobs were always a good thing, but she didn't understand why they had to come at the expense of taste and tradition.

A little bit farther along the road she passed the newest day spa to open. That would be of no use to her. She was the ultimate in low maintenance, partly by choice and partly by necessity. Once every six weeks or so she had her hair cut by a retired hairdresser who had worked for thirty years in Portland. Mrs. Snowman now worked out of her kitchen and charged twenty dollars for her services. Delphine hadn't had a manicure since college, when she used to go, occasionally, with Maggie to a salon in Cambridge. She didn't have the money for facials or massages; she had never even been inside the spa on Main Street, the first of the crop. Her daily boots had manure in their treads and were left at the front door. She had never set foot inside a gym, not even the Y in Wells. There was no need. Daily life had given her admirable muscles and stamina. Eating local had helped keep her forty-nine-year-old body more than serviceable. If she couldn't fit into the jeans she had worn at thirty-nine, she could still lift a bale of hay and toss it into the back of her truck. Today she was wearing a short-sleeved T-shirt, once bright orange and now a mellow melon color. Her hair, still thoroughly brown, was held in place by a navy bandana, tied at the back of her neck. She probably had close to fifteen bandanas, some at home, a few in the truck, more stashed in her office at the farm. You never knew when you'd need to keep your hair out of your face. She hadn't worn makeup in years.

Delphine turned off the busy main road. Traffic was almost non-existent on these back roads. Most tourists were strictly interested in the beach and in shopping, not in the farms and the woods out of which the farms had been carved. That was fine by her. On the right of the road was a mass of old lilac bushes. Lilac season was over, the purple and white blooms gone. Lilacs were one of Delphine's favorite flowers. Now, in August, the fields and gardens were teeming with orange and red daylilies, wild daisies, clover,

Queen Anne's lace (her mother's favorite), and buttercups. Sturdy cattails crowded the edges of marshes and tall, exotic grasses grew in great clumps on the manicured lawns of the wealthier residents.

A few minutes later, Delphine turned onto Ryan Road and finally into the dusty drive that led up to Crandall Family Farm.

Her parents' house, the house in which she had grown up, was a traditional telescope-style New England structure. It sat on a small rise, with the farm and front and backyard spread for several acres around it. Thriving hydrangea bushes with vividly purple blooms lined the left side of the house, while a variety of hosta plants flourished out front. Behind the house, from June to October various breeds of roses grew in wild profusion. Her mother had a way with plants, a trait that was exceedingly helpful if you lived on a farm.

Delphine admitted that from afar, the house and its surrounds looked like something out of a storybook—peaceful, idyllic, the sun always shining, an apple pie always cooling on a windowsill—but the life of a working farm was anything but a fairy tale. If a coyote or a fisher cat wasn't making off with a cat or a chicken, then a drought was killing the crops or Japanese beetles were infesting the beans or the blueberries or the tomato plants. Even the formidable Patrice Crandall, matron of the Crandall clan, couldn't entirely subdue Nature.

Delphine parked her truck alongside her father's ancient black Volvo in the front drive and went into the house for a second cup of coffee. No one was around; she assumed her parents had taken her mother's car to the family's diner earlier that morning. The house was beyond familiar. Delphine had known it for almost fifty years. It was more like a living being than a structure of plaster and wood. Her bedroom was still pretty much as she had left it all those years ago, when she had moved into her own house, a house her parents had inherited from a long-deceased relative. Jackie and her husband, Dave Sr., had bought their own home, as had Joey and his wife, Cybel. Neither seemed to mind that Delphine wasn't burdened by a mortgage as they were. Sibling rivalry wasn't something that plagued the Crandalls. When Charlie and Patrice died, their house would belong to all three of their children. It would never be sold, not if the siblings could help it.

In the large kitchen Delphine set about making a pot of coffee. What she didn't drink would not go to waste. Her parents were big coffee drinkers but not particular about blends and quality. Day-old coffee scalded in a saucepan was just fine by them. When the coffee was brewed she poured some into an old mug decorated with a picture of lupines and leaned against the sink to drink it.

Only hours remained until Maggie's arrival. She had given no other reason for her visit to Ogunquit than the need for a quiet vacation, some time off. Imagine—a vacation! For Delphine, there was no such thing as a vacation. She had too many responsibilities; there was no such thing as "time off." She knew it was uncharitable to feel so accusatory and petty. Everyone deserved a break from the routine, even if not everyone could get it. Still, Maggie's out-of-the-blue visit was an intrusion, an interruption of her life and her work. Delphine suddenly felt overwhelmed by resentment. There were plenty of other places Maggie could have gone for peace and quiet, one of those big resorts in the Caribbean, for example, or a secluded lakeside village in Vermont.

No, Maggie had chosen Ogunquit not because of its lovely beach and fabulous restaurants and pretty little inns. She had chosen it because of Delphine. And that worried her. Maggie was bound to bring up the end of their senior year of college. She was bound to have questions. She had had questions all those years ago, questions Delphine had been unwilling and maybe unable to answer. Delphine didn't want to talk about the past, especially not about those final weeks before she had come back home for good. She didn't even want to think about the past, and mostly she succeeded in keeping the memories at bay. Not having Maggie around as a reminder helped. There were months on end when Maggie Weldon Wilkes ceased to exist. And when a stray memory did pop up in Delphine's head, she ruthlessly shoved it back down.

She poured a bit more coffee into her cup and sipped it appreciatively. She suddenly remembered that back in college Maggie had been strictly a tea drinker. She wondered if that had changed and figured she might find out that evening at dinner. But she didn't want to sit lingering over coffee and dessert. She planned to get in and get out as quickly as possible without being rude.

And she would not be rude because it was her own fault she was in this situation. She could simply have told Maggie that now, this summer—never?—was not a good time for a visit, that summer in general was always the most hectic and even exhausting time of the year for the Crandalls. But she hadn't said anything other than, "Oh. Well. It will be nice to catch up." Or something like that, some lame and largely insincere response.

Delphine took a final sip of her coffee, washed the cup, and turned off the pot. Time to get to work. It was almost seven o'clock. She needed to speak to Jackie about one of the best-laying hens that had been acting "off," and then to Lori, Jackie's fifteen-year-old daughter, who was being trained up in the farm business, about a change in Lori's work schedule due to an unexpected party invitation. Before the day was out Delphine would also have spoken with and possibly seen her parents, her brother, her sister-in-law, and her brother-in-law, though Dave Sr. was not one for the phone and even when you were face-to-face with him he rarely spoke unless addressed. The other Crandalls were never far away, and while at times Delphine felt that she was suffocating, most times she found their proximity essential and right. Sometimes she thought that Harry, her boyfriend, was mostly with her because of her family. His children were grown and busy with lives of their own, leaving Harry, who didn't have any close friends or siblings or living parents, alone except for the Crandall clan.

Delphine left the house and walked the short distance to the office, located in a small outbuilding off the smaller of the two barns. *Another day,* she thought, though this one would not be entirely like the rest.

3

Delphine hurried home from the farm that evening, fed Melchior, who seemed happy to see her and then annoyed that she was rushing around and not paying attention to him, changed into clean clothes, and drove out again to the restaurant. She'd had difficulty choosing the place where she would meet her old friend. Or was Maggie really a former friend? More like a virtual stranger now.

Delphine wanted to keep this reunion of sorts away from the prying eyes of her small town; sometimes caring got mixed up with curiosity for its own sake. Of course, it wasn't as if Maggie was likely to be an embarrassment. Quite the opposite. Maggie had done very well for herself (Delphine had checked out her Facebook page and knew) and, to some eyes, was likely to make Delphine look fairly shabby. Anywhere they went there might be people who would remember Maggie and her parents. After all, the Weldon family had rented in Ogunquit for seven or eight years. True, Maggie hadn't been seen in town for a very long time, but someone with a good memory was bound to recognize her. Tall, blond, beautiful—Maggie Weldon had always stood out.

In the end Delphine had decided on the Cape Neddick Lobster Pond on Shore Road. She got to the restaurant first and was seated at a table off by itself a bit, a deuce near one of the many large windows that afforded an unobstructed view of the marsh, now at mid-tide. She was wearing a T-shirt, chinos, and on her feet serviceable sandals from L.L. Bean. The only jewelry she routinely wore was a watch—if that could be considered jewelry—an old, reliable Timex, and, on special occasions, a pair of small gold hoop earrings Jackie had given her for her fortieth birthday. Tonight, it seemed, was a special occasion.

After a few minutes, Delphine noticed a tall, slim, blond woman walk up to the hostess station. Maggie. Suddenly, she felt exposed and vulnerable. She had a mad desire to duck under the table. The hostess pointed in Delphine's direction. Maggie waved and with confident strides walked toward her.

Delphine felt herself begin to sweat. She couldn't remember when she had felt so awkward. Yes, she could. It was when she had first met Harry's children, both now in their early twenties. It was only a few months after she and Harry had started to date. There the awkwardness had been all around, and in an odd way the obvious fact that everyone—Harry, Delphine, Bob, and Mary—felt uncomfortable had eased tensions pretty quickly. That had been a bit of a miracle.

Delphine half rose from her chair and at the same time Maggie half bent to give Delphine a hug. The hug became a bump and they separated awkwardly, quickly.

"It's so good to see you," Maggie said as she took the seat across from Delphine.

"Yes," Delphine said, her voice sounding odd in her ears. "You too."

She was a bit disconcerted to see that Maggie was dressed so nicely, in a lime green linen dress and sling-back heels. That was nothing new for Maggie, she had always dressed well, but for the first time in the history of their relationship Delphine felt dowdy in comparison. A short-sleeved T-shirt tucked into belted chinos might be comfortable, but in no way was it an "outfit." She suddenly remembered that she had first heard that term—"outfit"—from Maggie's glamorous mother. It certainly wasn't a term her own mother, who owned one "church dress" and one pair of "good" shoes, had ever used.

"How was the drive?" she asked Maggie now. It was a requisite question to ask of a vacationer. And it filled what was becoming a long silence.

"Okay," Maggie said. "Not as bad as it could have been. Though I was surprised by how slowly the traffic moved through Wells. Route One was absolutely mobbed."

"A lot has changed. The summer population now gets to about twenty thousand, and that's in Ogunquit alone."

"Well," Maggie said, smiling brightly, "all those people mean money to the local economy."

Delphine was about to point out that all those people also meant littered sidewalks and noise pollution, but wisely didn't. The last thing she wanted was an argument. Things were uncomfortable enough. At least, for her. Maggie seemed to be at ease. That was nothing new, either. She had always been the more socially adept, easing the way for Delphine with her creative introductions, her ability to start pleasant conversations, and her skill at getting out of unpleasant ones.

"We should look at the menu," Delphine blurted.

"Okay." Maggie picked up her menu and glanced around the large, simply decorated dining room. "This place is so . . . unpretentious," she said finally. "Unassuming. I like the atmosphere."

Delphine wondered if Maggie really did like the "atmosphere" or if she was just being polite. Hadn't Maggie always been polite? Delphine thought that she had. So had her parents. Unfailingly polite, well dressed, and socially skilled.

"Well, it's quiet, generally," she said in reply. "At this hour at least, once the families from the camp across the road have had their dinner. And the food is good. Nothing fancy, but good. Actually, we supply some of their tomatoes. Crandall Farm, I mean. And some lettuces." Delphine lifted the dime-store reading glasses that hung on a cord around her neck and put them on her nose. "You're not wearing glasses," she noted.

"I'm wearing bifocal contacts these days," Maggie explained. "When I'm not wearing bifocal glasses. Glasses are so outrageously expensive, but I have such a weak spot for funky frames. Maybe it's because of those early years of having to wear ugly glasses. And then the eighties! What a nightmare! Frames that practically hung down to your chin. Ugh."

Delphine couldn't help but smile. Robert Evans, she remembered, had had perfect vision back when she had known him. He used to tease Maggie, albeit good-naturedly, about her thick lenses and ponderous frames. Delphine had seen him on television not too long ago and he had been wearing a pair of unobtrusive metal frames. Other than the glasses she thought he had looked almost entirely unchanged. She wondered what he would think if he saw her now, a forty-nine-year-old woman who looked decidedly different from the way she had looked when she was twenty-one. She pushed the thought away.

Maggie looked up from her menu. "You know," she said, "on the drive up here I realized we haven't seen each other since my wedding."

"Has it been that long?" Delphine said. She knew exactly how long it had been, but she didn't know what else to say. This was a startlingly new situation for her, sitting across the table from someone who had once meant so much to her. The only other person she had loved and lost—if "lost" was the right word, given the fact that in each case she had been the one to walk away—was Robert. And there had never been a chance of their meeting again. She had seen to that.

"Twenty-four years exactly, this fall. It's hard to believe."

"Yes," Delphine said. It was, actually, kind of hard to believe so much time had gone by since Maggie's wedding. A wedding to which Delphine almost hadn't gone. She had waited to accept the invitation until Maggie assured her that

Robert would be on an assignment somewhere in another part of the world. She forgot where. But she had always wondered why Maggie had invited him in the first place. Had she thought, maybe, that Robert and Delphine would reunite, lulled into reconciliation by the sentimentality of a big, traditional wedding? She supposed that she could have asked Maggie—she could ask her right now—why Robert had been invited. But Robert Evans was no longer relevant. The only reason he kept popping into her head these past few days was because of his association with Maggie. That had to be the reason.

A waiter came by, a local boy Delphine knew by sight—she thought he was in her niece Lori's class at the high school—and they ordered food, a lobster salad and a glass of wine for Maggie and fish and chips and a beer for Delphine.

"Tell me about your family," Maggie said, when the waiter had gone off. "I hope everyone is well. How's your brother?"

"Joey's good," Delphine said. "He's got a small-appliance repair shop in South Berwick." Maggie had had a brief crush on Delphine's brother one long-ago summer. He had been a big, handsome boy, then a robust young man, and now, in his early fifties, Delphine thought that he was still attractive in a slightly worn, grey-haired, burly kind of way. She wondered if Maggie would agree.

"Is he still married to—Cybel, is it?"

"Oh, yes," Delphine said. "Cybel works in a day-care center in Wells. Their son, Norman, is twenty-three now. He's married and lives in South Berwick. His wife is expecting a baby around Christmas. And I guess you wouldn't know about Kitty, Cybel and Joey's daughter."

Maggie shook her head. "No."

Delphine smiled. "She was a 'surprise child.' Kitty's eight years old. And needless to say, she's the apple of everyone's eye, especially her father's. And, well, of mine, too."

"I would think so! And do you have children?"

"No."

"Oh," Maggie said. "So it must be extranice for you having a little girl around."

Delphine didn't reply and Maggie wondered if she had said something she shouldn't have. She was rarely rude or inappropriate, but suddenly she felt that she might have been both.

The young waiter brought their food just then. When he had gone, they ate in silence for a few minutes. Delphine was hungry and happy not to talk. Maggie picked at her salad and wondered when Delphine would look up from her plate.

"How's Jackie?" she asked finally, tired of waiting. "I remember her as being so popular when we were growing up."

"She still is popular," Delphine answered, wiping her mouth with her napkin. "Everyone likes Jackie, even her own teenage children. And Jackie pretty much likes everyone, too. Even tourists." It was true. Most locals tolerated—and sometimes welcomed—tourists for the business they brought. Jackie seemed to like most visitors as actual people. "She works the farm with me, though she's much more of the hands-on, in-the-fields person. And she's directly in charge of our summer workers."

"Wow," Maggie said, eyebrows rising. "But she went to college, didn't she? Somewhere in South Portland?"

Delphine bristled. What did Jackie's education have to do with her involvement with the family farm? Of course. No one with a formal education, even one from a two-year community college, was supposed to get her hands dirty with manual labor. It amazed her that so many people really didn't understand how much intelligence and learning it took to farm successfully. And then there was intuition, a feel for the work. That, too, was important. "Yes," she said after a moment. "She went to college." That would be the end of it.

"Is she still married?" Maggie asked.

"The Crandalls don't do divorce. Not that there's any reason for Jackie and Dave Senior to be divorced. He owns a small contracting business. Norman works for him, actually. And Dave Junior, he's seventeen, he'll probably join the business when he gets out of high school. Lori, she's fifteen, she works at the farm with me after school, on weekends, and during the summers. I'm training her to take over someday, but that will be a long time coming."

"Wow," Maggie said again. "The Crandalls are quite the . . . enterprise."

"There's nothing new about that," Delphine said, unable to tell if Maggie had meant something critical by her remark.

"I guess I just never realized how . . ."

"Realized how what?"

Maggie shrugged, smiled. "Nothing. So, tell me about your parents? I hope they're well."

"My mother is good," Delphine said. "She's still doing the baking for the diner, taking care of the house, helping out with her grandchildren. And my father is good, too. The diner is almost always packed, so he keeps pretty busy with that. Neither has much to do with the farm anymore, since Jackie and I pretty much run everything. But they chime in on any major decisions. We all do, Joey, Cybel, Dave Senior. Like you said, we're an enterprise, a team."

"I have some fond memories of that diner," Maggie said. "There was that one really nice waitress, I can't remember her name. She had an old-fashioned beehive hairdo. It was almost Day-Glo orange. I had a yo-yo that same color. She used to sneak us cookies."

"Veronique," Delphine said. "She's actually a distant cousin of my mother's. Well, she was a distant cousin. She died a while ago."

"Oh, that's too bad. You know, I'd love to visit the diner while I'm in town. Maybe we could have lunch there one day."

Delphine hesitated. She never ate at the diner as a customer. To do so now, after so many years of working behind the counter, would feel somehow inappropriate. She couldn't allow her father's employees to serve her, a sometime colleague. "We're very busy in the summer," she said.

"But that's good, isn't it? I mean, busy means money coming in."

"Yes. Well, what about your parents?" Delphine remembered Mr. and Mrs. Weldon as a glamorous couple, especially compared to her own parents. Mrs. Weldon always wore a skirt or a dress, never pants, and often wore heels, even when sneakers would have been more practical. Her husband always wore a jacket when they went out in the evenings, no matter the heat. They had been good to her, generous and supportive, especially when it had come time to apply for college. Walter and . . . It took Delphine a moment to remember. Dorothy.

"My father's dead," Maggie said. "My mother lives in Florida."

"Oh." Delphine felt a prick of conscience. She would have sent a note of condolence if she had known. And she would have known if she hadn't walked away all those years ago. "I'm sorry about your father," she said. "He was a nice man. How long ago did he die?"

"Almost six years now," Maggie said. "He had a massive heart attack. By the time the ambulance got to the house he was gone. My mother moved to a condo down south a few months after he died. She's doing pretty well. Luckily, she doesn't have any major health problems."

"That's good. How's your brother?"

"Peter is fine. He's a successful corporate lawyer and his wife is a judge. They live in Marblehead. We don't see each other much." Maggie smiled a bit. "I don't know if you remember, but we were never really that close growing up and it seems that every year we drift further apart. It's okay, though. It is what it is."

Delphine said, "Oh." Her own sibling situation could not be more different. She saw Jackie and Joey several times a week, sometimes every day, and she liked it that way, even when Joey was in one of his grumpy moods or Jackie was being a know-it-all. And they seemed to like seeing her just about all the time, even when she was being whatever it was that annoyed them. A killjoy, Joey had once called her. Just last week Jackie had accused her of being uptight.

"So, tell me," Maggie said now. "Are you seeing anyone?"

Delphine took a sip of her beer. There was no point in trying to deny her relationship with Harry. It was a small town. Maggie would meet him before long in some way or another. Besides, she thought, it wasn't like Harry was some sort of freak. She had nothing to be embarrassed about. "I've been with someone for about ten years now," she said. "His name is Harry Stringfellow. He owns a house on Agamenticus Road."

"So you don't live together?" Maggie asked.

"No."

"Oh." Maggie smiled and sipped her wine.

"Your children. How are they?" Delphine hesitated, caught short by another sudden and embarrassing lack of memory. "I'm sorry," she said. "I'm blanking on their names."

"Kim and Caitlin," Maggie said easily, seemingly undisturbed by what might be taken as an insult. "They're both at a small college in San Diego. In fact, they're staying through the summer this year. They got decent jobs and an off-campus apartment with some friends, so . . . Unless I go out there in the fall I probably won't see them until Thanksgiving. That is, if they decide to come home."

"That must be tough. Being so far away from your children."

Maggie shrugged. "Not really," she said, aware she was lying to an extent. "I'm so busy with work I don't have time to miss them much. And the girls seem happy. I guess they got tired of life in the Northeast. And I guess they were through with living so close to Mom and Dad. I can't say that I blame them. At least, about the mom and dad part. It's perfectly normal for a child to want to get away from her family, experience life on her own. I mean, you raise children to be independent. It's natural that they leave you."

"Of course," Delphine said. "So, you said you wanted to come to Ogunquit for a quiet vacation." What Delphine really wanted to ask—but wouldn't—was: "So, what made you want to see me after all these years, the unnatural child who didn't, couldn't, wouldn't get away from her family?"

"Yes," Maggie said. "It's been an incredibly busy year and I had some vacation time saved and I thought, why not Ogunquit? It's peaceful and lovely and I could see Delphine while I'm there." What Maggie really wanted to say—but wouldn't—was: "And I want you to finally explain to me why you abandoned our friendship."

"You might not find it as peaceful as it used to be," Delphine said. "But like you said, more people means more money."

"Yes. So, tell me about yourself."

"Oh, there's not much to tell."

"No, really, what's going on in your life?"

Delphine shifted uncomfortably. "Well, work, mostly," she said. "You know, the farm, and the diner. I help out there when I'm needed, if a waitress has to take a sick day, that sort of thing. I've got the nieces and nephews and one or another of them always needs something." Then, and she had no idea why because it was a lie, she added, "It's all pretty unexciting."

Maggie shook her head. "Oh, I doubt that," she said. "For example, the farm. Tell me about what you do exactly."

"Well, we're certified organic now. And you've heard of CSA, Community Supported Agriculture?"

Maggie nodded.

"We raise chickens for the eggs. Free-range. We grow vegetables, tomatoes, lettuces, other salad greens, various kinds of beans. It can vary from year to year. Jackie and Dave Senior maintain an herbal garden, but that's just for family use. We've just started selling cut flowers for bouquets. And

Jackie and her daughter are learning how to make wreaths out of dried and preserved flowers and vines. We sell locally and at the summer and winter markets up in Portland. Sometimes we barter with other farmers or fishermen for their products." Delphine shrugged. "I guess that's about it."

"I think that all sounds very interesting," Maggie said.

Delphine shrugged. She assumed Maggie was just being polite, again. It didn't matter. "How about you?" she asked.

"Well, the same as with you, mostly work, though my job is a lot less . . . varied than yours. I'm at the second largest investment firm in Boston. And, let's see, I play tennis about once a week and I work out five days a week. I guess that's pretty much the sum of my life."

"And what about Gregory?" *At least,* Delphine thought, *I remembered her husband's name.*

"He's fine," Maggie said. "He's doing really well at work. He's a senior partner in his firm, which means he has to travel a lot. And, well, to be honest, things aren't what they used to be between us. Nothing major is wrong, though," she added hurriedly, with a flick of her wrist, at the same time wondering if that was really true. Not the trouble part but the "nothing major" part. "It's probably just the twenty-four-year apathy setting in," she went on. "The arduous middle years. It was probably bound to happen. This, too, shall pass. It is what it is."

If Delphine was remembering correctly, it was unlike Maggie to resort to a string of clichés. But maybe she wasn't remembering correctly. And people changed. She really knew very little, if anything, about the woman sitting across the table from her. Maybe Maggie was a bit nervous, after all. Why else would she have revealed to someone she hadn't seen in over two decades, that there was trouble in her marriage?

"I'm sorry," she said. "You're probably right. Everything will be fine."

"Oh, sure," Maggie said, with that same dismissive flick of

the wrist. "I know. Hey, the other day I was thinking about the time my parents took the two of us to see that musical at the Ogunquit Playhouse. For the life of me I can't remember what it was, but I do remember that when we came out of the theatre we were both totally convinced we were going to become actresses. Do you remember that?"

"No," Delphine said.

"Oh. Really? My mother made us get dressed up and we were both sure we were going to have an awful, boring time and then we wound up having a blast."

"I'm sorry. I really don't remember any of that." Delphine looked down at her watch. "I should probably get home. I go to bed pretty early. And I get up pretty early, too."

"Sure, okay," Maggie said, reaching for her bag. "Let me get the check. This is my treat."

"No, no. We'll split the bill. Please."

"Well, okay," Maggie said. "But next time it's on me."

No, Delphine thought, *it won't be on you. I can pay for my own meals.*

There was little conversation as the bill was asked for and then paid. Together, they walked out into the gravel parking lot. The evening sky was streaked with purplish clouds. The tide had come in a bit more since they had arrived and now the water of the Cape Neddick River lapped up against the shore. A small overturned rowboat rested close to a shed decorated with colorful buoys. The air was filled with the excited, happy shouts of kids from the camp across the road, some playing in the calm waters of the Cape Neddick Harbor.

"It's a beautiful evening," Maggie said. "I forgot just how lovely it is here."

"Yes," Delphine said. She lifted her hand in a sort of wave. She really didn't want to attempt another hug and hoped that Maggie felt the same. "Well," she said, "it was good seeing you again, Maggie."

Maggie smiled. "Thanks. It was good seeing you, too. But

we'll see each other again, soon. I'm booked at the hotel for several weeks."

"Of course."

"I was hoping we could spend some quality time together, really catch up, you know. I've missed you, Delphine."

Delphine hesitated. She looked away, a bit over Maggie's left shoulder. She had not missed her old friend, not in a very long time. She couldn't afford to be missing people. There were too many people right in front of her, in the present, who needed her. "Yes," she said, knowing her reply was inadequate but feeling helpless to respond otherwise. "But I do have to work. Every day, sometimes all day. I don't have much free time."

But Maggie was not going to be put off. She wouldn't allow herself to be so easily dismissed. Not again. "Oh, I know that," she said. "And I wouldn't want to interfere with your job. But I'm sure I could squeeze myself in some times. I mean, you must have an odd hour here and there, maybe in the evenings?"

Delphine forced herself to look directly at this person from her past, this person who seemed to badly need or want a connection. She managed a smile. "Of course," she said. "We'll . . . I'll make some time. Sure."

"Good. Well," Maggie said, indicating a sleek hardtop convertible, "this is my car. Good night, Delphine."

Delphine watched as Maggie got behind the wheel. She wondered how much a car like that cost—a Lexus of some sort, she saw—and if it was worth it. But "worth" might mean something very different now to Maggie than it meant to Delphine. Value was a subjective notion. Maggie waved as she drove off, back in the direction of her hotel.

Well, Delphine thought as she climbed up into her truck, *that was a disaster or pretty near to one.* But Maggie seemed determined to repeat the disaster. Vaguely, Delphine remembered this about Maggie—her persistence, her refusal to walk away from a friend even when she was being ignored or pushed along. She shook off the memory and pulled out of the parking lot onto Shore Road.

Before going home she would stop at the farm and check on that worrisome hen. Jackie, of course, would already have done so, but it was better to be safe than sorry, as her father always said. And then, before going to bed, she would read a few pages in the novel that was currently absorbing her—a mystery by C. J. Sansom, set in the time of Henry VIII—and work for a bit on her current knitting project, a fairly mindless one, a simple, lightweight scarf for her sister. It would be good to be home with Melchior where she could attempt to put thoughts of her dinner with Maggie—and of what might come in the weeks ahead—out of her mind.

4

The next morning Delphine was at her office at the farm by six-thirty. The air was already thick and sticky. It was going to be a hot day, and humid. She might even need to turn the air conditioner on when she got home, even if Jemima wasn't coming over. With all that fur, Melchior didn't do well in the heat, either.

Maggie, of course, had the option of spending the day in her hotel room in air-conditioned splendor. Delphine sighed. She thought about the awkward conversation they'd had last night over dinner. She thought about the glaring difference in their appearance, a physical difference that reflected a deeper divide.

Delphine turned on her computer and entered the password that would allow her access to the farm's financial information. She wondered if she and Maggie had ever really had anything in common. Adults had the freedom to seek out friendships in a variety of places and among a variety of people. But the social life of children was limited by so many factors. In her own case, school had been let out for the summer and there had been no money for her to attend a day camp. And then, Maggie had appeared, just down the road. Maybe proximity alone had made them friends. Maggie had been available to Delphine. Delphine had been available to Maggie. Maybe they had always been just accidental friends, meant to come together, have a few laughs, learn a few life lessons, and then move apart.

But then, Delphine asked herself, *if that was the case, why had it hurt so badly to walk away?* She shook her head as if that motion could toss off the disturbing thoughts.

"Aunt Delphine!"

Delphine looked up from her computer to see her niece, Kitty, standing in the doorway. Behind her stood her mother, Cybel.

"I hope we're not bothering you," Cybel said as they came into the office. "Kitty was just dying to show you the picture she made last night."

Delphine smiled and put out her arms. Kitty charged into them and hugged tightly. "Of course you're not bothering me," Delphine said. Often, when she looked at her niece she had the sense that she was looking at herself at Kitty's age. She was not alone in noting this. Everyone who met the two noted that the family resemblance was indeed strong. They had the same dark, unruly hair and the same big brown eyes. And there was something more, something indefinable, a common spirit maybe, a shared energy.

But lately, Kitty had been less energetic than usual. She was looking a little wan, too, a little pale. It worried Delphine, but she hadn't said anything as of yet to Cybel. Cybel and Joey were good parents. She trusted them to be on top of their daughter's health and well-being. And she hated the notion of intervening, which seemed more often than not to be interfering.

"It's a noodle picture," Kitty explained unnecessarily. "I dyed the noodles with food coloring, and when they were dry I pasted them on the paper to make a picture. It's you and me, see?"

"You're quite the artist!"

"It's like what the Impressionists do," Kitty said. "It looks all mushy up close, but when you look at it from far away it makes a picture."

Delphine raised her eyebrows. "How do you know about the Impressionists?"

"From a book in the library," Kitty replied. "The picture is for you, Aunt Delphine. You can put it on your 'fidgerator."

Delphine bit back a smile. She, too, had been unable to say "refrigerator" until she was almost ten. "Thank you so much. I'll put it up the minute I get home."

"Next up are woven friendship bracelets," Cybel said. "I'm glad we're still at the basic craft stage. I'm dreading the day she decides she's into sports. I'll have to take a second job to keep up with the cost of the equipment."

"Well, if she decides to take up knitting, instead, you know where to come. I'll teach her and she can use my retired needles."

Cybel put out her hand for Kitty to take. "Thanks. I'll keep that in mind. Come on, kiddo, let's drop you off with Grandma. Mommy has to get to work."

Kitty hugged Delphine hard—yes, Delphine thought, Kitty felt skinnier than usual—then took her mother's hand and left the office.

Delphine turned back to her desk. It was going to be a particularly busy day. When you ran a farm the notion of a "weekend" made as little sense as the notion of a vacation. Today there were bills to be reviewed—her own and the farm's—and an office inventory to plan. But as busy as she was, she found her thoughts returning to Maggie and their strange reunion the previous evening.

Ideally, of course, reunions should be about reestablishing a useful emotional or social connection; they should not devolve into a beauty or a career contest, though they usually did. Seeing Maggie's smooth face and unblemished hands at dinner the previous night had made Delphine highly conscious of her own physical flaws. This annoyed her.

She was aware that the sun and the wind and the cold had

done its work on her face and hands and arms. She had what was known as a "farmer's tan," pretty much year-round. There were lines at the corners of her eyes and around her mouth. There were dark spots on the backs of her hands and her cuticles were perpetually raw. She used sunblock, she used moisturizer, she even, at her sister's suggestion, used cuticle oil, but nothing that came in a tube or a jar or a little glass bottle, no matter how expensive (not that Delphine bought expensive products) or touted as miraculous, was going to effectively combat hours, days, weeks, years of sun and wind and cold. Then there was the housekeeping and the shifts at the diner, which sometimes involved loading and unloading the dishwasher and scrubbing the grill. Soft, unmarked skin was just not going to happen for Delphine, and until Maggie's arrival she had never thought of it as an issue.

Nor had her fingers ever felt so . . . inadequate. Next to Maggie's smooth, long fingers, wearing a considerable amount of diamonds, she thought her own fingers looked . . . juvenile. Adornment shouldn't be equated with maturity, she knew that, but somehow those sparkly rings seemed to Delphine like signs of achievement or success. Ridiculous. Vanity had never been a troublesome issue for her and she didn't want it to become one now. That would be a moral defeat.

Delphine suddenly looked up from the computer. One of the chickens, a light brahma, was standing in the open doorway, staring at her. If chickens could actually stare, and Delphine wasn't sure that they could. She smiled. "What's up, Lucy?"

Lucy had nothing to say for herself. Grandly she turned and strutted off. Delphine turned back to the computer. *I bet Lucy doesn't waste her time comparing the color of her feathers to the color of her coopmates' feathers,* Delphine thought. No, only humans, who knew the limited nature of time on earth and who should cherish it, were in fact so wasteful of it.

And that was what Maggie's visit to Ogunquit felt like to

Delphine, a waste of time. They had briefly caught up on the present. What were they to talk about now, the distant past, a past that, with a few exceptions, she was not eager to revisit? In Delphine's opinion there was no point to reminiscing. You couldn't recoup the past, should you even want to, and you couldn't change anything about it, except, maybe, for your feelings about it.

Besides, it didn't take a genius to know that in any relationship, a romance or a friendship, there had to be a give-and-take or the relationship would die. And what could she possibly offer Maggie after all this time? What could Maggie possibly offer her? There was simply no room in Delphine's life for someone she had already once abandoned, for someone whose daily life was so drastically different from her own. There had to be current commonality for a friendship to have a purpose.

Delphine sighed and rubbed her temples. She felt tired. *Maybe,* she thought, *I should just give in to the memories, just for a moment or two.* Like now, she was remembering so clearly the first time she had met Maggie. Forty years ago. Her mother had sent her up the road to the Lilac House with a welcome basket of homemade jams and pickles. Delphine remembered being a little nervous. She didn't meet many strangers. She knocked on the door and waited. When no one answered after a moment or two, she was tempted to leave the basket on the porch and run. And then the door had swung open. A tall, slim, blond girl stood there smiling.

"Hi," she said.

Delphine had been struck dumb for a moment. "Hi," she said finally, holding out the basket. "This is for you."

Maggie had taken the basket. "Thanks," she said, with an even bigger smile. "I'm Maggie."

Maggie's hair was smooth and shiny. Her clothes were pressed and new. Delphine, with her messy, uncombed hair and hand-me-down clothes, felt slightly in awe of this smiling, pretty person.

"I'm Delphine," she said. "I live on the farm down the road."

"Oh, good. I'll have someone to play with. I'm here for the whole summer. Wanna come in?"

Delphine hadn't really been sure that she did, but Maggie seemed kind of nice, so she shrugged, said, "Okay," and followed her inside.

Mrs. Weldon was in the kitchen. She was wearing a mini-dress and pink frosty lipstick. It was the first time Delphine had ever seen a mother wear a mini-dress or lipstick and she felt a little weird about it. But Mrs. Weldon was also very nice and accepted the welcome basket graciously. She gave the girls some grapes and lemonade and went off to continue unpacking. Delphine remembered sitting at the kitchen table with Maggie, popping grapes into her mouth and listening to Maggie chatter on about herself. Maggie told her that she had first been on a plane at the age of four. "My mom's parents live in California," she explained. "So we had to fly. The plane actually had an upstairs and a downstairs! And they showed movies and gave us food and everything."

Delphine was suitably impressed. She had never been farther from her hometown than Portsmouth, New Hampshire.

"Is Portsmouth nice?" Maggie asked.

Delphine nodded.

"Maybe I could get my mom to take us there someday. That would be fun!"

And right then and there, sitting at the kitchen table, Delphine had decided that Maggie was okay. Even if they were different in a lot of ways, so what?

The adult Delphine knew that kids seemed to have a natural ability to accept and appreciate what was put in front of them and ignore as unimportant issues that would give an adult pause. She had seen it with Norman, with Dave Jr., and then with Lori. She was seeing it now with Kitty. Kitty's best friend, Emily, spoke French at home. Kitty and her parents spoke only English. Emily's family was Jewish and the Crandalls were vaguely Christian. Emily had no use for reading while Kitty couldn't get enough of books. Emily was a classic tomboy. Kitty preferred skirts to pants. The girls got along like clams. Their parents waved at each other from a distance.

It was just like it had been with the Crandalls and the Weldons. By the second summer Delphine had understood that her parents and Maggie's parents were not going to be best friends. She remembered the adults being polite when they met and politely interested in each other's affairs, but they had never hung out in the evenings together in the fancy living room at the Lilac House or on the Crandalls' front porch. They had never gotten together for town events like the Fourth of July parade or the communal lobster dinners. For the Crandalls, Sunday mornings had meant early church services followed by a communal pancake breakfast; for the Weldons, Sunday mornings had meant sleeping late, and then coffee and the *New York Times*. Delphine's family had lived in the same house for generations. Maggie's parents had moved four times in the first six years of their marriage. The Crandalls didn't as a rule go to college. The Weldons routinely achieved degrees in higher education.

Sitting at her desk now, Delphine couldn't help but smile. If the adults had been content to be nothing more than polite neighbors, Maggie and Delphine had not. From the day the Weldons arrived in late June until the day they went home to Concord in late August, the girls were inseparable. They jumped rope on the deck behind the Lilac House and roller-skated up and down its lengthy front driveway. They did crafts on the Crandalls' front porch and got ice-cream cones at the shop in Perkins Cove. Mrs. Weldon would take them to the beach, where they would swim and play for hours while Mrs. Weldon perfected her tan. Sometimes, on Saturday afternoons, she would take all five kids to the movies in town at the Leavitt Theatre. While they watched the movie, Mrs. Weldon shopped or had a cocktail at a local restaurant.

Delphine never told her parents that Maggie's mother left them alone in the theatre. The secret was part of the fun. The girls watched television together, shows like *The Partridge Family* and *The Brady Bunch*. For a while, both girls had a big crush on David Cassidy. Sometimes, Mr. Crandall would let them help out with small chores at the farm. Mrs. Crandall taught them to bake, and on the weekends, when Mr. Weldon was at the Lilac House and not at work in Boston, he sometimes would take the girls and their brothers out on a rented fishing boat. When Delphine was old enough to work at the family diner, Maggie waited impatiently for her to come home from her shift so they could get back to the business of being friends.

And then, Delphine remembered, during the long months of the school year, through the rains of fall, the snows of winter, and the blossomings of spring, they had written each other letters. Maggie's were written on pink, flowery stationery, Delphine's on paper torn from a spiral notebook. Over the years, the letters became lengthier and more impassioned, revealing heartaches and sharing dramas and sketching out exciting plans for the following summer.

The sound of a cat yowling in the yard brought Delphine back to the present with a start. No. Even though so many of the memories were pleasant—she couldn't deny that—she could not allow the past to come flooding back like that. She wouldn't allow it. You gave memory an inch and it took a mile. Memories served no purpose other than to undermine a perfectly good present. Memory, like desire, could make you sick.

Delphine thought of Lucy and her feathered friends, who never wasted time with the past, who lived only for the moment at hand, and went back to her work.

5

Maggie flipped off the television—she had been watching a morning news show—and sighed. Since leaving Delphine the night before, she had felt unhappy. Their conversation had been at times awkward, at other times downright boring. And why had she even mentioned the trouble in her marriage? That had been inappropriate, really poor timing. Delphine had seemed so uncomfortable in the parking lot outside the restaurant. Maggie had had to force the issue of their getting together again. Overall, the evening had not been a great success.

She didn't know what she had expected. That Delphine would throw her arms around her? That in one magical instant they would regain the intimacy they had shared for so many years, until Delphine had gone back to Ogunquit and subsequently untied the bonds of their friendship for reasons that had never been clear to Maggie?

Of course not. But still, she had hoped for more . . . joy in their reunion. She had brought the aquamarine necklace with her to the restaurant, just in case things had gone well. She had hoped to explain—she still hoped to explain—why in the end she hadn't asked Delphine to stand up for her at her wedding and instead had asked a cousin she barely even knew.

They had never talked about this; Delphine had never confronted Maggie about her choice. She had just shown up at the wedding—she hadn't gone to the shower—with an impersonal gift from the registry and a card signed with only her name, no special note of support or love. That had hurt Maggie, but she thought that she might have deserved Delphine's anger, if it was indeed anger and not just lack of concern. Maybe, by the time of Maggie's wedding, Delphine had already completely left the friendship behind. Maybe she had shown up purely out of a sense of obligation or duty. If she was anything, Delphine was dutiful. She had learned that from her parents.

Maggie spent some time checking in with her office (there was one minor bit of direction to give to her assistant), her husband (he was in a meeting and said he would call her back), and her housekeeper (Mrs. Barnes had discovered an ant in the kitchen and had laid down traps). She considered checking in with her daughters but decided they would only be annoyed by her texting again, so soon after her last contact. Besides, she had nothing new to tell them. She drank a third cup of coffee and immediately wished that she hadn't. Her digestive system wasn't what it used to be. She brushed her teeth for a second time. When she came back into the bedroom the sound of a child's whoop of glee reached her ears. She crossed to the window and looked down on the outdoor pool below.

A mother, father, and their toddler, a boy, were together at the shallow end of the pool. The mother was pregnant; she sat on the side of the pool, her legs dangling in the cool blue water. The father, standing in the water, held his son tightly in his arms. Maggie smiled to herself. When children were small a parent's life was blessed with so much physical intimacy. It was of necessity, but it was miraculous all the same. That was one of the things she missed now, that physical closeness. But she had done her duty by her children, had raised them through infancy and childhood and adolescence, just as her own mother had done so neatly. Maggie sometimes wondered if her mother had felt a little lost when she and Peter had gone off to college and built lives apart from their parents. If she had felt lost, Dorothy Weldon had given no indication of that. She certainly would never have talked to her daughter about her private emotions. Emotions, Dorothy had taught, when felt at all, were best kept in check.

Maggie turned away from the window and stared blankly at the lovely hotel room before her. She felt deflated, depressed. She wondered if she had been wrong to come back to Ogunquit. She wondered if she should have gone somewhere else, far from Delphine and the past. She wondered if she should just have stayed home.

But what was there for her at home? Gregory would return from his business trip to Chicago and everything would be the same as it had been before he'd left. They would cross paths like the proverbial ships in the night. They would be perfectly polite to each other, exchange pleasant but largely meaningless chitchat, and eat most of their meals electronically connected to other people.

Maggie sighed. Her marriage had changed, no doubt about it. She had never thought she could feel so distant from Gregory. In some ways, he had become a stranger. She no longer knew what he really thought about things, what he really felt about things. And there was the lack of sexual spark, though that bothered her less than mass media told her it should. You could be having sex with your partner and be emotional miles apart. No, it wasn't just a lack of frequent or fantastic sex that was the cause or even the result of their drift. She really didn't think so.

Twenty-four years. They had married in October of 1987. She remembered Gregory making a joke about the start of their life together coinciding with the major stock market crash. Recently, Gregory had said something in passing about celebrating their twenty-fifth anniversary in Japan. He'd always wanted to go to Japan. Maggie didn't want to think about that upcoming landmark. It didn't feel like there was much left to celebrate.

She wondered now if her daughters would even remember their parents' anniversary. They hadn't last year, or the year before that. But maybe that was her fault, in a way. She had been happy, almost relieved, when Kim and then Caitlin had decided to go to college across the country. She remembered feeling a little bit guilty for wanting them out of the house at such a tender age, and she would never have forced them to leave if they hadn't wanted to go, but still, life without the girls living in the house had felt more free and unencumbered.

At first. For a while. But now, she missed her daughters, in spite of what she had told Delphine. She felt alienated from them, a feeling that had little to do with their living in California. But maybe the feelings of loneliness and alienation could be explained away by "empty-nest syndrome." Maybe all of her dissatisfaction could be explained away by the term "mid-life crisis." *Oh, Lord,* Maggie thought, *maybe I'm just one big cliché.*

And that was another problem, too, she thought, sitting on the edge of the king-sized bed. For so many years she had led an unexamined life, yes, a clichéd life. And hadn't someone said that the unexamined life was just not worth living? She just didn't think or wonder in the way she used to, back in college, back before graduate school, back before her marriage and the children and the long, long hours in the office and in the air, flying here and there to meet with clients and advise them on their financial futures. God, she hadn't even read anything other than business and news reports in ages.

Maggie got up from the bed abruptly. She felt she would go mad sitting there alone in this hotel room, whining to herself. She went over to the desk and picked up her iPhone. She sent a text to Delphine's cell. Texts were harder to ignore than calls. When no text came back, she grabbed her gym bag and headed for the resort's spa. A workout followed by a massage might help take her mind off the suspicions that she might be largely unwanted or unwelcome in her own life.

6

1973

Eleven-year-old Delphine stood behind the trunk of the towering pine tree at the very edge of the front yard, peeking at the Lilac House and waiting. Maggie had gone inside ages and ages ago. A flock of butterflies were madly flapping around in Delphine's stomach. She had never felt so nervous.

Finally, Maggie emerged from the front door and skipped down the porch steps. Delphine darted out from behind the tree and ran toward her friend.

"What happened?" she demanded. "You were in there, like, forever."

"Nothing much," Maggie replied, a small smile playing on her lips.

"Did you tell them about the broken window? Are we in big trouble?"

"Yeah, I told them about the window. But I told them it was my fault. I told them I was practicing my Frisbee throws by myself."

"What? But I was the one who threw the Frisbee into the garage window!"

"It doesn't matter. I told my parents that I did it and that I was sorry and they believed me."

Delphine was dumbfounded. "Why? Why did you lie to them?"

Maggie just shrugged.

"I can't believe you took the blame for me. You'll be punished, won't you?" Delphine asked.

"Maybe. But it won't be anything bad. Maybe, like, no TV for a week. That would be kind of bad 'cause I think John Boy on *The Waltons* is cute."

Delphine wrinkled her nose. "Gross!"

"You don't think John Boy is cute?"

"No way."

"Well, anyway, my dad usually feels so bad if he has to punish us that he lets us off the hook after about a day."

Delphine felt awful. The butterflies in her stomach had been replaced by a dull ache. "Still, you shouldn't have taken the blame for me. I should confess."

Maggie shook her head, making her blond braids fly. "No way. Your parents are way stricter than mine. They might not let us hang out together. Then what? Besides, it's no big deal. You'd do the same for me, right?"

"Sure," Delphine said immediately. She would. "Best friends forever. We swore. Remember?"

"Of course. Pinky swear."

They linked pinkies and swore again. "Thanks, Maggie," Delphine said. "I owe you."

"Whatever. Hey, want to ride our bikes over to the farm and see if those chicks are hatched yet?"

Delphine smiled. "Race you!"

7

Delphine didn't return Maggie's call until Sunday evening. She had ignored her text. That wasn't unusual. She didn't like texting. She felt stupid doing it; her fingers, usually so deft, in this case didn't want to obey her brain. She had mastered several difficult stitches and techniques with her knitting—she executed the difficult German Brioche stitch with relative ease—but mastery of the tiny telephone and its many options eluded her. Or maybe she was just being a stubborn holdback. The thought had crossed her mind.

Maggie had sounded very pleased to hear from her. Delphine had suggested they have lunch together at the farm the next day. Maybe a sandwich in her cramped little office might help prove to Maggie that she really was very busy and that she really didn't have any time to spend with her. Not much time, anyway.

Maggie arrived at Delphine's office a little before noon on Monday. She was wearing a sleeveless black linen blouse, white Capri-cut jeans, and pink kitten-heeled sandals. She carried a pink-and-black-checked linen bag. *City mouse visits country mouse,* Delphine thought, unconsciously pulling on the hem of her old green T-shirt.

"Thanks for asking me to lunch," Maggie said.

Delphine shrugged. "Sure. Everyone has to eat." She hefted a red cooler onto her desk and began to unload it. She had made the sandwiches at home, big hearty ones on whole-grain bread, filled with ham, cheese, tomato, lettuce, and slathered in mayonnaise.

Maggie, sitting gingerly in an old folding chair Delphine had indicated as her seat, refused to reveal her disappointment. She had been hoping for a light meal of chilled oysters and ceviche, maybe accompanied by a glass of vhino verde, on a restaurant patio overlooking the ocean. Instead, she was perched precariously on an ancient piece of outdoor furniture, being offered a sandwich the size of her head. But at least she and Delphine were together. That was what she had hoped for more than an upscale meal. She accepted the monstrous sandwich, unwrapped it, and then rewrapped half of it. The beverage choices were water or coffee. Maggie chose water, thinking it would come in a bottle. Instead it came from a tap. At least, Maggie noted, the plastic cup was clean.

As Delphine bit hungrily into her sandwich, Maggie let her eyes roam. "It doesn't look like much has changed since I was last here," she said after a few minutes. "The summer before we went off to college. The last summer my parents rented the Lilac House."

"Yeah, it's mostly the same," Delphine agreed. "The desk has been here as long as I can remember. My chair is fairly new, one of those ergonomic things. I got it on craigslist. And of course, the computer is new. In fact, I'm not sure we had a computer back then, back when you were around. I'd have to ask my father when exactly we changed over. I know it was Jackie's doing that we finally went electronic." Delphine gestured to her desk. "Though there always seem to be piles of paper . . ."

Maggie looked up to the plain, tan corkboard over the desk. On it were tacked various bills and other official-looking notices, a faded photograph of a dark-haired child on a pony—Delphine?—and a yellowed piece of paper on which the following words had been typed by a probably now ancient typewriter: " 'There is more to life than increasing its speed.'—Mohandas Gandhi." Maggie smiled to herself. *Tell that to my boss,* she thought. *Tell that to Gregory. Tell that to me.*

Delphine took another large bite of her sandwich and glanced at her friend sitting on the old folding chair that had been leaning against the back wall of the office for years. She had wiped it down before Maggie's arrival. Still, she was afraid that Maggie's white jeans were probably not going to be quite so white when she got back into her Lexus. She wondered if she should have warned Maggie that the office was not a pristine place and then thought, *Who would be silly enough to wear white around chickens, and mud, and farm equipment, much of which was at least partially rusted?*

"Do you play golf?" Maggie asked suddenly.

"No," Delphine said. "Why?"

"Well, because I'm staying at Gorges Grant I have privileges at the Cape Neddick Country Club. I thought that maybe we could play some golf. I remember it being a gorgeous course. Well, I've only seen it from the road, but . . ."

Delphine began to fold the wrinkled aluminum foil that had covered her sandwich. She would rinse the foil when she got home and use it again. After that, it would go into the recycling bin. "No, thanks," she said. "I've never played golf. I don't really have any interest in the game. And I don't really have the time." *Or the money,* she thought, *and I don't want you paying for me.* "Sorry. You could play alone. I've driven by the course and seen people playing alone."

Maggie smiled, but she doubted her smile looked anything other than lame. "Yes," she said, "maybe I will."

They sat in silence for a few minutes, Delphine sipping a coffee, until Maggie just couldn't stand it any longer. Did Delphine really have nothing to say to her?

"You know," she said, "the farm always seemed kind of, I don't know, like a giant outdoor playhouse. I mean, back when I was a kid. I don't think I ever realized that people actually worked here. Whenever your father let us help out with something it was an adventure."

Delphine laughed. "Oh, it's an adventure all right. Like when we don't get enough rain and the crops dry up, or when we get too much rain and the fields flood, or the cultivating tractor breaks down and we can't get a part for days."

"Then why do you still do it?" Maggie asked. "Why does your family keep farming? Aren't most small farms a losing proposition these days?"

Delphine felt challenged. "We do it because we've done it for years," she said, careful to keep her tone even. "We farm because we love it."

"I don't know. It just seems like it's so much work for so little return."

"Not everything in life has to be about the return, or about the profit," Delphine said forcefully. "Lots of times the journey is what's important, not the payoff at the end of the road."

But if the journey doesn't make you enough money to pay your mortgage, Maggie thought, *then you're out in the streets.* She let the subject drop.

"Are you going to eat the other half of your sandwich?" Delphine asked, getting up from her chair. Clearly, Maggie thought, lunchtime was over. She'd only been at the farm for about forty minutes.

"Oh, uh, no," she said. "I'm sorry. I just don't eat that much for lunch."

Delphine shrugged, picked up the abandoned half sandwich, and tucked it back in the red cooler. "I'll have it for dinner," she said, "with the vegetable soup I made last night."

Maggie just nodded. So much for evening plans. She would ask the concierge at the hotel to recommend a well-reviewed restaurant where she would feel comfortable dining alone. A restaurant with a good wine list and clean chairs.

"What are you doing tomorrow?" Maggie asked as they left the office and emerged into the noonday sun. "I know you're working, of course. But I'm sure you must have a bit of free time."

Delphine fought back a sigh. *This,* she thought, *is like being stalked.* Though stalkers were probably a lot less polite. It couldn't be healthy in the long run, but she supposed that "for old times' sake" she could share a few more awkward lunches in the office or on a bench in Perkins Cove. Not that she put much stock in "old times."

"Why don't you come by the house around nine tomorrow morning," she suggested reluctantly. "My neighbor Jemima is stopping by. We could have coffee."

Maggie smiled. "That would be great," she said. "I'd love to see your house. Oh, and I could show you mine. I've got some photos on my iPhone that were taken last year when we were thinking about putting the house on the market."

Delphine tried to imagine the sort of luxurious home Maggie and her family might live in. Would there be walk-in closets and an in-ground heated pool? Would there be central air-conditioning and a Jacuzzi in the master bathroom? "Okay," she said. "So, I'll see you then."

Delphine gave Maggie directions to her house and again watched as she drove off in her sleek, pristine car. She wondered what Maggie would do with herself for the rest of the day and felt momentarily guilty that she hadn't offered an invitation for dinner, that she hadn't even suggested some local activities that Maggie might enjoy. There was a new exhibit at the Barn Gallery, and another at the Ogunquit Museum of American Art. Neither place would threaten the whiteness of her jeans. She could take a drive out to the Nubble Lighthouse or go shopping up in Portland. Neither one of those activities would cause too much damage to heeled sandals.

She turned and went back to her desk. She had her own life to live and her own responsibilities to bear, and those responsibilities, copious though they were, did not include being Maggie Weldon Wilkes's social director.

8

It was almost nine o'clock on Tuesday morning. Delphine had been up since five and had already been out to the farm. Then she had stopped in to her parents' house for a second cup of coffee and to see how her father, who had a light cold, was feeling. Better, was the answer, though Patrice had convinced him to stay home that morning and let her handle the diner on her own. Then Delphine had driven to her brother's house to drop off a jigsaw puzzle—it was a picture of kittens in a basket—she had bought for Kitty at a yard sale. She had made it back home in time to welcome her closest friend in Ogunquit, Jemima Larkin, who would be coming by soon. Not that Jemima needed a formal welcome. Besides, even if Delphine wasn't yet home, Jemima had a key.

Delphine looked around her living room and sighed. She wished she hadn't invited Maggie to come by the house. Not that she was in the least ashamed of it; not at all, she was proud of her home. Still, in all the years she had lived there, no one other than family and a few select locals, neighbors such as Jemima and, of course, Harry, had ever been there. Delphine had come to feel protective of her privacy. There was a very satisfying feeling of safety and quiet and seclusion that she cherished when she was home alone with Melchior.

The house itself had been in the Crandall family since it was built around 1925. The first floor was comprised of a living room and a kitchen, off of which was a pantry that Delphine kept well stocked with dry goods and jars of her mother's sauerkraut, pickles, and blueberry preserves.

A staircase against the right-hand wall of the living room led to the second floor, where off a short, narrow hallway there were two rooms and a bathroom. The larger room, the one in the back, was Delphine's bedroom. The bed had an iron frame and foot- and headboard. On the bed was a quilt her mother had made for her one Christmas. Under the window sat an old oak desk, on which sat her laptop, a chipped clay mug containing pens and pencils, and a spiral-bound notebook. The pine dresser, both tall and wide, had belonged to her grandmother. On it were a framed photograph of Kitty and one of her parents on their wedding day. For many years there had also been a picture of Delphine on her graduation from Bartley College, but eventually that had migrated to a drawer. There were no framed pictures of Harry. On the wide pine board floor were two braided rugs that had been around since Delphine's childhood. She had a vague notion that her grandmother, her mother's mother, had made them, but she would have to check with Patrice to be sure.

The second room, the smaller one, faced the front of the house. It had no closet. The walls were painted white and the floor was painted robin's egg blue. This was where Delphine stored her many skeins of wool and knitting cotton, fleecy wools, and Shetland wool, and cotton wool blends; her various kinds of needles, wood and metal, circular and double pointed; and her collection of patterns, both new and vintage, that she found from all sorts of sources, from the Internet, to the Central Yarn Shop in Portland, to yard sales.

Against one entire wall stood a simple wooden bookcase, built by her brother. It was packed with books, some from her childhood, others from college, others she had bought at yard sales and secondhand bookstores over the years. Mostly there were the classics of the Western canon. With a few exceptions, Delphine was a traditionalist in her reading. There was an old, water-damaged copy of *Jane Eyre*. There was a paperback collection of Jane Austen's novels, none of which had cost more than two dollars. The showpiece of her collection was a complete set of the work of Charles Dickens. Published in the late nineteenth century, the books were tall and heavy and bound in dark green leather with tooled gilt writing. The works were printed in four columns per page, the print minuscule. She had found the set in an antique shop, at the bottom of a box of old, musty clothing. The set had cost six dollars. Sometimes she thought it was the best six dollars she had ever spent.

The bathroom was fairly small and dominated by an old claw-footed tub. Delphine had installed a shower, with Dave Sr.'s help, when she first moved in. Wood paneling, painted white, reached up the walls about a third of the way. Above the paneling, Delphine had painted the walls a pale mint green. The white towels were fairly worn, though the bath mat was new, a bargain Jemima had picked up for her at Marden's.

Delphine checked her watch. Almost nine o'clock.

"Ready for guests?" she asked Melchior.

He didn't reply. He was sitting on the back of the couch. It was one of his favorite perches because it gave him an unobstructed view of the front porch and, more important, of the hummingbirds fluttering madly at the feeder. Hummingbirds were okay—to Melchior, they looked like tasty snacks—but he didn't care for the crows that occasionally gathered out front. Some of them were almost as big as he was. When they began their awful screeching and cawing he retreated to the interior of the house. And if Melchior happened to witness a male wild turkey or, worse, a mother with her brood, strutting out of the woods behind the house, he charged under the living room couch. Maine coon cats were known as great mousers. Not Melchior.

Delphine straightened a large stack of library books. They were due back that day. Nancy, the town's librarian, did an excellent job of seeking out the books Delphine wanted to read, but the library's resources were limited. Delphine made a mental note to stop at the recently renovated library in Portland the next time she had reason to head north on a weekday. Jackie usually drove the produce to Portland for the summer farmers' markets on Wednesdays and Saturdays. Maybe one Wednesday she would join her.

Jemima arrived at five minutes to nine. She was wearing an oversized flowered shirt over a pair of baggy striped shorts. If Delphine's wardrobe was less than fashionable, Jemima's was a travesty of style. In fact, clothes seemed almost an afterthought to her. The only jewelry she wore was a slim gold wedding band, now embedded into the flesh of her ring finger, and a tiny silver-toned watch that had once belonged to an aunt.

"I made corn muffins," she said, holding up a plate loosely covered in tinfoil. "They're still warm." Of course, Jemima had made them from scratch; she was an excellent cook and baker.

Jemima was originally from Connecticut but had lived in Ogunquit for twenty-five years, ever since she had married Jim Larkin, a native of Norridgewock, Maine. Some people still considered Jemima as "from away," but in her own mind, which was all that counted with Jemima, she was a genuine Mainer. Jemima had three children. The oldest, a young man named Kurt, whose father was her first husband, was "on the road" at the moment, and that's pretty much all anyone knew. Occasionally, Jemima would receive a postcard informing her that he was alive, well, and currently in Alaska or Montana or Florida. The second child, a boy named Jake, was studying at the University of Southern Maine. Sarah, the youngest, was in high school and lived at home. Recently she had informed her parents that she wanted to go to college in California. "Roaming must be in their genes," Jemima had told Delphine, with a sad shake of her head. "Some ancestor of mine was probably a pioneer."

After Jemima had put the plate of corn muffins in the

kitchen, she returned to the living room just in time to witness Maggie pulling up to the house and parking next to her own thirteen-year-old Mazda. It was missing three hubcaps and part of the front fender had been eaten away by rust.

"Well, will you look at that car?" Jemima frowned, as if offended by the obvious display of wealth. "That must have cost a pretty penny."

"A lot of pretty pennies," Delphine said. "But I guess she can afford it. She has a big job in Boston."

Jemima murmured what sounded an awful lot like, "Big deal."

Maggie got out of the car carrying a large bouquet of flowers—lush pink peonies—wrapped in shiny cellophane. She paused for a moment to look up at the house. She was wearing a pair of slim-fitting tan Capri pants and a navy cropped blazer over a white T-shirt. Her flats and her bag were navy patent leather. Delphine couldn't help but survey her own clothing, thrown on without thought at the crack of dawn, clean, but not ready for prime time.

"I'll get the door," she said, before Maggie had time to knock. "Hey," she said. "I see my directions were clear."

"Perfectly." Maggie stepped inside and offered the bouquet to Delphine. "These are for you. I had no idea what your décor would be like, so I thought flowers would be a safe bet. But I guess I didn't think it through. You have such a lovely garden right out front."

Delphine took the bouquet. It was from the most expensive florist in town. "Thanks," she said. "I love flowers so—"

Maggie suddenly spotted Melchior. "Oh, my God," she said, her hand to her heart, "that cat is huge."

"His name is Melchior."

"Appropriate," Maggie said, as Melchior stood, stretched, and turned his back on the women.

Delphine smiled. "I forgot you're not a big fan of animals."

"No, I guess I'm not," Maggie admitted. "I remember that

massive dog you had years ago, when we were just kids. What was his name? I practically fainted the first time I saw him. He was up to my shoulder. Well, almost."

"Longfellow. My father named him after the poet. Longfellow was big," she told Jemima, "a Greater Swiss Mountain Dog, but he had the sweetest nature. I remember Joey teasing Maggie about being afraid of being in the same room with him. Anyway, Jemima, this is Maggie Weldon Wilkes."

Maggie reached out to shake Jemima's hand. Jemima hesitated, and then responded with a bone-crunching grasp and one hearty pump that made Maggie wince.

"So," Jemima said by way of greeting, "you don't have pets?"

Maggie shook her head. "No. I didn't grow up with pets. My mother didn't like the mess they made. When my girls were little they wanted a dog, but Gregory and I were on the road so much it just didn't make sense. Kim had a goldfish for a while. Or maybe it was Caitlin, I can't remember. It went down the toilet after a few weeks."

"My husband and I have three dogs," Jemima said, "all from shelters, and a tame raccoon. They're no trouble at all. We call them our fur children."

"A tame raccoon?" Maggie looked horror stricken. "I didn't think there could be such a thing. Don't raccoons carry rabies?"

"They can. But Ben is all right; he's had his shots."

Maggie's dubious expression betrayed her doubts about Ben the raccoon's health. She stretched the fingers of the hand Jemima had crunched and surveyed the living room.

"This room is charming," she said. "I love the fireplace. It must be so cozy in here in the winter."

"I mostly use the wood stove to heat the house," Delphine explained, laying the bouquet on a side table. "It can still be fairly cold upstairs at night, but I have plenty of extra blankets."

Jemima pretended to fan herself with her hand. "And it's as hot as hell in the summer."

"It feels cool now," Maggie commented.

"That's because Delphine finally caved and got an air conditioner."

Delphine shrugged. "I don't feel the heat as badly as some people."

Jemima smiled. "We make sacrifices for our friends."

Jemima, Maggie thought, must spend a fair amount of time at Delphine's house if Delphine bought an air conditioner for her. She looked between the two women and realized that she felt jealous of their friendship. Once upon a time, she had shared an easy rapport with Delphine. What had gone so wrong? Oh. Right. Delphine had walked away. And after a time, Maggie had ceased to follow. But she was back now and things could be what they once were. She truly believed that. Mostly.

Maggie's attention was drawn to the stack of books on the coffee table in front of the couch.

"You're still a voracious reader, I see."

Delphine smiled. "Yes. And I have to return these books to the library today."

"I could take them on my way out."

"Thanks, Jemima," Delphine said. "That would be a help."

Maggie peered more closely at the top book in the stack. It was a survey of the English Civil Wars. "I hate using the library," she said. "Number one, I just don't have the time to be reading on someone else's schedule. And the library is hardly ever open when I have the time to run in. And when you take a book out of the library you have no idea who's been touching it. I've found food stains and even dead bugs on the pages of library books."

"Well," Delphine said, hating the note of apology she heard in her voice, "new books are so expensive, especially the hardcover ones . . . I'm afraid I'd be lost without the library."

"And people up here are more respectful of public property than people in the city, I'd say," Jemima added, looking pointedly at Maggie. "We don't have those sorts of vandalism problems in Ogunquit."

Maggie tensed. She didn't like this woman at all. First she had tried to break her hand and now she was implying that she lived in a den of iniquity? "Then you're lucky," she said. "I suppose there are benefits to living in such an out-of-the-way place."

"Come," Delphine said a bit too brightly, "let me show you the rest of the house."

"That would be great," Maggie said.

Jemima followed the other two women to the stairs. Maggie wondered why she was coming along for the tour. Maybe, she thought, Jemima was scared to leave Delphine alone with the woman from the big, bad city.

Delphine led the way up the stairs and to the smaller, front bedroom. "This is a sort of catchall room," she explained. "My library and my workroom."

"Wow," Maggie said. "All the wool, the needles—is this all yours? I didn't know that you knit." She walked over to the worktable, on which several pieces in various degrees of completion were laid out. "You're so skilled. Look at all these different stitches. Delphine, your work is amazing."

Delphine shrugged. "Thanks. I took up knitting a few years after college."

"You sell your work, of course. These pieces are too beautiful to just give away."

Delphine wasn't sure she understood the logic in that reasoning but let it pass without comment. "Yes, I sell a bit in the summer. I have a sign I put on the porch. 'Blueberry Cove Designs.' It sounds a bit pretentious to me, but Jackie came up with it and, well, I guess it works. People stop by."

"But your house is kind of out-of-the-way," Maggie noted. "You can't get much traffic. And what happens if someone does come by and you're not home?"

"What happens? I don't know. They come back, I guess. If they're really interested."

"Do you advertise in other places, besides the front porch?" Maggie asked. "You know, signs in town, ads in the local papers, flyers in the hotels."

"No, not really," Delphine said. "Well, no, not at all, actually."

Maggie tried to hide her exasperation. "You should, Delphine. I mean really, your work is exquisite. How much inventory do you have? Do you design to order? I'm assuming you buy your materials wholesale—"

"Wait!" Delphine laughed. "Maggie, my knitting is not a big business. It's a hobby. I just like to knit. Well, I love it, really. But it's not my job."

Maggie didn't look convinced. She pointed to a completed sweater that hung on a padded hanger from what was originally meant to be a hat rack. "Please tell me this sweater is for sale. I want to buy it right now. I absolutely love the color. Blondes always look good in periwinkle. And the work around the collar is gorgeous. How much is it?"

Delphine felt a little panicked. "I can't charge a . . . an old friend."

"Yes, you can. I don't care what you say, Delphine, this is a business," she argued. "And it's special because it's all your own. It's not one of your family's ventures."

Jemima had said nothing during this exchange, but Delphine could feel disapproval, maybe unreasonable, emanating from her. She risked a glance and then hurriedly looked away from Jemima's frown. "I suppose I could offer a 'family and friends discount.' " She named a price significantly lower than what she would charge a stranger.

"Delphine! Don't be ridiculous. I feel like I'm stealing from you." Maggie held out the sleeves of the sweater and sighed. "It's so lovely. . . . Well, all right. I have cash."

Jemima's eyes widened as Maggie removed several fresh bills from her slim red leather wallet. The wallet, Jemima noted, was monogrammed. Without meeting Maggie's eye, Delphine stuffed the bills into her back pocket and proceeded to wrap the sweater in white tissue paper. Then she put the sweater into a plain brown shopping bag.

"You should have your logo on the bags," Maggie said. "It's an easy way to advertise."

"I'll show you the bedroom," Delphine said in response.

Maggie decided not to ask about a receipt. She suspected that Delphine probably didn't keep accurate accounts of her sales. She followed the other women down the short hallway to the back of the house. The bedroom, Maggie thought, had the comfortable look of a refuge, unlike her bedroom back home, which, thanks to the decorator she had hired, perhaps wrongly, looked more like an impersonal hotel suite than someone's personal sanctuary.

Maggie walked over to the old dresser and picked up the framed school portrait of a little girl. "Is this Kitty?" she asked.

"Yeah. That picture was taken last September, at the start of the school year."

Maggie looked from the photograph to Delphine. "She could be your daughter," she said. "The resemblance is so strong. It's like looking at you when you were a little girl."

Delphine smiled. "That's what everyone says."

"Has her appetite gotten any better?" Jemima asked, her voice low, as if to exclude Maggie from hearing.

"Not really," Delphine replied. "Maybe it's just the heat. Some people lose their appetite in the heat."

Maggie refrained from making a comment and replaced the photograph on the dresser. The women moved on to the bathroom. "A claw-footed tub," Maggie noted. "I'd love to have one, but our master bedroom and bath are contemporary. It just wouldn't work with our décor." *Our impersonal décor.*

Under her breath, but loud enough for Delphine to hear, Jemima muttered, "A tub is a tub."

"And that's the upstairs," Delphine said, leading the way back down to the first floor. "The house is small, I suppose, but it's big enough for me." *And for Harry when he spends the night,* she added silently. Harry had a drawer in the bedroom's dresser for a change of underwear and clothing, but there was no need for that to have been on the tour.

"So, Maggie," Jemima said when the women were back in the living room. "Is your husband here in Ogunquit with you?"

Delphine eyed her questioningly. She had told Jemima that Maggie was in town alone.

"No," Maggie said, "Gregory's in Chicago, on business. He's a partner in a law firm."

"My husband is an engineer. He's been put on part-time," Jemima added almost defiantly. "This economy is hard on a lot of people. Lots of us can't afford to be taking vacations."

"Yes," Maggie said. For Delphine's sake she would refrain from giving this Jemima person a tongue-lashing, or a smack across her face. "I know."

"Jim also forages for exotic mushrooms and fiddleheads," Delphine said, though what that bit of information could possibly add to the conversation she didn't know.

Maggie seemed puzzled. "He's a forager? But where does an engineer learn to forage? And isn't it dangerous, out there in the woods, with all the wild animals and poisonous plants? Who buys the mushrooms and fiddleheads?"

"Plenty of people," Jemima replied. "A lot of the local chefs. He does just fine."

"And what do you do?" Maggie asked.

"What do I do?"

"Yes, what do you do?" Maggie repeated. "I mean, for a living. What do you do for a career?"

Delphine winced. It wasn't the kind of question people around town asked each other. Maybe that was because everyone pretty much knew what everyone else did. Maybe that was because the question seemed somehow irrelevant, when better questions might be: "How are you doing?" and "Are you and your family well?"

Jemima, however, answered proudly. "I'm a mother of three children," she said. "And I work part-time as a waitress at Clay Hill. That's one of our best restaurants."

Maggie laughed a little. "Oh, I haven't waited tables since college! I couldn't do it now; I wouldn't last a night. I don't think I'd have the patience to deal with fussy customers. Waiting tables is really a young person's job."

Delphine tensed. Jemima smiled tightly. "Then it's lucky," she said, "that you don't have to do it."

Maggie blushed. She had spoken unthinkingly. "I'm so sorry," she said quickly. "I didn't mean to—"

"How about some coffee?" Delphine suggested, and made for the kitchen. "And we should get to those muffins before they're entirely cold."

Jemima and Maggie followed Delphine into the kitchen.

Maggie was shocked by the tiny size of the room. Her kitchen at home was at least four times the size of Delphine's. Not that it got much use, especially since the girls had gone off to college. The breakfast nook might as well not even be there. The grill was spotless with disuse. Mostly, on nights when they were home together, Maggie and Gregory ate dinner—something from a local gourmet take-out place—while sitting at the marble-topped kitchen bar, using their iPhones to text their colleagues.

The sink in Delphine's kitchen was narrow and deep. Maggie guessed it dated from the 1940s. The stovetop had only two burners, one quite small and the other not much larger. A quick glance around revealed a lack of dishwasher. An old-fashioned two-slice pop-up toaster sat on a small counter next to the sink. The front of the fridge, which had to be circa 1975, was covered with a child's artwork. Kitty's, Maggie guessed.

"I guess you don't cook much," she said to Delphine.

"Oh, I cook every night. Why?"

"Oh." Maggie shook her head. "Nothing."

Jemima took her plate of homemade corn muffins from the counter by the sink and placed it on the square kitchen table, a piece that seemed to dwarf the room. Delphine brought a fresh pot of coffee to the table and they sat. Maggie accepted a cup and that answered Delphine's question about Maggie's changed habits. She then took a muffin, sliced it in half, and ate half of one half, without butter or jam. In rapid succession, Jemima ate three muffins, with both butter and jam, almost, it seemed to Delphine, in defiance of Maggie's self-regulation. Delphine helped herself to one muffin and tried not to smile.

"You don't like corn muffins?" Jemima asked, a slight note of challenge in her tone, when Maggie had delicately slid her plate away.

"Oh, it's not that," she said. "They're delicious. It's just that I try not to eat too many carbs."

Jemima raised her eyebrows just a little bit and took another sip of her coffee. Delphine said, "My mother made this blueberry jam," and then realized that it was loaded with sugar, hence Maggie's rejection of it. *Fat, too,* she thought, glancing at the butter, *must be on the list of restricted foods.* Delphine pulled the hem of her T-shirt down in an unconscious attempt to hide a tummy that thoroughly enjoyed carbs and fat.

Jemima left soon after, taking the library books with her and wishing Maggie a safe trip back to Boston. *So,* Maggie thought, *this woman has no plans to spend any more time with me.* That was fine with her.

"I should be going now, too," Maggie said, when Jemima had driven off. "I'm sure you have a lot to do."

Delphine did have a lot to do and she did want Maggie to go, but at the same time she felt responsible for the tensions of the morning. Well, she knew she hadn't been at fault, but she had brought the two women together. Good manners dictated that she couldn't let Maggie go without a gesture of courtesy. Jemima was a tough cookie. She could take care of herself. Maggie, if memory served, and who knew if it did, was a more sensitive person.

"The pictures of your house," she said. "You said you were going to show them to me."

"Oh. Right." Maggie hesitated. The last thing she wanted to do right now was show Delphine photographs that would further emphasize the vast divide between their lives. Four bathrooms, three bedrooms, a den, a living room, a dining room, and a state-of-the-art kitchen as opposed to the cramped, if charming, quarters of a small old farmhouse. Maybe if Jemima hadn't poisoned the atmosphere with her bad attitude and made Maggie feel like a clumsy, critical interloper she could share the pictures without worry for Delphine's feelings.

"So," Delphine asked, "can I see them?"

Maggie shrugged. "Well, the thing is I thought the pictures were still on my iPhone, but I checked last night and it turns out I must have deleted them."

"Oh, okay," Delphine said. She had made an effort, and now she really did need to get back to the farm. "I'll walk out with you," she said, reaching for her keys, which sat on a small table by the door. She would deal later with the flowers Maggie had brought. With a farewell to Melchior, she pulled the door shut behind her.

9

Delphine sighed as she navigated the holiday traffic in the heart of town. She wasn't looking forward to an excursion with Maggie, but it was too late to cancel now. It was all because she still felt a bit guilty about Jemima's behavior toward Maggie the previous morning. She hadn't expected the two women to become fast friends, but Jemima's unpleasant attitude had been uncalled for. Then again, Maggie had been insensitive, with her comments about the library and waitressing and foraging and . . . And what if Maggie had had those pictures of her house in her iPhone? In retrospect Delphine was glad Maggie had deleted them. She wasn't sure she could have faked interest in an opulent and no doubt wasteful home.

Anyway, the guilt had compelled her to call Maggie and invite her to go along shopping that morning. And now she was at Gorges Grant, driving up to the hotel's entrance, where Maggie was waiting, once again in Capri pants and matching sandals and bag. Delphine was very aware that the other vehicles pulling up to the hotel were in far better condition than her old truck. And they weren't trucks.

"I put a towel on the passenger seat," Delphine said as Maggie climbed in, "so you wouldn't get your clothes dirty."

"I see. Thanks. So, where are we going? I love shopping." Maggie laughed. "Well, you know that. How many times did I drag you with me to the mall when we were in college?"

"I don't remember, but I'm sure it was too many times."

"What's on your wish list? Are we going to the outlets in Kittery?"

Delphine shook her head. "No wish list. No outlets. Just some things I need to get."

Things like a new rubber spatula, as Harry had accidentally melted her old one while trying to make a grilled cheese sandwich in her big old cast-iron skillet. She could probably get one for a decent price at the grocery store if she couldn't find one at Renys. A pair of jeans for her niece Kitty, as the pair she owned now was pretty worn out. And she would look for a new summer nightgown for her mother. The old blue cotton one she was wearing was practically threadbare. It bothered Delphine that her mother paid so little attention to her own wants. Not that she was much better at that, but she did spend some money on her wool and other knitting supplies. It didn't feel like splurging. It felt like a necessity, and the knitting did earn back some money. When she didn't undersell to an old friend.

"Oh," Maggie said. She wondered if Delphine had gotten around to putting those flowers she had brought her in water. She didn't want to ask.

A few minutes later, Delphine pulled into a parking lot on Post Road in Wells.

"Have you ever been to Renys?" Delphine asked as they got out of the truck.

"I don't think so." Maggie tried to feign enthusiasm but suspected she was failing. "We don't have Renys in Massachusetts. At least, I don't think we do. I usually shop at Lord & Taylor, and sometimes Louis of Boston. There are some nice boutiques on Boylston and Newbury Streets, too."

Delphine opened the glass door for Maggie and let her pass inside. "This place has been around since 1949. They've got fourteen stores around the state. And I'm pretty sure it's still family run."

"Oh," Maggie said. "That's nice."

"There's a fun phrase: 'If Renys doesn't have it, I don't need it.' "

Maggie smiled. She had no idea what she could say to that.

"You should also give Goodwill a shot while you're in Maine," Delphine said. She wondered if Maggie knew that she was teasing her. "There's a massive store out by the mall in South Portland, though there's probably one by you back in Lexington."

Goodwill, Maggie thought. *Thank God my mother isn't hearing this conversation.* "Oh," she said, "that's okay. I don't really need anything right now. . . ."

"Really, you can get some amazing bargains. I got Harry a pack of undershirts for three dollars. They're slightly irregular, but nobody sees them."

"Well," Maggie said carefully, "I think Gregory is all set with undershirts for now. . . ." And he would never consent to wear irregular anything, Maggie thought, not even undershirts. In fact, neither would she. What would be the point?

Maggie trailed behind as Delphine set about looking for her few items. It didn't take long. Clearly, she had never become a recreational shopper.

"There's nothing for you," Maggie said when Delphine's purchases were laid out on the checkout counter.

"I know. Oh, well, the spatula's for me."

"Don't you want anything . . . fun—for yourself?"

"Fun?" Delphine repeated. "No. I don't need anything right now. Except the spatula."

I didn't ask if she needed anything, Maggie thought. *I asked if she wanted anything.* "I saw a nice blouse back there," she said. "From what remained of the tag I think it might be a Talbots. It's a very pretty coral. It would look very nice with your coloring and your dark hair. Do you want me to show you?"

Delphine pushed her purchases farther along the checkout counter as the woman in front of her moved on. "No, that's okay," she said. "I've got plenty of blouses already. I don't wear them all that much, anyway. Mostly, I'm in T-shirts in the summer and flannel in the winter."

Maggie had nothing to say to that. The concept of shopping without getting a little something for herself was truly foreign. Just a little something, a little gift for the effort. Her mother had taught her all about giving herself little treats. *But then again,* she thought, *one needed disposable income for little treats. . . .* Maggie tried to remember if on any of those shopping trips during college Delphine had ever bought anything frivolous for herself. She didn't think that she had.

Delphine paid for her purchases. As they were leaving the store, two quite elderly women, walking arm in arm, were entering.

"The Simmons sisters," Delphine whispered as they approached. "You must remember them?"

"Of course I do," Maggie replied. "But I haven't thought of them in years."

Both ladies wore broad-brimmed straw sun hats, decorated with somewhat dusty silk roses, and immaculate white cotton gloves that came almost to the elbow. Martha's long flowered dress was drawn in at the waist by a narrow belt of cracked patent leather. Constance, a bit stouter than her sister, wore an identical long flowered dress without a belt. Both had blue eyes, now faded and somewhat milky. Beneath their hats Maggie could glimpse hair so white it almost glowed.

"Well, if it isn't Delphine Crandall," the thinner of the two women said in greeting.

"Martha, Constance, it's so nice to see you," Delphine said. "Do you remember my friend Maggie Weldon? She and her family rented the Lilac House for several years, way back in the seventies."

Martha put a gloved finger to the tip of her nose and tapped. "Oh, dear, now that was a long time ago. Sister, do you remember anything about a Weldon family?"

Constance repeated her sister's gesture. "Oh, wait now, something's coming to me. Yes, I do seem to remember Delphine having a friend from away. Yes, and I think her family used to stay at the Lilac House. . . ."

Maggie smiled. "Yes, that's me, Maggie Weldon. Maggie Weldon Wilkes now."

"Well, dear, you look just lovely. What have you been doing all this time?"

"Oh," Maggie said, "the usual, I suppose. Getting married, having kids, building a career." She didn't mention the regular Botox injections. She wasn't sure the Simmons sisters would know what Botox was. She wasn't sure Delphine would approve.

She's also been avoiding the library and carbohydrates, Delphine added silently, at the same time scolding herself for the stupidly critical tinge of her thoughts.

"We're just out for a little shopping," Delphine said, holding up her bag.

Martha's eyes widened and she looked suddenly years younger. "We just love to shop," she said, "ever since we were little girls, remember, Constance?"

Constance nodded enthusiastically. Delphine smiled. "Then we'll let you get to it."

The women exchanged good-byes and the Simmons sisters moved on inside the store. Delphine and Maggie climbed into the truck. Maggie carefully adjusted the towel so that her clothes were entirely protected from the cracked and dusty upholstery.

"How old are the Simmons sisters?" she asked.

"Oh, they must be getting close to ninety now," Delphine said as she pulled out of the parking lot and back onto the road. "Maybe they're over ninety. I don't know. I wonder if they even know. Sometimes I find myself forgetting how old I am. I guess age doesn't seem to matter anymore."

"Or maybe it matters too much. It was just a thought," Maggie added quickly. "I didn't mean to accuse you of lying.

Personally, I find myself hyperaware of my age. I think, I'm almost fifty and time is running out. It makes me feel a bit panicky sometimes, like I have to do something now—what, I don't really know, but do something different or make some essential connection before it's too late."

"Maybe you think too much about what's missing in your life. That's bound to make a person unhappy. I prefer to think about all that I have."

Maggie looked over at Delphine. "You never miss what might have been? You never find yourself wanting something you can't have?"

"No," Delphine said. "I'm content." She wondered if she was being entirely truthful with Maggie, and with herself. Of course she wasn't. But at this stage in their so-called friendship she didn't owe Maggie anything other than her company, if that. As to what she owed to herself, that was a question better left for another time. Like, maybe never.

They drove past a garden lush with roses and wildflowers, then a house with a bower of purple wisteria. They could make out the hammering of a pileated woodpecker in the distance, and the salty smell of the ocean on the late morning breeze.

"It's so beautiful here," Maggie said. "Really, Delphine, you're so lucky to live in Ogunquit."

"I don't dispute the 'lucky' part. But remember, you've never been here in the winter."

"I'm sure it's beautiful, all the pine trees covered in snow. It must be so romantic."

"Sure, nobody can beat us for perfect winter postcard scenes. But we've also got power outages and ice storms and high tides that flood homes, and then comes mud season. That's a real treat. The world is grey and brown for weeks. Not inspiring."

"Well, I guess you never really know a place unless you've visited in every season."

"Unless you've lived through every season," Delphine corrected, "not just visited. You can't really know a place until you've slogged through muddy fields just to get to work and shoveled piles of snow just to get out of the house and—"

"Okay," Maggie said with a laugh, "you've made your point."

Delphine nodded. "Off to the right, behind those trees, there's a parcel of land that's been in my family for hundreds of years."

"Really? I don't remember you ever mentioning that before."

"I was a kid when we . . . when we knew each other. I didn't understand the importance of heritage and history."

"I'm not sure many children really appreciate the past," Maggie said. "I mean, children don't have much of a personal past. Why would the average boy or girl be interested in a family's ancestry?"

"You're probably right. Anyway, that land means a lot to my family. It's a piece of living history. The ruins of the original Crandall house are still there. Well, barely. You can tell where the foundation was laid. My father has a piece of old glass that supposedly came from the original house. I don't see any reason to believe otherwise. And there's a lilac bush that's about a hundred and fifty years old. It still blooms every year. It's incredibly beautiful."

"Talk about having roots in the area."

Delphine laughed. "Yeah, that's the Crandalls. Old as dirt."

A few minutes later, Delphine dropped Maggie off at Gorges Grant and headed back to the farm. In spite of herself, she had actually enjoyed the time with Maggie. Somewhere along the way she had begun to feel almost comfortable. Not that it was like old times. Nothing would ever be like old times and that was a good thing. Delphine enjoyed exploring the past when it wasn't hers. Like, when it was re-created in historical novels about people she would never know, or when it was in stories about her long-gone ancestors.

That sort of past, other people's past, couldn't hurt. It might entertain or educate or even provoke, but it could never really hurt.

10

Later that afternoon Maggie called Delphine and suggested they meet for drinks after dinner. They'd had an enjoyable morning and Maggie was eager to capitalize on what she saw as a development in their relationship.

Delphine had hesitated. Going out with Maggie that evening would cut into her alone time, the time she spent knitting and reading with Melchior on her lap. In the end, and she wasn't sure why, she agreed to meet Maggie at seven, but only for a little while. Briefly, she considered asking Harry to join them. She had hardly seen him in the past week and maybe a friendly bar was a good venue for a meeting between Maggie and her boyfriend. Better, anyway, than the three of them being stuck in her living room with no distractions from what she felt sure would be an awkward scene.

But in the end she decided against asking Harry along. She wasn't entirely comfortable—well, she wasn't at all comfortable—with introducing the two, so why force the issue? And Harry didn't mind staying home. While he liked the occasional night out with some of the guys from work, he was really much happier in his armchair, with a can of beer and a copy of the day's paper.

Maggie suggested they meet at the Old Village Inn on Main Street. She had never been there. Back when they were teens, they had been more interested in places with a younger crowd and electronic dance music. Maggie recalled her parents having dinner at the Old Village Inn once or twice. Her mother, she remembered, had liked the décor—lots of antiques—and her father had liked "the generous pour." Maggie hadn't understood what that meant until she was in college.

Maggie was already seated at the bar when Delphine arrived.

"I have a habit of being early," she explained. "I think I get it from my father."

Delphine shrugged. "I guess it usually doesn't much matter if I'm early, on time, or late. I mostly set my own hours." *And,* she added to herself, *I'm not in the habit of going out to meet anyone of an evening.* Jemima never went out at night. Maybe once or twice a year Delphine and Jackie caught an early evening movie. As for dates with Harry . . . Well, they were few and far between.

Delphine ordered a beer and took an appreciative sip. "How was the rest of your day?" she asked.

"Oh, fine. I walked down to the Cove and did some browsing. I used the hotel's Jacuzzi. There's nothing like a Jacuzzi when you want to relax."

"I'll take your word for it," Delphine said.

Maggie turned completely toward Delphine. "That guy," she whispered, "the one at the end of the bar, the one wearing the Red Sox cap. Do you see him?"

Delphine nodded.

"He's had three drinks since I came in. Scotch, I think. That's three in less than half an hour. And without ice or a glass of water on the side!"

"That's Barry Franks," Delphine said. "He's known mostly as Old Barry, though I don't think he's even sixty. He's a regular."

"A regular drinker." Maggie frowned. "I wonder why he drinks so much. Maybe he's depressed. Maybe he's lonely or having a spiritual crisis."

"I don't think so." Delphine regarded Old Barry over

Maggie's shoulder. He was laughing and the man seated next to him, another local, put a companionable arm around his shoulder. "I think he drinks because he likes to drink. That is possible, you know. That drinking doesn't have to be a problem."

"A medical doctor or a psychiatrist wouldn't say so. They'd say he has an addiction. Alcoholism is a disease."

Delphine shook her head. "Doctors don't know everything, Maggie."

"They know enough to say he's destroying his liver, maybe even killing himself."

"Maybe he is," Delphine conceded, "but it's his business, isn't it? Old Barry doesn't have to answer to anyone but himself. He's got no wife, no kids, and no boss. If he wants to spend every night at the OVI drinking with his cronies, let him."

"But then how does he get home? If he's driving drunk then—"

"No, no," Delphine said, "he lives in an apartment around back. Besides, no one would let him drive when he's drunk. He's got friends, you know. People like him. People look out for him."

Maggie frowned. "People are enabling him is more like it. I'm sorry. I guess I can't be so nonchalant about it as you obviously can."

"I don't think I'm being nonchalant," Delphine protested. "It's just not my business to get all worked up about."

"Live and let live?"

"I suppose. In Old Barry's case, anyway. He's just a small-town character. One of many." *And,* she added silently, *you shouldn't judge him for it. Your standards are not ours.*

Maggie was wise enough to let the subject of Old Barry drop. What she really wanted to talk about with Delphine was the subject of their friendship. She had enjoyed the shopping trip, in spite of the fact that Renys wasn't exactly Lord & Taylor's. She had felt that Delphine had been a little more relaxed and welcoming than she had been since their first meeting.

Still, she hesitated. She didn't want to scare Delphine off by seeming too eager to bond. Maybe that's what had happened all those years ago. Maybe something she had said or done had scared Delphine back to Ogunquit, or at least, maybe Maggie had been part of the reason for her sudden retreat. She had lived with the uncertainty for so long she would almost believe any reason Delphine could give for her defection.

But Maggie Weldon Wilkes was not a quitter. She hadn't come all this way after all this time to skulk off no wiser than she had been when she'd arrived. "Do you remember," she asked now, "how we used to celebrate a 'pretend birthday' every summer? Because your birthday is in March and mine is in November we picked a day in the summer, a day we could share."

Delphine nodded. She did remember, but vaguely. She couldn't recall the date they had chosen and now, from the perspective of middle age, it seemed like a pretty silly thing to have done.

"And then for a while," Maggie said, "after college, we would send each other a card on that day. August fourth." That wasn't exactly the truth. Maggie had continued to send a card for a few years. Delphine had sent a card just once, that summer after graduation.

Oh, that was it, Delphine was thinking, *August fourth.* She wondered why had they had chosen that particular date. She had no idea. A bit of a line came to her then, from John Banville's *The Infinities,* a novel she had read the year before. "When I peer into memory's steadily clouding crystal . . ." Yes, the past was continually clouding over. Mostly, that was just fine with her.

"And then," Maggie was saying, her tone light, "we stopped. Or one of us stopped or forgot or got too busy and then the other one did, too. When was that? When did we stop caring about that shared birthday?"

"Pretend birthday," Delphine corrected. She felt as if she was being accused of negligence toward the friendship and she didn't like it. Yes, she knew all too well that she had withdrawn from Maggie, but it wasn't a crime for which she should be punished. The past was the past. If you didn't shed the past, like a snake shed its old skin, it would choke you to death. That was a lesson Delphine had learned from her mother, very early on. There was never any point in dwelling or pondering or moping or pining. It was always best simply to take a deep breath and look at what was directly in front of you.

"So, you don't remember why—" Maggie began.

"No," Delphine said. "I'm sorry."

"Okay. Do you want another beer?" Maggie asked. Her tone was neutral, hiding her disappointment in Delphine's reluctance to engage in a revealing conversation.

"All right," Delphine said, against her better judgment, just to be polite. "One more."

Maggie hailed the bartender and a moment later he delivered their drinks. Maggie slid the glass of beer closer to Delphine and took a sip of her wine. *One more try,* she thought. One more foray into the past Delphine seems determined to erase. "I still have the birthday cards you gave me," she said. "The real ones and the 'pretend' ones. And all of the letters you wrote to me during the school year, before we went to college. I'll admit I haven't looked at them in a long time. But I never threw any of them out."

Delphine shifted on the bar stool. "Oh," she said.

"Do you still have my cards and letters?"

Delphine took a long sip of her beer. Again, she bristled at the implication of—of what? Disloyalty? Unconcern? *Maybe,* she thought, *I'm being paranoid. Maybe my guilty conscience is being its own accuser.* Oddly, she hadn't known that she had a guilty conscience before Maggie's return. Not really. Maybe just a little. She put her glass down on the bar. "I don't know," she said, careful not to reveal her annoyance. "There's a lot of stuff at my mother's house, up in the attic. My stuff, Jackie's, Joey's. I don't know what she's thrown out and what she's kept."

"Oh."

"Excuse me." A tall man, dressed in a crisp, tailored long-sleeved shirt and expensive designer jeans, was standing just behind them. Maggie guessed him to be about forty. He was very handsome, in a way that reminded her of Jon Hamm, that actor from *Mad Men*.

"I don't mean to intrude," he said now, with a brilliant smile. "I've been sent on a mission by my colleagues." He gestured over his shoulder and Maggie saw a table of similarly good-looking, well-dressed men.

"Not at all," she said. The man placed the drink order for his table. Maggie raised her eyebrows at Delphine. Delphine shrugged.

"May I buy you ladies a drink?" the man said now.

Maggie smiled as brilliantly as he had. "Well, thank you very much," she said. She told him what they were drinking. The man gestured to the bartender again. "I'm staying at the Shoreman," he said. "They have a good bar. Maybe I'll see you there sometime? My name is Dan and I'm in town for two weeks."

"I'm Maggie. Maybe you will see me sometime."

Delphine coughed. The man smiled once more at Maggie and returned to his table. Maggie couldn't wipe the smile off her face.

"Wow," she said in a whisper, though the man was too far away now to hear. "No one's flirted with me in ages. And he's so good-looking!"

Delphine rolled her eyes. She had no patience for flirtation. She never really had. And they were adult women, almost fifty years old, in committed relationships. Neither had any business flirting, especially with a younger man. *I sound like an old fart,* she thought. "Whatever," she said.

Maggie was wise enough not to continue the one-sided conversation the man had interrupted. "Your friend Jemima seems like an interesting person," she said instead.

"She's had a bit of a tough go," Delphine said, preferring to let the choice of "interesting" pass. "Her first husband was a jerk."

"Maybe that explains it. She seemed to have a bit of a chip on her shoulder the other morning." *And those clothes,* Maggie added silently, *were a crime.* No good-looking man would be flirting with her any time soon.

Delphine refrained from pointing out Maggie's several social faux pas that might have heightened Jemima's bad attitude. "She's a good person," she said. "She works really hard. Her arthritis makes it hard for her to be on her feet a lot, so the waitressing job is tough on her."

"So why doesn't she quit?"

"And do what?" Delphine said. "She doesn't have a lot of options. Most people around here don't."

"Well, times are tough everywhere, that's for sure."

"They can be tougher here than a lot of other places." Delphine realized she had probably sounded defiant, but that was all right because she felt defiant. Maggie's bringing up those stupid fake birthday cards had put her on edge. Another line came to her now, from another novel that had made a deep impression on her, one that, given her by then ancient, defunct friendship with Maggie, had disturbed her. The novel was *The Evolution of Jane,* by Cathleen Schine. "Is there anything more petty," the line read, "more exalted, than a friendship between two girls?"

Delphine reached into her pocket for her wallet. "Look," she said. "I'd really better be going. It's getting late."

Maggie nodded and reached for her bag. She knew better than to argue. They had spent less than an hour together this evening. She had pushed too hard. She wondered if she had lost what little ground she had gained with Delphine that morning. She thought that maybe she had, and it made her feel bad.

On the way out of the restaurant, the handsome, well-dressed man who had flirted with her at the bar caught her eye and winked. Maggie couldn't help herself and winked back. She felt a tiny bit less bad.

11

1975

It was the summer after the Weldons' infamous European vacation. The girls had been forced to spend a whole summer apart, though Maggie had sent Delphine a postcard every week. But now they were back together again and all was right with the world. Delphine had looked forward to Maggie's arrival with an intensity that made her feel sick to her stomach. When the Weldon family car pulled up to the Lilac House, there had been much squealing and hugging and jumping up and down.

The first week had been bliss. The girls had revisited their favorite cloud-watching spot out in the field behind the Crandalls' main barn and they had ridden their bikes, new ones because they had outgrown the banana seat bikes, down to the beach. They had snuck out to the old movie theatre on Main Street, the Leavitt, and seen *Jaws,* even though their parents had told them they weren't allowed to. One night, Delphine had stayed over at Maggie's house. Another night, Maggie had stayed over at Delphine's. It was just like old times.

But then everything had gone horribly wrong. Suddenly, out of nowhere, Maggie had come down with a big, fat crush on Delphine's brother, Joey. Okay, at the same time Delphine had gotten a little, tiny crush on Peter, who everyone said was very handsome, so that was excusable. But Joey? Delphine was totally annoyed that Maggie, her sworn best friend, like-liked her totally gross and annoying brother. She felt betrayed. She didn't care if Maggie was miserable or if she got her heart broken. And she totally couldn't understand why it didn't bother Maggie one little bit that she, Delphine, had a crush—though not a big one—on her brother, Peter. She had never felt so confused in her entire life. She wished she had never met Maggie or Peter. She wished that Joey had never been born. She wished that everything could go back to way before these stupid crushes that were ruining her entire life.

The absolute worst had come when just the other day Maggie had said to her, "Can you imagine if we all got married someday! You and Peter and me and Joey? That would be so cool. We could have a double wedding!"

Delphine had been so horrified by this prospect she had been unable to reply. What she had wanted to say was, "No, that would not be cool. That would only be the worst thing to ever happen, ever." But the words just wouldn't come out. She just couldn't tell Maggie why the thought of her liking Joey upset her so much. Partly it was because she was afraid. What if Maggie got really mad and refused to be her friend anymore? Delphine felt that all sorts of bad things might come if she opened her mouth. Her mother had told her that most of what people said didn't need to be said. She wasn't really sure what her mother meant by that, but she thought the basic message was that it was mostly better to keep your feelings to yourself.

And now . . . Everything had changed back, just like she had wanted it to, but not really. Maggie was, in fact, miserable, her heart had indeed been broken, and Delphine found that she really did care about her, after all. Joey had come into the Crandalls' kitchen just that morning to find his sister and her friend at the kitchen table, eating Apple Jacks. Maggie had begun to choke and Delphine had been about to say something insulting to her brother, like "you smell like a monkey," when, braggingly, Joey had announced that Christina Brown, a girl his own age with a reputation for being "wild," had agreed to go out with him. Maggie's spoon had rattled to the floor and, oblivious, Joey had gone on to pour a glass of orange juice and chatter about how cool and pretty and popular Christina was—she had even gotten the new Bruce Springsteen album everyone was talking about, *Born to Run*—until Delphine had grabbed Maggie's arm, yanked her to her feet, and dragged her from the room. "Hey, I was talking!" Joey had called out to their retreating backs, still oblivious to the misery he had caused.

Hours later, her tears mostly dried, the bright red splotches on her face now pale pink, Maggie was recovering. The girls were in Perkins Cove, perched on a large, craggy grey rock by the water. The tide was low. A seagull stood about four feet away, eyeing them and waiting for the appearance of food. Off to their right, a father and his toddler son were squatting, peering into a tide pool.

"Do you feel better now?" Delphine asked tentatively.

Maggie sighed. "Yeah. I'm okay. I was being stupid, anyway."

"No you weren't," Delphine insisted. "Joey's the stupid one. If he can't see how much cooler and smarter and prettier you are than that Christina person, he's the moron. He's the chucklehead."

"I guess."

"And I am totally so over your brother, as of this very moment. Just so you know. Okay?"

Maggie could only nod.

"Look," Delphine said, throwing her arm across Maggie's shoulders. "Let's swear never to let a boy make us unhappy, ever. Okay?"

"Okay," Maggie said, wiping away a stray tear. "Pinky swear."

They linked pinkies and swore.

"But what if it happens, anyway?" Maggie said then, her voice a little wobbly. "Even though we swore, what if someday we just make a mistake? My mom says that love makes you do stupid things and that a girl should be very careful."

"Careful how?"

"I don't know, exactly," Maggie admitted. "Make sure the boy is nice before getting a crush on him, I guess."

"Well, whatever it means, we'll figure it out. Hey, you wanna get some ice cream? I have some money with me. I earned it at the diner this week."

Maggie smiled. "Yeah. I want a double scoop. Chocolate and chocolate chip. Even though my mother says too much chocolate makes your face break out. Potato chips, too. All the good stuff."

Delphine shrugged and climbed to her feet. "Who cares? I'm getting chocolate, too. With fudge sauce on top."

12

It was Thursday afternoon. Delphine had finished up early at the farm and was now in her workroom, but her thoughts weren't on the sweater she was making for Jemima's daughter. She was thinking about the call from Maggie she didn't want to return. She was thinking about the past. She was remembering. It was something she had been doing a lot since Maggie's arrival in Ogunquit. She wasn't exactly happy about it, but for all of her willpower, which was considerable, she didn't seem to be able to stop it.

Robert Evans. Maggie hadn't mentioned him by name yet, but she would. She would have to talk about him. In a way, she was the one responsible for Delphine's having met Robert. Without Maggie's influence, Delphine wouldn't even have gone to college in the first place, especially not one all the way down in Boston. It was her coaxing and support, along with a few well-chosen words of encouragement from Mr. and Mrs. Weldon, that had led Delphine to apply for admission to Bartley College.

None of the other Crandalls had gone to college but for Jackie, who was, at the time, commuting to a two-year community college in South Portland. But Delphine had had dreams, vague and unformed as they were. She had always been an avid reader; she had always wanted to learn more, to see some of the world outside of Ogunquit, a place that had begun to feel awfully restricting. She remembered now how

Maggie had spun tales of how much fun they would have if they went to the same school and maybe even got to be roommates. And Delphine had allowed herself to be caught up in those fantasies. It wasn't hard. She was an intelligent, curious teenager in a small town that didn't offer a whole lot of career options. Visions of freedom and adventure—never anything more specific than that—captured her imagination.

Delphine shifted on the hardback chair. She thought she might have to start sitting on a cushion before long, or buy another ergonomic chair like the one she had in the office. No one approaching fifty had a perfect back. Fifty. God, so much time had passed since she had waved good-bye to Ogunquit and headed off for Boston, an excited, naïve eighteen-year-old. Her parents, she remembered, had not been entirely supportive of the scheme. That's how they had seen Delphine's wanting to go to college—not as a plan or a stepping-stone but as a scheme, something not quite right, something slightly suspicious. Why, they had asked, did she need to go to college, anyway, especially a "real," four-year one? She didn't need a college education to help run the family farm or to wait tables at the diner. And who would pay for college? they wondered. They hadn't forbid Delphine to apply for admission, but they had made it clear that she could only go—assuming she was accepted—if she was awarded enough scholarships and loans to cover all of her expenses.

It had seemed like a bit of a miracle when both girls were accepted to Bartley. Delphine managed—just barely—to land the money necessary for tuition and room and board and, by the start of the second semester of freshman year, Maggie had charmed someone in the housing department into appointing them roommates. It was a fantasy come true, indeed, even if Delphine had to hold down two part-time jobs after classes to make it work. She didn't care. She was learning. Her world was expanding. She was having fun.

Together, Maggie and Delphine struggled through some classes and aced others. They helped each other study. They went to lots and lots of movies at funky little art theatre houses and went to concerts by local bands in minuscule clubs around Cambridge. Maggie lost her virginity to a skinny bass player in a funk band. Delphine lost her virginity to a moody poetry major from Belgium. They wrote term papers and took finals and argued, but only occasionally, about what new videos on MTV were the best.

And then came that life-changing night in the fall of 1982 when they met a handsome, charismatic young man named Robert Evans. They had gone to a play at the American Repertory Theater in Harvard Square and at intermission found themselves making small talk with Robert and two of his friends.

Delphine shifted again, but this time the discomfort was caused by the memories, not her aging back. Try as she might, she could never erase the memory of her first meeting with Robert Evans. She had noticed him even before he and his friends had come over to talk. He was tall and slim. He wore black jeans, a black leather jacket, and around his neck a long red scarf. His smile was big, his hair was dark and wavy, and his blue eyes were piercing and intelligent. When someone spoke, he focused those eyes and his attention on that person completely. He asked questions. He told a silly joke and laughed at himself for telling it. Robert Evans had presence.

When the lights flickered, signaling an end to the intermission, he suggested they go for coffee after the play. One of his friends begged off, but the other agreed, so an hour later Maggie and Delphine found themselves in a coffee shop with Robert and another guy, someone whose name they both forgot by the end of the evening. They talked about the play, a performance of Chekhov's *Uncle Vanya,* and discussed a local political scandal. Delphine told the guys that she was from Maine and Robert said he'd heard it was one of the most beautiful places in the United States. Maggie said that she was an economics major. Robert said that he had majored in history, minored in economics and political theory, and that he was now earning a graduate degree in journalism. He had been born in Boston and raised by parents he described as wealthy, well educated, and bohemian. His parents, he said, were currently living in Rome. When the bill came, he paid for all four of them.

In spite of the emotional pain it caused, Delphine could not help but smile at the memory of that long-ago evening. On the surface, Robert had seemed more of a match for Maggie, whose upbringing, except for the bohemian part, was similar to that of Robert's. But the heart was a wild and unpredictable thing, and within days of meeting in the lobby of the American Repertory Theater, Robert and Delphine had fallen madly in love. Within months, they were engaged. It was the very last thing Delphine had expected to happen—to meet, fall in love with, and plan to marry a man like Robert Evans, a man so completely unlike any man, or woman, she had ever known. She was happier than she had ever been. She was happier than she had ever imagined she could be.

Junior year became senior year. Maggie decided to go to business school after college. With an MBA she could achieve financial success and the benefits of that—travel, a lovely home, beautiful clothes, all of which she was already accustomed to having.

Robert completed his master's in journalism and was courted by several important media outlets. He took a month to travel throughout Eastern Europe, which resulted in a series of articles he was able to sell for a nice sum. The articles eventually became the core of his first book.

And while her friends planned for the future, Delphine began to realize that she had made a very, very big mistake. She began to panic. She put off filling out applications for law school or graduate school. She ducked Maggie's questions and avoided Robert's attempts at making detailed plans for their future together.

The thing was, she had always assumed she would move back home after college. But then Robert had come along and she'd fallen madly in love. Now he was on the brink of a big career, one that would take him all across the globe, one that might bring him fame and fortune. She knew he would never—could never—settle in Ogunquit. There was nothing for him there but Delphine, and she knew beyond a shadow of a doubt that she would never be enough for a man like Robert Evans.

She would never forget that one unsuccessful visit they had made together to Ogunquit. Robert had liked the beach but had been unimpressed by the town, the farm, and the Crandalls. The Crandalls had been equally unimpressed by Robert. It became increasingly clear to Delphine that a marriage to him would leave her stranded, alienated from her family and from her home. Her parents would never entirely abandon her, but neither would they welcome an outsider with open arms, and married to Robert, she would become an outsider.

As time sped on, Delphine knew she should end the engagement. But at the same time she worried that she might be making a decision based on fear of the unknown. Self-help books told her that she needed to face her future, not turn away from it. Maybe her future was really with Robert. She believed that he loved her. She loved him in return.

She experienced agonies of doubt. At one point, she was very close to asking Robert to marry immediately and without fuss at city hall. Then, after graduation, she would follow him to New York, where he had accepted a post at the *New York Times*. With this plan there would be little time for reflection or for running away. But the thought of what that would do to her parents stopped her. She could never hurt them by eloping. They might never forgive her and then she would be entirely lost, cut off, unmoored. She would never survive that.

The protest rally in the autumn of 1983 had decided her

once and for all. Rather, her reaction to the rally Robert had organized, her panic when the crowd got out of hand and then her moment of catharsis. But she hadn't had the courage to act on that revelation until the following spring. It cost her dearly to break things off with him, though she hadn't been able to convince him of that. She insisted he take back the ring, though he told her he didn't want it, he had bought it for her and not to give to some other woman. She left it in his apartment anyway. She apologized, and apologized some more. Hurt and angry and heartbroken, he had finally gone off to New York alone.

Delphine put her knitting on the worktable, got up from the unforgiving chair, and stretched. She walked over to the window and looked out at the front yard. Two large blue jays, a male and a female, were hopping on the lawn, screeching and searching for bugs. She watched them for a few minutes. And then she closed her eyes and leaned her forehead against the window.

Though she had deliberately forgotten so much of what had been said between her and Robert, some details, some conversations, were still bright and vivid in her memory. She wished the words would go away, but they never did. She feared they never would.

"I should have known this was coming," Robert had said. "Maybe I did, in a way. The fact that you never told me your parents' reaction to our engagement. The fact that I never got a congratulatory card or a call from them. My parents sent you a card, and a gift. I told them right away that we were getting married. I was proud of that. But you weren't proud of marrying me, were you? You never told your parents about our engagement, did you?"

"No," she had admitted, literally cringing with shame. "I didn't tell them. But it wasn't because I wasn't proud of you!"

"Then why?" The look on Robert's face had been an

awful mix of hurt and anger and sheer puzzlement. "Why did you keep our engagement a secret?"

She hadn't been able to answer right away. And then, Robert had said, "Because you never really saw our engagement as real, is that it? Because you never really believed in us."

Yes, she thought. *And no.*

"Why did you even say yes to my proposal?" Robert had asked.

"Because I love you."

"Then . . . why this? Why are you leaving me if you love me?"

"I want to marry you, Robert," she had said as firmly as she could. "I do. Please believe me. But I just can't."

"That's it? That's all the explanation you can give me? Is there someone else, Delphine?"

"No, no, of course there's no one else!" she had cried. "It's just . . . Robert, please forgive me. Please."

"Is there anything I can say to make you change your mind?"

She had lowered her eyes, unable to look into his beautiful blue eyes any longer. It was too painful. "No," she had whispered.

He had accepted her decision without further argument.

And that had been that. The end of an era. The end, in a way, of a life.

Delphine turned from the window to see Melchior sitting in the open doorway staring solemnly at her. She smiled. The present was what deserved her attention, not the past.

"Is it time for dinner already?" she said to him.

In response, Melchior turned and padded down the stairs.

13

It was early Thursday afternoon and Maggie was browsing in Abacus, a high-end store in the heart of town that featured original, one-of-a-kind work by artists and jewelry designers. The pieces for sale were lovely, but Maggie's mind wasn't registering much of what was on shelves and behind glass. Her attention was distracted by the past.

She had yet to bring up the topic of Robert Evans with Delphine, but she would before long. He was the elephant in the room. It would be impossible to ignore him forever. But if the mention of old cards and letters had shut Delphine down so effectively, how would she react to the mention of Robert? Not well, Maggie imagined. Not well at all.

It had come as a terrible shock to Maggie, Delphine's breaking off her engagement and moving back home to Ogunquit. It was the biggest crisis their friendship had sustained and it was a definitive one. Nothing was ever the same between them after that.

Maggie just hadn't been able to understand why, after her plans for marriage to a worldly, kind, and fascinating young man, Delphine would have voluntarily chosen to return to a quiet and decidedly unglamorous life in a tiny town. Back home, her life would be reduced, diminished. With Robert, it would be broadened and enriched. Robert Evans was what Mrs. Weldon would have called "a real catch"—handsome, intelligent, ambitious. He was even brave. Maggie remembered how he had handled the overly excited crowd at that rally in the fall of her senior year, how he had put his own life at risk to save the lives of others. Anyone with eyes could see that he was bound for public success.

"Oh, excuse me," Maggie said. She hadn't seen the woman she had just bumped into, even though she was pretty noticeable in a hot pink tracksuit, circa 1984.

"That's all right," the woman said nicely. "The aisles here are pretty tight."

Maggie smiled and vowed to be more careful. She didn't want to spend a thousand dollars on a broken ceramic bowl she wouldn't have wanted whole. She wondered if Delphine ever came to this store and almost laughed at the notion. For a thousand dollars she could buy out the stock at Renys.

Maggie walked toward the back of the store, past painted furniture and a display of jewelry made from sea glass and a collection of handmade wooden toys. None of it was of interest. What was of interest to her was Delphine's strange decision to go home to Ogunquit all those years ago. It had seemed like a betrayal of their friendship. In a way, she had been heartbroken. And it had only made things worse that Delphine was so evasive and sometimes downright silent when Maggie tried to talk to her, to offer support or consolation. For a long time, Maggie had felt rejected and angry and sad. Delphine hadn't seemed to care. Maggie had never let Delphine know just how upset she was. Pride had kept her silent on that score. Maybe it shouldn't have.

But eventually, inevitably, Maggie had stopped offering a shoulder to cry on. To be rejected time and again was humiliating. The demands of business school began to take precedence in her life and before long she had met a handsome, serious law student named Gregory Wilkes. Maggie felt her future opening up before her and it looked bright. She still thought about—and cared about—Delphine, but increasingly their relationship began to seem like a thing of the past. Maggie was a romantic, yes, but she was also Dorothy and

Walter's daughter. She had no intention of wallowing in a seemingly defunct past when an entire future lay ahead of her.

She finished her MBA and landed the first of several good jobs in investment banking. She and Gregory got married. They had a daughter, and then, another one. Maggie's mother was pleased. Gregory made partner. Maggie's father was pleased. They bought a large house in Lexington, then a larger one, with an in-ground pool and media room. They traveled to Europe, skied out west, and soaked up the sun in Anguilla. On the occasion of their fifteenth wedding anniversary, Gregory gave Maggie a four-carat diamond ring, an upgrade of her original engagement ring. It was heavily insured. Just as the house and the cars and the art—their entire lives—were heavily insured against disaster from without.

But sometimes trouble—if not exactly disaster—came from within. *Because here I am,* Maggie thought, looking blankly at a tall blown-glass vase that was selling for five hundred dollars, *all these years later, trying once again to make a connection with a person who effectively abandoned me.* She shouldn't have told Delphine that she had kept her cards and letters. Not yet, at least. It had probably scared her away, like the too-early revelation of the trouble in her marriage. Delphine hadn't answered a call she had made that morning. Maggie wondered if she would ever respond.

"May I help you?"

Maggie jumped a little and then smiled at the saleswoman at her side. "Oh, no, thanks," she said. "I'm just looking."

The saleswoman smiled back politely. "Just let me know if you'd like to see anything in one of the cases," she said.

Maggie nodded and the saleswoman moved off to approach another customer. A moment later, Maggie left the store and stood on the busy corner at the center of town, at a complete loss about what to do with herself next.

14

1977

"Hey," Maggie said from the porch.

Delphine clumped up the steps and threw herself into one of the white wicker chairs. "Hey." Her greeting was accompanied by a scowl.

Maggie raised an eyebrow. "Uh, something wrong?"

Delphine was wearing a scratch–'n'–sniff T-shirt. On it were the words "American Pie." Below the words was an image of a slice of pepperoni pizza. She'd been wearing it a lot, so the scent of the pepperoni was not as strong as it had been when she'd first got it for her birthday back in March. Maggie was wearing a thin, slightly crinkly cotton top embroidered with Indian designs. Both girls wore jeans. Delphine's were patched at the knees with similar fabric to hide holes. Maggie's were patched with stylized neon flowers, just for the fun of it.

"What's wrong," Delphine said, "is that I can't go to the concert."

Maggie shrieked. "What do you mean you can't go? You bought your ticket already."

"I know," Delphine said darkly. "It's my mother. She changed her mind."

"What? No way. She can't do that!"

"Uh, yeah, she can and she did. And please stop shouting."

"Sorry. I mean, I don't understand. What happened?"

Delphine sighed. "What happened is that my mother was talking to one of her friends at church, and this lady told my mother about one of her friends whose son had gone to a Dream concert and said that everyone was doing drugs. So, my mother told me that I couldn't go."

"But that's crazy." Maggie perched on the chair next to Delphine's. "Not everyone does drugs. We don't do drugs! Ugh."

"I told her that. But it didn't make any difference."

"Does she know my dad is driving us down to Portsmouth and waiting for us outside the club? Does she know the concert isn't even in a big arena?"

"Yeah, she knows all that. But she says it doesn't matter. People do drugs everywhere, she says."

Maggie abruptly stood and put her hands on her hips. "She doesn't trust you."

"She says she does trust me. It's that she doesn't trust other people."

"I can't believe this, Delphine. You worked all those extra shifts at the diner to pay for that ticket."

"I'm aware," Delphine said dryly.

"Look, do you want my mother or father to talk to her?"

"No! I mean, thanks, but that would make everything worse, believe me."

"What does your father say about this?"

Delphine sighed again. "Whatever my mother says."

Maggie sat back down again. "I can't believe this is happening. We were so looking forward to this."

"Well, you can still go."

"Are you crazy? No way I'm going without you."

"Your brother will be there," Delphine pointed out. "You can sit with him and his girlfriend."

"Uh-uh, no way. I'd have absolutely no fun without you."

"But what about your ticket?"

Maggie shrugged. "Maybe one of Peter's friends wants one. Or two. We could sell them."

"Isn't that called scalping? I think that's illegal."

"No, I think that's only when you ask for more money than you paid. I'm pretty sure."

"Okay." Delphine hesitated. "Look, are you sure you're okay about this? Really, I wouldn't be upset if you went to the concert without me."

Maggie rolled her eyes. "How many times do I have to remind you, dummy? We're best friends. Best friends stick by each other through thick and thin. For better or worse."

"I think that's supposed to be a marriage."

"Whatever. End of conversation. I'll talk to Peter this afternoon, see if he can sell the tickets for us. Okay?"

Delphine smiled. "Thanks, Maggie. I mean it. Thank you."

"You'd do the same for me. Hey, let's go cheer ourselves up."

"Okay. With what?"

"Ice-cream sandwiches? There are some in the back of the freezer. My father hides them back there hoping my mother won't see them and yell at him."

Delphine smiled. "That sounds good. If your father won't mind our stealing his ice cream."

"He can buy more. Come on. Oh, and *Laverne & Shirley* is on tonight. Want to watch it here?"

"Sure," Delphine said, following Maggie inside. She felt a little bit better already.

15

It was early Friday evening, about five-thirty, when Harry got to Delphine's house.

Harry Stringfellow, aged fifty-five, drove a truck for one of the largest building material suppliers in Maine. It was a good job in many ways, especially for Harry, who was too restless to last at a desk job.

He was a few inches over six feet tall and slim, though middle age had deposited a layer of fat on his belly that no amount of hard work seemed able to remove. His hair was thick and brown and beginning to go grey, as was his beard, which he wore a bit too long for Delphine's taste. His eyes were large and blue green. Recently, he had taken to wearing reading glasses, but like Delphine, his eyesight was generally good. Around his neck and hidden under his work shirt he wore a large silver cross on an old leather cord. The cross, he said, had belonged to his father, long dead. In the ten years Delphine had known Harry, he hadn't once passed the threshold of a church, but the cross never left his body and if anyone asked, he considered himself a Christian.

Delphine and Harry hadn't seen each other in a few days, which wasn't entirely unusual. Delphine was always busy. And Harry had filled in for a buddy whose wife had gone into early labor. Buck's route had taken him all the way to Augusta. According to Harry, the wife and baby were doing well and Buck now owed him a favor.

Harry put his empty lunch box on the coffee table. "I saw Ellen today," he said.

"Oh." No matter how many years passed, the mention of Harry's wife always came as something of an uncomfortable surprise. "How is she?" she asked.

"The same. The nurse said she'd had a bad night, though."

"Did she recognize you?" Harry liked—needed—to imagine that Ellen was aware of his presence. It meant a lot to him. Sometimes, often, Delphine wished that it didn't.

Harry nodded. "I think she did. Her doctor would probably say no, but he doesn't know Ellen like I do."

Delphine couldn't argue that point. Maybe Harry did know more than Ellen's doctors about the state of her comprehension. Even if he didn't, he would never admit that. He hadn't once been to a doctor in the ten years Delphine had known him, even when he'd sprained his wrist. Even when he'd had what anyone could see was pneumonia and spent almost three weeks wheezing and hacking. He could be distrustful of professionals. He could be stubborn.

"So," she said, "you're still determined to keep things as they are, even though Ellen has no chance of a recovery that would allow her to live a normal life?"

"If by 'keep things as they are' you mean am I determined to stay married to my wife and to visit her faithfully once a week, then yes. I am."

"But you say you love me, Harry."

"I do. Of course I do." Harry sighed and rubbed his palm over his forehead. "Del, we've been through this. I'm not divorcing Ellen. I made a promise at the altar to love and cherish her until death do us part. I can only give you what you've already got of me. I'm sorry."

Delphine took a deep breath. She wondered what had made her bring this up again. She knew how Harry felt. And she wasn't in the mood for a fight. Why again and why now?

"I'm sorry, too," she said, disappointed in herself. "I'll get dinner together. Dave down at the Cove gave me a couple of haddock as payment for the sweater I knit for his daughter's birthday."

But Harry didn't respond. He was already sitting deeply in his favorite armchair, the *Portland Press Herald* open on his lap. Melchior was perched on top of the narrow freestanding bookcase, one eye open and directed down at the top of Harry's head. Melchior was used to Harry by now, but that didn't mean that he liked him.

Delphine went into the kitchen to prepare dinner. While she got out the pans and bowls and knives she would need, she thought about how her romantic life had come to this . . . interesting state. The truth was that for a long time after Robert she had remained almost obstinately single. Though several men had pursued her, she had ignored them or turned them away. To any who asked—mainly, her sister and, for a while, Jemima—she said she didn't have any interest in dating. She said she wasn't lonely. She kept very busy, sometimes insanely busy, at the farm and at the diner. She was needed. She read voraciously and she learned to knit. Eventually, even Jackie stopped suggesting she go out on a date with one of the few local eligible bachelors. Jackie figured that her sister had her memories to keep her warm at night. You heard of such things, in old novels, women living on the fumes of a great love. And Jackie, perhaps rightly, had always assumed that Robert Evans had been her sister's great love. Not that Delphine had ever admitted as much. On the subject of Robert Evans she had always been very quiet.

And then, ten years ago, she had met Harry. As she cleaned and cut vegetables for the salad she thought about what had attracted her to Harry Stringfellow. She didn't quite know, beyond the fact of his basic good nature and his ruggedly handsome face, which even a too-long beard couldn't disguise. It was true that he was Robert's antithesis. He hadn't gone to college. He didn't read anything but newspapers and the occasional spy thriller. He didn't care about traveling farther than his brother's house in Framingham, Massachusetts.

He didn't like "fancy food." Sure, he didn't challenge her intellectually, but she got enough of that through her reading and through the occasional conversation with Nancy, the town librarian. And he held old-fashioned, some would say ridiculous or even distorted, notions about honor and duty—hence his refusal to divorce the wife whom he saw as blameless in their mutual misfortune. Well, Delphine certainly agreed that Ellen was blameless. Car accidents happened to the best of drivers.

She took the butter out of the fridge so that it wouldn't be too hard when they sat down to eat. Harry liked his butter spreadable. She tried to remember if Robert had liked butter but couldn't. Delphine felt oddly sad about this. She had never told Harry about Robert. There seemed to be no reason why he should know that as a twenty-one-year-old she had been engaged. And engaged to a man whom even Harry, with his narrow media choices, would probably know at least by name or by sight. There had been a profile in *Time* magazine a few years back. She had seen Harry flip through a discarded *Time* at Bessie's diner once. It was entirely possible that he would recognize the name Robert Evans.

The truth was that she feared Harry's reaction. Rather, she feared how his reaction would make her feel. She imagined several ways in which Harry might take the news. He might be uncomfortable with the revelation, feel he didn't measure up to her former fiancé. Or he might not care one little bit. He might even, she imagined, be incredulous. She could almost hear Harry saying, "What were you, of all people, doing with someone like this Evans fellow? What could you possibly have had in common?" He might even, she imagined, be unimpressed. She could almost hear him saying, "So? What's the big deal? He puts his pants on one leg at a time just like any other man."

Dinner was ready. Harry joined her at the table in the kitchen after washing the newsprint from his hands. Delphine brought the salad to the table. She had lightly breaded the haddock with panko crumbs. Earlier, Jemima had dropped off a loaf of molasses bread fresh from her oven. For dessert, there were blueberries with heavy cream. Harry liked to sprinkle sugar on top of his berries and cream. With his coffee, he took three sugars.

They ate in silence for a few minutes before Harry, having devoured his fish, said, "Oh, I've been meaning to ask, how are things going with that old friend of yours, the one from Massachusetts?"

"Fine," she said.

"Good. I'm glad you're having some fun. You work too hard, Delphine."

Delphine took a careful sip of her water. She hadn't said that she was having fun with Maggie. All she had said was that things were fine. Harry had heard what he had wanted to hear. She took a breath and tried to calm herself. She reminded herself that most men, at least the ones she knew, were poor listeners. And Harry was a good guy. She believed he had heard what he had wanted to hear, which was that she was having a fun time with her old friend. He cared about her.

And so did Maggie, Delphine suddenly realized. After all, Maggie had sought her out after all those years of non-communication. Her return to Ogunquit had to be due to more than mere curiosity, the desire to see up close and for herself how an old friend had fared. For better or worse, Maggie wanted to spend time with her. They might actually come to enjoy time in each other's company. Stranger things had been known to happen.

And, right there at the dinner table, for the first time in years and years Delphine remembered in her gut what the friendship used to feel like—the intensity of the emotional bond, the excitement of it, and the deep comfort it afforded. It was a fleeting moment of visceral memory but a powerful one.

She suddenly felt frightened. She suddenly felt liberated.

Things—what things?—might actually change a little if she allowed them to change. If she wanted them to change, and she wasn't sure that she did, but . . .

Delphine took a bite of fish and chewed carefully. She hadn't spoken to Maggie since they had met at the Old Village Inn two evenings earlier. She felt bad about not having returned her call. So what if Maggie was a little weird, holding on to every scrap of paper Delphine had ever given her? Some people were just pack rats. Some people were just hopelessly sentimental. That didn't make them bad.

Delphine cleared her throat. "I'm going to call Maggie after dinner," she said. "We'll probably get together tomorrow evening. Just so you know."

Harry nodded, engrossed now in buttering a thick slice of Jemima's molasses bread. Delphine wondered if he had heard her.

16

"Thanks for suggesting this place," Maggie said. "It's fun."

Delphine had, in fact, called Maggie after Friday night's haddock dinner and had asked her to meet her at Billy's Chowder House in Wells the following evening. The sprawling restaurant wasn't fancy, but as at the Cape Neddick Lobster Pound, the food was good, and the view of the surrounding marsh was magnificent whether the tide was coming in or going out.

They sat at the bar rather than at a table, which was Delphine's choice. She recognized many of the other customers, some locals from Ogunquit but mostly from Wells. It was a predominantly older crowd, with a few people well over eighty. Several large-screen televisions were mounted around the room, each one broadcasting a sports event. The bartender that evening, Kelly, was typical of all the bartenders at the restaurant—hardworking, friendly, and totally unflappable. Delphine suspected that half of Kelly's male customers, young and old, were a little bit in love with her.

"The onion rings are killer here," Delphine said. "But maybe you don't eat onion rings."

"Not as a rule," Maggie admitted. "But I suppose I could have one or two."

"One or two certainly won't hurt you. My problem is stopping after five, six, and seven."

Kelly came by then and took their drink order. She asked after Delphine's parents and Delphine asked after Kelly's three boys. She brought Delphine's beer and Maggie's wine and moved off to serve a middle-aged couple at the far end of the bar.

"Well," Maggie said, "since you seem to know everyone and everything in the area, I should ask you to suggest a local church I could go to. I try to go every Sunday. Well, maybe every other Sunday. Okay, at least once a month."

"You might go to St. Peter's By The Sea," Delphine suggested. "It's on Shore Road in Cape Neddick. It's Episcopal, but I suppose anyone visiting on vacation can attend a service. It's a beautiful old stone building, on top of a hill. It's very picturesque."

"Oh, how could I have forgotten about St. Peter's By The Sea? We passed it every time my parents took us out to dinner in Portsmouth. There was some Italian restaurant down there they were mad about. Anyway, yes, maybe I'll go to a service next Sunday. Thanks, Delphine."

"Sure. What church do you belong to back home?" Delphine asked.

"No one in particular, actually." Maggie sighed. "I don't know, I feel the need to go to church, but I don't like to get involved in the community aspect. That's why I'm always drifting from one place to another when things feel like they're getting too close." *Which is strange,* Maggie thought, *given the fact that I feel so isolated these days.*

"I don't remember your family going to church when we were kids, but maybe I just didn't notice."

"They only went on the big holidays," Maggie said. "Easter, Christmas, someone's wedding or funeral. I half think my mother just wanted excuses to dress up."

"And when we were in college," Delphine said. "You didn't go to church then, did you?"

"No, I didn't. It wasn't until the girls were born that I went back. Well, there wasn't much to go back to. I never had a religious education, so I was kind of floundering for a while. I guess I still am."

"Do you consider yourself a believer?" Delphine asked, thinking of Harry and his cross.

Maggie frowned down at her drink and didn't answer for some minutes. She couldn't answer because she really didn't know what to say. She wasn't in the habit of asking herself such a question: *Am I a believer?* Maybe she never had been in the habit of self-reflection, at least about spiritual things. Finally, she looked up from her glass of wine and said, "I don't know. Sorry. That's a lame answer."

"No, that's okay," Delphine said. "It was a difficult question anyway."

"Gregory never goes to church and my daughters stopped going with me when they were old enough to say no. I didn't really put up much of a fight. I can't force my kids to believe something I'm not even sure I believe."

"Of course."

"What about you?" Maggie asked. "Do you go to church?"

"No," Delphine said, "I don't. I haven't been inside a church in— I can't remember how long it's been. No doubt it was for a funeral. It might even have been my mother's cousin Veronique's funeral. My parents go every Sunday without fail. The rest of the family goes on occasion."

"Do your parents pressure you to go with them?"

Delphine laughed. "Maggie, I'm forty-nine. I think I'm a little too old to be pressured by my parents into doing or not doing something."

Maggie wondered about that. In her opinion, which, granted, might not be an entirely informed opinion, it seemed that her old friend was in some ways in thrall to her parents, as well as to her siblings and their kids. What she said was: "Parental pressure never really dies. I mean, even when the parents are dead, their influence lives on."

"Maybe. What sort of lasting influence do you think your parents have had on you?"

"Me? Oh. Well, in my case I guess it would be the need to succeed. And the need to be independent, which is pretty much the same thing, I think. But that's not a bad legacy, is it? Every time I achieve a goal in my career I automatically think of my father, and how proud of me he would be if he knew." She laughed. "I guess on some level I still think of myself as his little girl. With my mother, it's different. She was happy when I married and had my children. Any career success is, in her opinion, secondary to those achievements. For a woman, of course."

Delphine took a sip of her beer. She wondered if her parents were actively proud of her and why. Because she was dependable, reliable, because she hadn't gone off and made a life of her own? Or were they proud of her because of her achievements? She thought about the ways in which she had helped grow the farm and improve business at the diner. She had made their lives a bit easier, maybe even a lot easier. But the Crandalls weren't the sort of people who expressed their emotions in words. If Delphine ever asked her mother and father if they were proud of her, they would find the question absurd, unnecessary, and embarrassing.

"Here's Jackie," she said, as her sister came into the bar from the lobby. She was thankful for the interruption of her thoughts. "I didn't know she'd be here tonight."

"Hey! Look who's here! Gosh, this must be Maggie!"

Maggie found herself enveloped in Jackie's arms. She laughed and hugged back.

"It's just like old times," Jackie said. "The girls out together on a Saturday night." Jackie took the stool on Maggie's left, putting Maggie between the sisters.

It was the first time that Maggie had seen Jackie since her college graduation party in Boston. And before that, the one time Jackie had come to visit when Maggie and Delphine were seniors. Jackie had bunked on the floor of their dorm room. They had brought a picnic to the Common and taken a ride on a Swan Boat. They had gone for dinner to the Union Oyster House and splurged on oysters and pigged out on fried clams. Some guy they met at an Irish pub had pestered Jackie for her number, until she told him she had a rare and very contagious disease she had picked up while working with a pack of wild boars in Borneo. Later, the three of them had met up with Robert and some friends and had gone to a midnight showing of *The Rocky Horror Picture Show.* It had been a memorable weekend of non-stop fun.

Now, Jackie's once dark brown hair was liberally streaked with grey and pulled back into a loose ponytail. That and the long crinkly cotton skirt she wore, with flat, brown leather sandals on her feet, and big silver hoop earrings gave her the look of an earth mother. Her face was slightly gaunt, though the too-tight shirt she wore revealed that she had gained some weight over the years. The skin around her eyes was deeply wrinkled, as if she had spent too much time squinting into the sun. Her smile, though, was still bright and welcoming. Maggie found that if she focused on that smile, she could still see the Jackie of twenty-seven years before, the girl-next-door-sexy Jackie. But she had to focus really, really hard.

Jackie ordered a rum-and-Coke, the same drink she had been ordering since she was eighteen. She waved at someone she recognized across the bar. "That's Raymond Collins. He's a bagger at the Hannaford supermarket in York," she told Maggie.

"A bagger? But he must be at least seventy-five!"

Jackie laughed. "At least."

Maggie suddenly felt highly self-conscious. She knew she was privileged. Her life—and the choices she had made to build and maintain that life—afforded her luxuries. She felt bad that Jackie and Delphine had so little. She realized that she felt annoyed with and puzzled by them, too. She couldn't understand why two intelligent women had made the choices they had made, choices that prohibited the acquiring of the amenities, the niceties. And that poor man sitting across the bar, the bagger. What choices had he made that had led him to still be working at a job better suited for a high school kid? But maybe, unlike Maggie, he simply hadn't had many choices, or opportunities. *God,* she thought, *the shoes I'm wearing tonight could probably feed that old man for months. They could send Jackie to a spa for a facial and Delphine for a month of daily manicures.*

"Dave Senior's at home glued to the television," Jackie was saying. "There's a Red Sox game on. He probably doesn't even notice I'm not there."

"When he wants popcorn he'll notice," Maggie said. "At least, that would be Gregory."

"Oh, Dave Senior can manage the microwave by himself. Otherwise, he's completely incapable in the kitchen."

"I'm not very good myself," Maggie admitted. "When the girls were little we had a full-time nanny and she did most of the cooking. I mean, I could manage a box of macaroni and cheese, that sort of thing. But now that it's just Gregory and I and neither of us are home much for dinner—and rarely on the same days—well . . . cooking just seems like a waste of time and effort."

"With two teenagers at home," Jackie said, "I have to cook. Nothing fancy, but healthy stuff, for sure. And Dave Senior and I insist they eat dinner with us each night. It's hard to maintain the family unit, but we believe it's worth the effort. Even when the kids get whiny about it."

Maggie remembered lots of nights eating dinner without her father. She had assumed that most fathers came home after seven, had a cocktail, and ate a late dinner alone or with their wives. She and Gregory had been lax about their own family gathering around the table. Well, they had had to be. Their careers had demanded they be at their offices or on the road most days, rather than at home making dinner and helping with homework. At least the nanny had been there to make sure the girls were fed. Now, when the girls came home from college for vacations, they were rarely in the house other than to sleep.

"Do you have pictures of your daughters?" Jackie asked.

Maggie was startled. No one had asked her that question since the girls were babies. "Oh, sure," she said, pulling her iPhone out of her bag. "Let me just . . . Here. Here's Kim and Caitlin this past Christmas. We were in Colorado, skiing. One of my colleagues has a gorgeous chalet and couldn't use it this past year, so we were able to rent it for a song."

Jackie widened her eyes in a gesture of disbelief. "An opera is more like it. It's huge. Not for nothing, Maggie, but if this is the sort of place you can afford to rent for winter vacation, you must be doing all right. Good for you!"

Maggie blushed. "The condo was nice," she admitted. "Five bedrooms, media room, state-of-the-art kitchen—not that we used it much! There are some great restaurants out there. . . . Okay, here are the girls dressed up to go out one night without the parents."

Delphine looked at the two tall, slim young women on the screen. She felt bad that she hadn't asked to see photos before now. People's children were an integral part of their lives. She knew that. She remembered that Maggie had sent a birth announcement for each girl. She couldn't recall now if she had responded to the announcements with a card or a call. She doubted that she had. She felt like a bit of a rat. "They're both so pretty," she said honestly. "They look so much like you."

"And Gregory," Maggie said, "especially Kim, on the right. But then again, you only met him once, and that was so long ago. You probably wouldn't see a resemblance."

No, Delphine thought. *I wouldn't.* Of course Maggie would have wanted her to know Gregory, to deem him suitable, to give the thumbs-up when he proposed. A couple, even a couple who had been together for a long time, didn't exist in a vacuum. Part of what gave validity to a couple was the acknowledgment and respect of the community—of their friends and family and neighbors. She hadn't honored her friend's marriage as she might have, partly, maybe, because she was upset about not being chosen maid of honor.

But no, Delphine thought. *I'm lying to myself.* The reality was that being Maggie's maid of honor—and she would have felt duty bound to accept—would have meant being dragged back to the world she had rejected with such difficulty. It would have meant a further commitment to a friendship she had come to find threatening—and too strong a reminder of her life with Robert Evans. Being with Maggie meant being in the larger world. Delphine had chosen a smaller world, her own world. The two, she had believed, would not easily mix. Maybe she had been mistaken in that belief. Maybe.

Maggie was putting her iPhone back into her bag. "How is your niece, Kitty?" she asked. "I got the sense the other morning from Jemima that maybe she wasn't feeling well."

Jackie flashed a look at her sister and said, "Jemima is a bit of a drama queen."

"Kitty's fine," Delphine said. "Thanks for asking. Let's order. How about some steamers?"

"And onion rings," Jackie said.

Maggie smiled. "I'm in."

17

1979

The tension, the suspense, was almost unbearable. Delphine stared at the phone on the hall table, as if she could will it to ring. She thought it had been bad while she was waiting to hear from Bartley College. But that was nothing compared to waiting to hear from Maggie, to learn if she, too, had been accepted. It had been three days now, three long days of making deals with a god she wasn't even sure she believed in—"If you let Maggie get accepted, I promise I'll be a better person"—and of wishing on the first star of the evening. "Star light, star bright . . ."

The phone rang, startling Delphine so badly that she yelped. She snatched the phone from its cradle.

"I got in!"

It was Maggie. Delphine screamed. Maggie screamed. Delphine said, "Oh, my God!" Maggie said, "Oh, my God!"

When the screaming stopped, Delphine said, "I swear I wouldn't have gone if you hadn't gotten in, too." She meant it.

"I know, and I wouldn't have gone if you hadn't gotten in. A whole new world is opening up for us, Delphine. We're going to have so much fun; we're going to have so many adventures!"

"Yeah, but remember, I have to work between classes. It

won't be all fun and games. And I'm on a lot of academic scholarships. If I screw up, I'm out."

"Oh, please," Maggie said, "you'll be fine; you're always getting As, right?"

"Yeah, but college is going to be a lot harder than high school."

"Grrr! Can't you just be thrilled for a minute without thinking about reality?"

Delphine laughed. "I'll try."

"Good. Now all we have to hope for is that we get to be roommates."

Delphine rolled her eyes at the wall. "There's no way that's going to happen. It would be way too much of a coincidence."

"You're doing it again. Don't be so negative. Wonderful things happen sometimes. Look, we both got into the school we wanted, right?"

"Yeah. Okay, I'll keep my fingers crossed about the roommate thing."

"Good," Maggie said. "Man, I can't wait to meet some college guys. Everyone in my class is so lame."

"Ugh, here, too."

"Speaking of ugh, did anyone ask you to the prom yet?"

Delphine sighed, as if bored by the subject. "Yeah. But I said no."

"Who is he?" Maggie asked. "Is he really gross?"

"No, he's okay. I'm just not into going with someone just to go. I mean, why bother if the guy's not my boyfriend? Besides, it's a lot of money."

"Yeah, but you only have one senior prom," Maggie argued. "This guy in my physics class asked me and I said yes. We're not dating or anything, but we both want to go so we're going as friends."

"That's okay, I guess. But I'd rather pass."

"You're a romantic."

"No, I'm not. I'm a realist. I—" Delphine heard her

mother calling to her from the kitchen. "Look," she said. "I gotta go. My mom wants me to get off the phone. She needs me to help with the baking for the diner. She does all the prep the night before. Well, you know that."

"Okay," Maggie said. "I should go, too. I have this history paper to finish and my parents are taking us out to dinner to celebrate. Remember, start wishing for us to be roommates!"

18

Maggie got out of her car and looked up at the big, old house before her. Delphine had once told her that her ancestors had lived in the house since it was built in the 1850s. Since then, generations had come and gone, but the structure had remained and it had grown. It was what was known as a classic New England "telescope" house. The original house had consisted of two small rooms and a kitchen on the first floor, and a central staircase leading to four small bedrooms on the second. Above that, reachable by a pull-down set of stairs in the hallway ceiling, was an attic. Over time, two bathrooms had been added, as well as an extension behind the kitchen, one large room, now used mostly for storage, and connecting to a passageway that led directly into the main barn. On the outside, the house was simple white clapboard, with four-over-four windows and a steeply sloped roof.

There were two other buildings on the property, a smaller barn, off of which Delphine's office had been built, and a wooden shed that Maggie thought looked about to collapse in on itself. Cultivated fields of vegetables, fruits, and flowers stretched out behind and to the sides of the house. Chickens in a variety of breeds roamed freely, pecking at the ground for bugs and grass. A barn cat skulked in a stand of grasses, no doubt eyeing unsuspecting prey, like mice or chipmunks.

From what Delphine had told her, the cats had learned long ago not to mess with the chickens.

It was six o'clock on a Monday evening and the sky was still bright and blue. Maggie climbed the stairs to the porch. Delphine opened the door to her knock. How many times had they played this scene, Maggie coming over to the Crandalls' house, looking for Delphine, Delphine rushing to the door, eager to be with her friend? Only now, Delphine thought, the eagerness, at least on her side, was tempered by the long stretch of their separation.

Mrs. Crandall—Maggie would never be comfortable calling her by her first name—was in the living room. The older woman gave Maggie a brief but strong hug.

"It's good to see you again after all these years, Maggie," she said.

"It's good to see you, too, Mrs. Crandall. And it's good to be back in Ogunquit, in this house. There are just so many memories. . . ."

Maggie scanned the room. Framed photos of family members were lined up on the fireplace mantel, perched on tables, and hung on the walls. An antique brass lamp sat on an immaculate white lace doily on top of a wooden side table. A framed piece of old embroidery showing the alphabet and several small animals hung on one side of the fireplace. An oval braided rug in greens and blues covered a large part of the wood floor.

She smiled at Mrs. Crandall. "It's all so familiar," she said. "I feel like this room hasn't changed one bit. I feel like I'm twelve years old again."

"Well, we did have to replace the sofa," Patrice said. "The springs just wore out. I suspect it was all the jumping on it Joey did when he was young. But otherwise, yes, I'd say everything's about the same. 'Why fix what isn't broken?' I always say."

Maggie laughed. "My mother used to redecorate the entire

house every two years. It drove my father crazy. I kind of liked it. I'd come home one day from school and find my bedroom all colonial instead of modern. Good-bye, orange beanbag chair; hello, old-fashioned rocking chair. It was fun."

Delphine thought that living with such uncertainty sounded horrifying, but she kept her opinion to herself. Her mother, she knew, was probably calculating the cost of such continual home improvements and silently disapproving.

Jackie came downstairs then. She was wearing a knit sweater that Maggie immediately recognized as Delphine's work. She clearly had a unique talent and why she wasn't advertising it from the rooftops was anyone's guess. *Maybe,* Maggie thought, *before I go back to Massachusetts I can talk some business sense into her.*

"Let's go on into the kitchen," Patrice said. Mr. Crandall, a man Maggie was introduced to as Dave Sr., and a teenage girl introduced as Lori, Jackie and Dave Sr.'s daughter, were already sitting around the long wooden table that dominated the kitchen.

Patrice had made a roast chicken with sides of freshly picked Swiss chard and a plate of fresh sliced tomatoes with herbs. The bread she had baked that morning. For dessert, she had made a strawberry rhubarb pie. Maggie was pretty sure she had insulted Delphine's obnoxious friend, Jemima, by not scarfing down her corn muffins. She would not insult Delphine's kindly mother by refusing a piece of her pie. She would just add an additional half hour to her exercise routine the next morning.

Patrice brought a glass pitcher of homemade iced tea to the table and Charlie took it upon himself to pour everyone a glass. Maggie couldn't help but notice how worn Delphine's parents looked. It was a fair bet that Patrice had not been getting facial peels. Charlie's back was bent and his face was the reddened, leathery face of a man who had spent a lot of time outdoors in all sorts of weather.

"I don't remember the last time I had a home-cooked meal," Maggie said, taking a seat at the table. "I'm afraid neither Gregory nor I are much use in the kitchen."

"Well, you enjoy yourself," Charlie said. "My wife is the best cook around here."

Patrice waved her hand in a dismissive gesture and took her seat at the other end of the table. "I don't know if you remember, Maggie, but we say grace before our meals."

"Of course," she said. Following the example of the Crandalls, Maggie lowered her head and folded her hands. Patrice spoke a short, simple prayer, and with a sudden clatter of serving spoons on ceramic, dinner began.

Jackie sat to her husband's left. Lori sat to his right. She was a pretty girl, dark haired like her mother, but with her father's deep blue eyes. Dave Sr. was a bit of a surprise. At least, Maggie hadn't pictured vivacious Jackie being married to someone so quiet and, well, unobtrusive. He sat hunched as if embarrassed about his great height or his thinning blond hair or whatever it was that seemed to embarrass him. Maybe he was just shy. Dave Jr., who, Maggie was told, was even taller than his father, was playing basketball with some friends. Delphine had told her there was some vague hope of his having a career in the sport, but nobody was counting on it. Besides, he would always have a job at the farm, with his father, or with his uncle Joey.

Lori ate hurriedly and then, after kissing her parents and grandparents good-bye, she left for a babysitting job down the road. Her father would pick her up later. Maggie tried to remember when her own daughters had last kissed her before charging off on a date or for work. The Wilkeses weren't a very demonstrative family. Which was all right. Maggie hadn't grown up in a demonstrative household, and neither had Gregory, and yet both were successful adults. They were normal.

"We were so sorry to hear from Delphine about your father," Patrice said when Lori had gone. "May he rest in peace."

Maggie smiled. She didn't think that anyone other than Mrs. Crandall had wished that sort of thing for her father, an ostentatiously secular man. "Oh, thank you," she said. "Well, it's been a long time now. And my mother's doing well, so that's one less worry for us."

"Does she live with you?" Jackie asked.

"Oh, gosh no. She has a condo in Florida."

"All the way down in Florida. It seems a shame." Patrice's lips set in a thin line, a clear indication to her family of her disapproval, but not, it seemed, to Maggie.

"What do you mean?" she asked.

"Well, with her family up north . . . ," Dave Sr. said. Later, Maggie thought that this half sentence might have been his only contribution to the conversation.

"Oh, my mother has a great life down in Florida," she said. "Her condo development is gorgeous and she can use the pool and the tennis courts and there are organized excursions to the mall and the local amateur theatre. There are all sorts of things to keep her busy and dressing up." Maggie laughed. "I don't know if you remember how my mother used to overdress for every occasion. She even wore heels to the beach. Well, I can't say I haven't done the same!"

"But how often do you get to see her?" Jackie asked. "How often does she get to see her grandchildren?"

"Oh, often enough," Maggie said. "Gregory and I see her once a year. She doesn't really like to travel anymore, so we go down to Florida. There's a fabulous hotel close to her condo development. I guess Kim and Caitlin haven't seen her in a while, almost two years I think. Spending time with their grandmother isn't exactly their idea of a fun time. I can't say I blame them! When I was a kid I hated having to visit my grandparents."

Immediately, Maggie realized she had said something she

shouldn't have, that she had been insensitive, something she had been guilty of several times since coming back to Ogunquit. The Crandalls were grandparents, and from what she had heard and seen their grandchildren enjoyed spending time with them. "What I meant was—" she began.

Jackie mercifully cut her off. "What about Peter?" she asked.

"Peter? Oh, my brother and his wife don't have children. They never wanted a family."

"Yes, but does he visit his mother?"

"Peter and my mother never really got along all that well after he graduated from college," Maggie explained. "Honestly, I'm not really sure what happened. I'm not close to him, either. After our father died . . . Gosh, you know I can't even remember when Peter last saw our mother."

Charlie wiped his mouth on his napkin and then folded it neatly, tucking it half under his empty plate. "I lost both my parents before I was nineteen," he said. "I pretty much raised my younger brother and sister by myself. They both died young, too. I don't know why I'm still around."

Delphine patted her father's arm. "Well, we're glad you are, Dad."

Patrice turned to Maggie again. "Have you met Delphine's Harry?" she asked.

"No," Maggie said, "I haven't. I'm kind of wondering if Delphine's hiding him from me for some reason. I'm only kidding, of course."

Delphine felt her mother's and her sister's eyes on her. "He's been superbusy at work lately," she said, which was not really a lie. "I'm sure they'll meet soon."

The table was cleared then and dessert brought in. Maggie didn't find it hard to accept a slice of pie, though the coffee Patrice had brewed threatened to burn a hole in the lining of her stomach. When those plates and cups had been cleared, Delphine and Maggie offered their thanks and said their farewells.

"Your parents are so nice," Maggie said when they were in the front drive. "They're so . . . so different from my parents. Not that my parents aren't, weren't fine people, it's just that . . . Your parents seem so comfortable, so sort of homey."

"The grass is always greener." *For some people,* Delphine added silently. *But not for me, at least, not always.*

"Yeah," Maggie said. "I guess that's it. Most people want what they don't or can't have."

Delphine smiled. "Anyway, believe me, my parents are not as sweet as they appear. They're pretty tough people. I don't mean that they're cruel. It's just that they're the sort of people who have no patience with self-pity or whining and all that. Unless you're bleeding to death, they'll tell you to put on your own Band-Aid."

"I don't remember that about them," Maggie admitted, "from when we were kids. All I could see was how awful my own parents were. Not that they were really awful, but when you're a kid you have an overblown sense of what's fair and what's unfair. I must have accused my mother and father of being unfair hundreds of times before I left for college."

"And how did they react?" Delphine asked. Had she ever accused her parents of being unfair? She was pretty sure that she had never talked back to them.

Maggie laughed. "My father would pretend he hadn't heard. He'd just walk away. And my mother would say things like, 'I'm sorry you think so.' There was no negotiation between parents and children in my house."

"Or in mine," Delphine said. "But I think that was the norm back when we were growing up. Parenting styles have changed drastically since then. At least, from what I read and see on TV. My brother and sister have pretty much repeated my parents' style, with some exceptions. But there's no spoiling going on, that's for sure. Except, maybe, a little bit with Kitty, but that's mostly my fault."

Maggie thought of how she had raised her daughters and felt a little twinge of guilt. Sometimes, maybe too many times, saying yes had just been easier than saying no; sometimes backing off on a threatened punishment had just been less of a hassle than following through and having to deal with the tears and the shouts.

Maybe, she thought now, she had been unfair to her children—there was that word again—by being too lax with discipline, too ready to capitulate to their whims and threats of holding their breath until blue and hating her forever. Maybe she had made them into young adults with little sense of generosity or compromise or kindness, young adults who didn't know how to accept disappointment as a normal part of life, young adults who thought the world was their due. She certainly hoped not. But it was too late to change anything now.

Maggie gestured toward her car. "Well, I should say good night. I know you like to get to bed early."

Delphine shrugged. "I'm not sure that I like it so much, but I need it. Five o'clock comes early, as my father always says. Drive safe," she added, already walking toward her truck. "It's probably too early for drunken tourists to be on the road, but you never know."

"I will. You too." Before sliding into the driver's seat, Maggie checked her watch. Only eight o'clock. She felt somehow bereft. She had so enjoyed being at the dinner table with the Crandall family. She wasn't ready to be alone for the rest of the evening. She considered the idea of going out someplace nice for a drink, maybe some place in walking distance of her hotel so that she didn't have to drive. Maybe she would go back to the Old Village Inn. It was a friendly place and the other night there had been that table of handsome, well-groomed men. One of them, the one she had flirted with at the bar, Dan, had winked at her on her way out. She couldn't remember the last time a man had winked at her or made any sort of appreciative gesture.

Maggie got behind the wheel and headed back into the heart of town. When she got to the hotel she parked and went up to her room. *No,* she decided the moment she closed the door behind her. *I'm not going anywhere.* She felt. . . . restless, and to go out alone might potentially be stupid. She was upset to admit that she wasn't at all sure she could resist a temptation. As Mr. Crandall might have said, it was better to be safe than to be sorry.

She undressed, got into her nightgown, and crawled into bed. She wished she had brought a book to read. It was ridiculous that she hadn't. She picked up the remote and flipped through channels. The only show that seemed at all interesting was a documentary on the state of the continuing cleanup in the Gulf of Mexico after the massive BP oil spill in 2010. She watched for an hour, and when she finally turned out the light she had no idea of what she had just seen. She dreamed that night of her children.

19

The Burton brothers had been born in England but raised since the age of ten in New York City. Each had a master's degree in art history. Piers's specialty was seventeenth- and eighteenth-century European painting and Aubrey's was European ceramics. They owned the largest and finest antique gallery in Ogunquit and another, slightly larger gallery in Kennebunk. Both men, now in their forties, were gay and had been single at least since moving to Ogunquit nine years earlier. In a way, Delphine thought, the Burton brothers reminded her of the Simmons sisters, siblings devoted so intimately and happily to each other and to their work they might never break apart and marry.

"Thanks for suggesting we come here," Maggie said, climbing down from Delphine's truck in the parking lot outside Burton's Antiques and Curiosities on Tuesday morning. "I love browsing through old things. You never know what treasures you'll find."

She looked up at the massive white structure before them. Delphine explained that it had once been a dilapidated barn. The Burtons had rescued it, rebuilding and restoring and adding on until it was the impressive place it was today.

"I thought you might like it," she went on, "even though you said your house is contemporary."

"Oh, only the master suite. I paid a not so small fortune for each area of the house to have a different look and feel. I guess I have my mother's lust for decorating. That, or I have a fear of commitment."

Delphine smiled and thought about her own method of "decorating." Was someone giving it away for free? If it was a lamp, did it have a working switch and a clean shade? If it was a couch, was the stuffing still intact? If the answers to these questions were "yes," the pieces found their way into Delphine's house. Along with, of course, pieces inherited from her family.

Delphine and Maggie entered the building. Neither Burton was in sight, though the women's entrance was surely known to them. Security cameras monitored both floors of the shop. Every summer, without fail, the brothers caught at least one potential shoplifter. Interestingly, it was always a woman, middle-aged and well dressed, the last person one would assume to be a thief. There was never a need to call the police. The woman's subsequent embarrassment—after a requisite initial denial—was, the Burtons believed, punishment enough. That and the horrified look on her husband's face, if he happened to be with her and not outside in the car, waiting and bored.

The brothers stocked an enormous amount of objects, but there was a sense of order not always found in antique shops. Maggie looked around and noticed an exceptionally fragile wooden rocking horse on a shelf above the front counter. Immediately to the left of the counter, there was a selection of fine bone china plates, cups, and saucers in a glass-fronted cabinet. To the right of the cabinet were two end tables inlaid with marble mosaics. A brass standing lamp with a tasseled rose-colored shade caught her interest. She wondered why until she remembered that her grandmother had had one just like it.

"Do you collect anything?" Maggie asked, pointing to a portable display case on the counter, containing twenty or thirty enameled thimbles.

"Not really," Delphine said. "I mean, I do have an awful

lot of books, but I buy them without much of a plan. I don't set out to find a particular edition of a particular book. I don't think I could afford to. I just browse and see what I find."

"Interesting. I mean, I acquire all sorts of things, too, but I don't actually collect anything. My mother did. I remember that when I was about eight she was mad for these lovely little delicate ceramic horses. And then, suddenly, she lost all interest in them. I was horrified when she sold the entire collection to a stranger, someone who saw her ad in the local paper. I felt so sad for the little horses. I know, it's strange to feel sad for an inanimate object, but I did."

Delphine thought of Kitty and her intense feelings for her stuffed animals. Each one had a name and a history and was a treasured friend. "You were a child," she said to Maggie. "Maybe you believed they were somehow alive."

"I guess. The world was a whole lot more magical when we were kids, wasn't it. A whole lot more emotional, too, somehow. Sometimes that was painful. Like when the little horses went away to live with a stranger."

"Greetings!" From the back of the first floor two men were emerging. Delphine introduced them to Maggie.

Piers, the younger brother, was about five feet nine inches tall and on the chunky side. He wore it well, though, Maggie noted. His clothing—a dove grey silk suit—fit perfectly. His hair was thick and wavy and brown, brushed back off his forehead in a way that made him look a bit mischievous or rakish.

Aubrey, the older brother by three years, was a bit taller than Piers and quite slim. His appearance was neat, clean, and thoroughly dapper. He wore a white shirt with French cuffs and, over it, a brocaded vest. His polished leather slipons, Maggie saw, had to be Italian. His hair, a silvery grey, was worn just like his brother's hair. Together, they made an arresting pair. Maggie assumed—correctly—that they didn't do their clothes shopping locally.

Maggie asked where the paintings were displayed and both Burton brothers escorted them to the second floor. She was immediately drawn to a large painting sitting on a tall easel. It was a landscape in oil, showing a luminous clearing in a sylvan forest. The frame was made of carved and gilded oak. The artist had signed the lower right-hand corner. The date on the back of the canvas, written in an antique hand, was 1859. Piers informed her that the artist, who was English, had been a minor but relatively popular painter in his day. The canvas had been professionally restored and was in fine shape. The frame was original to the piece.

"It's absolutely gorgeous," she said. "I just have to have it. It will look perfect over the fireplace in the den. I've been meaning to change out the art in that room anyway. You get tired of looking at the same pieces all the time, don't you?"

Delphine shrugged. Her selection of art, if it could be called a selection and not a random mass, consisted of one small watercolor of Perkins Cove, done by a local minor artist; an embroidered sampler done by a long-gone great-grandmother; a framed poster of a Marsden Hartley painting owned by the Ogunquit Museum of American Art and bought at an end of the season sale; another framed poster, from a Winslow Homer show that had been at the Portland Museum of Art—that one hung over her bed—and several of Kitty's drawings, including the latest noodle picture, held to the fridge with magnets. Even if she wanted to "switch out" some pieces, she had no other pieces with which to replace them. For Delphine, fine art was going to have to remain in what big, glossy, expensive books she could find in the library.

"Unless the piece is a favorite," Piers was saying. "Then, of course, one never tires of its presence."

"Could you have it sent to my home?" Maggie asked. "My housekeeper can accept delivery. I don't want to risk it laying around a hotel room."

"Of course," Aubrey said.

Piers asked Maggie where she was staying while in town. When she told him, he turned to Delphine.

"Isn't that where you worked a few years back?"

"You worked at Gorges Grant?" Maggie asked.

Delphine attempted a smile. There was nothing to be ashamed of—nothing—but she would have preferred to keep this bit of personal information from Maggie. "Yes," she said. "I worked there as a chambermaid for a few months. Money was tight. We were having an awful summer. There were big rains for weeks on end. We lost a lot of our harvest. Even the chickens weren't laying properly."

"Fortunately," Aubrey said, "many of the merchants did quite well. Visitors were booked into town, and with the beaches a literal washout they had little choice but to shop and to eat."

"Which, unfortunately, didn't do anything to help Crandall Farm or any other local farm," Delphine added.

Aubrey frowned in sympathy.

Maggie looked back to the painting. She felt a spasm of guilt at spending so much money on something that wasn't strictly necessary to maintain life and limb. But as quickly as it had come, the guilt was gone, replaced by a feeling of annoyance, edged with a bit of defiance. It was her money. She had earned it; she had worked hard for it. Why shouldn't she spend it as she saw fit? If some people had to take on an extra job cleaning up after strangers, that was not her problem to solve. Still, she wished she hadn't learned about this bit of Delphine's life. She didn't like to be reminded of all about Delphine that was so foreign.

While Aubrey completed the paperwork for the purchase and delivery, Piers chatted with Delphine. He asked after her family and she told him about Kitty's worrisome lack of energy. What she didn't tell Piers was that only the night before Kitty had come down with a fairly high fever. According to Joey and Cybel it wasn't high enough to warrant a trip to the emergency room, but still, the news was upsetting.

"Does she eat enough?" Piers asked, a hand on Delphine's arm. "So often children don't eat properly, no matter what the parents attempt. Our dear mother used to make us the most delectable treats but no matter to Aubrey! He was such a fussy eater. Unlike me." Here Piers transferred his hand from Delphine's arm to his own substantial belly.

Delphine smiled. "Well, it's true she's never been much of an eater. She gets so distracted she forgets she has to actually finish a meal. Cybel's taking her to the doctor soon. Maybe he'll give her some vitamins or supplements."

The sale completed, the women took their leave of the Burtons and drove into the heart of town. "I could drop you off at your hotel," Delphine said, "or you could come with me to the library." *Even though,* Delphine added silently, *I know you don't care for libraries.*

Maggie smiled. "Oh, I'll come to the library with you. Thanks."

Delphine drove back into town and parked the truck a few yards from the Ogunquit Memorial Library. They were beginning the short walk to the building when someone behind them hailed Delphine. They stopped and were joined in a moment by a man Delphine introduced as Marc Pelletier, owner of Pelletier Farm.

"Glad I ran into you, Delphine," he said. "Looks like I'm going to be shorthanded for a run to the market in Portland next Saturday. You think Jackie and Dave Junior could bring up some of my onions and such, sell them at their stand?"

"I don't see why not. I'll have Jackie give you a call, set things up."

"Much appreciated. You interested in a couple of pork chops for a couple dozen of your eggs?"

Delphine laughed. "Always."

While Delphine and Marc caught up on local news, Maggie thought about the exchange she had just witnessed. Delphine had mentioned barter the first night they met, at the Cape Neddick Lobster Pound. The notion of bartering had struck Maggie as quaint, like something out of an old novel. But now that she thought about it she realized that it could make good sense, if you could figure out how to value a thing, if you could figure out what price to put on it and how to ensure that there was a fair exchange. Of course, there would have to be a level of trust between those bartering, and really, what were the guidelines for trust in such a situation? Proximity? Just because someone lived down the road from you didn't necessarily mean he was trustworthy. Of course, she thought, people could be shamed into keeping a promise, shamed into being trustworthy and honest. If you knew you were going to run into your neighbor on a regular basis, chances were you wouldn't want to cheat him because of the embarrassment that would follow if your deceit was found out. In the end, Maggie thought, a straightforward exchange of cash for goods seemed an awful lot easier.

Maggie refocused to hear Marc Pelletier saying good-bye and loping off. She followed Delphine into the beautiful stone building set on a perfectly groomed lawn. Delphine introduced Maggie to the librarian, Nancy Brown, and then went off into the stacks in search of a book, a first novel by a Maine writer. She had read about it in one of the local papers and was hoping it would be in. A moment after she had gone, a tall, generously proportioned woman with a mane of silvery hair came into the library carrying a brown paper bag.

Nancy smiled as the woman joined them at the checkout desk. "Glenda," Nancy said, "this is Delphine Crandall's old friend, Maggie Weldon. Her family used to rent the Lilac House, oh, many years ago."

Glenda shook Maggie's hand and smiled. "Hi. I'm Nancy's partner. Weldon, did you say? That sounds familiar. But my memory isn't what it used to be." Glenda turned back to Nancy and handed her the brown paper bag. "How does ham and Swiss cheese sound? With a big fat peach for dessert."

"Yummy." Nancy smiled. "Glenda brings me my lunch,"

she told Maggie. "It makes a pleasant break in the day for each of us."

"How nice," Maggie said, even as she smiled to herself at the thought of Gregory's coming to her office with a homemade sandwich in a brown paper bag. She would think he had lost his mind or had been replaced by an alien from a much nicer planet.

"Gotta run," Glenda said. "Souvenirs don't sell themselves."

"Glenda works in one of the gift shops in the Cove," Nancy explained when she had gone. "It can be a madhouse some days, but it's a living."

"I can imagine." Maggie gestured to the paper bag on the checkout desk. "Please don't let me disturb your lunch."

"Oh, lunch can wait. You know, Delphine uses the library more than anyone else in town. She's a great reader."

Maggie glanced in the direction of the stacks. "When does she get the time? I wonder."

"Oh, a reader will always find time for a book."

"I have to admit I haven't read more than two or three books a year in ages. I used to read so much more. . . ." Maggie shrugged. "Now, I don't know; I just don't. Aside from the news and business reports, that sort of thing."

Nancy shook her head. "They say the Internet and all those machines like Kindle are going to kill the book, but I say that's ridiculous. There will always be those of us who love the feel of paper between our fingers, the turning of pages."

"Will there?" Maggie said. "I'm not so sure. A few generations from now there might be kids who find anything but electronic media obsolete. To them, a book might be some quaint relic from the past, something rare and inconvenient."

Nancy's cheeks reddened. "I won't believe it."

Maggie wished she had kept her thoughts to herself. She wished that Delphine would hurry up and pick a book. Happily, just then Delphine emerged from the stacks with two fat volumes in her arm. One, she showed Maggie, was Peter Ackroyd's biography of William Blake. The other was a novel by Ross King titled *Domino*. The first novel she had hoped to find was out, so she asked Nancy to reserve it for her when it was returned.

When Delphine had checked out her books and said goodbye to Nancy, the women left the library. Just outside, they ran into a short, roughhewn sort of man whom Delphine introduced as Bobby Taylor. He was still quite muscular, though Maggie guessed he had to be in his late seventies or thereabouts. His face was deeply lined and deeply tanned. He wore a clean though threadbare shirt with the sleeves rolled up. There was an ancient tattoo on his left forearm, but Maggie couldn't make out what it represented. His pants were held up with suspenders.

Delphine and Bobby chatted for a moment or two about the weather and the volume of tourists as compared to the previous year—staples of local conversation—and then he went off into the library.

"He's a retired lobsterman," Delphine explained when the door had closed behind him. "He's one of the other avid readers in town, along with me and Tilda McQueen. Bobby was a close friend of her father and he's been with Tilda's aunt, Ruth, forever. Her 'gentleman caller,' I guess you could say."

"The name sounds familiar. McQueen. Would I have known them?"

Delphine considered. "Your parents might have, maybe through the museum or the Barn Gallery. Tilda's family owns a big old estate overlooking the water. Larchmere. Well, actually, her sister, Hannah, owns it with her wife, Susan, now that the parents are gone. They run it as a bed-and-breakfast. Her brother, Craig, is the manager. He lives there year-round. I guess you could say the McQueens are kind of an enterprise, too, like my family. Except they're originally from Massachusetts."

Which made them, Maggie knew, perpetual outsiders. "You know everyone around here," she said.

"Everyone knows everyone."

"I guess I don't remember that from when we were kids."

"I'm not sure it's something a kid would really notice, the dynamics of a community. Kids are pretty self-involved. Of necessity, I guess."

"Yeah, I guess so. Pretty much all I was concerned about those summers I spent here was catching lightning bugs and eating ice cream. And all my brother was concerned about was playing baseball."

"That reminds me," Delphine said. "I need to buy Sea Dogs tickets. I want to surprise Kitty. What says summer more than a baseball game and a hot dog?"

"And lightning bugs and ice cream. I'd love to go to the game with you. I haven't been to a ball game of any sort since the girls played soccer when they were in middle school."

Delphine hesitated. She had planned to take Kitty on her own, just the two of them, a special outing. She looked over Maggie's shoulder, glad to be wearing her sunglasses. "I'll have to check my schedule first and then check with Cybel. . . ."

"Sure," Maggie said quickly. "If it doesn't work out that's fine. Look, thanks again for introducing me to the Burtons and to Nancy and Mr. Taylor. Oh, and I got to meet Glenda, too. I appreciate your letting me hang out with you today."

"Of course," Delphine said, but she realized she felt a little bit annoyed. She wished Maggie wouldn't make herself sound so pathetic, like Delphine was doing her some huge favor by "letting" her hang out. And if Maggie really did see spending time with her as a big favor, something special, might that mean she was asking Delphine to shoulder the responsibility—the burden—of a real friendship? *Either that,* Delphine thought, *or I'm overthinking this entire topic.* It had been known to happen.

"Look," Maggie was saying, gesturing in the direction of

Gorges Grant. "I can walk from here back to my hotel. I'm kind of thinking I'll go for a swim."

Delphine nodded. "Sure."

There was an awkward moment of silence and then Maggie turned and began to walk toward the hotel. Delphine raised her hand as if to hold her back; then she let it fall. She turned and walked in the other direction, back to her truck.

20

At ten o'clock Wednesday morning, Delphine got a call from her father, asking her to work the counter at Crandall's Diner. One of the women who usually handled the lunch shift, Melissa, had had a minor accident on the way in; her car, while not totaled, had been hauled off to a garage and she was temporarily stranded. Delphine left a message for Maggie, canceling their plans to have lunch at the farm, and rushed off to the diner. The last person she expected to see walking through the front door an hour later was Maggie.

Delphine was not thrilled. She didn't particularly want Maggie to watch her serving sandwiches, wiping counters, and scraping dirty dishes. *At least I'm not wearing a hairnet and a too-tight polyester uniform,* she thought. *And it's not as if there's anything unworthy about the work.* It was just that—well, just that this was work time, not playtime.

There was one seat left at the far end of the counter, close to the door, and Maggie took it. She smiled brightly as Delphine came toward her, order pad in hand.

"What are you doing here?"

Maggie laughed. "What do you mean, what am I doing here?"

"Didn't you get my message?"

"Of course. That's why I'm here. I figured this way we could still see each other."

Delphine kept her tone neutral, but she could feel a flush

of anger rise in her cheeks. "I'm at work, Maggie. I don't have time to chat."

Maggie reached for a plastic-coated menu propped between the salt and pepper shakers. "Oh, I know," she said lightly. "I've just been wanting to have lunch at the diner, for old times' sake. I told you that."

An old-fashioned counter bell sounded. "I need to serve another customer," Delphine said, and walked to the other end of the counter. Maggie saw her speak to a young, dark-haired waitress with a tattoo of a rose on her neck. The young waitress came toward her and with a smile asked if she could take Maggie's order.

When the waitress had gone off, Maggie examined the diner she had remembered with such fondness. She couldn't be sure, but she thought that the high-backed leather benches in the booths in front were new, at least, new to her. In her memory she saw them as red. These were blue. Otherwise, everything looked much as it had; she was sure of it. On the counter, next to the cash register, was a display of glass jars containing preserved foods made by Mrs. Crandall from produce grown on the farm. There were several kinds of sauerkrauts and pickles. In slightly smaller jars were blueberry and strawberry preserves. A picture of a bull moose was taped to the wall behind the counter. A circular glass case displayed homemade cakes and pies. At the checkout counter, next to the cash register, was a bowl filled with those awful chalky white mints. Maggie shuddered, remembering how she once had stuffed a bunch of them into her mouth, thinking they would taste good. Candy was supposed to taste good, right? She hadn't meant to, but she'd spit out the half-crunched mints, horrified. Delphine had thought it was hilarious.

The young waitress brought Maggie's lunch then and hurried off to take the order of a new customer a few seats down the counter. Maggie had found waitressing difficult as a college student. She didn't know how Delphine had handled the stress at thirteen or fourteen. She remembered that her mother hadn't let her hang out at the diner on Delphine's shifts because she thought Maggie would be a distraction. Maggie didn't think that Delphine had ever complained about having to work while Maggie was free to play, to read, to goof off. She had been the one to do the complaining: "It's not fair I have to be all alone." Not fair. Maggie felt embarrassed by the memory of her selfish, immature adolescent self.

The man next to her at the counter ordered a whoopee pie and Maggie suddenly remembered the time someone had thrown a party at the diner. It might have been someone's birthday, but whatever the occasion, there had been a giant whoopee pie that Mrs. Crandall had sliced up like a cake. Maggie, Delphine, Jackie, and Joey had been the only kids there. A local band played old rock and roll and the adults danced like crazy. Delphine had even taken a sip of an abandoned beer. *But wait,* Maggie thought now. *Maybe Jackie was the culprit.* She couldn't remember now. Had it been a dare? Maybe. Maybe she had made up the whole story, her brain creating an event that was likely to have happened whether it did actually happen or not.

"I hope you enjoyed your lunch."

Maggie looked around to see Delphine's father, standing at her elbow. "Oh, I did, Mr. Crandall," she said. "It was excellent. But I really should be going, let someone else have this seat. I'll just get my check."

"No, no," he said, with a dismissive wave of his gnarled hand, "no charge for an old friend of Delphine's."

"Oh, but please, Mr. Crandall, I—"

"Now, we'll hear no more. You come by again anytime."

Charlie Crandall walked off to speak with a customer at one of the Formica-topped tables. Maggie felt bad. She didn't believe that the Crandalls could afford to be giving away business. It wouldn't do. She pulled a twenty-dollar bill from her wallet and gave it to the young waitress when she came by to clear the plates. It was a tip entirely out of proportion to Maggie's bacon, lettuce, and tomato sandwich and glass of iced tea. She tried to catch Delphine's eye, but Delphine was still down at the far end of the counter, busy cleaning away the remains of another customer's lunch. At the door, Maggie turned, but Delphine was no longer in sight, probably back in the kitchen. With a shrug, Maggie headed out into the parking lot. Overall, she was glad she had come.

21

1981

The first thing Maggie saw when she crawled out of bed that morning was a thick, neat stack of paper on the edge of her desk. It hadn't been there the night before. She stumbled over to the desk and saw next to the neat, paper-clipped stack her messy pile of handwritten pages.

"Hey."

She turned to see Delphine coming into their dorm room. Her hair was wet from a shower and she was wearing her fuzzy blue robe and a pair of men's brown slippers. Maggie had pleaded with her to get a prettier pair, like, a pair for girls, but Delphine insisted these were the most comfortable slippers she'd ever had. And they had cost next to nothing.

"You typed the whole thing for me?" Maggie asked, her voice still thick with sleep.

"Yeah. It was no big deal."

Maggie pointed at the desk. "Delphine, this is a forty-page paper! It's a huge deal! And you did this all after I went to bed last night?"

"Yeah," Delphine said with a shrug. "I'm fast."

"Wait a minute. If you were typing all night why didn't I wake up?"

"I took the typewriter into the hallway, down at the end by the bathrooms."

"You sat on the floor and typed a forty-page paper? For me?"

"Well, didn't you say you were going to have to turn it in late because you didn't have time to type it, and that you'd have to take a penalty on the grade? I just figured I'd help out."

"You're amazing," Maggie said. "I don't know how to thank you."

Delphine hung her towel on its hook behind the door. "Forget it. Remember back when we were like eleven or twelve and I broke a window on the garage behind your house and you took the blame for me?"

"I guess," Maggie said. "Sort of. Maybe I'll remember after coffee."

"Well, consider this payback."

"You really are the best friend a girl could ever have."

Delphine sighed ostentatiously. "I know. It's a gift; what can I say?"

"Seriously," Maggie said, "now I owe you."

"Let's not keep track. Everything evens out in the end with friends. I shouldn't have called this payback."

"Well, thank you, again. I mean it."

Maggie reached out and the girls hugged.

"Just promise me one thing," Delphine said when they parted.

"Anything," Maggie said. "Pinky swear."

"Don't be late for class!"

22

"Did you hear about the trouble Dave Junior got himself into last night?"

"Dave Junior? No, what happened?"

Maggie was in Ogunquit Sundries on Main Street Thursday morning, hoping to find cuticle cream, which for some reason she had forgotten to pack. She was peering down one of the narrow aisles when she overheard a bit of the conversation between two older women to her right.

Maggie didn't make it a habit to listen in on other people's conversations, but this was different: This was about her friend's family; it had to be. She turned and took a small step closer to the women, pretending to examine a box of Efferdent on the shelf in front of her.

"Well, I don't know if the police are involved," the first woman was now whispering. "But I did hear that his parents are absolutely . . ."

Her words were lost as the woman and her friend passed behind Maggie and moved toward the back of the store. She abandoned the search for cuticle cream and hurried outside. It was only nine o'clock, but already the sidewalks were filled with tourists. Maggie made her way to the corner and found a relatively quiet spot alongside the Bread & Roses Bakery. She called Delphine's house. When no one answered, she left a brief voice mail and tried Delphine's cell phone. Again, the call went to voice mail, and Maggie left another, similar message. "Hey, it's me. We had talked about maybe getting together today. Call me on my cell. Bye." She knew by now that Delphine would only ignore a text.

By ten o'clock Delphine hadn't returned Maggie's call. Maggie left another message; and at noon, another. Finally, beginning to worry in earnest, she got into her car and drove out to the farm. She found Delphine in the office, just rising from her desk chair. She startled when she saw Maggie.

"I thought I'd find you here," Maggie said. "Did you get my messages earlier?"

Delphine looked away, in the direction of the corkboard on the wall. "Yes. Sorry, I've been busy."

"You're always busy," Maggie said with a smile. "We had talked about maybe getting together today."

"I know, I'm sorry, but the day just got away from me." She passed a hand through her hair, which was messy and unwashed. "It'll have to be another time. I've got a lot to do."

Delphine walked past Maggie and out into the dusty yard.

"Wait," Maggie called. "Delphine. In town, this morning, I overheard some people talking."

Delphine came to a stop and slowly turned around. Maggie noticed that she looked suddenly exhausted, deflated.

"Talking about what?"

"I didn't hear it all," Maggie admitted. "Something about Dave Junior being in trouble."

"People should mind their own business." Delphine's voice was flat.

"By 'people,' do you mean me or those women I overheard in Ogunquit Sundries?"

Delphine hesitated, and then sighed. She felt she had been caught or defeated. "You'll find out about it anyway," she said. "Better to hear it from me. Last night Dave Junior got into a fight with some kid on vacation here with some friends. A kid around Dave Junior's age, seventeen. Too young to be drinking, but it seems that he had been. They were all hanging out in the parking lot at the beach. The kid started bad-mouthing one of Dave Junior's friends, a girl he goes to school with. Dave Junior asked him to stop, but the kid wouldn't. So Dave Junior hit him. The kid lost a tooth. His friends wanted him to call the police, but he refused. Just ran. Seems he's been in trouble before and his parents, who I talked to this morning, don't want to draw attention to the incident."

Maggie put her hand to her heart. "My God. Is everything okay now?"

"Everything will be," Delphine said firmly. "The parents want compensation. They want money for the tooth to be replaced. They don't have dental insurance. If we don't give it to them they'll call in a lawyer. I talked to a dentist in town, got some information on how much this procedure might cost, and I negotiated a deal with the parents. It's all taken care of. End of story."

"Delphine," Maggie cried, "that is not the end of the story! The parents don't want to call attention to the incident, but they're ready to hire a lawyer to sue you? No, you have to call a lawyer of your own. These people are trying to bully you. Who are they? What do you know about them? They could be con artists and—"

"Look," Delphine said, retreating a step. "We can't really afford a lawyer right now. Things have been kind of . . . tight. And we absolutely don't want bad publicity for our family. We'll pay what these people want and everything will stay quiet. They're not being unreasonable. Not really."

Maggie laughed in disbelief. "Not being unreasonable! Delphine, you're being pressured into a deal that's probably entirely unfair. If it were my daughter who—"

"Well, it's not your daughter," Delphine almost shouted, "and it's not your nephew. This is not your business, Maggie. You need to stay out of it."

"How can I stay out of it?" Maggie argued, undeterred by her friend's vehemence. "What sort of friend would I be if I didn't offer to help? Look, I could make a call. Gregory's probably too busy right now, but I know several other lawyers in Boston who could probably give you a cut rate, maybe even take the case pro bono—"

"I said, no. Thank you. Leave it alone, Maggie."

Delphine turned and once again began to walk off in the direction of the house.

Maggie couldn't help the words from spitting out of her mouth. "God, it is so frustrating dealing with you!"

Delphine whipped around. "Frustrating?"

"Yes, frustrating, because I don't understand why you do the things you do. I can't understand why you make the decisions you make. They seem so . . . They seem so self-defeating."

The look on Delphine's face chilled Maggie. "Then don't," she said, " 'deal with' me anymore. I didn't ask you to come back to Ogunquit."

Maggie felt as if she had been slapped across the face. Delphine's eyes were hidden now behind sunglasses. Her expression now was blank.

"You're right," Maggie said finally, weakly. "You didn't ask me to come back."

Delphine turned away again and this time Maggie let her go. *It's just like all those years ago,* she thought, *when Delphine walked away from our friendship. I've been rejected again. I've offered love and support and I've been turned away. When will I ever learn to give up?* She thought it was Einstein who said, "The definition of insanity is doing the same thing over and over again and expecting different results."

When Delphine was out of sight Maggie got back into her car and, drained of energy and purpose, headed back to her hotel room.

23

It was about nine o'clock on Friday morning. Delphine had been at the farm since early morning, as usual. But around eight-thirty she realized that she wasn't concentrating on her work. She was bothered by that conversation—well, that fight—she'd had with Maggie the day before. She left the office, got into her truck, and drove out to the beach. Maybe a brisk walk in the fresh air would help. She hoped that something would.

She began to walk toward Wells, high up on the beach close to the dunes. A local man, Wade Wilder, was fishing down by the shoreline, as he had done every morning since his retirement. Wade, who didn't like to eat fish, routinely threw back whatever he caught or gave it to a passerby. He was a nice man, but Delphine wasn't in the mood to talk to anyone. She put her head down and hoped that he didn't turn around and see her and think her rude for ignoring him. He was nice, but he was also a gossip. By afternoon everyone he had encountered would know that Delphine Crandall had snubbed Wade Wilder. The Crandalls had endured enough bad publicity in the past twenty-four hours.

This morning the sand looked as if it had been freshly groomed. The tide was pretty far out, exposing what seemed like miles of beach underwater at higher tides. Way, way out on the horizon Delphine could see a pleasure craft, maybe a for-daily-hire fishing boat. She had seen hawks and even eagles wheeling in the sky over the dunes, but this morning her only company was seagulls and three grey pigeons.

She rarely spent time at the beach, certainly never lying in a chair and soaking up the sun. She envied vacationers who could enjoy a slow walk on the warm sand or an afternoon frolicking in the waves without feeling guilty about being away from work. Well, maybe some, or even most, people on vacation did feel guilty or worried about being away from their jobs, but at least they had a vacation in the first place.

And there it was, the stirring of self-pity, an emotion she usually fought off with energy. The fact was that she was being absurd.

Yes, she definitely had been too harsh with Maggie, rejecting her offer of help out of hand, acting so defensively. But the truth was that Maggie's showing up after all these years had shaken her, had suddenly highlighted certain things about her life she had been content to leave in the shadows. It had made her remember things she had fought strenuously for over twenty years to forget. It made her question some of the choices she had made for her life. And she didn't like it.

A seagull screamed loudly overhead. Delphine startled. She had lived with the sound of seagulls all her life, and yet the harshness could still surprise her.

And yes, she was still a bit angry with Maggie for having shown up at the diner. Though really, Maggie had done nothing wrong. She was the one who had reacted badly. And she thought she knew why. Not long ago she had read an article about something called Social Comparison Theory. That was when people who started out at the same place, with pretty much the same advantages, tended, years later, to compare their achievements with those of their former colleagues. In her own case, she thought it likely that in the eyes of the "world," she had not measured up as a person with a college degree should have done. She wondered what Maggie saw when she looked at her. She wondered if Maggie judged her life as somehow unfulfilled, inadequate, wasted.

It was like those wrinkles on her face and age spots on her hands. She had known they were there. She had accepted them with some semblance of unconcern. But since Maggie had shown up, those wrinkles and spots had taken on significance; they had found a voice. They had become nagging, obvious reminders of the fact that she was almost fifty and had little to show for it, at least by certain standards. No husband, no children, no grandchildren. She hadn't traveled much, she didn't own her home, her parents did, and she hadn't even bought a new truck in ten years. That her life was the way it was due to choices she had freely made suddenly didn't seem to matter.

Delphine felt sweat trickle down her back and realized that she had practically been running. She slowed her pace, but her mind continued to race along a path she knew was dangerous.

What if all, she asked herself, or even most, of the choices she thought she had made freely had actually been forced upon her? The choice to leave Robert, the choice to come home to Ogunquit, the choice to let her friendship with Maggie die a slow death, the choice to work for the family farm rather than go to work elsewhere or establish her own business. Even the choice to stay with Harry all these years—could that have been foisted upon her in some way? She wondered if she had been living a life someone else wanted her to live. She banished the thought as preposterous. Because if the answer to that question was in fact yes . . .

The beach was beginning to fill with vacationers, parents lugging coolers and lounges, kids racing ahead trailing Boogie Boards, young, single people in barely there bikinis and low-slung trunks. She looked at her watch and saw that it was almost ten o'clock. She had been away from her chores for too long. Besides, Melchior would be waiting impatiently for his mid-morning snack. Delphine half ran back to the parking lot, where her big old reliable truck stood waiting amid a sea of SUVs and sports cars.

24

At the same time that Delphine was walking along the beach, Maggie was walking along the Marginal Way. She remembered fondly the times her father would take her there, special times when they could be alone together. After walking the entire length, they would stop at Harbor Candy Shop on Main Street. Her father had loved the hard round candies with the watermelon flavor. She had loved those green jelly candies in the shape of a leaf and with the flavor of spearmint. And those round caramels with the white icing in the middle. They'd never told her mother about the visits to the candy shop. Mrs. Weldon would not have approved.

Maggie stepped a bit off the path and looked out over the water. She had gotten her first kiss on the Marginal Way, under the partial privacy of a crooked old pine tree. The boy, whose name she had long ago forgotten, had been a tourist, in town with his parents for a week. They had met at the ice-cream shop in the Cove. The kiss, like the boy's name, was forgettable. Well, in retrospect it was, compared to other kisses she'd received later on, like Gregory's first, impassioned kisses. Now, Maggie couldn't remember the last time she and Gregory had really kissed, other than a quick peck on the lips or cheek, a brief greeting or a hasty good-bye.

She began to walk again, slowly. The Marginal Way was a just-over-one-mile-long path along the coastline, stretching from Perkins Cove to Ogunquit Beach. Only pedestrians were allowed, no bikes or Rollerblades or skateboards. The path was very narrow in parts, so strollers and wheelchairs and even slow-moving groups of tourists on foot could cause frustration to those behind. But the view of the magnificent Atlantic, and of the grey, craggy cliffs, and of the frantically eddying pools below, and of the soaring, cawing seagulls overhead made up for minor annoyances like oblivious tourists. The trees and shrubs along the Marginal Way were fantastically distorted by years of wind and rain. The people who had homes along the Marginal Way were blessed with a magnificent view year-round, even if in summer months that view included a steady stream of people in sneakers and baseball caps.

But at that moment, Maggie was largely alone, with just the distant, glittering ocean for company. It would have been nice to be walking with Delphine. Maggie remembered the summer her family had gone to Europe instead of coming to Ogunquit. Ancient stone castles with spooky dungeons, glorious old cathedrals with glowing stained-glass windows, magnificent museums filled with works by the people whose names Maggie had started to learn about in art class, charming cafés serving delicious pastries, crumbling ruins on which a kid could climb to her heart's content—it had all meant little or nothing without Delphine by her side, someone with whom she could giggle and take note and dream. Peter had been no company. He'd spent the entire time grumbling about not being able to play baseball and missing his favorite TV show.

A dragonfly darted by, close to her face, and then another. Maggie had been frightened of dragonflies when she was little. Once, she and Delphine had come across a dead dragonfly. It might even have been Maggie's first summer in Ogunquit. Somehow she had gotten up the nerve to kneel down next to it and see what it looked like up close. She had been amazed to find that it was beautiful. She hadn't been afraid of dragonflies since then. It was a sad way to learn a lesson, she thought now. To learn to appreciate something—someone—only after it had died.

Maggie sat on one of the benches along the path, placed there in memory of a person who had loved this spot on earth more than any other. She wondered how many people had chosen to have their ashes scattered from the cliffs. She had no deep attachment to this place, not like Delphine seemed to, anyway. She had wonderful memories of her summers in Ogunquit, this "beautiful place by the sea," but she would never consider living here year-round. She wasn't a victim of wanderlust, but neither was she a person who was passionate about place. Maybe that had something to do with her family having moved so often when she was growing up. Maybe that had something to do with her mother's passion for change and redecoration.

A massive seagull landed a few feet from her and cocked his head. "Sorry," she told him. "I don't have any food." The bird regarded her closely for another moment and then stalked away to find a person of value.

Maggie sighed. She was annoyed with herself. She was throwing herself at a person who clearly didn't want anything to do with her. She wondered what had happened to her self-respect. She wondered what Gregory would think of her chasing after Delphine. She had been too embarrassed to tell him the important reason she had come back to Ogunquit—to make a real and vital connection with someone. And that was sad, not to be able to trust your spouse with your uncertainties, your hopes, your fears, your loneliness. It was sad, but maybe it was also common. Maggie didn't know. She didn't have any close friends with whom she could talk about her marriage. She certainly couldn't talk to her mother about it. And Delphine . . .

How stupid she had been, keeping that aquamarine necklace all these years and then thinking that this summer, reunited with Delphine, would provide the perfect moment to finally present it to her. How stupid, how adolescent, how naïve she had been to believe that the two of them would come together as easily and as immediately as they had the summer before fourth grade.

That was something else Gregory didn't know about, the necklace or the hurt feelings that had prompted Maggie to withhold it from Delphine all those years ago. She had told him about the fact of the friendship, where it had started and how it had grown, and then how it had suddenly died. But she had never talked about the depth of pain Delphine's defection had caused her. Maybe she should have. Maybe she still could. Maybe it was too late. Maybe it just didn't matter what she felt.

Because it was true what Delphine had said. She hadn't asked Maggie to come back to Ogunquit, to return to the origins of their friendship. That had been all Maggie's idea, a misguided notion, a silly hope for the revival of what had once been an essential relationship, the central relationship of so many years of her youth.

Well, maybe she was partially to blame for Delphine's resistance to her friendship. Maggie suspected that since she had arrived in Ogunquit she had been making assumptions about Delphine's life, regarding it as inadequate, judging it against standards that simply didn't apply to a Crandall. Her offer of help for Dave Jr., her unthinking comment about waitressing that morning with Jemima at Delphine's house—none of that had been helpful, had it?

For all those summers they had spent together, and then, through four years of college, it had never really occurred to Maggie that she and Delphine were from such very different worlds. She had never really acknowledged the radical separateness of their lives. And it had certainly never occurred to her that those differences could one day become a problem.

Children, young people, didn't look for division; at least she hadn't. Love, even the love of a friendship, had truly conquered all.

No, a sense of division and separateness came with time and experience. Discernment became, in many cases, prejudicial or judgmental thinking. Maybe that was inevitable. If so, that was sad.

Suddenly, Maggie felt very, very tired. She got up from the bench and began the long walk back to her hotel. In Perkins Cove a monstrous tour bus was discharging a group of elderly people, mostly women, dressed in the unflattering clothes some nasty person in some snobby design studio thought elderly women should be resigned to wearing. A few of the women linked arms for support as they began to walk toward the water for a better view. Maggie felt her throat tighten, a prelude to tears.

Once she was on Shore Road, she fought a tide of mothers and fathers loaded down with beach gear, their children in brightly colored bathing suits and Crocs, jumping along beside them. Couples—women with women, men with men, women with men—some, the middle-aged couples, wearing matching T-shirts, others flashing new wedding bands and honeymoon nails, others visibly pregnant, still others merely teens. She felt she was the only person in the entire town of Ogunquit who was on her own.

It was with relief that Maggie shut the door to her hotel room behind her. She took off her shoes and lay down on the neatly made bed. Again, she thought that maybe she should cut short her visit to Ogunquit—her doomed visit to the past—and just go back home to Lexington. She could sell the aquamarine necklace there. There was a reputable family-owned jewelry store right in town that would probably buy it. The stone was a good one and the price of gold was still high. She couldn't imagine giving the necklace to someone else, one of her daughters perhaps. And she certainly couldn't imagine wearing it herself, not with all of the emotional resonance it held.

Maggie didn't make it a habit to nap. But now, she allowed her eyes to close and to stay closed. Before long, she was in a deep and dreamless sleep.

25

Delphine sighed and wiped her brow with the back of her hand. The afternoon was hot, not one on which she would ordinarily choose to mow a lawn, but she had made a promise to Jemima. Jim was away for a week on a job for his company up in the Greenville area, and Jemima's arthritis was acting up something fierce. While she could probably get the mowing accomplished, she would be the worse for it for days. Delphine was strong. Besides, it was what neighbors and friends did for each other, helped out in small but meaningful ways. It was just that it was really, really hot. . . .

When she had finished the job, Delphine, her bandana soaked with sweat and her arms aching, joined Jemima in her kitchen for a tall glass of iced tea.

"So," Jemima asked, handing a glass to Delphine, "is your rich friend still in town?"

"If you mean Maggie," Delphine said after taking a gulp, "then yes, she is." Then she wondered. For all she knew, Maggie might have gone back to Massachusetts. The thought disturbed her, but only slightly.

"I don't know how you can be friends with someone like that," Jemima said, transferring a large lump of dough from a stainless-steel bowl onto a flowered wood board.

Delphine drained her glass before asking, "What do you mean, 'someone like that'? Someone like what?"

Jemima hesitated, seemingly at a loss for the right words.

Then, she said, "Someone who takes a vacation without her husband. Who ever heard of a husband and wife taking separate vacations?"

"It doesn't seem so odd to me," Delphine argued. "Come to think of it, I seem to remember Maggie telling me that her mother went off on her own sometimes."

"And that car!" Jemima punched the dough with more force than necessary. "Who spends all that money on a car? If it gets you from point A to point B it should suffice."

"I bet in her business an expensive car is sort of a job requirement. You can't show up for a meeting with corporate presidents or important clients in a beater. Or in a truck like mine, for that matter."

"There's nothing wrong with your truck," Jemima said. "People put too much stock in appearances."

"Well, be that as it may . . ."

"And she wouldn't even eat a whole corn muffin! One little muffin!"

Now Delphine laughed. "Not everyone likes corn muffins, Jemima. Come on. And she did say she was watching her carbs."

"Watching her carbs! Ridiculous. She strikes me as one of those women obsessed with their looks, always on some fad diet. There are more important things in life, you know, than being skinny and shooting your face full of rat poison or whatever ridiculous thing it is those women do to look younger."

"Of course I know," Delphine said patiently. "And Maggie's not really like that. She's not shallow; she's just always been careful of her appearance. She's a very loyal person. She's very intelligent. You're just seeing one part of her."

The part you want to see, Delphine thought. *The part you need to see.* Maybe she, too, had been judging Maggie harshly, too quick to find habits and opinions she could condemn as different and so less valuable than her own. She thought about what had happened with Dave Jr. What had

Maggie really offered but access to professional help? There was nothing objectionable in that, unless you chose to be offended for your own muddled reasons, like a distorted sense of pride. Even the large tip Maggie had left at the diner. While going through the day's receipts, Delphine had discovered that Maggie's was missing. She asked Sue, the waitress who had served Maggie, about the receipt. Sue told her that Mr. Crandall hadn't charged Maggie for her lunch and that Maggie had left a twenty-dollar tip. Delphine had immediately seen the money as offensive, as an insult. Now, she thought that it was more likely to have been an offering of thanks and appreciation.

"More iced tea?" Jemima asked, wiping her hands on a kitchen towel and rousing Delphine from her brief reverie.

"Oh, no," she replied, "thanks. I should get going. I promised I'd help Jackie with some harvesting." She put her empty glass in the sink, said good-bye to Jemima, and let herself out the front door. *Maybe,* she thought as she walked to her truck, *I've been selling Maggie a bit short. Maybe.*

26

It was about five o'clock on Friday afternoon and Maggie was standing with ten or so other sweaty visitors to Ogunquit, waiting for a trolley to take her back to Gorges Grant. She had woken earlier from her mid-morning nap feeling disoriented and restless. She called Gregory and had an aborted conversation, as he was running off to a meeting. She sent a text to Kim and one to Caitlin. Neither girl responded. She left a voice mail for a woman back in Lexington, someone she had met on the tennis court, suggesting they get together for a game when she got back. She didn't really like Angela all that much, but you couldn't play a good game of tennis alone and Angela's skill level was on par with her own. Her company was, for lack of a better word, convenient.

And then, she had washed her face, reapplied sunscreen and makeup, changed into a lighter outfit, and headed into town. Ogunquit was a vacation destination. There was plenty to do, plenty to occupy the long, empty hours that stretched ahead.

First, she went to the Barn Gallery. There was an exhibit of local artists, and though many of the paintings and photographs and mixed media pieces were interesting and some even beautiful, Maggie was hardly moved. She considered seeing a movie at the Leavitt Theatre, a place she had fond memories of, but decided she wouldn't be able to focus on a story line. She walked on to Perkins Cove. In a store called

Swamp John's she bought a gold charm in the shape of a starfish. Kim liked starfish. She would give her the charm for her next birthday. She walked over to Barnacle Billy's for lunch in the shady garden. She ordered a lobster salad and a glass of wine, forgoing the infamous rum punch she had heard about back at her hotel. The food was fine, but Maggie ate without enthusiasm. The view of the boats docked in the cove was charming, but Maggie barely noticed.

When her meal was cleared away, she ordered a second glass of wine. Again, she considered cutting this visit to Ogunquit short and going back home to Lexington. But for what would she be returning home? And for whom? There was always her job. She could bury herself in work; there was a comfortable couch in her office, so she needn't bother to go home to an empty house at the end of the day. She could shower at her gym. Stash a change of clothes in her locker.

Maggie frowned. It was ridiculous, to be thinking about hiding from an empty house. It was her home. She had a right to be there and to feel welcomed, even if she was the only inhabitant. For God's sake, she owned the house. Suddenly, she'd had enough of feeling sorry for herself. What would her father say if he could hear her whining, self-pitying thoughts? And what would her her mother say? Maggie could almost see her frown of disapproval and disappointment.

She would not run home. She had come back to Ogunquit for a reason. She had lost Delphine once—maybe she hadn't fought hard enough for her—but she would not lose her again, especially not over something as ridiculous as a juvenile delinquent and a lost tooth. And she didn't really believe, not deep down, that Delphine wanted nothing to do with her. She couldn't afford to believe that, not yet, not until she found another home in which to place her trust and friendship, not until she found another source of emotional intimacy and strength. Maggie made her decision. She would approach Delphine one more time, and maybe one more time after that. The result would be up to Delphine and her willingness—her ability—to receive Maggie's friendship. But at least she would have tried.

After having finished the second glass of wine Maggie paid the bill and walked to the nearest trolley stop. Now, finally, a trolley was in sight. Once back at her hotel she would take a shower, put on clean clothes, and go someplace air-conditioned to get a drink. She had a very strong feeling that getting a little drunk was in order.

27

1982

Maggie sat at her desk in the dorm room she shared with Delphine. It was a Saturday night. She had no particular plans, other than flipping through the fashion magazine in front of her. Delphine would, of course, be seeing that graduate student, Robert Evans.

She had been dating him for almost a month. They were near to inseparable. If not for the demands of their professors—and both were on scholarships, so those demands were taken seriously—Maggie thought they would spend all of their time together, holding hands and staring into each other's eyes. It was enough to make Maggie sick. The fact that she felt bad about feeling so . . . jealous only made her feel sicker.

It wasn't right to be jealous of your friend's good fortune, even if that good fortune meant you got to spend less time with her and the time you did get to spend with her was largely taken up with talking about the good fortune. In this case, the good fortune was Robert Evans. You were supposed to be happy for your friend's happiness and she was, really. It was just that . . . It was just that she felt a little bit—just a little bit—abandoned. Left out. Ignored. Left behind.

Delphine came back from the bathroom down the hall. She was dressed in a pair of Levi 501 button fly jeans, black cowboy boots (they weren't real leather, so they had been affordable), and a white blouse, tucked in, and the sleeves rolled up almost to her elbows. Maggie noticed that she had actually managed to tame her hair into a ponytail. Delphine didn't like the big teased and lacquered hair so many of her classmates wore. Generally, Maggie thought Delphine looked like a throwback to the sixties, her hair long and messy and parted in the middle.

"Do you want to wear my leather jacket?" Maggie offered. "It's really warm. I heard on the news that this has been the coldest November in Boston since some time in the 1950s. I forget the exact year."

"Sure," Delphine said. "Thanks. I promise to keep it clean." And then, her tone suddenly anxious, she said, "You are happy for me, aren't you?"

"Of course I am," Maggie said firmly. "Now go, have a great time. I promise not to wait up for you."

"I'll tell you everything tomorrow, I swear."

"Okay. Wait," Maggie called, as Delphine was at the door. "You're going to a club out in Winchester, right?"

"Yeah. Some place called Space Bar."

"Is Robert driving?"

"I think so," Delphine said. "Why?"

"Don't get in the car if he drinks, okay? I know you really like this guy, but don't do anything stupid for him. Promise me."

Delphine put out her arms. Maggie got up from her chair and the girls hugged. "I would never do anything to risk our friendship, Maggie," she said. "Believe me."

"Best friends always."

"Pinky swear?"

Maggie laughed. "You are so silly. Okay, pinky swear."

When Delphine had gone—she had practically run from their room in her eagerness to be with Robert—Maggie lay down on her bed and stared up at the patched ceiling. It would be a long night if she stayed in. She could catch a movie. *The Blues Brothers* was playing in a revival theatre somewhere. People in her French class had been talking about it. She had never seen it and it was already a kind of cult classic. Or she could see *Gandhi.* That would keep her occupied for a few hours. And some girls she knew from her advanced statistics class were planning to hang out at Timmy O'Shea's, an authentic Irish pub on Boylston Street. The girls were okay. She could join them, even for one beer, maybe order some boxty wedges. She loved boxty wedges, even though her mother repeatedly warned her about the caloric dangers of anything made from potatoes.

Maggie sighed. She couldn't make herself decide on going out or staying in. She began to feel a bit pathetic. She wondered if she was too invested in Delphine, too reliant upon her for a social life. She had always considered them inseparable. Even when they were kids and she had gone back to Massachusetts for the school year, she had spent an awful lot of time writing to and calling Delphine and not so much time hanging out with the girls from her class. And what had Delphine done for friends all those years? Maggie realized that she didn't know. Delphine had never—or rarely—mentioned any other friend. Maybe she had been entirely invested in Maggie. Until Robert Evans had come along.

Maggie had liked certain guys, and some of them had liked her back. But she had never been in love, like Delphine was so obviously. Love meant the separation of friends. Love was going to divide her from Delphine. It wasn't fair. It shouldn't be that way, but Maggie had a bad feeling that it was that way.

She got up from the bed and took a step toward her closet. She intended to get dressed. She intended to go to that Irish pub. And then, she turned back and lay down on the bed again.

28

Maggie turned the Lexus into the Crandalls' front drive Saturday morning. Maybe she was being stupid or naive coming out to the farm again, trying one more time to make a connection with someone who didn't seem to want a connection at all. *But what the hell,* she thought. *I have nothing to lose except, maybe, my ignorance.*

She found Delphine at her desk, as she thought that she might. She knocked on the door frame and Delphine looked up. Maggie was relieved to see that she didn't look angry or even annoyed.

"I came to apologize," she said.

A very small smile appeared on Delphine's face. "Okay."

"I shouldn't have interfered with the Dave Junior situation. It's just that I didn't see it as interfering. I'm used to people coming to me for advice. I get paid for it. Still, I shouldn't have tried to tell you how to handle family business. I'm sorry."

Delphine's smile grew. "That's okay," she said. "I probably got too worked up about it. I'm pretty used to handling stuff on my own."

"Yes. I imagine you are. So, apology accepted?"

"Of course."

"Good," Maggie said. "That's a big relief."

Delphine hesitated, and then she said, "And, well, Maggie, I am glad that you're here. Really. I guess I'm just still a bit . . .

stunned that you are. Here. After all this time. In a way it seems unreal. I feel like . . . I feel like I don't know what I'm supposed to do or say."

"You're not 'supposed' to do anything," Maggie said. "And just say what you want to say. It's me."

It's me. Delphine wondered if Maggie had the right to assume that familiarity, that intimacy. *But maybe,* she thought, *I'm being too . . . prickly—again. Maybe I'm overthinking. And maybe taking on the responsibility of Maggie's friendship wasn't entirely a bad thing at this point. Besides, in a few short weeks Maggie would be going home and life could get back to normal.*

"Hey," Maggie was saying, "are you okay? Looks like you went away for a while."

Delphine shook her head. "Sorry. Look, I really do have to get back to work now, but maybe we could get together later?"

Maggie nodded. "Okay. I'll call you this afternoon and we'll figure something out." With a little wave and a spring in her step, she was gone.

29

At Maggie's suggestion the women met for a picnic on the beach that evening. She had brought sandwiches from the Village Food Market and, as a treat, two brownies from the Bread & Roses Bakery. She wasn't sure if alcohol was permitted on the beach, so she had brought two bottles of Pellegrino instead. Delphine brought a large, slightly threadbare blanket; she didn't own beach chairs. Maggie was wearing the periwinkle sweater she had bought from Delphine. It really did look good with her blond hair. Delphine was wearing a well-worn green sweatshirt.

The tide was coming in, so they sat well up the beach, close to the dunes. Most of the families with small children were long gone back to their hotels to shower, change, and find dinner. Only a few older couples and a scattering of teens remained.

"I can't remember the last time I did this," Delphine said when they had settled. "Had a picnic on the beach."

"I think if I lived in Ogunquit I'd come down to the beach every day, rain or shine."

Not if you had a life like mine, you wouldn't, Delphine thought.

They ate for a while in companionable silence. Delphine was always hungry and finished her sandwich quickly. The brownie didn't last long, either. She hoped that Maggie would eat only half of hers and pass the other half on.

"Tell me about Harry," Maggie said when she'd finished her sandwich. "I don't know anything about him, other than his last name and that he lives on Agamenticus Road. And why haven't I met him yet?"

"No reason," Delphine said. "He's just been really busy with work. He drives a truck for Charron Lumber. Besides that there's really not much to tell. We've been together for about ten years. I think I told you that already. He's a good man. He helps my father around the house when he can, you know, with the bigger stuff, shoveling snow in the winter, raking the leaves in autumn. Dad doesn't like to get on a ladder anymore if he can help it, so he calls Harry if Joey or Dave Senior aren't around."

"Well," Maggie said, "that's good of him, to be there for your family. So, are you planning on getting married someday? I know you don't live together, but it sounds like you have a pretty domestic kind of relationship."

Delphine had known this moment would come. And why shouldn't Maggie know the truth? Everyone else in Ogunquit did. "Harry," she said, "is already married. His wife is in a nursing home. She had a really bad car accident about twelve years ago. She wasn't found for kind of a long time, so there was oxygen loss. She has traumatic brain injuries. I really don't know all the details except that she can't function on her own."

"Oh." Maggie paused. "That's so terribly sad. But if she's incapacitated . . ."

"He won't divorce the mother of his children. He still loves her. He visits her once a week. So . . . We won't be getting married."

Maggie was silent for a moment, thinking. There was an obvious question to ask. What about when Harry's wife died, which for all Delphine knew could be at any time? Would Harry ask her to marry him then? Maggie hesitated a moment longer and then said, "Well, maybe I shouldn't ask this, but—"

"Then don't. Sorry. Lately . . . I don't know. It's become a bit of a touchy subject with me. Sorry."

"Lord, Delphine, don't apologize. I'd be upset, too, if—"

"I'm not upset," Delphine said. "Not exactly. Are you going to eat that brownie?"

"What? Oh, no, you can have it."

"We could share it."

"Sure." Maggie unwrapped the remaining brownie and broke it in rough halves. Delphine ate her half; Maggie rewrapped hers.

"I don't know how you can be okay with the situation," Maggie said finally. "Here I am interfering again. But don't you think you deserve more? I think you deserve more!"

"Be that as it may, you don't get into a fight with an enemy you can't beat."

Maggie thought, *This is just like when Delphine went back home to Ogunquit after college. She doesn't give life a chance. She doesn't try for anything. She just accepts what's put in front of her as all she's worthy of having.*

"Your life," she said, "could have been so much—"

"So much what?" Delphine interrupted, her tone challenging. "Better?"

"No. That's not what I was going to say. Other. Your life could have been so . . . other than what it is now."

"The same could be said for you," Delphine pointed out. "The same could be said for anyone. But I don't want my life to be anything other than what it is. My life is exactly what it should be." But Delphine wondered if she really believed that. Maybe she was just being defensive. She fiddled with the cap of her water bottle and wished they could be talking about something neutral, like casserole recipes. She liked casseroles.

"I wish I could say the same," Maggie said after a while. "That my life is exactly what it should be. But I can't, not anymore."

"Oh. I'm sorry. What would you change, if you could?"

Maggie chose her words carefully. "I guess I would like my marriage to be more . . . interesting. More passionate. But maybe that's not possible with Gregory, so maybe what I would change is the man. . . . I mean, maybe I would choose to be with someone else."

"Are you serious?" Delphine asked. "Are you thinking of leaving your husband?"

"No, no," Maggie said quickly, "of course not. I'm just—just thinking out loud. The thing is that lately I feel I could be happier. I feel that I could be—that I should be—more fulfilled. I'm not an old woman yet. I think I deserve some more excitement before I am an old woman and can't enjoy life like I could be enjoying it now."

"What do you mean by 'excitement'?"

"I don't know. That's part of the problem. I can't seem to think clearly about my life."

Delphine shook her head. "Change for its own sake is all well and good for the young," she said. "They have so much time to recover from their mistakes. But at forty-nine I can see sixty and even seventy, if I squint real hard . . . and I don't know. The abandonment of what's good if not necessarily wonderful in my life seems absurd, if not downright stupid."

"That's smart," Maggie conceded. "But maybe I don't want to be smart just now. I don't know. I just feel . . . restless."

And maybe, Delphine thought, *I'm just a big coward.*

"You know," Maggie said. She hoped to sound casual, though she had finally decided to bring up the name of the one person Delphine might not want to talk about at all. "I never told you this, but I don't know why I should be keeping it a secret. Robert contacted me a few times after you came back to Ogunquit. He was confused. He wondered if I knew more about your decision to end the engagement. Of course, I didn't know anything more than he did. And even if I had known more, I'm not sure I would have told him. It would have been betraying your trust in me as your best friend."

Delphine was silent. She had been expecting this conversation since Maggie's phone call back in the spring. That didn't make it any less surprising or comfortable. "So," she said finally, "you didn't tell him anything?"

"What was there to tell? It didn't make much sense to me, either, your ending things with Robert and going back home. After a couple of calls I told him he should just contact you directly. Did he?" Maggie asked. "Did he ever call, or write? Did you ever talk to him again?"

Delphine couldn't answer right away. How could she possibly explain what it had been like for her those first months back home in Ogunquit, the disturbing mix of relief and heartache, knowing she had done the right thing yet feeling that she was going to curl up and die because of it?

"No," she said finally. "We never spoke again. He did write to me, twice. Maybe three times, I don't remember. It was in that first year. But I never responded."

"Why?"

Delphine shrugged. "It was over. What was the point in writing back? What else could I say to him?"

"Did he want you back?" Maggie asked.

"Yes."

"And?"

"And I couldn't go back to him. I didn't want to." That was a bit of a lie, but Delphine had never talked about this to anyone. She had thought that she never would. And now, all these years later . . .

"God, Delphine," Maggie said, "didn't you feel any regret, not even a little? You were so in love with each other. It took every ounce of my will not to be jealous of you two. Sometimes, I failed pretty miserably."

Delphine looked out at the water. The tide was inching its way up the beach. More people had gone home, leaving them virtually alone with the seagulls searching for any scraps of food left behind.

"All right," she said finally. "Yes, I did feel some regret. Of course I did. I did want to go back to him, a little. For a while . . . For a while I was still in love with him."

Maggie sighed. "It must have been so hard for you. Honestly, Delphine, why? Why did you end things with Robert and come back here? I know I asked you this at the time, but I have to ask it again. Did he cheat on you? Did he hurt you in some way?"

"No, no," Delphine said. "Robert was . . . perfect. Perfect for someone else. I . . . I had to be here, in Maine, in Ogunquit, with my family. I was needed. That's all."

"Couldn't you have married Robert anyway, and visited your parents a few times a year, even once a month?"

"It wouldn't have been the same thing," Delphine said firmly. "Besides, Robert didn't like it here. He felt it was too . . . provincial."

"I just can't believe you broke up over a little thing like where to live."

"It's not a little thing," Delphine replied vehemently. "You don't understand what this place means to me."

Maggie looked at her closely. "I guess I don't. So explain it to me."

"I don't know if I can. Just take my word for it. I needed to come back here. The world I would have had to live in with Robert would not have been my world at all. I would have been . . . lost."

They sat in silence for a long moment. After a time, Maggie said, "Robert was—he is—a wonderful man. He makes a huge difference in the world. He's a man worthy of being loved. I'm sorry, Delphine, but I don't think I'll ever understand how you could have walked away from the love of your life."

The love of my life, Delphine thought. Had Robert really been the love of her life? Or was the love of her life this beach, this town, this land? Was it her family? She really didn't know. She didn't think that it mattered.

"I saw Robert on TV not too long ago," Maggie was saying now. "He was one of the people being interviewed for a documentary on China and its changing workforce. It was on PBS."

"I saw that show, too." What Delphine didn't say was that she watched every documentary and interview and that she read any article with any connection to Robert Evans. She had bought all four of his books. They were in the bookcase in her workroom, hidden behind the collection of Dickens's work. She wasn't entirely sure why she felt the need to keep them hidden away.

"How does it feel," Maggie asked, "watching, listening to the person you were once so in love with?"

"I don't know," Delphine answered with a small laugh. "Weird. I feel like I'm watching a stranger, but at the same time I keep thinking, I know he has a little mole on his right shoulder and all those other people at home watching him don't know that. It's like I have privileged information. Frankly, it makes me a bit uncomfortable."

"I think he dyes his hair."

"What? No, I don't think Robert would be so vain. He's a serious journalist, not some silly, shiny anchorman."

"Not vain?" Maggie laughed. "Are you kidding me? Robert Evans has a lot of good qualities, but humility isn't one of them! He was always sneaking a look in a mirror. It didn't really bother me because he was always nice to me and, more importantly, he treated you really well. It used to make me laugh, though. I don't think he realized everyone saw him checking himself out."

"I don't remember his being concerned with his appearance," Delphine said. "Are you sure about that?"

"Of course I'm sure. And of course you never noticed. You were in love and love is blind. If you had married him, lived with him, I'm sure that after a while your eyes would have been opened. But maybe not. I mean, if you and Robert had married, maybe your influence would have cured him of his vanity. At least, helped him keep it in check."

"Maybe," Delphine said. "But it's all moot now. There's no point in speculating about what might have happened."

The two women were silent for a while. The sun was sinking and now the final few remaining sunbathers were packing up. Delphine was remembering that about a year after coming home to Ogunquit she had thrown out Robert's letters, all of them, even the ones he had written her when they had first started to date. She had been determined to purge her present life of her past. Now, she almost—almost—wished that she had kept the letters, not necessarily to read them again (that might be too painful) but just to hold them. His words, on paper he had touched, written especially for her. At least she would have something tangible of a time that, while frightening, had also been magical.

Maggie was thinking not of the past and Robert Evans but of the present and Harry Stringfellow. "You know," she said, breaking the silence between them, "technically speaking Harry's cheating on his wife with you. He's an adulterer, though I suppose not a lot of people would really blame him. Still, if he's so devoted to his injured wife, then why is he sleeping with another woman? You can bet she doesn't know about you."

Delphine sighed. "I'm not sure she's capable of understanding anything much about life outside her own head."

"That's not the point," Maggie argued. "Look, I'm certainly not perfect, but—"

"Let's change the subject, please."

"Just one more question. Is that why you and Harry don't live together? Because he's not technically single?"

Delphine hesitated before answering. "No," she said. "Harry would move in with me in a minute if I asked him to. It's not that. It's just that my life . . . I don't really know how to say it. My life is very busy. It's very full. People—a lot of people—rely on me for a lot of things. I like to close the door behind me at night and be alone. I need to be alone." *My home, my house,* she added silently, *is all I really have to call my own. But if I really had Harry, if Harry would marry me, would I still want to live on my own?* She thought that the answer might just be yes.

"Well," Maggie said, "I can't say there weren't times when the girls were younger when I would have killed for a place of my own, even a small closet, any place with a door. And a lock. Maybe an armed guard outside. But now . . ."

"Now, what?"

Maggie shrugged. "I don't know. Now, I think I'd appreciate someone barging in on my quiet time."

"But you don't live alone. You live with Gregory."

"Yes. But sometimes, you can feel very lonely even with someone else in the same room. Somehow, that feels worse than being really alone. It can make you feel . . . desperate."

Yes, Delphine thought. *I know exactly how that feels.*

"You know," Maggie said, her tone thoughtful, "I don't know if I can call Gregory the love of my life. I mean, I do love him and he loves me; I'm sure of that. We fell in love once, a long time ago. And he's stuck by the family, which is more than you can say for a lot of men. He's been a very good father. The girls have wanted for nothing. My mother adores him. But . . ."

"But what?"

"But he's not like your Robert. I mean he's not to me what Robert was to you. He's not my big passion."

"Are you sure?" Delphine asked. "Maybe you're rewriting history because some of the magic has gone from the relationship. I doubt that even if Robert and I had stayed together we would have still been so madly in love now. Maybe we would have been more deeply in love, more settled, maybe even more devoted to each other. But maybe we would be divorced. I don't know."

Maggie thought for a few moments and then said, "No, I

don't think that I am rewriting my history. I think that some people just don't ever find a great passion with another person."

"Then maybe your passion is your work," Delphine suggested. "Or your children."

Maggie wasn't sure about those, either. She loved her daughters, of course, but she was also aware of being—of having been—anything but a helicopter parent. And as for her career, well, in truth it was more of a means to an end than something fulfilling in its own right. Maybe it hadn't started out that way, but that's what it had become.

"I don't know about me," she said finally. "Maybe I just haven't found my one great love yet. Or maybe it's right in front of me and I just can't see it."

Delphine looked at her watch. It was already eight o'clock. The food was eaten, the water bottles empty, and the sun was almost entirely down. She got to her feet. "I really should be going," she said. "I have some paperwork to do tonight. I can't believe we've been here for so long."

Maggie got to her feet, as well. "Enjoying yourself isn't the same as being negligent, you know."

Delphine shrugged. "I know. Now, let me fold the blanket. And are you going to eat that half of a brownie or what?"

30

"That was just delicious, Delphine," Maggie said. "Thank you."

"No problem," Delphine said, stacking the plates in the sink to wash after Maggie had gone. "I like to cook. And I like an appreciative eater."

It was Sunday and Harry had gone to visit his daughter in Falmouth. Delphine had invited Maggie for dinner, something that felt like a big step, though to what end she wasn't quite sure. Much to her surprise, their conversation about Robert Evans had resulted in a slight but significant melting of her resistance to Maggie's friendship. She wanted to make a meal for Maggie; she wanted Maggie to enjoy an evening in her home.

She had made a fish and corn chowder (with a bowl set aside for Melchior), accompanied by a salad and whole-wheat rolls her mother had baked that morning. Maggie had brought a bottle of wine, a sauvignon blanc, and though Delphine didn't know much about wines, she knew enough to realize that this wine was good.

After dinner they retreated to the front porch. It was small, especially compared to Delphine's parents' front porch, but it was big enough for two people to enjoy a warm evening with a cooling breeze. An enormous butterfly bush with large pink flower spikes grew along one side of the porch. In the day-time, bees and hummingbirds and of course butterflies swarmed it. Now, at seven in the evening, life on the wing had gone home. Hollyhocks, orange and magenta, grew at the base of the porch, close to a patch of black-eyed Susans. A large pot of basil sat on the wooden rail of the porch. Between the two wicker armchairs stood a small round wicker table and on it two glasses of iced coffee.

"I don't know how you can do that," Maggie said, pointing to the bag of yarn by Delphine's foot. "Talk to me, look out at the view, and knit all at the same time. It seems almost like magic."

Delphine laughed. "More like practice."

"I tried to learn to knit once, when Kim was a baby. I was horrible at it."

"It takes a feel, I think," Delphine said, "to be good and to enjoy it."

They sat in companionable silence for some time. Delphine found that she liked this, sitting on her front porch with someone by her side. Harry wasn't a porch sitter. Neither was Jemima. Truth be told, Delphine didn't allow herself this pleasure often, and when she did, she was always alone.

She glanced over to Maggie, whose head was resting against the back of her chair. She looked utterly relaxed. Delphine wondered if she had the right to speak freely about something that had been worrying her. Well, she thought, Maggie certainly thought she had the right to probe into her life, so . . .

"You were flirting with that man the night we were at the Old Village Inn," Delphine said. "The one who came to the bar to order drinks for his friends."

Maggie raised her eyebrows. "And?"

"Well, flirting is harmless, not that I've ever really enjoyed it. Maybe I just never knew how to do it right."

"You didn't."

"Be that as it may . . . That first night you came to town, and then again last night, on the beach, you talked about your marriage not being what it used to be. That maybe Gregory is not the love of your life. I feel I have to ask. You're not planning on having an affair, are you?"

Maggie laughed a bit too loudly, in a misguided attempt to cover her embarrassment. "Oh, no, no, not at all," she said. Well, that wasn't really a lie. She wasn't actually planning on having an affair. Which was not to say that the thought hadn't crossed her mind lately. But she wasn't at all sure that an affair would serve any purpose other than to be a selfish quick fix. She and Gregory had been closer once upon a time, sure. Maybe they were experiencing an inevitable drifting apart, something most if not all long-term couples went through. Maggie didn't know if it was possible in her case to reverse that drift, but even if it wasn't, a divorce would make a lot more sense and be a lot fairer to everyone involved than an affair.

"Good," Delphine said. "I just wanted to go on record as saying I think having an affair is never a good idea. And yes, I know you're thinking I'm applying a double standard, given my situation with Harry."

Maggie was eager to get off the subject of affairs, and of Harry, of whom she had a pretty low opinion, so she said, "No, I understand you. Hey, did I tell you I went to the big Bartley College reunion event? Gosh, that was three years ago already."

Delphine nodded. "I remember getting the announcement in the mail. Along with a request for a donation."

"But you didn't go."

"No. And I didn't send any money. My money is needed right here."

"Yes. There were rumors Robert was going to be there. It was going around that he was planning to give a talk or something. Nothing was official. Anyway, in the end he didn't show up."

"Oh."

Maggie looked keenly at Delphine. "I would have liked to have seen you at the reunion. I suppose I should have called you, let you know I was planning to be there."

Delphine smiled vaguely. She hadn't wanted to attend the reunion for several reasons. Robert was one of them. The chance of running into him after all those years was too frightening. Maggie was another reason.

And the third reason was almost as daunting. She had been afraid that people she had known at Bartley might judge her for choosing the life she had chosen. All those classmates who had probably gone on to perform great public works and to make tons of money might look at her life as devoid of merit or value. Other people's opinions mattered to Delphine, though she wished that they didn't, at least not the opinions of strangers. It was a character weakness she continually fought and one she vigilantly kept hidden.

"The past is the past," she said finally. "There's not much point in going backwards."

Maggie shook her head. "I don't agree. I think that celebrating what was is a good way to, I don't know, assess the present and plan for the future."

Delphine thought about that. If that was the motive behind Maggie's return to Ogunquit—to assess her present life in light of what had been and then to make plans for a happier, more fulfilling future—had she been successful? Would she be? By the time she left for her home in Lexington, would she really feel she had accomplished something by spending evenings on Delphine's front porch?

Maybe. Still, Delphine doubted that a return to her own past would have any great transformative effect on her future. Everything was pretty much fine as it was and would go on being fine, or it would not. What would happen would happen. There was a limit to what anyone could do about her present, let alone what she could determine about her future.

Maggie rose from her chair. "I'll be right back," she said. "It's 'that time' of the month."

Delphine continued to knit, enjoying the feel of the wool between her fingers. She hadn't hit full-blown menopause yet, either. Neither had Jackie, though she seemed desperate for it to come and go. "I've had my kids," she told her sister. "I'm done. I can't wait for the whole system to shut down." Delphine didn't feel quite so eager for her own reproductive system to shut down, in spite of the fact that she knew she would never be having children. Her feelings about the whole thing were complicated. She chose not to explore them too intensely.

Maggie returned and sat back down with a sigh. "If perimenopause is this annoying, I can't imagine what full-blown menopause will be like. I never know what to expect."

"I'm not looking forward to it," Delphine said, "that's for sure."

Maggie took a long sip of her iced coffee. She wondered if Delphine ever felt that she had wasted a great opportunity by not having children. Maybe someday she would ask her why she had never started a family of her own. Maggie herself had had children almost automatically. There she was, married, financially secure—so why not get pregnant, too? Starting a family had been more like fulfilling a social imperative than following a dream. Not that she had any regrets, but she imagined she might have been perfectly happy not having had children. She wondered if many other women felt as she did. It wasn't the sort of thing you shared casually. The Mommy Police were everywhere.

"Penny for your thoughts," Delphine was saying.

"Oh, I was just thinking about menopause. My mother calls it mental pause. Seriously, she claims her memory simply failed her during those years."

"My mother never mentioned anything about going through menopause," Delphine said. "Of course, she must have experienced it, but I don't remember noticing anything different about her behavior."

"Your mother is stoic. I can't see her bitching and moaning about hot flashes or heavy bleeding."

Delphine laughed. "No, that's definitely not my mother's style. She could have a fork stuck in her head and she'd try to pretend it wasn't there."

"Not my mother. God, she became such a drama queen about the whole thing. My father walked on eggshells for years. Even Peter and I suffered. Maybe that's going to happen to me. Maybe I'll become an unbearable bitch. Poor Gregory."

"Don't think about it," Delphine said. "Don't anticipate anything about menopause, good or bad. What's going to happen is going to happen. And then, it will be over."

"Now you sound like a stoic. And a bit of a defeatist, too."

Delphine shrugged.

"What is that you're making?" Maggie asked.

"A coat, actually. Lori tells me that long coat-like sweaters are 'in' this fall. She showed me some pictures from a magazine and here I sit, knitting a coat."

"You're a good person, Delphine Crandall."

Delphine shrugged. "Better I make it for her than she waste the money she should be saving for college."

"So, Lori's planning on going to college?"

"I don't really know," Delphine admitted. "I'd like to see her continue her schooling after high school. But it's her decision."

"You could encourage her."

Like Maggie and her parents encouraged me, Delphine thought. "Yes," she said. "I do encourage her. So does her mother."

"That's good." Maggie checked her watch and got up from her chair. "Well, I suppose I should be getting back to my hotel. You'll want to read whatever tome it is you're currently reading."

Delphine grinned. "I was an English major. With a minor in history. And one in art history."

"All big-volume subjects, yes." Maggie rose and stretched. "Thanks, Delphine," she said. "I had a lovely time."

Delphine hesitated a moment. And then she said, "Me too."

31

Delphine came into the house from the office around two o'clock Monday afternoon to help her mother assemble and price items for a tag sale at her church. The sale would, hopefully, pay for new prayer books. The ones in current use were old and falling apart; some were even being held together by rubber bands. Delphine brought with her a child's purple cotton sweater and three wool scarves, one in the "potato chip" stitch, her donation to the cause.

The two women set to work in the living room at a rarely used formal dining table Patrice had inherited from an aunt. On the table were some of the items to be sold. There was a package of doilies made by one of the older churchgoers; a handmade rag doll with buttons for eyes; two wood birdhouses painted in red and yellow; and a variety of other items Delphine couldn't imagine anyone wanting, let alone paying money for. But there was no accounting for a person's taste. She was sure Maggie was reminded of that every time she looked at Delphine's clothing.

"Where's Kitty?" Delphine asked her mother.

"Out in the barn with Jackie and Lori," Patrice said. "She wanted to see the new kittens. Their eyes have just opened."

"Did she have lunch?"

"Of course. Though she didn't eat very much."

"How does she seem to you?" Delphine asked.

Patrice frowned. "I don't like to interfere with a parent's child-rearing decisions."

"What do you mean?"

But Patrice just shrugged.

"She has a big bruise on her leg," Delphine said. "What's that from?"

"I saw it. But I don't know how she got it. Neither does she. I asked. Kitty's not usually clumsy. So, how long is Maggie going to be in town?"

"I don't know," Delphine said. "She hasn't been specific. I know she's accumulated a lot of vacation time."

Patrice folded a crocheted quilt contributed to the sale by a Mrs. O'Connell. "I think that woman has some figuring out to do."

Delphine laughed. "Don't we all?"

After a moment, Patrice said, "Some more than others."

Delphine didn't respond. She wondered if her mother was implying that her younger daughter needed to fix her life in some way.

"There's something lost about Maggie," Patrice went on, "for all her fancy clothes and sophistication."

"How do you mean 'lost'?" Delphine asked.

"Every summer, she was glued to you from the moment her family got here until the moment they left."

"Yeah, but wasn't I glued to her, too?"

Patrice shook her head. "It wasn't the same. There was something almost desperate about her need for your friendship. Sometimes, it made me worried. Like she wasn't getting any attention at home or that something was missing. I don't know. You know I don't like to interfere."

Delphine reached for a pile of dish towels a local woman named Mrs. Bubier had sewn for the sale and began to fold them. For all the years of their friendship she had seen Maggie as the more assured, the more self-sufficient, of the two. Maybe she had been wrong. Or maybe something had changed. Maybe loneliness was what was behind Maggie's pursuit of their old friendship. She had talked a bit about loneliness, hadn't she? Loneliness, and feeling restless and confused.

"Why haven't you introduced her to Harry?" Patrice asked, interrupting Delphine's thoughts.

"No reason."

"Delphine, there's no point in lying to me and you know that."

"Fine," she said with a sigh. "I just don't think they have anything in common."

"Why should that matter? I think you're afraid Maggie will find that Harry doesn't measure up. Well, sure, his manners are a bit rough at times, but he's a good man, not very exciting, but that sort of thing doesn't matter in the end."

Delphine bristled. Didn't she deserve someone exciting, someone with good manners, someone who "measured up"? *I guess not,* she thought. *At least, according to my mother.*

Delphine had never talked with her mother, or her father, about Harry's marital situation. They knew, of course, about Ellen; everyone in town did. But if either of her parents had a problem with Delphine's being with Harry, they weren't saying. Now, for the first time, Delphine wondered if her mother really cared about her happiness. She wondered if her mother, and her father, really valued her properly. How could they, Delphine thought angrily, if they weren't bothered by the fact that their daughter was dating a married man?

If she and Harry were actually dating, because "dating" implied a journey leading to an end—to a breakup or to a committed union. Delphine had realized long ago that their relationship was stagnant—it wasn't progressing and it wasn't regressing. It just was. Which might be okay if the big circumstances were satisfying, but they weren't. Not anymore, not for her.

"Look, Mom," she said. "Harry hasn't even asked me

when he's going to meet Maggie. I don't even think he cares. Which is fine. She'll be gone in a few weeks, anyway."

"Who will be gone?" It was Kitty, come in from the barn through the kitchen. Her cheeks were flushed. Delphine recognized her T-shirt as one she had given her, pink, with a picture of a glittery fairy on the front.

"My friend Maggie," Delphine explained. "She's in Ogunquit visiting. She lives in Massachusetts."

"Oh. Is she staying at your house?"

"No. She's staying in a hotel."

"Why, if she's your friend? Why isn't she staying with you, like a sleepover?"

Delphine thought, *Because I didn't want her to visit me. I didn't ask her to come.* "It's just better this way," she said lamely. "Hey, guess what? I have a big surprise for you."

"What is it?" Kitty grabbed her hand. "Tell me, tell me!"

"You and I are going to a Sea Dogs game!"

"Yeah!" she cried. "When?"

"In three weeks. You think you can wait that long?"

"Mm-hmm. I'm a good waiter. Grandma, can I have a glass of water? I'm really hot."

Patrice casually brushed her hand across her granddaughter's forehead. She didn't let Kitty see her frown. "Of course you can. Here, let me go with you. Maybe you'll want a nice nap soon, too."

"Grandma! I'm not a little kid anymore!"

Patrice and Kitty went off to the kitchen. Delphine continued to fold Mrs. Bubier's dish towels. She had bought only two tickets to the ball game. She wasn't quite sure what she would say to Maggie if she asked about the tickets. Of course, the best thing to do would be to tell her the truth, that she wanted a special day alone with her niece. But Maggie could be so sensitive. She thought again about her mother's opinion of Maggie as lost or lonely but was interrupted by Kitty and her grandmother coming back into the living room. Kitty was clutching a glass of water.

"Can I get a souvenir?" she asked Delphine. "I have two dollars in my piggy bank."

Patrice frowned. "You don't need a souvenir, Kitty. You don't want to be wasting your money."

"Oh, Mom, come on." Delphine smiled at her niece. "Don't worry; we'll get a souvenir."

"Yeah!" Kitty yawned hugely. "I'm gonna sit on the porch with my book," she said, and tramped out through the front door.

Patrice frowned. "You spoil her."

"Not badly. Besides, everyone deserves to be spoiled a little."

Patrice gave her daughter a close, questioning look. "Do you really believe that?"

Delphine wasn't sure. She had spoken without thinking. Robert had been good to her, but he hadn't spoiled her. She wasn't sure she would have let him if he'd tried. Her parents certainly hadn't spoiled her, far from it. The one person in her life who had come closest to really spoiling her, to being indulgent, to giving her above and beyond what was strictly necessary for contentment, was Maggie.

"I don't know what I believe," she said, bothered by this thought. "Let's finish up here. I have to get back to the office."

32

Maggie looked at the Ogunquit Museum of American Art with appreciation. It was a long, low, attractive white building set on a cliff overlooking the ocean. There was a charming garden out back and on the lawn in front of the museum there was a well-groomed pond surrounded by reeds, and several large wood sculptures of animals, created by the artist Bernard Langlais. Maggie remembered going to the museum as a child and being frustrated by the fact that her mother wouldn't let her touch—let alone climb on—the animals.

Maggie and Delphine had come this Monday evening for an event to benefit a small, privately run art program for high school kids with talent. Maggie was wearing a form-fitting sleeveless lilac-colored linen dress that came just below her knee. Her sling-back heels and clutch were black. Delphine wondered just how many suitcases Maggie had brought with her. She hadn't seen Maggie wear the same outfit twice since she arrived.

Delphine had been understandably nervous about her own clothing for the evening. She knew through the Burton brothers that the people who went to these events at the museum, particularly the older ones, dressed in their finest summer clothes. The men wore jackets and ties, no matter the heat. The majority of women wore dresses or skirts, many of them with panty hose. Briefly, Delphine had thought about asking Maggie to come over to the house and help her put together something suitable, but the thought of Maggie sorting through her closet seemed too . . . intimate. Too much like those college days when Maggie had helped her dress for a job interview or dates with Robert. They weren't in college now. Their friendship was something very different from what it had been, back when they had undressed in front of each other and held back each other's hair when they were sick.

In the end Delphine had gone to Jackie's house and together they had assembled what they hoped might pass for respectability, if not for sophistication. Jackie was a little bigger than Delphine, but two safety pins helped solve the problem of the coral-colored crinkly cotton skirt. She wore a T-shirt of her own, one of the newer ones, and over that one of her own hand-knit cotton sweaters in a deep green. That had been Jackie's idea. "It'll be great self-promotion," she'd said. "Plus, it looks good." On Delphine's feet she wore a pair of Jackie's nicer sandals. She had even allowed her sister to apply a coat of pale polish to her toenails. "Really," Jackie had scolded. "You could put a little effort into your appearance. Take a cue from Maggie."

"I asked for your help tonight, didn't I?" Delphine had replied.

Jackie had eyed her sister critically. "Well, it's a start."

"How did you get these tickets?" Delphine asked now, as she and Maggie entered the museum. "I don't think you mentioned. If you did, I forgot."

Maggie explained that a guest at Gorges Grant, an older man, had given her the tickets. His wife wasn't feeling well, he'd said, and they wouldn't be able to use them.

"He wouldn't accept money for them," Maggie went on. "I'll make sure I do something nice for them in return before they leave."

"Not everyone needs a favor to be returned."

"Of course not. But I'd feel bad if I didn't reciprocate. And how could buying them a dinner hurt?"

Delphine didn't believe that kindness needed to be rewarded, but maybe, she thought, it should be rewarded, at least, sometimes.

"Why don't you have a membership?" Maggie asked when they had walked down the short flight of steps into the main room. Ahead of them they could see the vast Atlantic through the glass doors leading onto a patio and sculpture garden. "This is such a wonderful museum. And it's very well respected."

"It wouldn't be worth it. I don't come all that often, usually just once or twice a season."

"But what about a family membership? There are a lot of you Crandalls. Maybe there's a membership for extended families."

"No one else in my family is into art," she admitted. "Honestly, I'm not sure either of my parents has ever been to a museum. The only literature my father's ever read are the poems of Longfellow. I'm not criticizing them. It's just the way they are."

Maggie heard the tension in Delphine's voice and imagined how lonely she must be. She was like an exotic bird among a flock of dull grey pigeons. Harry was the biggest of those pigeons. "Let's get a glass of wine," Maggie suggested.

They joined the lengthy drinks line on the back patio. "That's Tilda McQueen over there by the rosebushes," Delphine said. "She's the tall, slim woman wearing the yellow skirt. I told you about her family and their house, Larchmere."

"She's another great reader."

"Yes. She was widowed some time ago and when she got remarried she reverted to her maiden name. Oh, and over there, to her right. That's her sister, Hannah, the one with the red hair, and her wife, Susan."

"The ones who run Larchmere as a bed-and-breakfast."

"With Hannah's brother, yes. And there, the little man in the seersucker suit, that's Alan Horutz. He's very nice. He owns a fun little shop you might like to check out while you're in town, quirky stuff, crafts, antiques—anything that catches his fancy."

"You really do know everyone, don't you?" Maggie said.

"Life in a small town is not a life of privacy. I'll bet someone who lives in a big apartment building in New York or Boston has more privacy than we do."

"Privacy of a different sort," Maggie said. "It doesn't feel so private when you're crammed into a subway car with hundreds of strangers."

"None of whom know anything more about you than what you happen to be wearing at that moment."

"Point taken."

Drinks in hand they reentered the museum. Almost immediately, Maggie noticed a woman across the room staring quizzically at them. She looked to be in her early forties and, Maggie thought, very well preserved. She was wearing a pair of fitted very low-rise beige cuffed pants and a shrunken black blazer over a tiny white T-shirt. Her pointy-toed stilettos were black. Her small clutch was a supple white leather. Maggie recognized her shoulder-length hair as high-quality salon blond. Her jewelry was simple, gold, and expensive. And she was making her way determinedly toward them.

"Delphine?" she said from a few feet away. "Delphine Crandall?"

"Yes." Delphine glanced to Maggie and then back to the woman. "I'm sorry . . ."

The woman held her left hand to her chest as if to prove identification. Maggie estimated the central diamond in her engagement ring to be about three carats. "Lauren Jenkins," she said. "Remember me?" She turned then to Maggie. "And don't tell me you're Maggie Weldon!"

Maggie smiled. "Oh, of course, I remember now." She turned to Delphine. "When we were kids, remember? Lauren used to hang out with us sometimes."

Lauren laughed. "Tag along with you is more like the

truth. It was good of you, really, to let a little kid follow you around."

"I haven't seen you in ages," Delphine said. "Didn't you move away after high school?"

Lauren nodded. "My parents were not pleased about that, let me tell you. But I just had to get out. So I went to Boston and took what jobs I could get and lived in crappy little apartments in bad neighborhoods and survived on ramen noodles and had an awful lot of fun doing it."

"Have you been living in Boston all this time?" Maggie asked. "You know that Delphine and I went to Bartley College there."

"Really?" Lauren said. "No, I didn't know. But no, long story short, I started taking computer classes and eventually I started to get better jobs and working my way up and then I met my husband at one of the law firms I worked at as an administrative assistant. He's older than me; he was already a partner, well, a junior one at the time. After we got married I was able to a get a degree and we've had a pretty good life since. We lived in California for a while, and now we're back in Ogunquit. Well, partially. We still have a condo in the South End and Jason's going to work part-time from our home here, part-time at his office. Plus, the condo is a place for me to stay in Boston when I just have to go on a shopping spree!"

Delphine smiled lamely.

Maggie said, "That's great, Lauren, really. It sounds like things worked out really well for you."

Lauren turned her brilliant smile—very good veneers, Maggie thought—to Maggie. "So, what are you doing here in Ogunquit?"

"I'm visiting Delphine. I live in Lexington."

"How nice, that you've stayed friends all this time. That's really special." Lauren looked back to Delphine. "So, does your family still have the farm and the diner?"

Delphine nodded.

Lauren brushed her hair back from her face with a manicured hand. "I feel I appreciate this place so much more for having been away for all those years, you know? And I really feel like I've been welcomed back. Frankly, I was a bit nervous about getting a cold reception after having been gone for so long, but I guess once a native always a native."

Delphine still said nothing. She remembered her own homecoming. It was as if nothing had changed. It was as if she had never left. She was back in her old bedroom, expected to show up at the table on time for dinner and at the diner on time for her shift. People in town greeted her as if she had never been away. No one but the current librarian ever asked her about her years in Boston. If she had something to show for her college education, no one wanted to know what it was.

"I never would have met my husband," Lauren was saying now, "or gone to China or even lived on the West Coast for that matter if I'd stayed here in Ogunquit after high school. I know I would always have felt that I was missing something if I'd stayed on." Lauren laughed. "And I would have been missing something—my life!"

From across the room an older woman Delphine recognized as one of the major patrons of the museum was waving Lauren over to her side. With a good-bye and a wave of her own, Lauren hurried off to join her.

"Imagine running into her after all these years," Maggie said. "Did you know she was back in town?"

Delphine shook her head. "No. This must be her big debut, this party."

"Yes. She certainly was . . . exuberant. I don't remember her as being so . . . exuberant."

"She's happy," Delphine said, fingering her borrowed skirt. "She's made it."

Maggie shrugged. "She's just one version of 'making it.' There are lots of other versions. Like your version and like mine. Hey, let's look at the art while we're here. It seems a shame to come to a museum just to chat with a self-obsessed airhead."

"Sure," Delphine said. She felt a surge of gratitude toward her old friend. "I'll show you my favorite painting on permanent display."

33

"I still don't know why you wanted to come to a hardware store."

It was Tuesday and Maggie and Delphine had each just pulled into the parking lot at Eldredge Lumber & Hardware on U.S. 1 in York. Delphine was there because she needed a new tape measure. Melchior had chewed through the old one. Maggie, it seemed, was there because she was bored.

"I didn't necessarily want to come to a hardware store," she explained. "But I have some time to kill before my massage, so I thought, why not, I'll hang out with you."

"You know that sounds pretty pathetic, don't you?"

Maggie laughed. "Yeah."

"Do you even own a hammer?"

"Gregory's got one. He's got all the requisite tools—saws, hammers, screwdrivers—down in the basement. He's very handy."

"Have you ever even hung a picture?" Delphine asked as she opened the door to the store and they went inside.

"Of course I've hung pictures. But for the expensive art in our home I hire a professional to do the framing and the hanging."

"You don't trust Gregory to hang pictures? I thought you said he was handy."

"He's handy enough," Maggie said. "But when the art is worth thousands of dollars, I take no chances."

"Playing it safe," Delphine commented.

"When it comes to things of value, absolutely."

"I think the tape measures are down this aisle," Delphine said, pointing ahead. And then she muttered something that sounded an awful lot like, "Shit."

"What?"

"Nothing. It's Harry and my brother."

Maggie looked at the two men who were coming toward them. One was very tall, with a longish beard. The other was shorter, stocky, and clean shaven. Both men were wearing trucker's hats, work pants, and T-shirts. Around the shorter one's neck hung a pair of sunglasses. Their boots looked too big and clunky for summer. Maggie had an unpleasant image of sweaty, swollen feet. The tall man smiled at Delphine as he approached.

"Del, what are you doing here?" he asked. Maggie noted that his hands were calloused and rough, the hands of a man used to manual labor.

Delphine attempted a smile in return. "I could ask you the same thing, I guess."

"Getting some wood and some other stuff for the project me and Joey are working on."

"I needed a tape measure."

"I could have loaned you one of mine."

"It doesn't matter. Um, Harry, this is Maggie. My friend."

The tall man now looked at Maggie for the first time. He seemed to be appraising her. Finally, he nodded.

"Hi," Maggie said, not quite sure of what had just happened. "It's nice to meet you."

Harry nodded again. No words, no handshake, no smile.

"And you remember Joey," Delphine said, her voice betraying a slight note of desperation.

"Of course," Maggie said. "It's nice to see you again, Joey."

Joey Crandall smiled and tipped his hat. His hands, too,

were work worn. "Nice to see you, too, Maggie. Never would have recognized you."

Maggie laughed a bit. "Have I changed that much?"

Joey's face turned a little red. "Nah, it's just that it's been a long time."

"Yes," she said. "It has."

Joey Crandall had nothing else to contribute. The conversation, such as it had been, seemed over. Maggie found it hard to believe that she had once had a crush on him. He seemed nice enough but . . . *Maybe,* she thought, *I liked him because he was there. Maybe it was a crush of convenience.*

"Well," Joey said, stepping past them, "I'm gonna go look for those nails we need."

The three of them, Delphine, Maggie, and Harry, stood together, Harry the apex of an awkward triangle. Maggie smiled lamely. Harry's eyes wandered over her head.

"Maggie lives in Lexington," Delphine said. "Massachusetts. And she grew up in Concord. I don't know if I told you that."

Harry nodded. Delphine's face was flushing.

"Yes," Maggie said, with a bit of an awkward laugh. "Home of the Transcendentalists. And all those writers. Emerson. Hawthorne. Alcott."

"Don't forget Thoreau," Delphine said with a jauntiness that far exceeded what the situation called for.

"Who could forget Thoreau?" Maggie replied.

Harry looked at Delphine. "These people famous or something?" he asked.

Delphine's expression froze.

"I'll wait for you outside," Maggie said. She didn't bother to say good-bye to Harry.

She walked quickly to the front door and into the parking lot. She felt slightly shocked. Delphine had told her about Harry, the big, important parts, the fact of his mentally incapacitated wife, his adult kids, and his helpfulness around the Crandall house. But still, seeing him in person, face to face, had disturbed her. Clearly, there was much about Harry that Delphine hadn't told her, like the fact that he was ignorant of the history of American literature, which should matter enormously to Delphine, and the fact that he could be downright rude. If she tried really hard—and she did—she could not have imagined a man more opposite Robert Evans than Harry Stringfellow. *What in God's name,* she thought, *is Delphine doing with that man?*

A few minutes later Delphine joined her in the parking lot, a small brown paper bag in hand.

"It was nice seeing Joey again after all these years," Maggie said, hoping they could avoid the topic of Harry entirely, and aware that they couldn't.

"Yeah. He hasn't changed much, really."

"Yes."

Delphine sort of smiled. "So, that's Harry."

Maggie sort of smiled back. "He's . . . tall. I hadn't imagined him to be so tall. I don't know why."

"Yeah, he's about six-three."

"Oh. Are his kids tall, too?"

"The boy is. Bob."

"Oh." Maggie made a show of looking at her watch. She was afraid that if she stood there a moment longer she would say something she would regret. "Oh, look at the time. I have that appointment for a massage back at the hotel, so . . ."

"Of course. And I've got to get back to the farm."

"We'll talk soon. Bye, Delphine." Maggie walked off in the direction of her Lexus.

Delphine climbed into her truck. She didn't start it immediately. She felt unnerved, embarrassed, uncomfortable—something, a whole lot of things. She had to think clearly. She had to get out of the parking lot before Harry and Joey came out of the store. She started the truck. As she pulled out of the lot she saw the men in the rearview mirror, just getting into their trucks.

Delphine headed in the direction of the farm. An awful

truth assailed her as she drove. She was embarrassed of Harry, whether she was right or wrong to be. She was embarrassed of herself, too, for having chosen to be with someone so unsuitable in so many ways. She wondered what Maggie must think of her now. She wondered if Maggie had any respect for her at all.

Delphine sighed. There were certain people with whom you just didn't want to reconnect because you just didn't want them to be a witness to the person you had become. The fact that those people were witnesses to someone you had once been was now an embarrassment, whether that former you had been better or worse, more or less successful. That was one of the reasons she had never gone to a Bartley College reunion. That was the major reason she had not wanted to see Maggie Weldon again. That Maggie would make a comparison between the past and the present was inevitable. It might be unfair of her to do so, but it would be natural.

As Delphine drove she wondered if she, too, had been comparing the Maggie of their youth, the Maggie of her memory, to the woman in the diamonds and the Lexus. She thought about that and realized that Maggie really hadn't changed all that much. At least, not in ways Delphine could detect. Maybe she hadn't been looking hard enough. It was a question she couldn't answer.

Delphine waved as she passed Marc Pelletier in his truck. He waved back. She wondered what Maggie had thought of their negotiations outside the library, a couple of pork chops for a couple of dozen eggs. She wondered if everything that Maggie was witnessing, if everything she was experiencing here in Ogunquit, would cause her to abandon the quest for a renewed friendship.

No, Delphine thought, even if Maggie was finally aware of the many differences between them, she would not allow those differences to create a divide. She had made it clear that she believed the concept of a shared history to be important.

And when being totally honest with herself, something that was hard for her, Delphine believed that, too. It had to be important. So much in today's society was disposable, the new favored over the old, friendships discarded over Facebook or Twitter, electronic devices replaced every few months, fads frantically adopted and just as frantically rejected. Something had to be of long and lasting value.

Delphine stopped the truck to let a family of tourists dash across the road. The father carried folding chairs under both arms, the mother clutched two enormous beach bags, and the son dragged a Boogie Board along the pavement. Something about the scene made her smile, in spite of the troubling cast of her thoughts.

No, she thought, as the family reached the sidewalk and she started again to drive, *there is no valid reason for me to walk away from this friendship with Maggie. She isn't hurting me. She's unnerving me, but that's really my doing, isn't it? It's how I'm reacting to her, it's the power I've given her as my judge, when in fact I'm really the one doing the judging . . . of my own life and of hers.* Because even if Maggie had always enjoyed and valued the finer material things, only now was Delphine unfairly critical of her for it. And only now, since Maggie's return, had Delphine become critical of her own life, too. She didn't yet know if that self-criticism was unfair or if it was wholly justified.

Running into Lauren Jenkins at the museum hadn't helped, with all that talk of the great and exciting things she had been able to do because she had gone out into the wider world. Running into Harry today hadn't helped, either. He had been rude, even if his rudeness had been inadvertently caused by his social awkwardness. He had betrayed an ignorance of a subject that was important to Delphine. He probably didn't even know how important books were to her. But maybe that was her fault. Maybe she had never made it clear to him. Why?

Lauren Jenkins, and Harry Stringfellow, and her own emotional discomfort—none were good reasons for leaving the fledgling relationship she and Maggie seemed to be establishing. Lauren was a stranger who should have no power over her. Harry was a good man at heart. As for her own feelings . . .

She remembered now that not too long ago, while browsing through a magazine of psychiatric medicine at the doctor's office, she had read about a study of friendship patterns. The researchers had found that for women, the preferred method of ending a friendship was what they called "slinking away." It was admittedly a cowardly way to end a relationship, but it did allow a person to avoid a confrontation. That's what she had done, slunk away from her friendship with Maggie all those years ago, because a confrontation hadn't really been possible. Maggie had done nothing wrong. She had remained a loyal and steadfast friend for over ten years, throughout their childhood and young adulthood. How could Delphine possibly have explained why she felt the need to—well, to run away and hide? Maggie, she thought, tenacious, loyal Maggie, would never have accepted her reasons as anything other than excuses, and lame ones at that.

There, ahead, was the farm. Delphine sighed and pulled up into the front yard. She hoped that there was still a bottle of ibuprofen in her desk. The headache that was coming on was threatening to be a big one.

34

1983

It was a warm May evening. Maggie was at her desk working on a final term paper when Delphine got home from her date. She looked up to see her roommate grinning hugely, her hair messier than usual and her cheeks flushed.

"You look like the cat who ate the canary," Maggie said. "What happened?"

"Robert asked me to marry him. Look."

Delphine stuck out her left hand. On the ring finger a solitaire diamond sparkled in a slim platinum band.

Maggie screamed and leapt from her seat, knocking over the chair in the process. She launched herself at Delphine and together they screamed some more and jumped up and down until Maggie could hardly breathe. She grabbed Delphine's hand and pulled her over to the bed. They sat facing each other, knees touching.

"Oh, my God," Maggie said, her eyes shining with tears. "I can't believe this is really happening. You two are going to have such an exciting life; I just know it. You'll travel and meet all sorts of interesting and influential people. Wow."

"Yeah," Delphine said. "I guess."

"What do you mean, you guess? I know so! Robert Evans is going places, you mark my words."

And that would mean she would be going with him. Delphine felt a wave of panic rush over her. Where would he be going? Would it be far? Would it be too far away from her home and her family? Would she be lost along the way?

Delphine was aware of Maggie prattling on, but she heard none of the words distinctly. She was remembering the one visit she and Robert had paid to Ogunquit. They had stayed at her parents' house, of course, Delphine in her old bedroom and Robert in Joey's old bedroom. She hadn't dared sneak into Robert's room in the middle of the night, though he had wanted her to, and she wouldn't let him sneak into hers, either. Robert thought her deference to the "delicate" feelings of her family quaint. In his family, there was no such delicacy or, as Robert might prefer to say, no such antiquated so-called morality. He had been raised in a home that prized liberality and unconventional interests.

The visit had not been a great success. In the end Robert had come away with a view of the Crandalls as oppressive and narrow-minded. He had said as much, though in more politic terms. And the Crandalls, with the possible exception of Jackie, had come away with a view of Robert Evans as utterly foreign and condescending. He had used words they had never heard and had refused, however politely, to go with them to church. He had gone all over town looking for the *New York Times* when the local Sunday paper might have done just fine. He had shocked Patrice when he happened to mention the cost of the apartment his parents were renting in Rome. He had offended Charlie when he admitted he had very little skill with or interest in power tools.

"Hey, where are you?" Maggie was saying. "I've been talking about your wedding and you're, like, totally spacing."

Delphine tried to smile. "Sorry. I guess I'm feeling a little overwhelmed."

"We should get some champagne. Wait, did Robert have champagne? Oh, my God, I haven't even asked how he did it? Did he get down on his knee? You have to tell me everything. I bet it was so romantic!"

Delphine smiled again, but this time the smile was a bit wobbly. It had suddenly occurred to her—like a slap on the cheek—that by accepting Robert's proposal of marriage she had set in motion a train of events she could in no way control. Her life would, she felt—she knew—be molded into the form of Robert's life. He was the one with direction and plans and passions. She would be one of those passions, a partner, yes—Robert was no dictator—but a partner in an enterprise she had had nothing to do with creating. She thought of her parents again and her stomach clenched in panic.

"I'll tell you all about it in the morning," she said now to Maggie. "I suddenly feel like I'm going to fall asleep on my feet."

35

"Coffee is almost ready," Delphine called from the kitchen.

Maggie smiled to herself. The way the Crandalls made their coffee, she would be sure to add plenty of milk. "Okay," she called back.

Delphine hadn't had the time to see Maggie on Wednesday, as Jackie had been home sick with a twenty-four-hour bug, which put Delphine on double duty. And late in the afternoon Harry had called to say that his son and one of Bob's buddies were in town and were coming to Delphine's house with him for dinner. Ordinarily, she wouldn't have minded hosting Bob and a friend, even on such short notice, but this time it annoyed her, Harry's easy assumption that she was available to cook for and clean up after three people, one of them a stranger, after a long, hard day of work. She could have said no to Harry. She should have said no, especially after the way he had treated Maggie in the hardware store, whatever the cause of his rudeness. But force of habit had been too great for her to resist. "Sure," she had said. "No problem."

And now, this Thursday evening, she could have enjoyed a typical evening alone at home, with her knitting and her books and Melchior, but instead, almost unthinkingly, she had picked up the phone and invited Maggie to come over after dinner for coffee.

It had been raining on and off all day, and the air felt

heavy and wet. In deference to Maggie, Delphine had turned on the air conditioner, but the dampness still pervaded the house.

"Too bad it's raining," Maggie said as Delphine came into the living room. "We could have sat on the porch. Gregory and I have a back porch. Well, it's more of a deck, really. It surrounds the pool and overlooks the yard. It's very nice, but there's something so charming about a front porch."

"You could add one to the house," Delphine suggested, placing a tray on the coffee table. The tray contained cups, a creamer, a sugar bowl, spoons, and a plate of homemade oatmeal raisin cookies. Maggie knew the cookies would wreak havoc on her diet. She also knew that she would be eating at least one.

Maggie shook her head and sat at one end of the couch. Melchior was snoozing in a ball on an armchair across the room. "I don't live in the kind of neighborhood where people porch sit of an evening," she said.

"That's their loss," Delphine said. "Anyway, we need the rain. A lot more of it, too. The crops are suffering."

"I can't imagine my life being so directly affected by the weather. I don't understand how people can choose to live, say, on a major earthquake fault line. I would be anxious all the time. And those poor people who have no choice but to live in a flood zone. Do you remember what happened in Pakistan last year? There's no control over Mother Nature, only the possibility of a smart or a timely reaction."

Delphine smiled. "Welcome to the world of the farmer. We're very good at anticipating disasters."

"Yes. You're not at all insulated, are you? I mean, from the big things, the 'acts of God.' "

"We're right out there on the front line of life in a lot of ways." Delphine sat on the other end of the couch. "Those earrings are amazing," she said. "I'm sorry I didn't notice them before."

Maggie touched her right ear. "Thanks. Gregory gave

them to me. They're rose gold and the drop is a pink tourmaline."

"Tourmaline is Maine's state stone. Were they a birthday present?"

"Our last anniversary, actually. Gregory is very good about giving gifts."

Delphine laughed. "Harry doesn't 'do' gifts. Of course, he'll accept gifts. He just doesn't give gifts."

Maggie didn't find anything about Harry's lack of gift-giving skills funny. She had not been able to stop thinking about Harry—more precisely, about Harry and Delphine—since the encounter at the hardware store. She knew as well as she knew her own name that Delphine should not be with Harry Stringfellow. Maybe he would be fine for another woman—or not—but he was not fine or good or healthy for Delphine. She deserved so much better.

"What did Harry do before driving a truck?" Maggie asked, taking a sip of milky coffee and eyeing the cookies.

"Lots of things. Some carpentry, some house painting. He still does odd jobs for friends. He and Joey are working on a small building project for Joey's business accountant. Lots of people around here have more than one occupation going at a time. Like Jemima's husband and his foraging. You have to make ends meet in whatever way you can."

"Yes." Maggie paused. "Did you ever meet Harry's wife?" she said then. "I mean, before the accident?"

Delphine shook her head. "No. I'd never met either of them, which is kind of odd given life in a small town. And I certainly have no reason to meet Ellen now. She might not even know that I was in the room. And the last thing I would want to do is upset her."

"Yes," Maggie said, "I suppose there would be no point in going to see her. But what do you know about Ellen? Does Harry talk a lot about her? I mean, about what she was like before the accident."

"She was, he says, a perfect wife, a perfect mother, and a

perfect person. He's never said anything more specific—or less hyperbolic—than that. And he's never said anything remotely critical of her."

Maggie frowned. "How nice of him."

"It is nice of him. He respects her."

They sipped their coffee in silence for a moment or two.

"I'll be right back," Delphine said then. "I want to show you something." She loped up the stairs to her bedroom. When she came back down she handed Maggie a three-by-five white-bordered photograph.

"This is Ellen," she said. "It was taken shortly after they got married or started dating, I don't know which. I guess she was about nineteen."

Maggie looked up from the photo. "How did you get this? I can't imagine Harry giving it to you."

"No." Delphine sighed. "I can't believe I'm telling you this. I took it from his house. It's a copy. He has one in a frame, in his bedroom. This was loose in an old family album. I don't know why I took it. It's not like I look at it all the time or anything. It's just . . ."

"Go on," Maggie said gently.

"I guess in some ways I have to remind myself that she's real. That there's a reason why Harry isn't . . . available and it doesn't have anything to do with me being—being not worth it or deficient in some way."

"I think I understand." Maggie looked back down at the picture. She did understand, sort of, but she found the situation so awfully bizarre that she felt almost physically ill. "What do your parents think about the situation with Harry?" she asked after a moment. "And what does Jackie think?"

Delphine reached out for the photo and slipped it into her shirt pocket. "My parents don't seem to care either way. I mean, they like Harry. I think they like the fact that I have a man around when I need him. They've never said a word to me about Harry being married. Honestly, I don't know if they're aware that he refuses to get a divorce. Who would have told them that, if not me? Certainly not Harry."

Maggie felt the anger creep up into her cheeks. The Crandalls might be nice people, but they didn't want half enough for their daughter. As far as Maggie could tell, they just wanted Delphine's free labor. They didn't care if she was happy or fulfilled as long as she could sling hash and bail their grandson out of trouble and keep the books for that stupid old farm.

"And Jackie?" she asked again, trying to keep her tone even. "And Jemima? What do they think?"

"Jemima believes that everyone has a right to make her own decisions. She doesn't question my choices. She just accepts them."

"That doesn't mean she doesn't have an opinion."

"Well," Delphine said with a shrug, "if she has one she's keeping it to herself."

"Let's get back to Jackie. She was the only one of your family who liked Robert. Am I remembering correctly? I can't imagine she thinks you're getting a fair deal in this Harry situation."

"I made my choice. And please stop calling it 'this Harry situation.' "

"You say it, too. 'The Harry Situation.' Anyway, choices can be reversed. You can un-choose, you can make a different choice."

"Did I say I wanted to do that?" Delphine said. "I don't want to leave Harry. There's no real reason for me to leave him."

"Okay," Maggie said, though she didn't really believe Delphine and she could easily come up with several very good reasons for her to leave Harry. "But you still haven't answered my question. What does Jackie say about this . . . situation?"

Delphine smiled in spite of herself. She remembered Maggie's badgering her about all sorts of things when they were young, from combing her hair to not spending every waking hour outside of class with her head in a book. Maggie was tenacious when she cared; that much hadn't changed.

"You really don't give up, do you?" she said.

"No. Not when it's something important."

"Jackie thinks I deserve someone who can be fully devoted to me. She likes Harry, mostly, but she doesn't like his divided loyalties."

"His loyalties aren't divided, Delphine. His loyalties are to Ellen, his legal wife."

"And to me," Delphine argued. "He's loyal to me in his way."

In his way. It was one of the oldest excuses in the book, Maggie thought. *I love you in my way. My way happens to include a nightly slap across the face, but hey, at least I'm being true to myself.*

"What do his children have to say about their father's relationship?" she asked.

"They've both urged him to get a divorce," Delphine admitted. "They like me. They love their father. They feel he could be happier."

"But still he clings to his marriage. In other circumstances that would be admirable. If he wasn't having sex with you, for example."

Delphine felt stung by the truth of that remark. "You don't have to be so brutal about it," she said.

"I'm sorry." But Maggie thought, *I'm not sorry I said that.*

"I think," Delphine said after a moment of thought, "that Harry is afraid to move on. He's already lost so much. If his marriage to Ellen is officially gone, another huge part of his life will be gone. So, he stays married to her."

Maggie made a noise like a harrumph. "The marriage would be gone but not forgotten," she pointed out. "He'd get over it. And he'd get over her. But he'll never get over anything this way, not by clinging to something that's defunct. He's behaving like a coward, Delphine."

"Don't say that about him."

"I'm sorry. Again. But can't you see that it's true?"

"No," Delphine said firmly. "I can't. Harry's just making the best of a bad situation. Like we all have to do."

Maggie didn't know how to reply. Delphine sounded so resigned. Had no one taught her how to stand up for herself, how to fight for her needs, her wants? Patrice and Charlie had been conscientious parents, certainly. Their children hadn't lacked for the basics, for food and for shelter. But at least with their youngest child they seemed to have dropped the ball when it came to teaching a respect of self.

Maggie sipped her coffee. When they were little and then all through college she had looked up to Delphine as the stronger, the more adventurous, of the two and maybe she had been strong and adventurous when they were young, but something had changed. Somewhere along the line of her life Delphine seemed to have lost sight of her own worth. If one of Maggie's daughters ever got involved in a situation like the one between Delphine and Harry, she'd be furious. Well, they never would make such a masochistic choice in the first place. She had taught them self-esteem; she had taught them the value of holding out for what was best. She had taught them, but had they heeded the lessons? Strong, intelligent women were not immune to making disastrous mistakes when it came to men. She doubted that would ever change.

"Could I have another cup of coffee before I head back to the hotel?" Maggie asked. She felt unable, too disturbed, to continue with the conversation about Harry and Delphine and Ellen and their weird, unhealthy ménage à trois.

"Sure." Delphine practically leapt from the couch and headed for the kitchen. Maggie reached for a cookie and guessed that Delphine, too, was done with the topic for the night.

36

"Where's Harry tonight?" Maggie asked when she arrived at Delphine's house Friday evening after a solitary but pleasant dinner at the hotel. She brought with her a bottle of wine and a box of chocolates from Harbor Candy Shop. They were dark chocolates, supposed to be good for you, something about antioxidants. She would allow herself one, maybe two, and leave the box with Delphine, not because she doubted her own willpower but because she was pretty sure no one else ever brought Delphine a box of good candy.

"Working," Delphine said. "He gets off at midnight and he'll go straight home."

At least, Maggie thought, *he doesn't insult Delphine with a midnight booty call.* That showed a little class. Class, or middle-aged exhaustion.

The women were together to watch Robert Evans as a guest on a popular evening talk show. Maggie had seen the listing online and suggested she and Delphine watch the show together. Delphine, too, had seen the listing, but she had planned to watch the show alone, as was her habit. But Maggie had insisted, even suggesting they watch in her hotel room, on the large wall-mounted high-definition television. Delphine won a small battle—they would watch at her house—but she lost the war.

They settled on two inherited easy chairs in front of the television, a nine-year-old twenty-two-inch Panasonic set

Delphine had bought from Jemima's neighbor who was upgrading to a flat screen. Melchior watched them from the exact center of the couch.

Delphine turned on the television. A commercial for an insurance company was playing; for some reason she couldn't immediately fathom, the actors in the ad were riding on a merry-go-round.

Maggie laughed. "This commercial reminds me of that time the three of us, you, me, and Robert, went to that county fair in Topsham. Remember, we got sausage and peppers and funnel cakes and ice cream and we were all sick as dogs the next day. I think it was the sausages. Ugh. I'd totally forgotten about that fair until this commercial. Robert won you a hideous green bear."

"Yes," Delphine said. She did remember that day. For a while, the three of them had been close, a trio of comrades, loyal friends. And when Delphine had left Robert, the friendship between Robert and Maggie had not been able to survive. *Every act has a consequence,* Delphine thought. *I didn't seem to understand that for a long time. It would be wise not to forget that hard-won lesson.*

The show began. After a brief survey of Robert's career, the interviewer, a man in his forties with the requisite perfectly groomed hair and unobtrusive suit, said, "Your work as a political journalist, a social analyst, and as a whistleblower of sorts has been enormously important."

Robert Evans, his own hair artfully messy, dressed in an open-necked shirt and no tie, smiled graciously. "Thank you," he said. "At the risk of sounding pompous, I must agree with you. I consider my work an important civilian duty."

"Though it's a duty that has put your life in danger on more than one occasion."

"That's true," Robert acknowledged. "But let me quote President Theodore Roosevelt: 'Far and away the best prize that life has to offer is the chance to work hard at work worth doing.' Let's just say I've learned to duck when a gun makes its appearance."

The interviewer chuckled politely. Maggie smiled and glanced at Delphine. Delphine was looking straight ahead at the television.

"I can't say," Robert went on, "that I don't take issue with people who don't make 'the big sacrifices' in their life's work. Of course, not everyone has the opportunity to make a big difference, even if he or she wants to. And there are plenty of people who work at whatever pays them enough money to make ends meet, people who simply can't afford to take risks. But there are plenty of people out there perfectly equipped to sacrifice some of their time and resources for others but who are simply too lazy or self-involved to do it."

Delphine wondered what Robert would think of the work she did every day, of the sacrifices she had made and continued to make. She wondered if he would find them lacking. She wondered if he would judge her to be too lazy or, if not self-involved, then cowardly. Well, she would never know.

The show went to commercial and Delphine lowered the volume.

"He's right," Maggie said. "The work he does is so incredibly important. It must require so much sacrifice. You can't have a normal life when you're always on the road, going off to dangerous places." Maggie paused before adding: "Though he is a tad self-inflated."

Delphine nodded. "Oh, he's definitely self-inflated. Maybe you were right; maybe he always was vain. But I guess to be a celebrity you pretty much have to have an ego strong enough to stand up to criticism."

"Oh, of course. And for all the good, humanitarian work he does, he is also a celebrity."

"Do you think your work is important?" Delphine asked.

Maggie considered before answering. "I don't know. I suppose it is important to my clients. And my salary certainly helps my family. But it helps in what feels like such an indirect, impersonal way. A check comes in and another goes out. I guess it's fair to say that my work has become minimally and only occasionally satisfying."

"That's too bad."

"It could be worse," Maggie said. "I could be out of a job like millions of Americans. But what about you? Well, I don't even have to ask, do I? Of course you consider your work important."

Delphine nodded. "I do. I mean, even when my work on the farm or in the diner isn't personally fulfilling, it still has meaning because through it I'm helping my family. And the work is direct. It's not at all impersonal. That matters to me."

The women sat quietly for the duration of the commercial break. Delphine was recalling a quote she had read about Dorothea, the heroine of *Middlemarch* by George Eliot. The quote was from a biography titled *George Eliot: The Last Victorian,* by Kathryn Hughes. She had copied out the quote in the notebook she kept by her bed. She had read it so often she knew it by heart. ". . . in the tiny 'unhistoric acts' of goodness which she performs within her limited circle a ripple of influence has been set in motion which may eventually lap the edge of the world."

She liked to think that in her own life she was like Dorothea, devoted to the work of the here and the now. She believed that a person didn't need to perform her life in an arena. A small theatre would do, even a plywood stage on a backyard lawn with no sound system but that produced by her own vocal cords.

Or, she wondered now, as a commercial for yet another oddly named drug with thousands of negative side effects was ending, was that all just an excuse for cowardice?

"The show's back," Maggie said, and Delphine raised the volume.

The interviewer led off. "So many people," he said, "and let's say Americans in particular, consider work as merely a means to money, fame, material goods. What is your take on the contemporary culture of mindless acquisition and what even in this depressed economy can be seen as foolish spending?"

Robert seemed to consider his answer for a moment before speaking. Both Maggie and Delphine assumed the hesitation was for show. Robert was a practiced speaker. "I think," Robert finally said, "that we all, as moral individuals and as citizens of the world, not only our country, have the responsibility of debating the important questions about our purpose on this planet, our responsibilities toward ourselves and toward others. We need to ask ourselves questions like: Who determines if the work is worth doing? What are the criteria for worthwhileness and value? Personal satisfaction or public purpose or both? Does the person doing the work determine its value or does the person benefiting from the work do the determining?"

Robert paused and the interviewer nodded, his face set in a studied frown of interest.

"And," Robert went on, "we need to ask ourselves: What's more important, the process of our work or the results the work brings? And again, who has the right to make such a determination? We each need to grapple with these questions and to come to a strong, moral position. I mean, what's wrong with our culture when a devoted teacher in an inner-city school makes so much less money than a reality TV starlet? Our value system regarding work and reward is sadly distorted."

Robert Evans went on in this vein for some moments more. And then the interviewer thanked him for being a guest on the show and announced the segment to come. Delphine turned the television off.

"Well, that was interesting," Maggie said. "Not very informative, but interesting."

"It was a self-promotion piece, that's all. I'm not sure he actually answered the interviewer's questions. Though I do agree with him about the need for a reevaluation of—well, of value in American culture."

"Yes. I suppose I haven't given enough thought to . . . Well, too much of anything, lately."

"Daily concerns can easily get in the way of larger issues," Delphine said. "It's hard to balance priorities."

Maggie smiled. "You're nice to let me off the hook for lazy thinking. So, what did you feel this time, listening to Robert pontificate?"

Delphine considered before replying. "Well, I know for certain that I'm not in love with him anymore. I can still see why I was drawn to him, certainly, though the animal attraction, the gut level feelings just aren't there anymore. Those feelings haven't been there for a long time. Which is good or my life would be pretty pathetic. It would be a waste."

"Yes," Maggie said.

"Sometimes when I watch him," Delphine continued, "I feel as if the person on-screen isn't really Robert. I feel like I'm watching an actor play the role of Robert Evans. It's hard to explain. And then," Delphine added with a smile, "there are those times when I think about that little mole on his shoulder. . . ."

Maggie smiled back. "He's probably had it removed by now, in case a paparazzi catches him without his shirt."

"You're probably right." Delphine got up and fetched the box of dark chocolates from the coffee table. "But right now all I'm interested in are these." She sat back in her chair, took a chocolate, and passed the box to Maggie.

Maggie bit into a piece. "This is fantastic," she said. "Wow."

"Harbor makes their candy on-site. The smell alone makes me swoon. Not that I buy much from them, but at Halloween I go in to get some treats for Kitty."

"Hey," Maggie said, "I don't know why I didn't suggest this earlier, but maybe you'd like to come use one of the pools at my hotel. You could bring Kitty, too."

"Oh, no thanks. Kitty doesn't really like the water much,

and I haven't gone swimming since—well, since I came back to Ogunquit after college."

"But you loved to swim! You were great in the water, a proverbial fish. You weren't even afraid of big waves, while I was cowering back on the sand."

"Yeah," Delphine said, "but things just got really busy for me, so . . . I don't know. I just . . . stopped."

"Do you miss swimming?"

Delphine considered for a moment. "I haven't really thought about it. But yes, I think that sometimes I do."

"Really, Delphine," Maggie said, "why does the notion of recreation cause you such concern?"

"I wouldn't say it causes me concern, exactly. Anyway, it doesn't matter because I don't even own a bathing suit."

"You could borrow one of mine."

Delphine eyed her friend. Maggie was longer all over, as she always had been, and now also at least fifteen pounds lighter than Delphine. "Thanks," she said, selecting a third chocolate, "but I'm not sure that would work out."

"Oh. Sorry. But if you won't come swimming with me, then promise you'll take a day trip with me soon, okay? Even a half a day, if you can't handle the idea of eight hours away from work."

"It's not that I can't handle the idea of being away," Delphine argued. "It's the reality, the consequences of being away that worry me."

"You don't run the farm alone; you told me that. Other people can pick up your slack or deal with an emergency. You have a cell phone. You won't be going across the globe, only maybe to, I don't know, Kennebunkport. We could go someplace nice for lunch."

Delphine paused. She couldn't deny that the thought of getting out of town, of having lunch somewhere other than her desk, was tempting. "When?" she asked.

"Whenever you want," Maggie replied. "Look, I'm sure even the saintly Mr. Evans takes a vacation now and then."

Delphine smiled. "I'd have to look at the calendar, check with Jackie about things. I'd need to make sure that Lori can cover for me and that Dad has a backup if he needs someone at the diner. Maybe Dave Junior could help out, too."

"See? You've got a full staff ready and waiting. So, you promise you'll look at that calendar soon?"

"Yes," Delphine said after only a moment's hesitation. "I will. I promise."

Maggie grinned. "Pinky swear?"

It took a moment for Delphine to grasp the reference, to remember. She smiled.

"My own words are coming back to bite me," she said. She held out her pinky. "Okay, pinky swear."

37

1983

"No more nukes! No more nukes!"

The chanting was growing louder, more frenzied by the moment. Though the autumn night was chill, Delphine felt herself begin to sweat. She could barely see Robert, up on the makeshift stage, bullhorn in hand. Suddenly, the crowd around her surged and for a brief but terrorizing moment she felt her feet lift off the ground. She was being moved against her will. She was being carried without her consent by people who were strangers to her, people who were increasingly becoming out of control. Voices were rising in anger. She heard a girl scream. In the next moment her toes touched the ground and in a surge of animal instinct she managed to turn around and begin to claw her way through the press of bodies, yelling, "Get out of my way!" and, "Let me go!" She fought her way back through the crowd of protestors, back toward open space, all the while aware of Robert's voice booming through a bullhorn, calling for order, demanding a return to calm.

She tripped over a stray branch and fell, skinning her knees all the way through the thick fabric of her pants. She struggled to her feet and continued to run, harder than she had ever run before. She didn't care about nuclear weapons. What did nuclear weapons have to do with her, with a girl from a small town in Maine? She ran into an alley between two of the college buildings and skidded to a halt on wet brown leaves. She leaned against a brick wall and tried to catch her breath. She thought she might be having an anxiety attack. This could not be her life. Running away, hiding like a fugitive . . .

There was no way she could go back there. Later that night, Robert would want to know what she had thought of the rally. She would have to lie to him, maybe tell him she had been forced to go home because she'd come down with a migraine, though she had never had one before. Maybe she would say she had gotten suddenly sick to her stomach, something she'd eaten for lunch hadn't agreed with her. Because how could she tell him the truth, that in one flash of insight she had known that she didn't belong in his world, in the world he was entering with such energy and courage? That world was too frightening, too uncertain, too volatile, too not the world in which Delphine knew she needed to live.

But she loved him so much, she wanted to marry him, to have children with him someday; she wanted to grow old with him. She owed him the truth. She owed him the chance to argue with her, to persuade her, to come to a compromise with her. Maybe if she admitted to being afraid that her life might be subsumed if she fully entered his world he could help her to not be afraid, he could help her to adjust, to learn, to understand, to stand strong and preserve her identity against his.

No. She knew she was not strong enough to withstand him. Robert was like a force of nature. If she told him the truth, her truth, he would talk her out of believing it, and she would be forever lost. She would have to lie, at least for a while. She would have to buy some time. She would have to work up the courage to leave. Slowly now, her knees stinging where she had skinned them, Delphine pushed off the wall and made her way back to her dorm in the chilly dark.

The next morning the local papers would hail Robert

Evans as a true leader. One paper even went so far as to label him a hero. College administrators would hail him for getting the excited crowd back under control and for organizing the protest in the first place. Halting the proliferation of nuclear weapons was a worthy cause and few would argue with that fact. Robert had accepted Delphine's lie—a migraine—without suspicion and was extremely solicitous of her health, glad, too, that she hadn't been badly hurt when the crowd had gotten temporarily out of control. Skinned knees would heal. Maggie, too, had offered to bring her tea and aspirin and a wet cloth, whatever would help.

For Delphine, Robert's and Maggie's care and concern was like a torture. Once they each had left the dorm room she turned her face to the wall, embarrassed to have run away, ashamed to have lied to the two people, aside from her family, she loved the most, the two people who most loved her. The pressure inside her was building. Something would have to be done, and soon. She just hoped she could find the necessary courage to do it.

38

"Knock, knock."

Delphine looked up from the computer screen. "Hey, I didn't expect to see you out here, especially not so early on a Saturday morning."

"Sorry." Maggie stepped inside the office. "I woke up at six and couldn't get back to sleep. I had breakfast, went to the gym, and here I am. Am I in the way?"

"Nope. I'm just finishing up these accounts."

"Where is everybody?" Maggie asked. "I didn't see any cars out front."

"Jackie and Dave Junior are up at the farmers' market in Portland. Lori's in the house; her dad dropped her off. She's working on another wreath. They should sell nicely in the fall. My father's at the diner and my mother took some meals to Mr. Kneeland on Karfoil Road."

"Who's he?" Maggie asked.

"Right, you wouldn't know him. He's a native, about eighty now I'd say. He lost his wife a few years ago and the poor man's been getting frailer by the minute. A bunch of the locals share the work of checking in on him every day, bringing his meals, doing some housekeeping. I go over when I can, which is not very often. I should really get better about that."

"I'm sure there are plenty of other people around to take care of him," Maggie said.

"One more never hurts."

Maggie just shrugged. "How's Kitty?"

"Fine. Cybel took her to the animal park in York. She's been going on and on about it since one of the kids on her street went last week. I wanted to go along, but, well, these accounts don't balance themselves. I'll try to take her again before the end of summer."

Maggie brushed some dust off the seat of the folding chair and sat. She had learned not to wear white to the farm. "Delphine, can I ask you a question?"

"If I say no you'll ask it anyway."

Maggie laughed. "Probably. Why didn't you ever have kids? You're so good with them and you've got a built-in babysitting service right in your own family."

Delphine closed the file on which she was working and frowned. "I don't know. Well, that's a stupid answer."

"I'm sorry. We don't have to talk about this, especially so early in the morning."

"No, it's okay," Delphine said, swiveling in her chair to face Maggie. "I guess that growing up I never really had a burning desire to be a mother. I don't know why. And then, when I was with Robert, honestly, the thought of having children with him was something so far in our future it almost didn't seem a real possibility. I think if things had worked out between us, we would have had a family. But I don't really know."

"I don't think Robert has any children, either," Maggie said. "None that I've heard of, anyway. I did read once that he's divorced."

"A lot of men in his position would probably have abandoned kids all over the globe. But Robert isn't that kind of person. At least, he wasn't when I knew him. He respected the idea of family and he was nothing if not responsible."

"Yes. So, what about after Robert, when you came back here? Did you ever think about having a child then?"

Delphine shrugged. "Well, after Robert, I guess I thought

that when it was the right time or when the right things were in place, I would probably have a child." Delphine paused and gave a halfhearted smile. "But time just passed, and I got older and the right man, whatever that means, just didn't show up, or maybe he did and I didn't recognize him. And then, I met Harry and he certainly didn't want any more children, so . . . Here I am. Aunt Delphine."

"But is that enough," Maggie asked, "to be an aunt?"

Delphine shrugged. "It's had to be. There's no point in bemoaning what isn't."

Maggie wasn't so sure she agreed. "Delphine," she said, "you're so good to other people. You're always there when someone needs you. Haven't you ever wanted things for yourself, things only for you? Haven't you ever been selfish, just once, done something that was only for your own benefit?"

Yes, Delphine thought, *I have been selfish, once. I went off to college. I was away from my family and from the farm for four years. I fell in love. I had my chance. And once is enough. It's had to be enough.*

When Delphine didn't answer, Maggie said, "You never got the chance to travel or to be wild and crazy or to—"

Delphine interrupted. "No one forced me to come home after college," she said. "I chose to. And I was welcomed." She laughed. "Really, Maggie, it's not so bad when the people you love, love you back."

"Of course not. It's just . . ."

It was just, Maggie thought, that the motives behind the Crandall family's welcome seemed pretty selfish. Of course Charlie and Patrice wanted their daughter back home. They wanted her free labor. Delphine had made service and resignation her motto.

"Would you prefer that I be miserable?" Delphine asked with a smile.

"Oh, don't be silly. But it would make me feel better if I

could be one hundred percent sure that you really were happy, if I could be sure you didn't have regrets."

Delphine looked briefly down at her hands, folded in her lap. When she looked up again, Maggie thought she saw a trace of tears in her eyes. But maybe not.

"I never said I don't have regrets," Delphine said. "Everyone has regrets. If a person says she has no regrets about something she did or didn't do, she's lying. It's just that I don't dwell on the past."

"As simple as that?" Maggie said.

"Yes."

But Maggie wondered if it was. Delphine seemed to want to erase or ignore or deny the past, or parts of it, rather than not dwell on it. And here she was, dragging Delphine down memory lane and forcing her to remember every little bump along the way.

And yet Delphine was still here, still talking, answering questions, asking her own. She hadn't walked away again or told Maggie to clear off. That had to mean something, that maybe she did, deep down, want to engage with the past. Or, at least, that she wanted to engage with Maggie in the present.

"Do you want to help me clean the chicken coop?" Delphine said then, standing up and startling Maggie from her thoughts.

Maggie's eyes widened. "Oh, no, thanks, I don't think I could; I don't know how to—"

Delphine laughed. "Only kidding. You'd ruin your manicure."

"Well," Maggie said, getting up from the folding chair. "I'd better let you get to that coop. Are we still on for later?"

"Barring any unforeseen disasters, yeah. Meet you there at four."

39

The Lilac House hadn't changed much since the last summer it had been rented by the Weldons. The lilac bushes growing on both sides of the house were thriving. The enormous pine at the foot of the long front drive had escaped destruction from several major storms. The drive had been repaved, the house repainted, the roof repaired. Other than those basic improvements, the house looked exactly as Maggie remembered it.

Maggie sighed. It was late Saturday afternoon and she and Delphine stood at the foot of the driveway, looking up at the house, now occupied by a family with small children if the evidence of the three-wheeled bikes on the lawn could be trusted. "God, this place brings back such memories," Maggie said. "I miss those days when we were just kids, healthy, happy, innocent. Do you ever miss them?"

"I don't know," Delphine said. "I don't know if I actually miss being a kid. I remember the summers we spent together, maybe not as much as you seem to, but . . . I guess today, right now is good enough for me." *Most times,* she added silently.

"Yes, but the past was idyllic. Really, if life could always be like it was during those summers. I can't remember one rainy day or one bad thing happening. There must have been rainy days and something bad must have happened at some time. But it's all perfect in my memory."

" '. . . memories are injected after the fact with subsequent wisdom. Such is the treachery of this path upon which you have so thoughtlessly set me . . .' "

"What's that?" Maggie asked, turning to Delphine.

"Lines from a book, Arthur Phillips's novel *Angelica*."

"And is that what I've done?" Maggie said musingly. "Barged into your life and set my old and unsuspecting friend on the torturous path of remembering—of reconstructing, of reconstituting—the past."

Delphine didn't answer that question. Instead, she said, "Do you remember the summer when that fisherman died? We were in our teens. His name was Johnny Boyd. He was married and had two little children under five. It was a freak accident on his fishing boat. It was awful. Everyone was talking about it, even your parents. I remember they donated to the emergency fund his friends started to help his family pay for the funeral expenses."

"No," Maggie said. "I have absolutely no memory of that. How terrible for his poor wife. And his children, of course."

"It was horrible. I'll never forget it." Delphine turned to face Maggie. "Why do you only remember the good things? Or mostly the good things?"

"I don't know," Maggie admitted. "Maybe because the good things meant more to me. Maybe I didn't experience the bad things as so bad. I don't know."

"You're nostalgic by nature. But nostalgia just whitewashes everything," Delphine said. "Which can be convenient, of course. But it's still a lie."

"But is it the kind of lie that can hurt someone?"

"Yes," Delphine said. "I think it is."

"What, I wonder, is the opposite of nostalgia?"

Delphine thought about that a moment before answering. "I'd say it's appreciating that what you have right now is pretty darn good, even if it's not perfect."

"I think," Maggie said, "that the opposite of nostalgia is a refusal to acknowledge that some things about the past were actually better than they are now."

"That's another one of the ways in which we're different."

Maggie shook her head. "You're always focusing on our differences. Why can't you focus on our similarities?"

"Like what?"

Maggie rolled her eyes. "Oh, please. Like the fact that we're both women. That we're the same age. That we share so many memories. I don't know, like the fact that we love each other? There's a lot we hold in common, Delphine."

Delphine wondered. Did she, indeed, love Maggie? She knew that once upon a time she had; she had loved and cherished her and knew that without Maggie her life would be terribly diminished, almost unthinkable, really. But now, did she love her now, in the present? She thought that maybe she did. But she wasn't sure she wouldn't be lying if she spoke the words.

The front door opened just then and a young pregnant woman came out onto the porch, carrying a watering can.

"Why don't you ask her if you could go inside," Delphine suggested. "You could see if anything's changed."

Maggie shook her head. "No, that's okay. This is enough."

Delphine smiled to herself. Maggie didn't want pointy reality to burst the delicate bubble of memory. Well, that was okay.

"Come on, then," she said. "We'd better go before that woman calls the police on us for loitering."

40

1984

"So, I've absolutely decided I'm going for an MBA and not a law degree. I've signed up to take the GMATs and I've picked the two schools I'm going to apply to. My father thinks it's the best way to go, get the MBA now, rather than while I'm working at a full-time job, even though most companies will pay for it." Maggie laughed. "My mother just wants to know why I'm not engaged yet, like you."

Maggie and Delphine were at a café on Boylston Street. It was about three o'clock on a Wednesday afternoon in January. Maggie was drinking herbal tea and Delphine was largely ignoring a cup of black coffee.

"That's good," Delphine said.

"I can't decide yet if I want to go to Northeastern University or Boston University. I mean, each program has its strengths and specialties. Well, first, of course, I have to get accepted! And assuming, of course, I don't blow the GMATs. I've signed up for one of those practice courses. It's expensive, but I think it's a good idea in the long run."

"Right."

Maggie touched Delphine's arm. "Hey, I ran into Robert at the library earlier. He told me about the fantastic offer from the *New York Times*. It's so exciting for him. And for you, too, of course."

"I guess."

"What do you mean, you guess?" Maggie looked more closely at her friend. "What's up, Delphine?" she asked. "You seem so out of it lately."

Delphine felt, in the pit of her stomach, a ghost of the panic she had experienced at the protest. "Nothing's up," she lied. "I'm fine. I just don't really want to talk about all this stuff right now."

Maggie gave her the stern schoolmarm look. "Don't tell me you haven't talked to your advisor yet about your future."

"I will."

"Delphine, what are you waiting for?" Maggie leaned in closer, her tone urgent. "You need to be applying to graduate schools. You need to be interviewing for internships. You need to make some decisions. There's a lot of competition out there. You don't want to be left behind."

"I know; I know! Stop pestering me." Delphine shot a look at the two guys at the table closest to theirs. She was afraid she had raised her voice. Neither of the guys seemed to have noticed.

"I'm not pestering," Maggie said. "Well, maybe I am, but I'm doing it for a good reason. I care about you. I don't want to see you miss an opportunity."

Delphine took a deep breath. She hated that word, "opportunity." Graduate school, an internship, a big corporate job. None of that sounded like an "opportunity." It sounded like a nightmare. It sounded like someone else's life, which was pretty much the same thing. "I'm sorry," she said. "I didn't mean to be all pissy. I'm just feeling a bit overwhelmed. I mean, there's the wedding and—"

Maggie interrupted her. "What do you mean, the wedding? You haven't even set a date. You shouldn't be stressing about it. You should just try to focus on the next step in your career. One thing at a time, Delphine. Graduate school, a good internship, then a job. Robert's not going anywhere.

Well, he might be in Eastern Europe or somewhere exotic for a while, but you know he cares about you getting your career off the ground. He's not going to abandon you."

"I know he's not going to abandon me," Delphine protested. "That's not the point at all."

"Then, what is the point?"

Delphine shook her head. *The point,* she thought, *is that I'm the one who's going to abandon Robert. Either that, or I'm going to have to abandon my life.*

"Nothing," she said. "The point is nothing."

41

"That's the second time in two hours you've checked in with Lori. Don't you think that if there was something wrong she would call you?"

It was a Tuesday afternoon and Maggie and Delphine were just leaving the Harraseeket Lobster Pound on the Freeport Town Dock. They had had lunch there, lobster rolls and onion rings. The onion rings, which were sweet, more like onion donuts, were Delphine's idea. Maggie had eaten two, which was two more than she would have eaten if she were alone or with Gregory.

"It can't hurt to let her know I can be home as soon as possible if anyone needs me," Delphine argued.

"Did it ever occur to you that you're just annoying her?"

Delphine put her phone in her pocket. "What?"

Maggie sighed. "I know it took a lot of arranging to get the afternoon free. Can't you please just try to enjoy yourself?"

"I am enjoying myself."

"Really?"

Delphine smiled. "Really."

They walked to the Pound's small parking lot. Delphine hadn't seen Maggie in a couple of days. Work had kept her occupied during daylight hours. She had spent Sunday evening with her parents and Monday evening with Harry.

There was a finite amount of Delphine to go around, and she tried hard to give every person a fair portion.

They drove—they had taken Maggie's car, at her insistence—into the heart of Freeport to visit some of the outlet stores. This was another concession to Maggie. Delphine would have preferred to hurry back to Ogunquit, crisis or no crisis. She had already spent enough money—too much—on lunch. There would be no more spending money on luxuries.

"Look at this," Maggie said. "This would look perfect on you." They were in the Jones New York store. Maggie was holding up a simple, fitted cotton blouse with French cuffs. The color reminded Delphine of her mother's homemade peach ice cream.

"It's pretty," Delphine admitted, "but where would I wear it?"

"You can wear it when you're out with me."

Delphine looked at the price tag. It wasn't outrageous by any means and the idea of buying the blouse suddenly seemed dangerously appealing. But after a moment she said, "I'd rather spend the money on Kitty. She could use a new pair of sneakers."

"Can't her parents buy her new sneakers?" Delphine gave Maggie a look of reproach. "Maybe I shouldn't have said that. None of my business."

"She's still not feeling well. Kitty, I mean. And she's lost weight. I'm worried. A child shouldn't be losing weight."

"Maybe it's 'growing pains,' " Maggie suggested. "Kim went through a period like that. I think she was in fourth grade. She shot up like a weed and I had to practically force-feed her ice cream to keep her weight in step with her height."

"But Kitty's only eight. She's prepubescent. No, I don't think she's having growing pains, whatever they are."

"So, didn't Cybel take her to the doctor?"

"Yeah," Delphine said, "Dr. Waters, and he couldn't find

anything wrong with her. But I convinced Cybel to take her to see someone in Portsmouth, at the hospital. I found this doctor online and did some checking. Her reputation as a pediatrician is really strong. Dr. Waters is okay, but he should have retired long ago."

"It's probably nothing, you know."

"Yeah," Delphine said. "Hopefully."

"Hey, I just had a brainstorm. Let's go off to Boston for an overnight, maybe even a whole weekend. What do you say? Just us two, a real girls-only getaway? It will be like old times, only better."

"Why will it be better?" Delphine asked.

"You're impossible! I don't know; it just will be. Come on, what do you say?"

Delphine struggled. She really didn't want to give a categorical "no." She didn't. But the idea of committing to an overnight excursion was frightening. Maybe it shouldn't be, but it was. This one afternoon in Freeport felt enough like playing hooky to last her quite some time. Still, she had so enjoyed the four years she had spent in Boston. Things were different now, of course. So much had changed, and she didn't mean that restaurants had come and gone. But she could visit the museums and take a stroll through the Public Garden and get a fun souvenir for Kitty. . . .

"All right," she said. "But only if everything goes okay today and there are no disasters when I get back. Then, I'll consider it."

"Delphine, I'm not asking you to go away with me for a month."

"It's not easy for me, Maggie; you know that. I have responsibilities."

"It's like you're like the president of a country, I swear, or the general of an army. You're the self-appointed leader of the Crandall enterprise. You take on too much responsibility for too many people, Delphine." *And get too little appreciation in return,* she added silently.

"Someone's got to do it."

"Why you?" Maggie demanded. "Or, why always you? Jackie's perfectly capable. So is Joey, I'm sure. And there's Lori and Dave Junior." She refrained from suggesting Harry's name.

"Yes, but . . ."

"But what?"

But I'm nobody, Delphine thought, *if I'm not the person that everyone counts on. That's just the way it is with me. That's just who I am. Rather, it's who I've become.*

"But nothing," she said. "And I'm not buying that blouse, so you can put it back where you found it."

"You could wear it when we're in Boston."

"No. You're assuming we even get to Boston."

Maggie sighed. "All right, all right. I guess I can't win every battle. But I am taking you to the Coach outlet next."

Delphine reached for her phone. "Let me just call Lori again."

42

"It's exactly what you need, Delphine," Jackie said. "You haven't had a real break in years. Go to Boston and go crazy. But not too crazy. We need you back home."

When Maggie had dropped her at the house that afternoon Delphine had gotten into her truck and driven immediately to the farm. She wanted to talk to Jackie about the idea of an overnight trip to Boston before she lost the nerve.

"You're sure you can handle things without me?" Delphine asked, half hoping her sister would change her mind. "If you have any doubts at all I'll tell Maggie I can't go."

Jackie had given her a look of mock annoyance. "Are you saying you doubt my ability to run this place for twenty-four hours?"

"No, no, it's not about that. I—"

Jackie had grasped her sister's arm. "Go to Boston," she said. "Please."

Delphine had then gone directly to her office and called Maggie. Maggie was thrilled. They would leave the following Tuesday morning and return to Ogunquit on Wednesday evening. That gave Delphine plenty of time to prepare everyone for her absence. Maggie would search online for a deal at a decent hotel. Delphine wondered if she had a bag big enough and nice enough that would satisfy as a suitcase. When she had gone off to college she had stuffed her belongings in duffel bags her mother had gotten at Renys. She didn't think it would be appropriate for a grown woman to bring a duffel bag into a nice hotel. And it might embarrass Maggie. But no, she thought. Maggie might tease her about carrying scruffy luggage, but she wouldn't be embarrassed. As Delphine had told Jemima, Maggie wasn't shallow, in spite of her interest in appearances.

Delphine left the farm around six-thirty and went home. She fed Melchior, who then retired to the living room couch, and made a light dinner of salad greens, tomatoes, hard-cooked eggs, and chickpeas. She took the plate upstairs to her desk and opened her laptop. While she ate, she would browse the Internet for current information about Boston.

Boston. Where she and Robert Evans had met. Well, Cambridge, to be precise. That afternoon on the drive back to Ogunquit, Maggie had asked her what she would do if Robert walked into town that very day, declared his undying love, and asked her to go away with him. The question, hypothetical as it was, outrageous as it was, had given her pause because she had never posed it to herself, not once in all the years since she had last seen him at Maggie's graduation party. Though Robert had offered, Delphine had not let him see her off at the bus station days later.

Maybe, Delphine thought, eating her salad and staring unseeingly at the screen of her laptop, she would try to get in touch with him. It wouldn't be that hard. He was a public figure; he probably had a page on Facebook or some other social or business networking site. She could write to him at one of the magazines or newspapers in which he regularly published. She could write to his book publisher. There was nothing holding her back but her own fears. There never had been. She had set the obstacles all along. Like when she hadn't gone to that Bartley College reunion. She had been afraid that if she ran into Robert she would suddenly realize that she had made the wrong choice all those years ago. She was afraid she would be overwhelmed by regret, and forced to live rest of her life in misery.

But now . . . Delphine wondered if she really had the strength to come face-to-face—or e-mail to e-mail—with Robert without it resulting in disaster. She didn't know. And she had no idea of what she might say to him. Still, she could reach out if she wanted to. The possibility was there. But why would she want to? What would be the goal, the hope behind this? She could offer another apology, whether he deserved one or wanted one. She could offer a simple greeting. "Hey, just thinking of you and hope you're well." She wondered what she might want from Robert in return. An acknowledgment that she existed for someone out in the larger world, if that even mattered. A kind word of forgiveness. She really didn't know.

Of course, there was the possibility that Robert might not respond at all. He might no longer care about her. He might still be angry. He might send her a nasty note, decrying her lack of courage, demanding to know why she hadn't responded to his letters all those years ago, declaring his regret at ever having met her. She thought she might not ever get over that kind of rough dismissal.

Delphine shook her head. She would take no chances with her peace of mind. It was better to concentrate on the immediate future, her trip to Boston, than to speculate about a reunion of sorts she was pretty sure she didn't even want, a reunion Maggie had forced her to consider. She put her empty dinner plate aside and went to the Museum of Fine Arts site. There was a show of portraits by early American itinerant painters there, and she had always loved portrait painting. Maggie might like that, too. There was an exhibit at the Isabella Stewart Gardner Museum she would like to see, terra-cotta sculptures of the Italian Renaissance. She wasn't sure how Maggie would feel about that one. She found a secondhand bookstore on Beacon Hill that might be worth a visit, even just to browse if she found she couldn't afford the prices, which was likely. She had absolutely no idea of what restaurants were popular and she assumed that Maggie would want to eat at upscale places rather than pubs and diners, so there might be some tension there. But they would deal with the food situation together. They would compromise.

Compromise. That was one thing that neither she nor Robert had been willing or able to do. He had known who he was and what he wanted from his life. So had she. Delphine thought about her relationship with Harry and wondered what Harry was giving up or doing without in order to be with her. Nothing, at least nothing that she could see. As for herself . . . But sacrifice was necessary in a relationship, wasn't it?

She thought about the fact that she and Harry had never gone anywhere, not once in the ten years they had been together. Harry had no interest in seeing other parts of the country, certainly nothing south of Massachusetts. When he visited his brother in Framingham, he went alone. He had never asked if Delphine would like to spend a weekend in Montreal or Greenville or even Portland. And she had never asked him to go away with her.

Delphine shut down her laptop and sighed. She supposed she should tell Harry pretty soon about her plans to go to Boston with Maggie. She looked at her watch. He was working right then; she could call him on his cell, though he didn't like to talk on the phone while driving. She could leave a message on his home phone. But something held her back. She realized that she was a bit afraid of telling him. Harry had never mentioned his meeting Maggie in the hardware store. Whatever he thought about her, it wasn't friendly. But even if he didn't like the idea of Delphine's going away with Maggie, and he wouldn't, there was nothing he could do about it. She wasn't a child and he wasn't her parent. She wasn't his wife, someone who would be expected to consult a husband about an impending vacation. She was a free agent as far as Harry was concerned. She could do what she liked.

And then there was Jemima. She would tell her about the

trip the next time she saw her, which might not be for a day or two, as Jemima had accepted a few additional shifts at the restaurant. Suddenly, in her mind's eye, Delphine could see the look of disapproval on Jemima's face, the unfounded look of suspicion or criticism. She might be forced to explain or defend her decision to leave town. . . .

Jackie, as a matter of course, would tell her parents and the other Crandalls. Delphine's sense of apprehension grew. There would be disapproval, puzzlement, possibly concern. She wondered if her family would be right to be concerned about her. She wondered if she was doing the right thing in going away or if she was, after all, making a big mistake.

Because one little step in a new direction might just lead to a whole series of steps in that new direction. She might lose the staid and comfortable life she had known for so long, the life she had worked so hard to create and to maintain.

Delphine got up from her desk and began to pace. She was aware of a growing knot of tension in her shoulders. She was aware of a headache stealthily approaching. She was aware of her stomach jumping nervously.

She couldn't do this. She couldn't go away with Maggie. It wasn't too late to call off the whole thing. Maggie probably hadn't yet booked a hotel, and even if she had, people canceled reservations all the time. And if there was a cancellation fee, Delphine would pay it, as a reminder of her folly, as a punishment for risking the status quo.

Maggie would be mad. What reason could she possibly give her for backing out, other than the usual excuses she'd been reciting for weeks? Jackie, too, would be puzzled, ask questions, would pry into her motives for canceling. Jemima would smile knowingly.

Delphine felt her heart racing and sank onto her bed. She realized she was allowing herself to come close to a full-blown panic attack. She had gone from reasonably, even happily planning the trip to chaos in mere minutes. She hadn't felt so out of control of her thoughts and emotions for years.

She felt ashamed of herself. She was a grown woman, not a child. She knew she should not be so afraid of disappointing others, fearful of their opinions about her. She knew she should not base her actions, her decisions, on the desires of other people. She knew that if even one night away from home was frightening her so badly there was something deeply wrong with her life.

I want to go to Boston with Maggie, she told herself, and it was the truth. "I want to go," she said to the room. "I want to go."

She concentrated on breathing slowly, deeply. *It's only one night away, part of two days,* she reminded herself. *It's not as if the farm is going to fail because I'm not there for a few hours.*

You are afraid, a voice in her head said. *And you are also hubristic. You believe you are of great importance to so many people. Your ego is at stake.*

The thought upset her. She had never thought of herself as a self-important, puffed-up person, but that didn't mean that she wasn't. That was the problem with the idea you had of yourself. It usually didn't take much introspection for that idea to be shaken and shown as faulty or even false.

Delphine shook her head, rubbed her temples. It was time to stop thinking, or doing whatever destructive, unproductive thing it was she had been doing for the past minutes. There would be time later, someday, maybe, to examine her life. Now was not the time.

She took a deep breath and got up from the bed. She took her dinner plate down to the kitchen. She poured herself a glass of iced tea, swallowed three ibuprofen pills, and went back upstairs. She took a cool shower. She rubbed her arms and legs and neck with a lavender-scented moisturizer Jackie had given her for her last birthday. She felt a bit calmer.

She went into the bedroom and slid under the thin summer covers. She willed her mind to be still. Within a few seconds Melchior jumped from the floor and landed on her stomach.

She grimaced until he settled between her thighs. Maybe she should put him on a diet, she thought, if only to prevent him from rupturing one of her organs. While she was away in Boston Jackie would feed Melchior and clean his litter and assure him that his mommy was soon to return. But even with Jackie's good care, Melchior would be furious with Delphine and find some way in which to punish her once she was back.

Delphine smiled down at him. Cats were like people in that way, or people were like cats. No one liked being left behind, particularly without a good explanation. She turned off the light and closed her eyes. To the darkness—to herself—she vowed that she would try her very best not to leave Maggie behind ever again.

43

Maggie was in her hotel room that Tuesday afternoon, trying to decide what to do for dinner, when Delphine called. She had been prepared for Delphine to retreat from the idea of an overnight trip to Boston. When Delphine instead said, "Yes, let's do it," she was stunned.

"You mean it?" she asked.

"Yes."

"So, I can go ahead and book a hotel?"

"Make sure to look for a bargain."

"Of course. Delphine, I am so happy, really. We're going to have such a good time."

Delphine hadn't answered immediately. When she did, what she said was, "I hope so."

When Maggie hung up she went immediately to her laptop and began the search for a nice hotel, something Delphine could afford and something she herself could tolerate. She quickly found a few options—she was a well-seasoned traveler, used to hunting out deals—and made a choice. She put the room on one of her credit cards. She and Delphine would discuss money later.

She realized that she was hungry, even after the rather large lunch she'd had, and at about five-thirty went out to Black, the sushi place in town. She wondered if Delphine liked sushi. It was something she would ask her on the drive down to Boston. Delphine would be a captive audience. She would have to listen to Maggie's questions and opinions whether she wanted to or not. Maggie smiled at the thought. She wondered what music Delphine listened to these days. The radio in her truck was never on. Maybe it didn't even work. Well, Maggie was open, as long as she didn't have to drive to rap or, God forbid, heavy metal.

After a good meal of sushi, sashimi, and green tea, Maggie bought a bottle of wine at the Village Market and went back to her room. She got undressed and into a nightgown, opened the bottle of wine, and poured a glass. She settled on the comfortable couch and put on the television, though there was nothing in particular she wanted to watch.

She stopped on a reality show that had something to do with fashion. As she watched tattooed, spiky-haired young people throw fits and bits of fabric, she felt almost giddy with the idea of a girls' night away. She felt like a college kid again, unencumbered by responsibilities other than getting to class on time and achieving a passing grade. She felt like a high school kid again, looking forward to a long summer with nothing more to do than lie on the beach and watch the boys. She had no desire to call her husband or to e-mail her daughters. She knew she should check in with the housekeeper about the ant situation but just didn't want to. She felt as if she was about to embark on the pursuit of a guilty pleasure, something wrong but wonderfully exciting. She barely knew it, but she was reveling in that great gooey mess called avoidance, and its dangerous cohort escapism.

Maggie flipped to another channel, unable to bear the antics of the fashionistas. Another reality show, this one with scantily clad men and women throwing themselves through the air as though they were having a fit. They were supposed to be dancing. Whatever. It was only visual background for her thoughts.

And what she was thinking right now was that she had achieved something of great value that afternoon. She had won Delphine's trust. She was proud of Delphine for taking this step, and she was grateful. One little night away. It seemed so minor, but she knew that for Delphine it was something major; it meant something more than what it was on the surface. What, exactly, that was, Maggie hoped to discover.

Her excitement was suddenly tempered by the realization of a responsibility. She was the one who had suggested the trip, who even had pressured Delphine to agree to it. She would be careful with her in Boston. She wouldn't push her about leaving Harry or standing up to her parents or buying some new and decent clothes. And she would not suggest they stay a second night, as much as she might want to make that suggestion.

Maggie smiled to herself. They were definitely taking her car. No way was she going to drive into the city in that rusty old truck. Imagine what the hotel's valet would think when Delphine handed him the keys!

Yes, Maggie thought, taking another sip of wine, it would be a road trip à la Thelma and Louise, but without the murder and the suicide and the high-waisted jeans. So maybe Thelma and Louise was a bad comparison. Instead, they would create new heroines, be stars in their own chick flick, two women out on the town, childhood best friends now cohorts in middle-aged fun. She would convince Delphine to let her take them out for a fabulous meal at one of the city's best restaurants. She would order champagne. She couldn't remember if Delphine liked champagne, but what the heck, she'd drink the whole bottle by herself if she had to.

They could even, if they wanted, pay a visit to Maggie's home in Lexington. But that visit might have to wait for another time, and Maggie was convinced there would be another time, and another after that. Maybe someday she could convince Delphine to fly to Puerto Rico with her for a few days. They could drive out to Rincon and feast on fresh seafood and watch the gorgeous young surfers. There was nothing wrong with looking, was there? Maybe she could persuade Delphine to go to New York City. It was magical at Christmastime and they could spend hours in the Metropolitan Museum of Art, and the Whitney, and the Guggenheim, and MOMA and the Frick—Delphine loved portraiture—and they could . . .

One step at a time, she reminded herself. Dealing with Delphine was like dealing with a timid woodland creature. One false move and she would run away. It hadn't always been that way, but it was that way now.

Still, she would bring the aquamarine necklace to Boston and give it to Delphine there. There was no way Delphine could find a necklace threatening to her autonomy or whatever it was she was so fiercely protecting. The entire trip would be a celebration of the rebirth of their friendship, a friendship that had first been born forty years earlier.

Maggie turned off the television—a waste, anyway—and got up from the couch. She recorked the half-empty bottle of wine and put it in the mini-fridge. Then she went into the bathroom and completed her before-bed rituals—makeup removal, nighttime moisturizer, expensive under-eye cream—and crawled into bed. For a while she was too happy to sleep. Imagine! Too happy and excited and eager to sleep. That hadn't happened since she was a girl, looking forward to a trip to an amusement park or her birthday party or presents left by Santa Claus under the tree. She smiled in the darkness of the room. "Thank you," she whispered. "Thank you."

44

It was Wednesday afternoon and Jackie had stopped by Jemima's to deliver a carton of eggs. She didn't entirely like Jemima Larkin. She found her to be a bit too self-righteous, without the intelligence to back it up. That and on occasion, as Jackie had said to Maggie, a drama queen. But there was no denying she was a good friend and neighbor to Delphine, so for her sake Jackie was friendly. Well, she was friendly with pretty much everybody. It was her nature and her policy.

Jackie followed Jemima into the kitchen. Jemima's house was spotless, as if all the energy she saved by not catering to her appearance went into the care of her home. Jackie could have done without the faint but consistent aroma of ammonia, but hey, that was Jemima's problem.

"I ran into Delphine's friend in town this morning," Jemima said, pouring a cup of coffee for Jackie. "Maggie. She told me that she and Delphine are going to Boston for a night. She just rushed right at me and blurted the news like she had something to prove. Like she expected me to faint or start screaming or something."

Jackie hid a grin. The rivalry between her sister's two friends was amusing in some ways, though she wouldn't want to see it flourish. Nothing good would come of this sort of jealousy between women.

"Well," she said, "I guess she's just excited."

"Excited! She's not a kid. She's a grown woman for God's sake and she should act like one."

Jackie declined to comment. But Jemima wasn't finished. "I don't know what's gotten into your sister since that woman showed up. She's acting different. I mean, why didn't she tell me about this Boston thing?"

Maybe, Jackie thought, *because she knows you would have tried to talk her out of it.* What she said was: "They're old friends. They were inseparable for years. Delphine's just having some fun. She's fine. Frankly, I think she needs a break. Sometimes I think she's going to just, I don't know, fade away with nothing to show for her life."

Jemima shook her head. "That's not right to say. Delphine does so much for everyone around her. She's a vital part of this community."

"Yes," Jackie agreed, "she is and she does; she's almost entirely unselfish. But what does she have for her own? She doesn't have a husband. She doesn't even have a boyfriend who's fully committed. She doesn't have kids. She doesn't have any friends in Ogunquit but you and me, and I'm her sister; I almost have to be her friend. And Delphine won't concentrate on her knitting, which in my opinion could make her a small fortune, because she's always so tied up doing things for other people."

"She's happy," Jemima stated emphatically.

"Is she?"

"She's content."

Jackie considered this for a moment. "I think that maybe she was, before Maggie came back. Maybe Maggie will shake her up, light a fire under her again, get her moving."

And then what? Then Maggie would leave Ogunquit and return to her life in Boston and what would happen to Delphine then, without her immediate influence? For a moment Jackie wondered if maybe Jemima was right about Maggie's being bad for Delphine, but she dismissed the thought. If

Maggie were a drug fiend or a criminal, then yeah, she'd be a bad influence.

"I'm glad Delphine has someone like you as a friend," Jackie said now, "someone so fiercely loyal and protective. I am. But you know she's got to live her own life and make her own mistakes. You can't keep her from making choices, good or bad."

"Of course I know that," Jemima snapped. "I just don't know what that Maggie person is after. She wants something from Delphine, but for the life of me I can't see what it is."

This was a new thought for Jackie. It hadn't occurred to her to impute a motive to Maggie's reappearance other than the desire for a vacation in a relatively quiet beachside town. A town that just happened to be home to the friend of her youth, but Jackie had assumed all Maggie wanted was a respite from a high-powered, high-pressure career and to spend a few weeks reminiscing. That was all.

"Well," Jackie said, putting her empty cup in the spotlessly white sink, "Delphine will figure everything out for herself." She hoped that that was true. "I've got to be going. Thanks for the coffee."

45

The last of Wednesday's dinner dishes had been washed, dried, and put away. Patrice, Charlie, Joey, and Jackie were in the living room. Patrice was sewing a button on one of her husband's work shirts. Charlie was reading the local daily paper. Joey was drumming his fingers on the arm of his chair.

"What do you think of Maggie?" Jackie, who was leaning against the mantel, asked her brother. She knew that he and Harry had run into Maggie and Delphine at the hardware store. Delphine hadn't told her. Joey had.

Joey shrugged. "She seems okay. Sort of different from how I remember her, but I can't really say how. She's pretty."

Jackie sighed. "Men. They're so articulate."

Charlie folded the paper and placed it on the end table by his chair. "Why does Delphine need to go to Boston anyway?"

"Because she wants to," Jackie said. "Because she's having a nice time with a dear old friend."

Patrice frowned. "Well, she knows this is our busiest time of the year. I don't know what she's thinking."

Jackie sighed. "Mom, when was the last time Delphine had a break, even a full day off? Lori's doing great learning Delphine's job. She knows the computer system almost as well as Delphine does. We'll have everything under control while she's gone. Come on; she deserves this little vacation."

"Well, I don't know about 'deserves,' " Patrice said. "And

for that matter, when was the last time any of us had a day off? Answer me that."

"Then maybe we're doing something wrong," Jackie snapped. "Really, Mom, what's the problem with some time for relaxation? It's normal. It's healthy."

"Even God rested on the seventh day." Joey rose from his chair and reached for his baseball cap. "Though this guy's gotta get up early tomorrow. I'll be heading home now."

"How is Kitty feeling?" Patrice asked. "Did she like those oatmeal cookies I made her? I could make another batch for her tomorrow."

Joey adjusted his cap unnecessarily. His mother wouldn't want to hear that he had eaten them after Kitty had nibbled on one and put it down. "Sure," he said. In truth, he was very worried about his daughter but uncomfortable talking about her. He and Cybel were taking her to another doctor, someone Delphine had found for them in Portsmouth. He'd be glad when all this was over and Kitty felt like her old self again. He didn't enjoy feeling helpless, and the thought of anything being seriously wrong with his daughter made him feel nauseous.

"I'd better go, too," Jackie said. "I need to walk Bandit." Jackie grabbed her bag and followed her brother outside. She needed to get away from her parents and the house that could sometimes feel like a prison.

She got into her car and waved as her brother pulled out of the driveway ahead of her. Maggie's surprising visit. Jemima's fierce dislike of her. Harry's dislike of her as well, something Jackie had also learned from her brother. The incident between Dave Jr. and the boy from away. Kitty's weight loss and exhaustion. Jackie had an increasingly bad feeling that life for the Crandalls was tending toward some sort of crisis, and she had absolutely no idea of how to prevent that crisis from coming.

46

1984

Delphine and Maggie sat side by side on a bench in the Public Garden. It was mid-day and the April sun was surprisingly warm. Maggie was watching a family of tourists stroll by, two parents, a grandmother, and three teens, one sullen, one semisullen, the third and youngest plugged into his Walkman, singing aloud, oblivious to his siblings' moods. Delphine was looking down at her clasped hands.

"I have something to tell you," Delphine said finally.

"Okay." Maggie tried to smile but couldn't. "I figured something was up when you asked me to go for a walk. Since when do we just go for a walk unless it's on the beach?"

Delphine continued to look down at her hands. "I ended things with Robert."

"You what?" It was the last thing Maggie expected to hear. The very last thing.

"I broke up with him. I gave him back his ring."

Maggie looked to Delphine's left hand as if for confirmation. "Oh, my God!" she cried. "Why? I can't believe this is happening. What went wrong? My heart is racing. Please don't tell me he cheated on you."

"No, no, nothing like that. He didn't do anything. It's me. I just . . ."

"What?" Maggie pressed. "Don't tell me you're not in

love with him because I just won't believe that. I can't believe that. I know things have been stressful and all, with exams coming up, but . . ."

Delphine didn't reply. Her decision had nothing to do with love or with exams. But she couldn't tell Maggie about the night of the protest, the realization, the epiphany she'd had. She wanted to tell her, but she just couldn't. "I'll be going back to Ogunquit for a while," she said. "I need some time to clear my head." That wasn't exactly the truth. In her heart she knew that she was returning home forever.

"Please, talk to me," Maggie begged. "Let me help. Oh, my God, you must be feeling so awful." Maggie wiped away her tears and reached for Delphine to give her a hug. Delphine scooted away. She couldn't bear to be touched right then. Maggie felt stunned by this rejection.

After a moment, she asked, "How is Robert taking this?"

"Okay. I mean, he was very upset." Delphine paused as tears threatened to steal her voice. But she refused to cry, not now, not again. "But he's a strong person," she said finally.

"I bet he's devastated. I'm sure you broke his heart." Maggie didn't care if she was being cruel. She was angry with Delphine and hurt and confused and so very sad.

Delphine didn't answer. She had never felt so bad about something she was doing and at the same time so sure that what she was doing was right. It was like she was split in two inside. It hurt. It hurt to breathe.

Maggie sighed. "I have to know. Did you ever submit those applications for graduate school? Or did you just say that you did?"

"Why would I lie to you?" Delphine said. But she had lied and she knew why she had.

"Honestly, I don't know," Maggie answered. "I'm your best friend. I've been your best friend since I was eight years old. But I have no idea what's going on with you anymore, or why you're doing the things you're doing."

"I'm sorry," Delphine said. "I'm sorry you're upset."

"Are you?" Maggie snapped. "Did you tell Robert you were sorry? And if you did, was that a lie, too?"

No, she thought. *It wasn't a lie. I am so very sorry.* Delphine got up from the bench, and without looking back to Maggie, she walked off in the direction of the dorm.

Maggie put her face in her hands and cried.

47

Delphine stood in the middle of her bedroom. The closet door was open, as were all the drawers in her dresser, except for the one in which Harry kept some clothing. She and Maggie wouldn't be leaving for Boston until the following Tuesday morning; mid-week hotel rates were cheaper. It was only Friday evening, but Delphine was determined to choose clothes now and avoid a last-minute crisis. Not that the process of choosing what to wear in Boston was going to be easy, even days in advance of their departure. Nothing, nothing she saw in a survey of her clothing looked appropriate for hanging out with fashionable Maggie in the city. *Maybe,* she thought, *I should have watched an episode or two of* Sex and the City. *Maybe,* she thought, *I should have bought that blouse Maggie wanted me to buy at Jones New York. Rats.*

The home phone rang. Delphine turned her back on the disaster and went to the extension in the workroom. It was her mother.

Delphine listened. Her head began to buzz strangely.

"Okay," she said finally. "I'll be there soon."

Slowly, carefully, she replaced the receiver, then picked it up once again. She dialed Gorges Grant and was connected to Maggie's room.

"Maggie," she said. "It's Delphine."

"Hey. What's up? Your voice sounds . . . strangled or something. Is everything okay?"

Delphine couldn't speak for a moment. She wouldn't let herself cry, not now, or she might never stop. Finally, she said, "It's Kitty, my niece. She . . . We just got word that she has cancer."

Maggie's grip on the phone suddenly tightened. "Oh, no, Delphine, I'm so sorry. How bad is it?" she asked. "Where is she going to go for treatment? Does she—"

"I don't know the details yet. But look, Maggie, I have to cancel the Boston trip. I'm sorry."

"But . . . why? I mean . . ."

"I just have to."

"Of course," Maggie said after a moment. "I understand. Look, are you at home? Do you want me to come over? I could pick up some food and we could talk or—"

"No. Thanks. My mother needs me at the house."

"Wait, Delphine—"

"Good-bye, Maggie. I'm sorry about the trip. Maybe it wasn't such a good idea after all."

"What?" Maggie suddenly felt nauseous. "Look, Delphine—"

But she had already disconnected the call.

48

At nine o'clock Saturday morning, Maggie left a message on Delphine's cell phone and one on her home phone. She debated calling Mrs. Crandall but decided that it was too soon after the family's terrible news. Delphine was the one she should be talking to.

Now it was only eleven a.m. Time was moving way too slowly. That or she wasn't moving quickly enough. Maggie grabbed her bag and without much of a conscious plan left the hotel. The sidewalks were teeming with tourists. The street was jammed with cars. Maggie was largely oblivious to everyone and everything.

She found herself outside the library. *Why not?* she thought. She went inside and found the librarian alone at the desk. The room had that familiar library hush, which could be so soothing or, in moments of tension like this one, so maddening.

"Hi, Nancy," she said.

Nancy looked up from her computer and smiled. "Oh, hello. You're Delphine's friend. Maggie, is it?"

"Yes." She attempted a smile in return but failed.

"How can I help you?" Nancy asked. "Are you here to find a particular book?"

"No, thank you," she said. "I was just wondering if you had heard anything about Kitty Crandall."

"Oh." Nancy's expression darkened. "Well, nothing more

than that the poor little girl is ill. I believe she has a form of leukemia. Glenda ran into Jackie earlier at the post office."

"Oh. Okay."

Nancy gave Maggie a slightly puzzled look. "Why don't you ask Delphine for more news? I'm sure she'll tell you all that's going on."

"Yes," Maggie said. "I should do that. I just didn't want to bother her. . . ."

Nancy reached out across the desk and patted Maggie's hand. "Why would you be a bother, dear? You're old friends. I'm sure you're a comfort to her."

Maggie smiled, though she felt tears threatening. "Yes," she said. "Well, thank you very much. I should be going."

She walked back to the hotel, past souvenir shops, through throngs of people in shorts, flip-flops, and baseball caps. This time, she was brutally aware that most everyone she passed seemed happy, oblivious to the crisis at hand, to the local child who was facing months, maybe years, of pain and misery. She had an awful urge to shout out at them all, tell them to stop smiling and eating chocolate-covered blueberries and buying crappy souvenirs and to just listen. "A little girl is sick!" she wanted to shout. "And I don't know what to do!"

At Gorges Grant she picked up her car, and she drove out to the Burton brothers' store. Maybe they would know something more. Maybe they could do something; maybe they could help her to do something. She found Piers dusting a bust of an anonymous Roman woman. Aubrey, he explained, was away for the day on a buying trip.

"I hope there was no problem with the delivery of the painting," Piers said when they had exchanged greetings.

Maggie felt momentarily stupid at having come. "Oh, no," she said, "my housekeeper signed for it. It's safe and sound. I came because— Well, have you heard about Kitty Crandall?"

Piers's face immediately assumed an expression of great

and genuine sympathy. "Oh, yes, it's such a shame. A sick child, and such a lovely little girl, too. Is there anything worse?"

"No," Maggie said, "there isn't. Have you heard anything new? I mean, I talked briefly with Delphine last night, but she hasn't answered my calls all morning."

Piers reached out, as Nancy had done earlier, and patted her arm. "She probably just needs some space right now. The Crandalls are a tight unit. They close ranks when things get difficult. But they'll get through this time of crisis. Try not to worry."

Maggie attempted a smile. "Easier said than done, I'm afraid. But thank you, Piers."

They said good-bye and Maggie got back into her car. She sat there for a moment, lost. She badly wanted to go out to the farm but had a strong instinct that it would be a very wrong thing to do just then. She had made enough wrong steps already this summer.

The rest of the afternoon was a trial of patience. She bought herself an expensive linen jacket she didn't really like and certainly didn't need. She ordered a salad at a restaurant and couldn't eat it. She wandered down to the beach, but the crowds tore at her nerves.

Finally, she went back to her hotel, where she decided to call Gregory. She wasn't at all sure she would reach him, or, if she did, that he would have the time to talk. But cut off from Delphine, she didn't know whom else to reach out to.

Gregory was available, but only for a few minutes, he said. She told him about Kitty and about Delphine's having canceled their overnight trip to Boston. "She wouldn't even talk to me," she said. "She just hung up and she hasn't called me back today though I've left several messages."

"Maggie," Gregory replied, "she's probably in a bit of shock. I wouldn't take anything she does or says right now too seriously."

"No, but it's so strange," Maggie argued. "She said our trip to Boston was probably a bad idea all along. I don't know what's wrong with her. I don't know how to explain it. It's like her family is more important to her than absolutely anything else in the world, even her own self, her own needs."

There was a beat of silence before Gregory finally spoke. "Okay. Uh, Maggie? What are you saying, exactly? That I should care more about you and the girls?"

"No, no, God, Gregory, this has nothing to do with you!" Maggie cried.

"Then . . . I'm sorry, I'm not really understanding why you're so upset. It's terrible about the little girl, of course. But I don't understand why someone's not calling you back immediately is affecting you so much."

Maggie massaged her forehead. It did little to relieve the pain storm gathering there. "Forget it," she said. "It's nothing. Look, sorry I called."

"It's all right. Keep me posted. Do you think that you'll be coming home earlier than planned? I booked a golf trip for next weekend. And it looks like I won't be back from Chicago until Wednesday. There'll be plenty of privacy for you if you decide to head home now that Delphine's busy. You'll have the whole house to yourself."

"Great," she muttered.

"I have to go now, Maggie. Hang in there, okay?"

She said good-bye and ended the call. She went over to the window. The pregnant woman she had seen on the first morning of her stay at Gorges Grant was at the pool again, this time alone, reclining on a lounge, reading a book. Maggie had a crazy urge to go down to the pool and ask the woman if she could sit with her. *This is how lonely I feel,* she said to herself. *I would ask a total stranger for her company.*

Maggie sighed and turned away from the window. It had been an awful day. She couldn't remember ever feeling so frustrated. She had to do something productive. She opened her laptop and went online to research childhood leukemia. She didn't have much information to go on in terms of the specifics of Kitty's situation, but information was power and if there was anything she could do to help Delphine and her family, she would. In spite of Delphine's best efforts to keep her out.

49

It was an unusual gathering for a Saturday morning. With the exception of Charlie, who was at the diner, the other adult Crandalls were gathered at the family home. Even Jackie was there; Dave Jr. had gone up to the Portland market without her. Kitty was on the last play date she might have for some time. The mother of the little boy who lived next door had been instructed to let the children watch a movie on DVD. No running around, nothing risky. Infection and easy bleeding were now things to be seriously avoided.

Patrice was in the kitchen. The others were seated or standing around the living room. Delphine was pacing.

"Look," Jackie was saying. "The doctors told Joey and Cybel that Kitty's current white blood cell count is not half as bad as it could be. That's a good sign. And the leukemia hasn't spread to her brain or to her spinal cord. That's another good sign. We have to stay positive."

"That's easy to say," Delphine muttered, "not so much to do."

Dave Sr. cleared his throat. "I read that the current survival rate for kids with ALL is now about eighty percent."

"That's twenty percent less than perfect." Delphine turned to her sister-in-law. "What exactly have you told her?"

"She knows she's sick," Cybel said. "She knows she has something called ALL. She doesn't need to know the details. Not yet, anyway, not until we know more."

"Has she asked?" Delphine demanded.

"Well, yes, sort of, but—"

"Have you told her she could die from this?"

"Delphine!"

She ignored her sister. "Does she know she has cancer?" she persisted. "What do a bunch of initials mean? Nothing."

"Technically," Jackie said, "it means 'acute lymphoblastic leukemia.' "

"That means even less than initials to a child, a bunch of big words."

Joey sighed. "Delphine, what's your point? Why are you fighting us?"

"Does she know she might get sicker before she gets better?"

"We'll tell her everything the doctor and the social worker advise us to tell her." Cybel got up from the easy chair in which she had been sitting and reached out a hand. Delphine ignored it. "I know you're upset, Delphine. We all are. This feels like a nightmare. We're just going to have to trust the experts to tell us what's going on."

"And pray." That was Patrice. She had come in from the kitchen, wiping her hands on her apron. "There's a fresh pot of coffee. I suggest everyone have some and try to calm down."

"That would be directed at me."

Patrice nodded firmly. "Yes, Delphine, it would."

The family regrouped in the kitchen. Delphine poured a cup of coffee, took a sip, and put it down. She could barely keep down water, not since learning that her Kitty was sick.

"I just wish we knew what caused this," Joey said. "I wish we knew if this is somehow our fault."

Jackie gave her brother's arm a squeeze. "Of course it's not your fault. Don't be ridiculous."

"The doctor told us no one really knows for sure all the risk factors. But still . . . I'm her father. I want to know if there's anything I could have done to protect her from this."

"Some people think that this can happen because the mother was over thirty-five when she gave birth." Cybel wiped at her eyes with a napkin. When she spoke again her voice was wobbly. "This could be my fault. Kitty was such a surprise. . . ."

"Listen, all of you." Patrice's voice was commanding. "There's no point now in playing a guessing game or pointing fingers. Or," she said, looking pointedly at Delphine again, "in fighting amongst ourselves. What we do now is stick together and do what we have to do to make Kitty better."

Jackie turned to her brother. "When does Kitty start chemo?"

"Day after tomorrow," Joey said. "It's a fast-growing cancer, so the doctor said she'll need to start treatment immediately. This will be the first phase only. It'll be pretty intense. The doctor says it'll go on for about a month."

"All right then," Patrice said. "Let's sit down and work out a schedule for relieving Joey and Cybel while they're at work. Dave Senior, get me that pad of paper on the counter, will you?"

Suddenly, overcome with exhaustion, Delphine sank into a chair at the table. She felt a hand on her shoulder. It was her sister's.

50

The morning sun was strong as Maggie pulled into the yard of Crandall Farm on Sunday. She got out of the car and knocked on the open door of Delphine's office.

Delphine looked up from her computer and then back at the screen.

"I'm pretty busy right now," she said.

"You're always busy," Maggie countered, not for the first time that summer. She had noted the dark circles under Delphine's eyes and her wan complexion. "That's no excuse. I've been so worried since I last talked to you. How is Kitty feeling? Tell me what's going on. How are you holding up?"

Delphine continued to focus on the computer screen. "There's no need to worry," she said. "Everything is under control."

"That's impossible," Maggie said. "Nothing can be under control. You've just gotten some rotten news about someone you love."

"Thanks for the reminder."

"Why won't you talk to me?"

Delphine sighed and finally looked back at Maggie. "What's there to talk about? Kitty is sick and we're dealing with it. There's no point in going on about it."

"I'm not 'going on' about it," Maggie argued. "I just want to talk about this, with you. And I think you need to talk to me."

Delphine didn't reply.

"You can't avoid me," Maggie said, her voice rising with frustration. "You have to talk to me. I'm your friend, Delphine, your best friend."

Delphine continued to say nothing. *I never said that I was your best friend,* she thought, *not in a very long time. I don't have a best friend, not anymore. I don't need one.*

"I have money, Delphine," Maggie went on. "If your brother and his wife need it, it's theirs. I want to help."

"You assume we need help," she said now.

"Yes. I'm sorry if I'm assuming incorrectly, but I don't think that I am. So please, I can write a check right now. I did some research online. . . . She has leukemia, is that right? That's what Nancy told me. Treatment could go on for some time, for years even. It's going to cost and keep on costing. Now, I don't know the details of Joey and Cybel's health insurance, assuming they have any, but—"

"No." Delphine rose from her chair. "The Crandalls don't take charity."

"Charity!" Maggie laughed in disbelief. "This isn't charity!"

"Then what would you call it?"

"One friend helping another."

Delphine crossed her arms across her chest. It was not a usual gesture. "No. Thank you, Maggie, but it's impossible."

"I don't understand," Maggie said, with another small, frustrated laugh. "Is it because I offered to help with money? I can explain that. I'll be leaving before long. I don't live here. I can't be making casseroles for the parents. I can't be around to take turns sitting with Kitty or driving her to and from the hospital. Money is what I can offer, and if it's not as good as being a good neighbor I'm sorry; I am."

"Money," Delphine said tightly, "is only part of why I don't need your help."

Maggie shook her head. "You think money is somehow evil or wrong, don't you?"

"It's not good," Delphine replied, "not usually."

"Delphine, money is amoral. It has no meaning in and of itself. None. It only has meaning through its use. If you take this money you can help relieve your family's suffering. Then, the money becomes good. You've made it good."

"No, Maggie. That's my final word on the subject. We don't need or want your money."

Maggie felt her anger rising. "But you'll take someone else's money? Is that what you're saying?"

"The subject is closed."

"It's like all those years ago," Maggie cried. "And it's like when Dave Junior got in trouble. You're shutting me out again when I'm trying to help you."

Delphine felt a slight tingling in her head, her blood pressure rising. "I don't know what you're talking about," she said.

"Of course you know what I'm talking about," Maggie said fiercely. "It's become a pattern with you. Something troublesome happens in your life and you run away from me. Maybe you run away from everybody, I don't know. But I don't care about everybody; I only care about me. Do you have any idea how I feel when you turn me away? All I'm trying to do is help. You're my friend. You owe me the right to offer my help. You owe me—"

"Nothing!" Delphine shouted, her arms dropping to her sides. And in a slightly quieter voice she said, "I owe you nothing."

Maggie felt as if she had been kicked in the stomach. Tears flooded her eyes. She felt nauseous.

"I really have to get back to work," Delphine said, turning toward her desk, her back to Maggie. "So why don't you just go."

51

It was Sunday afternoon and Maggie was miserable. She had wandered aimlessly in town, then, annoyed by the press of vacationers, walked down to the beach, hoping to find a small, quiet spot where she could be alone. It was difficult, but she found a place about halfway down to Wells, up against the dunes. She sat directly on the sand, heedless of her expensive linen pants. The water was silvery in the sun. Seagulls cawed madly, circling above a scattering of beached clams.

She sighed heavily. To think she had been stupid enough to want to present Delphine with that aquamarine necklace on their trip to Boston. That necklace had become a tainted reminder of past joy, a macabre relic of a once-revered living thing. What had she been thinking, that she would give Delphine the necklace as a prize for good behavior, as a reward for being her best friend again? She supposed that if she really cared about Delphine and not more about her own need for the friendship she should give her the necklace anyway, for old times' sake, for the sake of selflessness. And then, she should walk away for good.

A shout of laughter brought Maggie's attention to the moment. A group of about six young people were setting up chairs and laying out blankets a few yards to her right. *So much for peace and quiet,* she thought. She got up, brushed off her pants, and walked back to Main Street, intending to go directly back to the hotel, by trolley if one came by.

As she reached the corner of Beach and Main Streets, she saw Jemima Larkin parking her car outside the Village Food Market. She didn't like Jemima and she strongly suspected that Jemima didn't like her, but she was feeling close to desperate. She had to make some connection with Delphine, no matter how tenuous.

"Jemima," she called when the woman had gotten out of her car. "Wait."

Jemima looked up to see Maggie hurrying toward her. "Yes?" she said when Maggie was a few feet away.

Maggie attempted a smile but couldn't muster one. "I want to ask you something," she said. "I want to know if you can explain to me why Delphine won't accept my help for her family."

Jemima smiled blandly. "Why don't you ask her that?"

"I have asked her. Of course I have. But she won't give me an answer." That was a bit of a lie. Delphine had given Maggie a firm and strongly worded answer. But it wasn't an answer she wanted to accept.

Jemima folded her arms across her ample chest. "You need to understand something," she said. "You're not one of us. You don't belong here. It means nothing that your parents rented a house here thirty years ago or however long ago it was. That doesn't make you belong."

Maggie laughed. She felt helpless. "That's crazy," she said.

"That's the way it is."

Jemima's smug smile was maddening. "You weren't born here," Maggie said, ashamed at engaging this horrid person in an argument but unable to keep silent. "Delphine told me so."

"I married a native," Jemima spit. "And this is not about me."

Maggie shook her head. "Why do you dislike me so much?"

"I have no opinion about you either way," Jemima lied. "But I do know that you're not good for Delphine."

"That's even crazier! I've known Delphine for almost all of my life!"

"You used to know her. But whoever it was you once knew is gone. Long gone."

Maggie felt Jemima's words like a slap. She suspected that this awful woman might be right. Maybe she had been supremely foolish, seeing what she wanted to see, imagining a Delphine who didn't really exist.

"Delphine is not a child," she said finally, her voice shaky. "I think she can decide for herself who's good and who's bad for her."

Jemima worked to hold back another smug smile of triumph. "I think," she said, "that she already has." She turned and walked off in the direction of the bakery.

After leaving Jemima, Maggie found herself on Shore Road. She had been driving aimlessly for over an hour, largely unaffected by the beautiful old homes with their gardens lush with flowers, by the vistas of the silver blue Atlantic, by the marshes with their dense clumps of wild grasses. She didn't want to go back to her hotel. She didn't want to walk through town. She felt, alone in her beautiful car, like more of a stranger to Ogunquit than ever. This place, with all its contradictions and quirks, with its fiercely independent locals and its wealth of natural splendor, was not hers. Maggie Weldon Wilkes was an interloper.

Jemima Larkin had said as much earlier that day. Her words continued to taunt Maggie as she wandered. "You don't belong here." "You're not good for Delphine." Maybe she was right, Delphine's ornery neighbor. At that moment Maggie felt that everybody was right, everybody but her. At that moment Maggie felt that everybody belonged somewhere specific and special, everybody but her. She was brimming with self-pity. She was bitter with self-recrimination.

She passed a big old pile of a house that Delphine had pointed out to her the week before. It had been in the same family for generations, Delphine had told her, as had the Crandalls' farmhouse. Vaguely she noted the elaborate nineteenth-century carriage mounted in the front yard. Last week she had exclaimed over its pristine quality. Now, it seemed just useless and forlorn. She turned on the radio and almost immediately turned it off again. She wasn't in the mood for music or for the learned opinions of pundits. She felt fidgety, and then lethargic, and in the next moment fidgety again.

Her mind returned to the awful encounter with Jemima. The most hurtful thing Jemima had said to her—also perhaps the most truthful—was that the person Maggie had once known was no longer. That the Delphine Maggie had remembered or imagined was a phantom, a chimera, a myth. Whatever she was, she wasn't real. Maggie had been laboring under a delusion. How had she come to this point in her life, a point where her need for companionship was so great she had created a fantasy and then proceeded to believe in it as real? *Stick to financial futures, Maggie,* she told herself sternly, *and leave the world of interpersonal relationships to people more qualified to make and keep friendships.*

A tour bus passing way too fast in the opposite lane startled Maggie back to the moment and she became aware that she was now coming up on a lovely sprawling hotel, more of a resort really. "The Shoreman," a sign proclaimed. The name sounded vaguely familiar, and then she remembered it was where the man she'd met at the Old Village Inn said he was staying. Funny, that she should be passing it just now, when she was feeling so low and almost despairing, when only weeks ago really Dan—yes, that was his name—with his chat and offer of a drink had made her feel so good, so . . . noticed.

Maggie turned abruptly into the long driveway of the hotel, causing the driver in the car behind her to lean on his horn. She winced. She'd given no notice of her intention to turn off the road and should have waved an apology but didn't, and drove on toward an empty parking space. When she turned off the engine she sat there, her hands still on the wheel, as if stunned. *What am I doing here?* she asked herself, while at the same time justifying her last-minute decision—if it could even be called a decision—to . . . To what? She reached for the key, which was still in the ignition, intending to start the car and drive off again, but instead she removed the key, on its Tiffany silver key chain, and dropped it into her bag. *I'll just peek in at the bar,* she told herself, stepping out of the car, adjusting her sunglasses, smoothing her slacks. *I'll just peek in—Dan said it was a nice place—and maybe if he's there I'll say hello and have one drink and then I'll go back to my hotel. And if he's not there, I certainly won't stay. Either way,* Maggie thought as the automatic doors slid open to admit her to the lobby, *I'll be in my bed before long and this horrible day will be over.*

A hotel employee in a navy and white uniform pointed her in the direction of the bar. Maggie thanked her with a smile. She peered into the room—dark, but not overly so, decorated with the requisite amount of nautical accoutrements, including a large anchor hung on the back wall—and saw that aside from the bartender and an older couple at a small table in a corner there was no one there. *I'll just leave now,* she thought. And she walked into the room and over to the bar, where she slid onto a bar stool upholstered in red leather.

The bartender, a tall man in his twenties with a shaved head, placed a cocktail napkin on the bar in front of her. "What'll it be?" he asked pleasantly.

"A martini," Maggie said. "Gin."

"I'm sorry. I can't do this." Maggie rose quickly from the couch and began to button her blouse.

The handsome man from the Old Village Inn, Dan, lay back on the couch, his own shirt untucked and partially unbuttoned. They were in his room at the Shoreman. It was close to midnight. "Hey, come on," he said. "I thought we were having a good time."

Maggie ran her hand through her hair and scanned the room for her bag. "No. I mean . . . I just have to go."

Dan—she hadn't asked for his last name—laughed in disbelief. "So you're just a tease, is that it? I spend the whole evening buying you drinks for this? Nice."

"No." Maggie grabbed her bag from the top of the dresser and turned toward the door. "I'll give you money. You don't understand."

"I don't want your money. What I want is—"

"I'm sorry!"

"You know," Dan called out as she tore open the door, "you're too old to be playing games."

Maggie ran down the hall, through the lobby, and out through the hotel's automatic doors. She got into her car—she was vaguely aware that she shouldn't be driving after all she'd had to drink—and fumblingly inserted the key in the ignition. Tears coursed down her cheeks as she drove off in the direction of her hotel. She felt self-loathing and fear and panic. She half wished she would be pulled over by a policeman, that her career would be destroyed, her life ruined. "God," she muttered as she drove, her hands gripping the steering wheel, "what has become of me?"

52

"I thought you'd be at the farm." It was late Monday morning. Jemima stood at Delphine's front door, a plate covered loosely with aluminum foil in her hands. "I was just going to leave these in the kitchen."

"I was at the farm earlier," Delphine said, gesturing Jemima inside. "I came home for a bit. Bad headache."

"You're not eating enough. I understand why, but you can't afford to make yourself sick. There are too many people relying on you, Delphine."

"I know." Of course she knew. She was never unaware of her responsibilities to her family.

"I brought you these nice cinnamon rolls. They're still warm. Do you want one now?"

"Maybe later," Delphine said. "Thanks, Jemima. I do need some coffee, though. The ibuprofen didn't help much."

The two women went into the kitchen. Jemima directed Delphine to sit and she brought her a cup of coffee from the pot warming on the stove.

"I ran into your friend Maggie in town yesterday," she said, sitting across from Delphine. "She started questioning me about you."

Delphine took a sip of her coffee before answering. "Questioning you about me? What do you mean?"

"She wanted to know why you wouldn't accept her help. By which I assume she meant money."

"What did you tell her?" Delphine asked warily.

Jemima shrugged. "I told her that she should ask you that. She said that she had."

"What else did you say to her?"

"Nothing. What would I have to say to her?"

Plenty, Delphine thought. Jemima wasn't known to hold back her opinions, even when she should. And there were times, not often but on occasion, when Delphine felt smothered by Jemima's friendship. She was a possessive woman. As far as Delphine knew, Jemima didn't have any other close friends, not in the Ogunquit area, anyway. But she was also a reliable person and that wasn't to be discounted.

"I think I'll have a cinnamon roll after all," Delphine said.

Jemima beamed. Soon after serving a roll to Delphine, she took her leave, satisfied that she had done her duty.

When she had gone, Delphine poured another cup of coffee and sat back at the table. She was a little bit angry that Maggie had interfered by questioning Jemima, but at the same time she acknowledged a small feeling of gratitude for her persistent concern.

Delphine sipped at the coffee and thought again about Maggie's two recent and generous offers of help. She wondered if she had ever cared as much for Maggie as Maggie claimed to care for her. She wondered if there was something about her that made her recoil from real, messy intimacy. And if there was something . . . wrong, then why? She had backed away from marriage to Robert. Maybe there were more reasons for that decision than wanting to return to Ogunquit. She had let go of, neglected, the friendship with Maggie. She was with a man who would not marry her. She lived alone. She was not in the habit of asking anyone for help. She wasn't sure she could even recognize a situation in which asking for help would be a smart thing. She often felt oddly removed from her current relationships with Maggie, Jackie, and Jemima, even when they were enjoying each other's company. She often felt as if she were a spectator and not a participant in her own life.

Delphine put the piece of foil back over the plate of cinnamon rolls. It was nice of Jemima to have brought them. Nice and typical. Her friendship with Jemima, though strong and consistent, didn't have much to do with shared feelings and dreams. It was a serviceable, workaday kind of thing. They did favors for each other. Jemima passed along coupons for cat food and Delphine picked Jemima up from the car repair shop when her old car broke down, which it routinely did. Jemima made chicken soup for Delphine when she got her annual winter cold. Delphine mowed Jemima's lawn when Jim couldn't get to it. It was all good stuff, very neighborly, but not necessarily intimate. At least, it didn't feel intimate to Delphine. Not that she knew what intimacy was, she reminded herself, not anymore. Maybe, she never had. Not even with Robert, because she had never been entirely truthful with him. And intimacy was about nothing if it wasn't about being truthful.

Maybe, she thought irritably, *I'm just not cut out for intimacy.* And if intimacy was what Maggie was really looking for, well, she wasn't going to find it with Delphine. Maggie might be a good person, but she was also a problem. She had caused Delphine to spend too much time away from her work, from her responsibilities, from her family.

Delphine didn't believe in divine retribution—she didn't believe that some unnamable all-powerful being had struck down her niece as punishment for Delphine's neglect of her family duties—but at the same time she couldn't help but feel that she had tempted fate by planning to go away. And for what? To have "fun"? What did "fun" mean, anyway? Who, other than children, deserved to have fun?

Well, she thought, *now that I'm not available to be Maggie's playmate, she should just go home where she's actually wanted.* Assuming Maggie was wanted at home, and from what she'd told Delphine about the current state of her marriage, maybe she wasn't wanted there, either.

Delphine felt an unwelcome rush of guilt. Just the other night, just before she had learned of Kitty's diagnosis, she had sworn never to leave Maggie behind again. What had happened to that vow? What had happened to that promise she had made to herself as well as to Maggie? Had she made it lightly, falsely?

Delphine rubbed her temples. *What has become of my life?* she asked herself. *How have I wound up here, in this place of isolation, so confused and so alone?*

The answers to those questions were not going to be found at the kitchen table. In spite of the throbbing in her head, Delphine went out to her truck and headed back to the farm.

53

1984

Patrice and Charlie did not drive down to Boston for Delphine's graduation. Delphine was not surprised or upset by this. They had never visited her in Boston; she couldn't see why they would start now, on the eve of her homecoming. Jackie alone represented the Crandall family. She presented Delphine with a Cross pen she had spent months saving up for. Joey had sent a card.

That evening, after the ceremony, Maggie's parents threw a big party in the rooftop bar of a sophisticated downtown hotel. Delphine and Jackie were there. Maggie's brother, Peter, now in law school, was also there, as were several of Maggie's classmates and a large group of the Weldons' friends and business colleagues. When Robert Evans showed up shortly before ten o'clock, bouquet in hand for Maggie, Delphine grabbed Jackie's arm and together they slipped out the far door of the room.

"It must have been a pretty bad breakup," Jackie had whispered to Delphine as they rode the elevator to the lobby. "You aren't even talking to each other?"

Delphine had only nodded. No one in her family, not even Jackie, had known of the engagement. She had asked Maggie not to mention Robert at all to her sister. Maggie had complied.

Early the next morning Jackie had driven back to Maine with most of Delphine's belongings. Delphine was staying on in Boston for another two days to say good-bye to a few people with whom she had worked for the past school year. She was sleeping on the couch of a fellow graduate who had rented a small apartment in Allston. Robert had offered to see her off at the bus station when she was ready to leave. She still wasn't sure she would let him.

She met Maggie for lunch at a diner they liked, close to their dorm. Today, neither young woman had much of an appetite. Delphine's tuna salad sandwich sat largely untouched. Maggie picked at her Greek salad.

"Thanks again for inviting Jackie and me to the party," Delphine said after a long silence.

"Of course. I looked around for you when the party was over, but I guess you'd already gone."

Delphine looked down at her plate. "Yeah, well . . ."

"Right."

"Good luck in graduate school," Delphine said, after another long pause.

Maggie smiled a bit. "Thanks. I'm going to need more than luck, though. Business school's going to be pretty tough."

"You can handle it." *She will,* Delphine thought. *Maggie can handle anything.*

"Did I tell you I'm going to be living at home and commuting to school?"

"Oh." Delphine took a sip of her now lukewarm coffee.

"Yeah," Maggie said. "I just couldn't imagine being roommates with anyone other than you."

Delphine felt a prick of conscience. "Well, that's probably the economical thing to do," she said. "Save the money you'd have to spend on room and board."

"Yeah. So, when do you think you can get back to Boston to visit?"

Delphine looked a bit over Maggie's shoulder when she answered. "I don't know," she said. "I'll have so many responsibilities when I get home, especially now that it's summer. It's our busiest season at the farm and at the diner."

"Yeah. Okay. Well, let me know. I'll be busy, too. My internship starts next week."

"Okay. So, I guess we should get the check. I have to get going."

"Oh." Maggie fiddled with her fork. "You're sure you don't have time to catch a movie or something? *Amadeus* is playing downtown. Or maybe we could just—"

"No," Delphine said, reaching for her wallet. "I really have to go. I have a bus to catch this afternoon." That was a lie. She wasn't leaving Boston for two more days.

Maggie reached across the table to touch Delphine's arm but then withdrew her hand. "Delphine," she said, lowering her voice, "look. I . . . I know I promised not to bring this up again, but I can't help it. I just don't understand why you're doing this. Please tell me it's temporary; tell me you're coming back to Boston for good or that you're getting back with Robert. Please tell me you just need a bit of a break before you get back to your real life."

Delphine felt her hands begin to shake and put them in her lap, out of view. She fought hard against the feelings that might break her determination to live the life that was meant to be hers. Not Robert's life. Not Maggie's idea of what her life should be. "My real life is back home," she said firmly. "In Ogunquit, with my family."

Maggie shook her head. "I'm sorry. I just can't believe that."

"I can't help what you believe," Delphine said evenly.

"I feel miles apart from you right now." Maggie's eyes were misting over. "I feel like I'm talking to a stranger."

Delphine sighed. "Maggie," she said, "I really have to go. Take care of yourself."

She put a five-dollar bill on the table and hurriedly walked to the door of the diner. When she was on the sidewalk, she let the tears come, let them stream down her cheeks unchecked. It was the last time she would cry for many, many years.

54

"How long until dinner?"

"About half an hour," Delphine called.

It was Monday evening and Harry was seated in his favorite armchair, reading the paper, watched by Melchior. Delphine was in the kitchen, halfheartedly cooking their meal. The headache was still there, in spite of more ibuprofen.

While she stirred a pot of brown rice she was thinking about the time she had lived with the Weldons, the summers before her junior and senior years of college. Paying room and board to Maggie's parents had been cheaper than renting an apartment, and their house was clean and spacious and comfortable. Back then, Delphine hadn't felt in the least bit beholden or embarrassed, but now, in the wake of Maggie's offer of money—not even a loan but a gift—the memory of that arrangement, a memory so long buried, maybe even forgotten, rankled. Maggie had said that money itself was amoral, that it was good or bad only in the way in which it was used. In Delphine's opinion, money was mostly bad; it tempted people to make stupid decisions and to create arbitrary divisions between themselves and others.

When dinner was ready, Harry came into the kitchen, washed the newsprint from his hands, and joined her at the table. He had nothing to say. Delphine was glad to be left alone with her thoughts, unhappy though they were. It was only when she brought coffee and a slice of blueberry pie to the table that a conversation began.

"I'll be visiting Ellen tomorrow when I get off my shift," Harry said, wiping his mouth with a napkin.

"Fine. Did you pick up my winter coat from the dry cleaner's?" Delphine rarely bothered with a dry cleaner, but she didn't have the capacity at home to clean certain items like comforters or wool coats. Harry had offered to fetch the coat. She hadn't asked for his help.

"No," he said, loading his fork with another bite of pie, "I forgot. I'll pick it up tomorrow."

"You said you would pick it up today."

Harry swallowed. "Look, Delphine, I forgot. You don't need it right away anyway. Winter is months away. What's the big deal?"

"The big deal," she said, slowly and emphatically, as if talking to a naughty child, "is that you promised. The least you could do is say you're sorry."

Harry sighed. "I'm sorry."

"Don't say it if you don't mean it, Harry."

Harry put his napkin on the table next to his half-eaten dessert. "Look," he said. "Maybe I'd better just go, spend the night at home."

Delphine stared down at her plate. She fought the urge to ask him to stay, at least to finish his meal. She fought the urge to offer to pack up the uneaten pie, send it home with him. "Yeah," she said. "That's probably a good idea. Sorry, Harry. I'm just—"

Harry got up from his chair and came across to her. He leaned down and kissed her on the forehead. "You're just exhausted. Try to get some sleep, Del. I'll talk to you tomorrow."

She sat at the table while he let himself out. When he had gone she cleared the plates and glasses and silverware off the table. She left them in the sink for morning, which was not her habit. She took a bottle of Jack Daniel's from under the sink. It had been there, untouched, for over a year. She poured herself a shot. She sat back down at the table. She wished Harry wouldn't call her Del.

55

Jackie pulled into the gas station across from the post office. She was surprised to find Harry's truck there. She thought Delphine had told her he'd be spending the night at her house. Maybe she'd misunderstood. She hadn't been thinking all that clearly since Kitty's diagnosis.

She got out of her car and called, "Harry, hey."

Harry, who was standing at one of the pumps, looked over his shoulder. She thought he looked tired, maybe a bit sad, but it was hard to tell for sure in the uncertain late evening light. "Oh, hi, Jackie," he said. "Any more word on Kitty?"

"The same. We won't know anything more for a few days. There are more tests to be run." Jackie sighed. "Good thing Delphine hadn't left for Boston already. We need her here."

"What?" Harry asked. His expression was puzzled.

Jackie smiled. "What do you mean, 'What?' "

"What did you say about Boston?"

"Boston. You know, the overnight she and Maggie—" Jackie stopped talking as the truth hit her. "You didn't know?" she asked unnecessarily.

Harry's lips were tight. He shook his head, one brief time.

"I'm sorry, Harry. I'm sure she . . . Damn. I'm not sure of anything. Look, I've got to get home. . . ."

"Me too. Drive safe, Jackie."

Jackie touched his arm. "Yeah. You too, Harry."

Harry got into his truck and drove off. Jackie filled her gas tank, got back into her car, and called Delphine on her cell. Delphine didn't answer. Jackie tried again and then called the home phone. There was no answer to either attempt. Fine. Delphine was avoiding her. Since when, she wondered, had her sister become a liar? Jackie tossed her phone into the passenger seat and sighed. That was harsh. Delphine was in trouble. Clearly, she needed help of some sort, but Jackie had no idea what sort. *That crisis I felt looming,* she thought as she pulled out of the gas station. *Looks like there might be a part two.*

56

It was Tuesday morning, the day and the time they were supposed to have left for Boston. Instead, they were standing in an almost-deserted section of the Hannaford parking lot in York. Delphine wanted privacy when she talked to Maggie, but she hadn't wanted to ask her to her home.

"Why did you want to see me?" Maggie asked, her tone wary. The idea of meeting in a parking lot had struck her as a little bit insane. Either Delphine was crazy or she was selling drugs on the side.

"I wanted to ask if you had already booked us a room in Boston," she said. "If there was a cancellation fee, I'll pay it."

"What? No, no, there was no cancellation fee. Is that why you asked me to meet you here? You could have just called me."

Delphine took a deep breath. "I also wanted," she said, "to tell you that you don't have to worry about us." What she didn't feel brave enough to do was apologize for having treated Maggie so harshly the last time they had met.

"What do you mean?"

"I mean that you don't have to worry about our needing money. We've decided to sell a bit of our land. The parcel is worth a lot. The money should pay for . . . a lot."

"What parcel?" Maggie asked.

Delphine hesitated, anticipating Maggie's reaction. "The

one I told you about. The one where the original Crandall house stood."

"The one that's been in your family since the eighteenth century?" Maggie shook her head. "But that means so much to you, to everyone in your family!"

"It's fine," Delphine said steadily. "A child's life is worth more than a piece of land."

"Of course, but . . ." And then Maggie had an inspiration. *Why not?* she thought. She didn't need to talk to Gregory about it first. They had each maintained a separate bank account since their wedding, in addition to their joint holdings. She might need to get a small mortgage, but that was fine. She made money. She helped other people to make money. She knew how to handle it. "Look," she said. "Why don't I buy the land? I can afford to let it alone. Your family can farm on it, build on it, or just keep it as is, whatever you want."

Delphine was thoroughly taken aback. In spite of Maggie's earlier offers of help, she really hadn't expected this third attempt. "No," she said firmly after a moment. "Thank you. My father has already made a deal with the Burton brothers. They've been wanting to build a new house. . . . The parcel is perfect for them."

"But . . . wouldn't you rather sell it to a friend? Wouldn't you rather sell it to someone who will let you use the land in any way you want to so it won't feel like such a loss?"

"We'll be fine," Delphine insisted. "We'll pull together. We always have and we always will."

Maggie felt hurt, left out, angry. She felt stupid for having cared. Again. Maybe she had no right to feel all those things, but she did. "You'll regret having sold away the land," she said. "I know it."

"You don't know anything of the sort!" Delphine cried, suddenly unable to keep her falsely calm façade in place.

"I know stubbornness for the sake of—for the sake of stubbornness when I see it," Maggie shot back. "I know false pride."

Delphine fought the urge to shove Maggie, to slap her face, to lash out. "What gives you the right to judge my life and my actions?" she yelled. "Why do you presume to think you know what's best for me? You know nothing about me, Maggie; you think you do, but you never really have."

"That's not fair!" Maggie protested loudly. She didn't care if anyone else in the stupid parking lot could hear. "I've known you since we were little. I probably know you better than anyone else outside your family. I certainly know you better than Harry knows you!"

"Leave him out of it."

"Better than your parents, then. You never even told them you were engaged to Robert!"

"How did you know that?" Delphine felt shocked, exposed, her anger tinged with fear.

"He told me," Maggie said. "When he was calling me for a while just after you went back to Ogunquit. He was really hurt by that, not that you cared. Not that you cared about anyone but yourself."

Poor Robert, Delphine thought. *Everyone is so concerned about poor Robert's feelings. What about my feelings? Who was there to help me when I came back to Ogunquit with a broken heart?*

Maggie. That's who had been there. Rather, that's who had tried to be there for her. And routinely, deliberately, Delphine had pushed her away.

"I'm sorry for him," she mumbled. She felt deflated, suddenly devoid of all purpose or intent. "I'm sure he's over it by now. I'm sure he's forgotten all about me."

"Well, I never did," Maggie said. Her voice was low and tight. "I never forgot about you." *But maybe I should have,* she thought. Without another word, she turned, walked over to her car, and left Delphine standing by her dirty old truck.

57

Delphine had gotten to Cybel and Joey's house around ten that Wednesday morning. She had volunteered to stay with Kitty while her parents met with another specialist down in Portsmouth.

Shortly after Joey and Cybel left, Jemima arrived, bearing a tuna casserole and a large deep dish of lasagna.

"Cybel and Joey need to be eating," she said. "This way they don't have to worry about cooking for a while. I'll roast a chicken for them later in the week."

Delphine thanked her and put the casseroles into the freezer.

"What does your friend Maggie have to say these days?" Jemima asked, not at all casually.

"About what?"

"About Kitty, of course. After you turned down her money. I mean, her 'help.' "

Delphine sighed. She really didn't want to talk about Maggie with anyone, let alone with Jemima, especially not after what had happened in the parking lot. She felt terribly embarrassed about that encounter. She wondered if she was losing her mind. "She said that she was sorry for Kitty, and for us."

"She hasn't tried to interfere again, has she?"

"No," Delphine lied. "And please don't say anything to anyone in my family about her offer of help."

Jemima shrugged. "Fine. I'd better be going. I'm on the lunch shift today."

"Be careful," Delphine said, which was what she always said when Jemima was going off to work.

"Always am."

When she had gone, Delphine joined Kitty in her bedroom. She was sitting cross-legged on her bed surrounded by stuffed animals. Delphine had given her most of them. They each had a name and a story. The room itself was a riot of pinks and purples—everything from the bedspread, to the curtains, to the walls. Cybel kept the room as tidy as she could, but Kitty wasn't very neat by nature. There were piles of books from the library on top of a small bookcase filled with her own books, many also gifts from Delphine. A poster of fairies was taped to one wall. Art supplies—crayons, watercolors, brushes, and pads of paper—were stashed in a milk crate Joey had spray painted purple. A pile of string in a variety of colors sat on Kitty's desk. Next to it were a few friendship bracelets she had already completed.

"Hey," Delphine said. She sat next to Kitty on the bed and picked up one of the stuffed animals, a beige puppy. His name was Puppy. There was a Doggie and a Kitty—of course—and several Bearies. A lamb was called BaaBaa. A rabbit was called Bunny.

"Hey," Kitty said. "Can we still go to the Sea Dogs game?" She looked tired, Delphine thought. And a little bit scared.

"I don't know," Delphine answered honestly. "We'll have to see what the doctor says. If we can't go this summer we'll go next summer for sure. Okay?"

"Promise?"

"Promise. I'll even do a pinky swear."

"What's that?"

Delphine showed her. "So, you swear to get all better, and I'll swear we're going to a Sea Dogs game."

They linked pinkies and swore.

"Is my hair gonna fall out?" Kitty asked suddenly.

Delphine panicked. She didn't know just what or how much Joey and Cybel had told their daughter and she wanted to respect their decisions, even if she didn't necessarily agree with them. "Who told you your hair was going to fall out?" seemed like a neutral way to answer.

Kitty shrugged. "Everyone knows that's what happens when you're really sick. This boy in my class, his mother had cancer last year, and she went bald and wore these scarves wrapped around her head."

"But her hair grew back, right?"

"Mmm-hmm."

"I heard that when your hair grows back when you're all better it's even prettier than it was before."

"Really?"

"Yup. But try not to worry about it, okay?"

"I'm not worried," Kitty said in a slightly defensive tone. "Is your friend still visiting you?"

"Um, yeah."

"Can I meet her?"

"Well, I'm not sure when she has to go back home."

"Oh." Kitty frowned. She seemed to be considering something. "Does she have pretty hair?" she asked then.

"Yes. She does."

"What color is it?"

"Blond. When we were kids it was almost the color of jonquils. You know those flowers, right?"

"They grow in our garden out back. And Grandma has them. Will my hair grow back the same color as it is now?"

"I think so." Delphine looked keenly at her niece. "Hey, are you sure you're not worried about losing your hair?"

Kitty reached for Bunny and without meeting Delphine's eyes said, "Well, maybe a little."

"It might not even happen, you know. And if it does, I promise to sew you the coolest, prettiest scarves. Or maybe you'll want some funky hats. Or you could get both."

"Maybe."

"Hey, want to play a game?"

Kitty shrugged.

"I'll go pick something." Delphine got off the bed and began to rummage in the tiny overstuffed closet. She heard the front door open and her brother call out, "We're home."

"Daddy!" Kitty cried, and raced from the room.

Delphine stood alone in Kitty's room, a board game in her hand, and fought the urge to sob.

58

Later that afternoon there was a harsh knock on Delphine's front door, the kind made with a well-shod foot rather than a hand.

Delphine was surprised to find her mother standing on the porch, holding a large cardboard box in her arms. "Mom," she said. "I wasn't expecting you."

"I just have a minute. I'm off to Joey and Cybel's." She came into the living room and put the box on the floor just inside the front door. "Keep that off your nice furniture. I dusted it off, but the grime is stuck there."

"What is it?" Delphine asked.

"Last night," Patrice said, "I couldn't sleep at all. I just had to do something. Nervous energy, I suppose. So I went up to the attic to do some sorting and came across this old box. It's yours. I thought you might want to look through it."

"Oh," Delphine said. "Thanks."

"Let me know if there's anything in there we can sell at the church fair. Well, I have to run. Come by for dinner if you want, about six. I'm making a pot roast."

When her mother had gone Delphine eyed the big cardboard box. The last thing she was in the mood for was a stroll down memory lane. That was Maggie's sort of thing. But a vague curiosity urged her to kneel down and open the flaps on top of the box. Her mother was right. The box felt soft and grimy.

One by one, Delphine removed the contents. An apron she had begun to embroider and neglected to finish. A chunky ring of pink and orange plastic, maybe Lucite, in the shape of a heart. A mood ring that had become permanently black. A naked plastic baby doll she had called Baby Mary. A threadbare Raggedy Ann doll wrapped in plastic. A furless pink rabbit she had named Bunny, just as Kitty had named her toy rabbit. An incomplete collection of tiny plastic furniture for a tin dollhouse she had shared with Jackie.

At the bottom of the box, squeezed between a yo-yo and a pair of roller skates with leather ankle straps, was what looked like a jumble of dirty string. Delphine pulled it free. It was the macramé bracelet Maggie had made for her the first summer of their friendship. Over time, the strands of cotton fiber had worn away and the bracelet had come apart. Over time, other gifts had been given and received, but this dirty, torn bracelet would always have the distinction of being the first gift of the friendship.

The dubious distinction. Delphine tossed the bracelet back into the box, wiped her hands on her jeans, and with her foot shoved the box against the wall.

59

At the same time that Delphine was rejecting a walk down memory lane, Jackie was seated in a back booth at Bessie's diner in the center of town, waiting for Maggie. Maggie had asked Jackie to meet her. She needed to talk. She hoped their conversation would be more enlightening—and less insulting—than the conversation she had had with Jemima Larkin.

Maggie arrived a moment later and walked back to the booth where Jackie was sitting. "Thanks for coming," she said, taking a seat across from her.

"Sure," Jackie said. "I don't have much time, though. Sorry."

"No, I understand."

When their coffee had been brought to the table, Maggie told Jackie about her offer to buy the Crandalls' land, about Delphine's rejection of that offer, and then about the awful fight they had had in the parking lot. Jackie wasn't quite sure how to react to it all. Maggie's offer, for instance. That was almost unbelievably generous. And a little bit crazy, as was Delphine wanting to meet in a parking lot. For a moment Jackie wondered if one or both of the women were having some sort of nervous breakdown.

"I'm sorry about the fight," she said finally. "And your offer . . ."

"It's sincere."

"I believe you."

Maggie took a sip of her coffee. "It's the same thing that happened when I offered to find Dave Junior a lawyer when he got into trouble with that other boy. Delphine rejected my help without even considering it. I told her I might be able to get someone to handle the case pro bono, but that didn't seem to matter."

Jackie shook her head. "She didn't tell me you had offered to help us with Dave Junior's trouble, either."

Maggie smiled ruefully. "She has a habit of keeping secrets. I don't know why."

"Well, thank you. Thank you for your concern about my family. I wish Delphine had told me so I could have thanked you earlier."

"Will you consider letting me buy the land?"

"It's a generous offer, Maggie," Jackie said sincerely, "and I appreciate it; I really do. But Dad's already promised to sell to the Burtons. It wouldn't be right to go back on our word now. Thank you. You're a good person."

Maggie blushed. "Delphine and I were always there for each other. Until she came back here after college."

"That was a long time ago, Maggie," Jackie pointed out. "Delphine's used to being on her own. You can't expect her to be someone she no longer is."

"Do people really change that much?" Maggie said. "Can they really become entirely different from who or what they once were? I just don't believe that. Or maybe, I can't believe that. I won't let myself."

Jackie shook her head. "I can't talk philosophy, Maggie. I just know what I see."

Maggie hesitated. *Well,* she thought, *why not? What else do I possibly have to lose? Certainly not my dignity. I seem to have given that up some time ago.* "Maybe you'll think I'm a sentimental fool," she said. "Maybe I am one." And she told Jackie about the aquamarine necklace.

"So, it's in my hotel room right now," she finished. "Hidden away in the lining of the drapes. It's something my father taught me, how to hide valuables when traveling if there isn't a safe in the room."

"Wow," Jackie said. She was touched by Maggie's keeping the necklace for all these years. But she was also worried about the obvious depth of Maggie's loneliness and what Jackie saw as desperation. She thought now about Jemima's question: What did Maggie want from Delphine? It seemed as if Maggie had placed all of her hope for happiness, love, and emotional fulfillment in Delphine's hands. Jackie did not believe that was a burden her sister could, or wanted to, handle.

"I wish," she said now, "that I could tell you that everything will be all right between you and my sister. But I can't guarantee anything, Maggie. Delphine—well, lately, she's been . . . Your coming back here has shaken her up, I think. I don't know if that's good or bad or something in between. And I'm not saying that anything is your fault. Just that I can't speak for Delphine. I'm sorry."

"I know." Maggie reached for her bag. She had taken up enough of Jackie's time. "Thank you for listening to me, Jackie," she said. "I appreciate it."

60

At about ten o'clock on Thursday morning, Delphine opened the front door to find Harry standing on her porch.

"I thought you were working today," she said. It wasn't the nicest of greetings, but she was startled by his unexpected presence.

"I switched a shift with Buck," Harry said. "I need to talk to you."

Delphine stepped back and Harry followed her into the house. "Okay," she said. "But I have to get back to the farm soon. I only came home to get some papers I'd forgotten this morning."

"I know. I went to the farm first. Your sister told me where to find you."

Delphine gestured toward the kitchen. "Do you want some coffee?"

Harry shook his head. He remained standing, hands shoved into the front pockets of his jeans. From the couch, Melchior watched, eyes narrowed. A sliver of fear ran down Delphine's spine.

"Why didn't you tell me about this Boston trip?" Harry demanded.

Delphine's heart began to pound. "I'm sorry," she said. "I meant to. I guess I just . . ." But she didn't know what else to say.

"I don't understand, Delphine. How was I supposed to find out? When I showed up at your house for dinner and found that you were gone? Do you have so little respect for me that you were going to leave town without telling me?"

Harry was right. Her behavior had been appalling. She had shared a bed and, to a large extent, a life with this man for ten years and she had been prepared to skip town—albeit for only a night—without a word of warning or explanation.

"I'm sorry," she said again. "I am. I was wrong. I don't know what I was thinking."

Harry laughed bitterly. "I know what you were thinking. That good old Harry doesn't have any feelings. That he wouldn't worry, that he wouldn't try in every way he could to find you. Damn, Delphine."

"Really, Harry, I'm sorry."

Harry sighed and took his hands from his pockets. "I don't know what to say, Del. I don't know if I can accept your apology."

"I'm sorry," she said again. "It's just that . . . Lately, I don't know . . . Lately, I feel so angry with you. Angry with myself, too, I guess. I just wanted to be . . . away."

"Angry at me?" Harry seemed truly puzzled. "What have I ever done to hurt you? I've been honest about my marriage since day one. I've never lied to you. I've never cheated on you. How have I hurt you?"

Delphine lowered her eyes for a moment. Maybe Harry was, indeed, blameless. Maybe she was the one who had been hurting Delphine Crandall all these years.

"I know you're a good man," she said, looking back to him. "I know I should respect your devotion to your wife, and I do, really, but what do I get out of all this? A friend, yes, a dinner companion, even a lover, but . . . It's not enough. I'm just not . . . happy."

Harry threw his hands into the air in frustration. "God,

Del, why didn't you ever tell me you're not happy? Am I supposed to just guess what you're feeling? I'm not a mind reader, you know."

"If I had told you, what would you have done about it?" she challenged.

"Whatever I could do."

"Which doesn't include marrying me."

Harry paused before asking, "Is that what you really want, Del? To be married to me?"

Delphine rubbed her forehead. "Honestly," she said after a moment, "I don't know what I want, Harry. Not anymore, anyway."

Harry went to the front window and stood with his back to Delphine. "It's that friend of yours, that Maggie somebody or other. Ever since she's come to town you've been different. Discontent, touchy."

"This has nothing to do with Maggie," Delphine said firmly. Though, of course, in some way it had everything to do with Maggie, and she knew it.

"I don't believe that." Harry turned back around to face her. His expression was hard. "I think you two have something in your past that's, I don't know, not right. It's like you've got your own secret club, just the two of you. I don't know who you are anymore, Delphine."

I don't know who I am anymore, either, she answered silently. She had a powerful urge at that moment to tell Harry that she had once been engaged to the famous journalist and political commentator Robert Evans. That who she once had been was Robert Evans's love. But she said nothing.

Harry sighed. "I'm leaving," he said. "Call me when you've figured yourself out."

Harry slammed the door behind him. Melchior hissed. Delphine walked into the kitchen. She didn't know why. She didn't blame Harry for being angry. She was angry, too. She was also scared.

She didn't like confrontation and yet in the past few weeks her life had been riddled with confrontation. She didn't like change and yet in the past few weeks her life had been rattled and bruised by change.

She looked at Kitty's noodle picture, taped to the front of the fridge. Suddenly, she felt overcome with exhaustion. *Life,* she thought, *is so stupidly unfair.*

61

There was another knock on the front door. Delphine shot to wakefulness. When Harry had gone she had taken some ibuprofen and lain down on the couch, Melchior pressed against her legs. Within minutes she was asleep. Now she checked her watch. *Damn.* She'd been asleep for almost an hour. She had to get back to work.

She struggled upright, annoying Melchior, and walked to the door. She opened it to find Maggie standing there.

"Hi," Maggie said.

Delphine sighed. First her mother, then Harry, and now Maggie. Three unadvertised visits in the space of two days. It pissed her off. She was losing control of the life she had so carefully constructed. "What are you doing here?" she said.

"I wanted to see how you were coping," Maggie said. *And I'm a brave and sometimes foolish person.* "I went out to the farm first. Jackie told me you had gone home to get something."

"I'm fine," Delphine said shortly. "I'm grabbing a cup of coffee and going back to the farm."

"Could I have a cup, too?"

Delphine shrugged and turned toward the kitchen. Maggie followed her inside the house and shut the door behind her.

"How is Kitty?" Maggie asked on the way to the kitchen.

"Fine. As good as she can be."

Delphine poured the rest of the morning's coffee into a saucepan and put it on the stove to heat.

Maggie took a seat at the kitchen table while Delphine fetched cups. "I talked to Gregory," she said. "He's still in Chicago. Of course, he feels terrible about Kitty. I tried to tell him how I was feeling about . . . Well, about everything that's been going on between you and me. But he didn't understand at all. Somehow he managed to make it all about himself. I mean—"

Delphine slammed a cup onto the table. "Stop it!" she cried. "I'm tired of hearing about your petty problems! All those years and you never even sent a postcard from your fancy vacations, never even called to see how I was doing, and now when you finally have a problem—you're bored in your marriage! Poor you!—you come running for my help. What in God's name do you want from me? What?"

Maggie was stunned. For a moment she felt physically afraid. She took a deep, steady breath and then, ignoring the distortions in Delphine's accusations, she said calmly and quietly, "I want you to be my friend."

There followed an awkward silence. Maggie looked down at her hands. Delphine rubbed her temples and then turned off the flame under the bubbling coffee.

"Don't you have any other friends?" she asked finally, tiredly.

"Not like you."

Delphine almost laughed. "I think you misjudged us, Maggie. I think you thought we were something we were not."

"No," Maggie insisted, looking back up at Delphine. "I haven't misjudged us."

"I can't be who you need me to be. Your sister, your twin, something more, a soul mate. I'm not who you remember. I'm not who you think I am."

Maggie rose to her feet. "Then, who are you? Tell me."

Delphine stepped away. "I wish you had never come here. Why don't you go back to where you belong?"

"I'm not sure I know where that is anymore."

"I'm sorry for you," Delphine said, "I really am. But I can't help you."

"No," Maggie said, and the tone of her voice was different now. Cold. "Of course not. No one can help you, either. Certainly I can't. Good-bye, Delphine. I won't bother you again."

Maggie walked quickly through to the front door and closed it firmly behind her. Delphine stood rigidly still for a full minute and then, as if compelled by a force she could not name or control, she ran into the living room and over to the old cardboard box her mother had found in her attic. She knelt beside it and rummaged through the detritus of her childhood until her hand closed on the dirty, frayed macramé bracelet Maggie had given her all those years before. She would cut it to shreds; she would stuff it in the garbage. She would burn it out behind the house; she would tear it to pieces.

But the moment she saw the bracelet clutched in her hand, she fell from her knees to the floor, flooded with a sense memory of love, literally knocked over by a wave of emotion. Later, she would recall this moment as one of supreme catharsis, similar in a way to the cathartic moment she had experienced at the protest rally all those years earlier. But at the time, she simply thought she might die.

Sitting on the floor of the living room, clutching the old gathering of string, Delphine cried, deep, painful sobs. She cried for the sake of the love she once bore her friend. It had been a real, living thing, their friendship, and she had in effect murdered it. They had grown together from childhood to womanhood and all that life together had to count for something in the present. At the very least, the reality of the friendship deserved respect.

She cried, desperately hoping that Maggie would forgive her. She cried for Kitty, for her own blighted maternal life, for the child she had never been wise enough to have. She cried for Harry and for Ellen, for the marriage that had been stolen from them, and she cried for his devotion to what was only a memory.

And she cried for her own broken heart. She had never allowed herself to properly grieve for Robert and the love they had shared. She had loved him so much, with such an intensity and such a joy. It had been a once-in-a-lifetime love that she had killed before its time. The realization of such accumulated loss threatened to overwhelm her. She lay down on the floor now and curled into a ball. She felt a warm pressure against her back and realized that Melchior had come to sit with her. She stayed on the floor for a long, long time.

62

1987

"Delphine."

Delphine turned. She had been hoping to leave the reception unnoticed. It didn't matter that she say good-bye to the bride. Well, maybe it did, but she was desperate to avoid an emotional scene, for her sake as well as for Maggie's.

Maggie stood there, magnificent in a confection of a pure white dress, a veil falling to her waist. In each ear a diamond sparkled. She was wearing more makeup than she usually wore, which somehow emphasized rather than disguised her natural beauty. Delphine had never seen Maggie look like this, so perfect, not even at parties. She felt as if she were looking at a character from a book, a princess about to ride off into the sunset on a white stallion. Self-consciously she fingered a button on the faux satin jacket she had borrowed from a neighbor back home. *I'll never be like Maggie,* she thought, but what exactly that meant she didn't know.

"I haven't had a moment to say hello," Maggie said. "The whole day has been a whirlwind. The whole week, actually."

"Being a bride is a busy job."

Maggie laughed a little. "I know. My feet are killing me. Are you having a good time?"

"Oh, yes. The food was very good."

"Yes. My mother and I went to five tastings before we finally chose the caterer."

There was an awkward pause. Delphine fought the temptation to look at her watch. Maggie twisted her wedding rings with her thumb.

"Gregory seems very nice," Delphine blurted.

Maggie laughed. "Well, I wouldn't be marrying him if he weren't!"

"Of course. He seems very devoted." Maybe she had meant to say "attentive." She had never met Gregory before today. How could she really know anything about him?

"He is," Maggie said. "He's a very loyal person. It was one of the things that made me like him so much."

Delphine blushed. She was all too aware that she had, in a way, been disloyal to Maggie. But she had abandoned Maggie to save her own life. And that was excusable. It had to be.

"It was a beautiful ceremony," she said then.

"Thanks. I wanted something traditional. And my parents were adamant about nothing weird. Since they paid for everything I couldn't really argue."

Delphine smiled a bit. Jackie had paid for her own wedding. So had Joey. Her mother had worn a friend's dress to her own wedding. She had returned the dress, freshly laundered and pressed, the next day.

"The band's rendition of 'With or Without You' was interesting."

Maggie smiled. "My parents had to make some small concession to me. At least I didn't choose it as my wedding song. My father strongly prefers Johnny Mathis to U2."

There was a moment of silence. Neither woman seemed to know what to say. Delphine focused on the standing ashtray outside the door to the ballroom. Maggie fiddled with her rings again. Finally, Delphine spoke. "Well, I really do have to be leaving."

"So soon?" Maggie said. "I mean, I haven't seen you in

three years. And we haven't even cut the cake. And I still have to throw my bouquet."

"Yeah. Sorry. It's a long drive back. And my father needs me to work the diner first thing in the morning. We open at five."

Maggie seemed about to further protest Delphine's leaving, but then all she said was, "Okay. Sure. Drive safely."

"I will."

"Delphine? Thank you for coming."

"Sure." Delphine raised her hand in a wave and before Maggie could attempt a hug she turned and walked quickly toward the hotel's grand entrance hall.

Maggie watched her go. She thought of the aquamarine necklace in its pale blue velvet case, tucked into a dresser drawer in the bridal suite. It should have been Delphine's. It would have been if . . .

"Maggie! I've been looking all over for you." It was her mother, resplendent in a sea foam green chiffon gown. "It's time to cut the cake!"

Maggie wiped a tear from the corner of her eye. Dorothy sighed mightily.

"Oh, look, now you've smudged your mascara. Come to the ladies' room and we'll fix it. What are you crying about anyway? This is the happiest day of your life."

If it is, Maggie thought, allowing herself to be steered in the direction of the ladies' room, *then why do I feel so miserable?*

63

It was Friday afternoon, around three o'clock. Delphine knocked on the door of room number 22. Ordinarily, the policy at the hotel was to not let visitors up to the rooms, but the staff at the front desk of Gorges Grant knew Delphine and waved her on.

"Yes?" came a voice from within the room.

Delphine cleared her throat. "It's Delphine."

A long moment later the door opened. Maggie gestured for her to come inside. A suitcase was open on the king-sized bed, half filled with lingerie and shoes in plastic cases. A bulging garment bag hung on the inside of the open closet door. Maggie had been packing to leave Ogunquit. Delphine wondered if she had been planning to tell her.

"I'm surprised to see you here," Maggie said, careful to keep her tone neutral and even. "I thought you had no use for me."

Delphine nodded. "I know. I know. Look, Maggie . . ." Suddenly, her head began to buzz and her eyesight to dim. "I . . ."

Maggie rushed forward just as Delphine began to sway. "Are you okay? Here, sit. Let me get you some water."

Maggie helped her into a large armchair. Delphine felt too weak to resist Maggie's ministrations. She gulped the water Maggie brought from the bathroom and tried to breathe carefully. "I'm sorry. I haven't really been eating since . . ."

"It's okay; just breathe. And when you get home, have some protein. Scramble some eggs. Don't be stupid."

Delphine looked up imploringly. "I'm so sorry, Maggie," she said. "I'm so sorry for everything. Can you ever forgive me?"

Maggie didn't smile when she spoke, and her tone was matter-of-fact. "Yes," she said. "I forgive you."

"So easily?"

"I didn't say it's easy. But my acceptance of your apology is sincere."

Delphine nodded. "Thank you. I don't know if I deserve your friendship anymore, but I would like to try to earn it back."

"Okay," Maggie said. She sat on the edge of the king-sized bed. "How do you suggest you go about that?"

Delphine sighed. "By telling the truth."

"Always a good place to start."

Delphine paused for another moment before saying, "There's something I should have told you a long time ago. Do you remember the protest rally Robert mounted in our senior year? The one against nuclear weapon proliferation, the one that threatened to get out of control?"

"Of course," Maggie said. "He averted what could have been a disaster. As it was, only a few people were really hurt."

"I didn't have a migraine that night. I was at the rally and I ran away. I panicked and ran. It came to me like a revelation, an epiphany. I suddenly knew, standing in the middle of that crowd, that I couldn't marry Robert. I knew I belonged in a smaller, quieter world. Not in his world."

Maggie shook her head. "Okay," she said slowly. "But why did you lie to me? Why did you lie to Robert? Why?"

"I was ashamed," Delphine said, her eyes filling with tears. "I thought you both would think me a coward."

"Oh, Delphine. We loved you. We might have helped you.

We might never have lost each other, all of us, if you'd been able to be honest about what you were feeling."

"I know," Delphine said. "I know that now."

The women were quiet for some time. Finally, Maggie said, "You know, if I'd known why you'd ended things with Robert, if I'd understood, our friendship might not have withered away."

"I know," Delphine said, despair in her voice. "I know. Look." From the pocket of her work shirt she took the frayed and dirty macramé bracelet. "Do you remember this? It's the only part of our past that I have left."

Maggie reached out for the bracelet and turned it over in her hand. "You have the memories," she said with a smile.

"Not as many as you do."

"Yeah, well," Maggie said, handing the bracelet back to Delphine, "I think we've established that I might have a flair for embellishing memories. That and a well-developed case of selective memory."

"Maybe that's not such a bad thing," Delphine said. "Maggie, I'm sorry that I said those awful things to you. I don't know what was wrong with me. Well, maybe I do. I don't know, really. I just know that I'm sorry."

Maggie smiled a bit. "Me too. Maybe I should have tried harder to keep in touch with you. But after a while the continued rejection just wore me down. Look, I know life happens and people change and all. . . . But some people are meant to be together forever; I believe that. I believe that about us."

"And you came back here to make sure that we would be."

"To be honest," Maggie said, "I don't know if I had any coherent thoughts about coming back to Ogunquit. I know I wanted to find something. . . . And to escape something, even temporarily . . . Maybe it was some long-buried or -ignored instinct that made me want to seek you out. An instinct for . . . home, in a way."

"Or for security and acceptance. Not that I've shown you much acceptance these past weeks . . ."

"We've both been judgmental," Maggie said. "And maybe a bit stupid. We know that. And I think we know why, now."

"When your own life isn't great, criticize someone else's."

Maggie laughed. "God, we've been idiots. On our own and together."

"We've also been smart," Delphine said. "Let's not go crazy with the blame. I am happy with a lot of things in my life. I am proud of some of the decisions I've made. Just . . . not all of them."

"Yeah," Maggie said. "Me too. Having the kids, that was a good decision."

"And marrying Gregory?"

"Well, once it was the right decision, but maybe it's not anymore. I guess I need to get working on that before any more precious time goes by. And what about not marrying Robert?"

"Good decision," Delphine said emphatically, "one hundred percent. Getting involved with Harry, staying in a stagnant relationship for so long . . . Not so much."

"Will you leave him?"

"Probably," Delphine said. "I don't think staying on is a real choice anymore. We had a . . . a conversation. I said some things. . . ."

"Be prepared to miss him. But don't let the missing lead you back into trouble."

"I won't," Delphine agreed. "Actually, I suspect I'll get over him pretty quickly. Look, promise me you won't do anything rash, like tell Gregory you want a divorce before you really explore all the options. A marriage is a pretty big thing to toss away. And I know I have no right to be preaching to you since I never managed to get married."

"You have every right to advise me," Maggie said. "You're my friend."

"Okay, so go to therapy. Talk to him honestly. Do something. It would be a shame to lose a relationship worth keeping." Delphine smiled ruefully. "Look what happened with us."

"What almost happened, you mean. I promise to do everything I can to fix things in my marriage."

Delphine smiled a watery smile. "Pinky swear?"

"Of course. You know," Maggie said, "I've been thinking about what you said about the Boston trip not being such a good idea. And I think you were right. I think I was so insistent upon the idea of our . . . running away because I wanted to escape from my unsatisfying life into a nostalgic past that doesn't even exist, that never existed. I think I was trying to make nothing into something real. I've been guilty of magical thinking."

Delphine nodded. "And I was so afraid to 'run away' because of what might have happened after. Because all sorts of things might have started to change. I was slightly terrified, actually."

"No one really can go home again, can they?"

"Well, I did. In a lot of ways."

"Maybe you never really left home in the first place," Maggie suggested. "Maybe that's why your life has worked out as well as it has. And it has worked out well in many respects. I'm sorry I didn't understand that."

"My life is hardly perfect."

"I wonder if anyone would know if her life was perfect. I mean, maybe it's part of human nature to be discontent, to always want something else or other. Unless, of course, you're a saint or a Zen master or something."

"Perfect would be boring, I suppose," Delphine said.

Maggie laughed. "I think I'd like to try boring. I'm getting too old for drama. It's not all it's cracked up to be. Really, these past few weeks have exhausted me."

"And even the most amicable divorce is bound to bring drama."

"I get it; I get it." Maggie got up from the bed. "Look, let's go get you something to eat. You look awful, totally worn-out. You can't drive in that condition."

Delphine smiled. "You know, suddenly I'm starved."

"And I'm picking up the tab."

"And I'm too tired to argue."

64

Delphine pulled her truck into her brother's driveway late Saturday morning. Joey was at work, but Cybel was home with Kitty.

"Thanks for letting me come along," Maggie said as she climbed out of the passenger seat.

"Well, Kitty asked me about you. She wanted to know why you were staying in a hotel and not with me, since you're my friend. Like a sleepover."

"What did you tell her?"

Delphine shrugged. "Something lame. But she also wanted to know if she could meet you before you go back home."

Delphine knocked on the front door, and a moment later Cybel let them in. Delphine introduced Maggie to her sister-in-law.

"Kitty's in the living room," Cybel said. "I'm letting her watch TV as a treat. Usually, she's not allowed to watch TV during the day. But now . . ."

Maggie touched Cybel's arm. "Yes," she said gently.

Cybel smiled and wiped her eyes with the back of her hand. "I'll go get us something to drink. You can go on in."

They found Kitty sitting on the couch, eyes glued to a cartoon on the television.

"Hey," Delphine said. "What are you watching?"

"Johnny Test."

"Is it good?"

Kitty shrugged. "It's okay. I like the dog."

"I've brought my friend Maggie to meet you. Remember, you asked?"

Kitty looked away from the television and nodded. "Hi," she said.

Maggie sat on the old armchair next to the couch. "Hey, Kitty. Wow, you look just like your aunt!"

"I know. Are you Aunt Delphine's best friend in the whole world?"

Maggie hesitated a moment before saying, "I think so."

"Yes, Kitty," Delphine said, "she is."

"I have a best friend, too. Her name is Emily."

"Oh?" Maggie smiled. "What's she like?"

Kitty smiled. "Awesome. She's not here right now, though. She went to visit her cousins in Montreal."

"You must miss her."

Kitty nodded. "Mm-hm. She sent me a postcard. And I'm making her a friendship bracelet for when she gets back."

Maggie looked to Delphine, then back to Kitty. "You know, your aunt and I made each other friendship bracelets when we were kids."

"Cool." Kitty's eyes drifted back to the cartoon.

Cybel came in then with a tray of glasses. "I hope you like iced tea," she said. "It's unsweetened, but I have sugar if you'd like."

Maggie smiled. "Unsweetened is fine, thank you, Cybel."

The women chatted about nothing in particular and avoided any mention of Kitty's illness. Joey was having difficulty getting payment from a new client of his small-appliance repair business. Patrice had heard that the family who had owned and operated one of the gift shops in town was thinking of selling to someone from New York. The news had cost her a sleepless night. Dave Jr. had a new girlfriend of whom Jackie didn't approve. She must be pretty horrid, Maggie thought, if not even Jackie, who liked everyone, disliked her. That or Jackie was just being an overprotective mother, something Maggie didn't know an awful lot about.

There was a lull in the chitchat and Maggie nodded toward Kitty. Her eyes were fixated on the screen, her mouth open. "I think we've lost her," Maggie whispered.

"That's why we're usually pretty strict about letting her watch TV," Cybel explained. "They really do get addicted. That's all some of the kids at my day care talk about, their favorite TV characters. It's depressing."

Delphine and Maggie agreed. And then Delphine suggested they leave and let Cybel get back to whatever it was she had been doing when they'd arrived. "Cleaning the kitchen," she said with a tired laugh. "Joey's a great husband, but he can't clean worth a lick."

"Call me if you want some help," Delphine offered. "I'm a whiz with a mop."

They got back into the truck and drove toward Delphine's house.

"Kitty's a very nice little girl," Maggie said.

Delphine nodded. "Joey and Cybel are good parents. I wish Norman was a bit more attentive to his little sister, but the age difference makes it hard. And with his own wife pregnant . . ."

"Maybe once the baby is born things will change," Maggie suggested. "Kitty will have a new niece or nephew. Maybe she'll enjoy helping to take care of the baby."

The thought made Delphine smile. Kitty surviving to be an aunt. Maybe it was a long shot, but she hoped not. She so hoped not.

"You know," Maggie was saying now, "for a long time I thought I must have done something wrong or hurtful to you. And that was the reason why you didn't pursue our friendship after you came back here. But it wasn't about me at all, was it?"

"No," Delphine replied promptly. But then she reconsidered. "Actually, yes. It was about you in the sense that you had come to represent for me a life I just couldn't live. I guess in a way it was painful to be around you. That sounds horrible, I know. Even when you came back, this summer, at first I didn't want you to be here. I was afraid of—of having to remember everything. Afraid that maybe I had made the wrong choice after all, all those years ago, and that seeing you would make me realize it."

"I had no idea my coming here this summer would be so monumental for you," Maggie admitted. "And so monumental for me, too. I probably should have." Maggie paused and then said, "Be honest with me, okay? After college, when you came back to Ogunquit, did you care at all about how I might be feeling? Did you ever think that I might be hurt by your walking away?"

Delphine sighed. "Honestly," she said, "no. Or not much. I thought you were so strong, far stronger than me. I didn't think you would suffer just because I moved away."

"You more than just moved away. It felt like you were abandoning me, and our friendship. I felt . . . devastated."

"I never really wanted the friendship to end," Delphine insisted. "That wasn't my goal."

"Then why did you shut me out?" Maggie asked. "I'm not angry, really, not anymore. I just want to understand."

"I was thinking only of what I needed to do to get myself away from—from everything, without losing courage. I knew I had made the right decision in coming back to Ogunquit. I knew it. But it was hard. Sometimes, it was very hard."

Maggie shook her head. "I wish I had known even that. It would have helped me to cope."

"I was being selfish."

"Yes. But sometimes a person needs to be selfish. I know that now, but back then I didn't quite understand it."

Delphine pulled into her driveway and parked. "I have some wine," she said when they had gone inside. "I know it's good because it's the same as what you brought that time, the sauvignon blanc. I made a mental note."

"Yes, please," Maggie said. "A glass of wine would be perfect right now."

"We can sit on the porch if you'd like," Delphine said, but Maggie had already gone back outside and settled in one of the wicker chairs. Delphine fetched the wine and glasses and returned a few minutes later. Melchior watched them through the window from his perch on the back of the couch.

Delphine opened the wine, poured them each a glass, and settled into her own chair with a sigh.

"Okay?" Maggie asked.

"Yeah. Just . . . tired."

"You have reason to be."

"Yes. You know, since my—well, my breakdown on the living room floor the other day, I've been thinking about friendships. Friendships are habits, aren't they? At least, they become habits. And habits aren't neutral; they're either good or bad. I believe that our habit, this friendship, is a good habit. I didn't always understand that."

"Our friendship is a habit of affection. A habit of love."

"Yes. And no one chooses to break a habit of affection, do they? It sometimes just happens, for any variety of reasons, but a person doesn't just say, 'Hey, I think I'll not love this person anymore.' So I guess what I'm saying is that maybe all those years when we were out of touch—my fault, I know—I was still really your friend. Maybe the friendship wasn't dead, it was just . . . dormant. Maybe the love was still there, just . . . sleeping."

Maggie smiled and took a sip of her wine. "You think too much and I don't think enough."

Delphine smiled back. "Do we balance each other out?"

"I think that's yet to be seen."

They sat in silence for a while. The air was clear, the humidity low. A hummingbird was feasting at the butterfly bush. Maggie thought she heard the lapping of waves in the distance but realized she might just be imagining that.

"I've also been thinking," Delphine said after some time, "about what happened to me. Or what I let happen to me when I came back home. I realize now that as time went on I seemed to matter less for myself than I once had. What I wanted, the things I didn't have, the things I hadn't yet done . . . Everything grew less important. What was in front of me—duties to my family, the demands of daily life—all of that stuff seemed to step forward to obscure my view of myself somehow. Delphine Crandall got increasingly less bright and insistent until she was only a grey, shadowy person. I thought that meant I had grown up. Now, I'm not so sure."

"Yes," Maggie said carefully. "It can be hard to pay proper attention to yourself, to value yourself, when other people need and rely on you."

"I became the person everyone needs. Sometimes, that's not such a great person to be."

"I don't think I've ever really been that person. I've never had to sacrifice my selfhood for anyone. Oh, maybe to some extent when the children were small. But not now, not any longer. And Gregory . . . Well, I don't think that Gregory needs me, either. I'm not sure he ever has, aside from being someone he could have kids with, someone he could buy a big house with, someone he could travel with. I could probably be substituted with one of a thousand other women!"

"Please, Maggie," Delphine said gently. "I don't think you should assume that Gregory doesn't love you for who you are as an individual. I don't think you should speak for him. Ask him what he feels."

"I suppose you're right. But I think I might be afraid to hear what he has to say."

Delphine smiled. "That is always a problem with communication, isn't it? Having to hear what the other person has to say."

"Oh, yes," Maggie agreed. "So, are you thinking that you might want to start paying some attention to yourself? Making sure that some of Delphine Crandall's needs are finally met?"

"Yes," Delphine said after a moment. "I think so. I think that maybe I went too far in the direction of service. I think that I want to do more with my knitting. I think that I do good work and I want to share that with more people. I do want to travel a bit, though honestly, I don't even know where! And the whole thing with Harry . . ."

"The Harry Situation."

"Yeah. I know now for sure that it's not right, not fair to me."

"Good for you. It'll be hard—change always is—but I believe in you, Delphine. I always have." Maggie paused for a moment. "Look," she said then. "I know you don't like it when I try to give you things."

Delphine smiled. "If by 'things' you mean money, well, yeah. But that's my issue. I do appreciate the good motives behind your offers. I do now, anyway."

"Yes, well." Maggie put down her wineglass and took a rectangular pale blue velvet box out of her bag. She handed it to Delphine.

"What's this?" Delphine asked.

"Open it."

Delphine lifted the cover of the hinged velvet box to reveal the aquamarine necklace. "It's beautiful," she said, looking back to Maggie. "But I don't understand."

"It's your birthstone. Aquamarine."

"But it's not my birthday."

Maggie took a deep breath. And then she told Delphine about the necklace. She apologized for not having asked Delphine to stand up for her at her wedding. She apologized for not having given her the necklace all those years ago.

"You've been carrying this around for twenty-four years?" Delphine asked when Maggie had finished.

"Well, technically it's been in the back of my lingerie drawer."

"That's why the box smells like perfume."

"Chanel, actually."

Delphine looked down again at the necklace and then smiled. "It doesn't exactly go with my T-shirt and jeans."

"Pooh. Here, let me put it on for you." Maggie got up and fastened the necklace around Delphine's neck. She fished a compact mirror out of her bag. "Here. Take a look."

Delphine peered at her reflection in the compact mirror and smiled again. "It's perfect," she said. "I don't have anything else like it."

"So," Maggie said, "you're not refusing this gift?"

"No." Delphine reached for her friend's hand. "I'm accepting it. I can't fight you anymore, Maggie. I don't want to. Thank you. Thank you for everything."

Maggie squeezed Delphine's hand. "You're very welcome," she said.

65

"You promise to be in touch?"

The two women were sitting on Delphine's front porch again. It was about ten on a Sunday morning. The air was fresh, a bit cool, hinting of autumn. Melchior was inside, enjoying a nap. Eating breakfast had really taken it out of him.

Maggie smiled. "I promise. As soon as I get home I'll send you an e-mail."

"Pinky swear?"

"Pinky swear."

"So," Delphine asked, "what are you going to do now?"

"I still have some vacation time," Maggie said. "I'm going to go pay my mother a visit. It's brutal down in Florida at this time of the year, but . . . Well, I'll survive."

"Stay inside. Keep the air-conditioning up high."

"Oh, I will."

"You know, Maggie," Delphine said suddenly, "you're a lot braver than I am."

"Oh, I don't think I'm very brave at all."

"You take chances. You always have. You took a chance in coming here this summer."

Maggie shrugged. "Well, I think you're just as brave as I am, Delphine, if not more so. How can I say this? I think it can be much harder to choose to value what you have than to pursue what you don't have, just because it's out there. Does that make sense?"

Delphine laughed. "Maybe."

"And you'll keep me posted about Kitty's progress?"

"Here's hoping there is progress."

"Hey," Maggie scolded, "you have to stay positive about this, for her sake if not for your own. No, wait, definitely for your own sake. You need to take better care of yourself, Delphine."

"It will take some learning."

"You're smart," Maggie said. "You can learn if you want to. Oh, on another topic entirely, will you recommend a book for me to read? I've so neglected my reading these past few years. I don't even know where to begin."

"Just one book? I could recommend a reading program for the rest of your life. Why don't I send you an e-mail with some ideas? Do you want to give me some parameters?"

"Why don't you choose for me," Maggie suggested. "I need to break out of this uncomfortable comfort zone I've been in for way too long."

"All right. And please say hello to Gregory for me. Though he doesn't really know me."

"He'll get to know you through me. He already knows you're important."

"Do you think he'll like me?" Delphine asked. "I am pretty rough around the edges these days."

Maggie smiled. "He'll love you. Gregory's a pretty easygoing guy when he's not wearing his lawyer's hat. Which isn't all that often, but maybe we can work on that. Well," she said, getting up from her chair, "I'd better get on the road."

Together they walked to Maggie's car. Instinctively they hugged, and it felt absolutely right.

"Bye, Delphine," Maggie said, slipping behind the wheel.

"Drive carefully," Delphine said.

Delphine watched and waved until Maggie's Lexus was out of sight. "I miss you already," she said to the air.

Epilogue

A friend is one to whom one can pour out all the contents of one's heart, chaff and grain together, knowing that the gentlest hands will take and sift it, keeping what is worth keeping, and, with the breath of kindness, blow the rest away.

—Arabian proverb

One year later . . .

It was early evening, around five o'clock on a Wednesday. Delphine was in her workroom. She had finished at the farm around three and come home to work on a project, a fairly elaborate hat, scarf, and glove set for a client. Around her neck she wore the aquamarine necklace Maggie had given her. She wore it all the time, only taking it off when she showered. Neither of her parents had asked where she had gotten the necklace. Delphine wasn't really sure they had even noticed it. Jackie, of course, knew the whole story. Jemima eyed it suspiciously. She knew it certainly hadn't come from Harry, but she refused to ask about it.

Waah. Melchior, who had been sitting at Delphine's feet, stood and stretched. He had settled at twenty-two pounds and was as imperious and demanding as ever. Delphine didn't know what she would do without him. " 'Waah' to you, too," she said. Melchior rewound himself and plopped back onto the floor.

Delphine went back to knitting. It had been almost exactly a year since Maggie had gone home to Massachusetts after her weeks in Ogunquit. Not long after that, Delphine had been browsing the Internet and had come across a quote from Albert Schweitzer. "At times," he said, "our own light goes out and is rekindled by a spark from another person. Each of us has cause to think with deep gratitude of those who have lighted the flame within us."

And that's what Maggie had done. She had rekindled Delphine's inner spirit when it had been nothing but a pile of cold, stubborn ash. If at times it had seemed an impossible task, Maggie had nevertheless persevered. Maybe she had revived Delphine's spirit for selfish reasons—she wanted, she needed, her friendship. It didn't matter. Either way, Delphine felt alive again for the first time in a very long time.

And maybe, just maybe, she had done the same for Maggie. At least, Maggie was admittedly happier than she had been last summer. Through therapy and hard work she and Gregory were rejuvenating their marriage. She told Delphine she had learned that if she felt disconnected from others in her life, it was her responsibility to remedy that, and walking away from the most solid relationship in her life, her marriage, was not the way to make repairs. At least, it wasn't the way in her case. She and Gregory were taking cooking classes together. He had been able to cut down on his business travel. If the success of their reunion seemed a bit of a miracle, then so be it. "I believed in miracles when I was a kid," Maggie told Delphine. "Why not now as an adult?"

They had even adopted a rescue dog, a small mutt who had been found wandering the streets of Roxbury. Somehow, Maggie had overcome her fear of animals, at least, of animals that could fit in the palm of your hand. When Delphine first saw a picture of Barney on Maggie's Facebook page she laughed out loud. Melchior was easily three times his size. Gregory, it turned out, was even more devoted to little Barney than his wife was. If Barney was a late-in-life substitution for the human children who were now largely grown, that was fine, too.

As for her relationship with those two largely grown children, Maggie had admitted that she didn't feel very optimistic about the possibility of becoming best friends with her daughters. But only time would tell. She had twice been to visit her mother since her summer in Ogunquit. She was still church-surfing but reported that she was narrowing in on a particular community. She continued to read the books that Delphine recommended and they discussed the more controversial ones via e-mail or phone. Sharing books was one way toward reestablishing a bond that worked for their present and that they hoped would sustain them in their future. And both Delphine and Maggie wanted a future together.

But if Delphine and Maggie were meant to be together forever, Delphine and Harry were not. Shortly after Maggie had left Ogunquit, Delphine and Harry had officially ended their long relationship. Harry had seemed pretty relieved to be let go. No man wanted to be with a woman who found him disappointing. Harry's ego had been at stake. Still, Delphine bet he missed her cooking.

She had been surprised at how easy it was to get on with her life. It was almost as if Harry had never really made an impression on her. That was scary—to realize that for ten years you had been with a person you could so easily live without. Both Harry and Delphine had been responsible for the faulty state of their union. She knew that even if he didn't. They had each lacked the ability to communicate and to commit. Convenience was not the same as intimacy, though it often pretended that it was. She had learned that the hard way.

Most important, she had begun weekly visits to a therapist in Portsmouth. She wanted to explore and hopefully come to understand what might have become a habit of passivity and resignation. She wanted certain things about her life to be different. She wanted to be happy. At first, she had told no one about seeing the therapist. After several sessions, she'd worked up the nerve to tell her sister, who, predictably, was thoroughly supportive, and then Maggie, who was both supportive and impressed. Delphine was working toward someday telling her parents and the rest of the Crandall family. She had kept enough secrets in her life. Still, she thought that she might never tell Jemima. There were some people who saw therapy for emotional or psychological issues as a sign of moral weakness. Delphine suspected that Jemima was one of those people, but maybe she was doing her friend a disservice. The decision to tell or not to tell could wait until she felt stronger, until she learned not to care so much about what other people thought of her.

Thus far, things had been going well, but progress was slow. She was determined to stick it out, though, because the alternative—the sort of half -life she had been leading—was unacceptable. Almost too late she had realized that the two people in her life to whom she had been most drawn—Maggie Weldon and Robert Evans—were people "from away." Both were distinctly different from her in so many ways, but both spoke to an essential part of her. Both Maggie and Robert had given her love. They had opened vistas for her, pointed out possibilities. Almost too late she realized that she needed—and wanted—something outside of the comforts and restrictions, beyond the joys and the limitations, of home, even if the form that took was a strong relationship with an "other."

As for a romantic relationship, well, that would have to wait until Delphine got right with herself. And when she did, she was not going to sell herself short. She would rather live alone forever than be allied with someone who couldn't or wouldn't give her his loyalty. And next time, she was going to rely on Melchior's opinion, as well. If he gave the guy a malevolent yellow-eyed stare, the guy was history.

Delphine put down the half-finished glove she was working on and stretched. She then turned to her laptop and opened her e-mail. Two new orders had come in since the morning. "Yikes," she said to Melchior. "Mommy's going to be busy." He opened one eye, and then closed it again.

With Maggie's help Delphine had expanded her knitwear business. The first step had been admitting that it was an actual business and not only a hobby. She now advertised in Ogunquit and the neighboring towns and had a Facebook page and a designated e-mail address for communicating with customers. At first, she had been uncomfortable marketing her work, but once she got into the groove she found the habit of self-promotion less unappetizing than she had feared. Plus, there was great satisfaction in making a sale and satisfying a customer. Okay, there was that old desire to serve, but that was fine. She didn't ever want to become a selfish person. She just wanted to be someone who knew how to take care of her own basic emotional needs.

Gradually, she was cutting back on her hours at the farm. Lori was increasingly showing an interest in the behind-the-scenes working of the family business. But Delphine still hoped that her niece would opt for college before settling down. Delphine was doing what she could to encourage Lori's studies, and Jackie, too, was urging her daughter to set her goals if not higher, then perhaps wider or farther afield than her mother and her aunt had done. Lori had said something about getting a degree in agricultural studies or maybe a degree in veterinary medicine.

Dave Jr. had graduated from high school that spring and was now working with his cousin Norman for Dave Sr.'s small contracting business. He still helped out at the farm on weekends. Norman's wife had had the baby, a boy they named Thomas. Kitty was fascinated by the little guy and loved to play with him, though for health reasons her access to Thomas was sometimes restricted.

The good news was that Kitty had responded remarkably well to the first and then to the second round of chemotherapy prescribed for her ALL. She was now undergoing maintenance therapy that, the Crandalls were told, might last for two or three years. She was not entirely out of the woods but getting better all the time. Her illness—and Maggie's reappearance in Delphine's life—had taught her that there were experiences she simply could not and should not try to handle on her own. She was learning to allow herself to be vulnerable. She was learning that "vulnerable" didn't have to mean "weak."

Delphine picked up her needles again. She was also learning to say no to clients with unreal expectations or repeat clients who were ridiculously late with payment. That newfound toughness she had to attribute just a little bit to Jemima's influence. She had been known to scold unpleasant customers at the restaurant. Because she was the best waitress on staff, her boss took her righteous indignation in stride.

Jemima's wandering son, Kurt, had returned for an unspecified amount of time, and while she grumbled about having another mouth to feed and another messy person to pick up after, she was, in reality, very happy to have her oldest child back home, even if it was only for an undetermined amount of time. There had been a subtle shift in Delphine's relationship with Jemima since Maggie's visit the year earlier. A slight degree of formality had crept into their friendship. Jemima stopped by unannounced less often and waited for Jim or one of her children to mow the lawn rather than ask Delphine to do it. And she never mentioned Maggie, though she knew, through Jackie, that Delphine was regularly in touch with her. Delphine wasn't really bothered by this new dynamic. She was still a person who focused on the present rather than the past, even if she was learning that the past couldn't and probably shouldn't be ignored.

The Burton brothers had begun work on their new home on what had been the Crandalls' ancient plot. Piers had shown the architects' design to Delphine when she had last visited the shop to say hello. The house would be magnificent but no McMansion. The Burtons had been careful to respect not only the land itself but also the history and the spirit of Ogunquit. The house would be a welcome addition to both the landscape and the town. The fact that the land was no longer a part of the Crandall legacy hurt; Delphine couldn't deny that. But at least the land—and the old lilac bush—was in good hands, and that counted for something.

Delphine occasionally wondered if Robert would have found Ogunquit as provincial and uninteresting all those years go if he had met residents like the Burtons, and Nancy and Glenda, and Bobby Taylor and the McQueens and not just her own family. She couldn't be certain.

What was certain was that Robert Evans's glorious career had become even more glorious since his capturing yet another international humanitarian prize back in March. There were rumors online of an HBO movie to be made about his work in the Middle East. He was spotted at the Academy Awards escorting a very young woman in a very tight dress. His hair was still suspiciously without a trace of grey. Watching him pose and smile for the cameras, Delphine was more certain than ever that she had been right to leave Robert Evans. They never would have survived as a couple. They were better off without each other, Robert working for change in his wide world and Delphine working for the good in her more proscribed world. Still, a little part of her would always love him, even if only in memory. She would always wonder if a little part of him still loved her. But she would not contact him. That, she felt, would be foolish. It would serve no purpose. She had, however, taken his books from behind the Dickens volumes and put them on a shelf as she would any other book. There was nothing to hide; there had never been anything to hide.

Thinking of couples, Delphine thought now of poor Ellen, Harry's wife. She continued to live her sadly diminished life, and as far as Delphine knew, Harry continued his weekly visits to her. Word around town was that he had recently begun to date another woman, a single mother in her late thirties. Delphine wished the new girlfriend well. She assumed the woman was a good cook. Delphine hadn't run into Harry since this latest development in his romantic life and wondered if he would mention the new girlfriend when she did run into him. She might have to kick him in the shin with her dirty old work boot if he did.

Delphine's eye caught a stack of papers on the worktable, orders already placed for Christmas gifts. A day or two after Christmas this year she would be leaving Ogunquit for her second holiday visit to Maggie's home in Lexington. The two days she had spent with the Weldon Wilkes family the year before had been wonderful. Gregory was a kind and welcoming host. Kim and Caitlin were home for a month between semesters and Delphine had felt deeply touched by the very fact of these pleasant and intelligent young women. Maggie had done something extraordinary; she had given birth to new life and had raised two fine human beings. Spending time with the family, Delphine had felt keenly her own regrets about not having a child—regrets she had admitted to her therapist—but she hadn't let those regrets ruin her visit. Though eager to see Melchior and Kitty and to get back to work, she had also been a bit sorry to leave Lexington.

They had seen each other again in May, when Maggie had driven up to Ogunquit for four days. She stayed with Delphine, and though Delphine had offered her use of her bedroom, Maggie had insisted she was fine sleeping on the living room couch. On the second morning Maggie awoke to find Melchior crouched on the back of the couch just above her head, staring intently at her. Her first instinct was to throw off the blankets and run from the room. But then she realized that he was purring. Melchior wasn't intending to eat her face. He was saying, *You're okay. I accept you.* She was still a bit freaked out by him but no longer actually afraid.

Maggie and Delphine had kept mostly to themselves during that visit, getting together only once, briefly, with Jackie. One night they got slightly—well, maybe more than slightly—drunk on the rum punch at Barnacle Billy's. Ice-cream cones helped the sobering-up process. One day they drove to Portland to see an exhibit at the Portland Museum of Art. Afterwards, they had lunch at J's Oyster, an old dive bar and local favorite, right on the water. In the afternoon they took the ferry to Peaks Island. Whenever Delphine had to stop in at the office or the diner, Maggie shopped at the outlets in Kittery and Freeport. And they talked. Maggie told Delphine how close she had come to cheating on Gregory with the man they had met at the Old Village Inn. Delphine admitted that she had lied to Maggie all those years ago. She hadn't applied to graduate schools. Maggie had figured as much. They talked about fear and about courage. They talked about family and expectations, both real and imagined.

Now, they were planning that long-awaited trip to Boston the weekend after Labor Day. Delphine would meet Maggie at the hotel around seven o'clock Friday evening and drive back to Ogunquit on Sunday night. They would have lunch one afternoon at Union Oyster House, in memory of that long-ago weekend when Jackie had visited them during their senior year. They would visit the museums, take a walk through the Public Garden, and maybe, if there was time, go to the aquarium. Maggie had promised to forgo a visit to the mall.

If anyone asked them, both Maggie and Delphine would say that their friendship was not what it had been when they were children or even what it had been when they were young women. It was something better. It was a friendship fully chosen, something they had fought for and won, and the friendship was more appreciated now than it ever had been because each knew there was nothing accidental or circumstantial about it.

Delphine's cell phone rang. It was Maggie's special ringtone.

"It's me," Maggie said.

"I know. I just got two new orders."

"Congratulations. I picked up the tickets to a play at the ART. It's a production of *A View from the Bridge*. Sound okay?"

"Maggie, I haven't been to see a professional troupe's performance in over twenty years. We could be seeing *A Charlie Brown Christmas* and I'd be happy. What's all that noise?"

Maggie laughed. "That's Gregory, in the kitchen. He's making—I should say he's trying to make—a soufflé. We learned about soufflés in our last class."

"You're sure he doesn't mind that we're staying in a hotel and not at your house?" Delphine asked.

"Are you kidding? First, he's totally supportive of my having a good friend. And second, he gets to be alone with Barney. I totally expect Barney will be wearing a little doggie outfit when I get home, hat, booties, and all."

"I think it's adorable Gregory's so into the dog. But . . . booties? In the summer?"

"I know. I've created a monster."

There was a loud, metallic crash, followed by a louder, "Damn!"

Maggie sighed. "I'd better go and check on the chef."

"Good idea. Talk tomorrow."

"Good night, Delphine. Say hello to Melchior."

"Good night, Maggie. Love to everyone."

Delphine hung up. She looked fondly at the mass of fur at her feet. No matter how deeply asleep he was, the mere whisper of the approach of food could rouse him.

"Is it dinnertime?" she asked her sleeping cat softly.

Melchior bolted to his feet. *Waah,* he said.

Delphine laughed. "Then let's go to the kitchen."

Please turn the page for a special Q & A with Holly Chamberlin!

Q. *Summer Friends* is your ninth novel and you've also written four novellas as part of collections for Kensington. How has your writing process changed over the years?

A. Well, I wish I could say that the writing process has gotten easier, but I can't. If anything, it's more exhausting than ever because I've become more exacting with my writing. I've set higher standards; whether I've been successful in meeting those standards, only the reader can judge. One thing hasn't changed. From the beginning I've never been hesitant to delete entire chapters if necessary. I suspect the habit comes from the years I worked as an editor. If it doesn't work, toss it.

Q. What is the most difficult part of the writing process for you?

A. Without a doubt, it's plotting. A plot comes to me in painful dribs and drabs. Sometimes, only a month away from my deadline, the plot is still filling in. Oscar Wilde said something about his characters being able to do nothing but talk. Not that I'm comparing my lowly skills to Mr. Wilde's considerable ones, but my characters also seem to want only to talk, never to do. Maybe they're just lazy. Maybe I'm just lazy.

Q. Do you ever have a problem finding jumping-off ideas for the novels?

A. Ideas are easy to come by. You just need to keep your eyes and ears open. Making an idea personal and meaningful by attaching it to the life of a particular character is the challenge. My novels aren't about ideas; they're about people or characters. At least, that's what they're supposed to be about!

Q. In *Summer Friends* you present two women who were very close from childhood through college but who have been largely absent from each other's lives for over twenty years before one of them decides to seek out the other in an attempt to recapture the old relationship. Were you able to draw on your own experiences for this aspect of the story?

A. I'm afraid that the idea of two old friends reuniting after a breakup that occurred under murky circumstances hit very close to home for me and caused a lot of retroactive shame and embarrassment. There are several people I feel I've treated carelessly over time and I can find no really good reasons for my behavior. At least, from the perspective of the present I can find no good reasons for letting certain friendships drift away. That said, the particular story of Maggie and Delphine is entirely fictional. I don't write about myself or about those close to me. Though I might steal their names for characters, the resemblance ends there.

Q. In several of your novels, including *Summer Friends*, you talk about the notion of nostalgia. Why do you think nostalgia warrants discussion and exploration?

A. Anyone who attempts to deny, bury, or ignore her past is in for a rude awakening. And anyone who attempts to whitewash, sugarcoat, or actively reshape her past is also in for a tough time. The past, one's personal and family history, is a powerful thing and it's almost impossible—maybe entirely impossible—to avoid some degree of distortion or self-deception when confronting it in the present (which is today, and then will be tomorrow, and then will be the day after that, ad infinitum), but I firmly believe it's worth the effort to remain conscious while attempting to do so. So, nostalgia—yeah, it's a bad thing. But if you can scrutinize and question a happy memory and in the end still find it happy, you're lucky. Keep it.

Q. You have lived in Maine since 2003 and before that in Boston for about seven years. You're originally from New York City. I'm wondering if you personally can relate to Delphine's deep attachment to her birthplace after having left your own.

A. The answer to that is yes, I certainly can relate to Delphine's love of her hometown. I swore I would never leave New York. I couldn't at all conceive of my life lived elsewhere. But clearly, my attachment to place didn't turn out to be as strong as Delphine's, because I left New York at the age of thirty-three, albeit crying all the way to Boston. For a while the sense of loss was very hard to bear, but thirteen or so years later, happily married to the man for whom I left New York, I've finally adjusted and am glad to be living in Maine, which boasts a very proud people and has a wonderfully distinctive character. Plus, my mother now lives down the block and she's a very strong reminder of home!

Q. Above all else, what keeps you sane during the largely solitary process of conceiving and then writing a novel?

A. My cats. If each day I can squeeze in an hour in my favorite reading chair with Jack, Betty, or Cyrus on my lap, I'm okay.

A READING GROUP GUIDE

SUMMER FRIENDS

Holly Chamberlin

ABOUT THIS GUIDE

The suggested questions are included to enhance your group's reading of Holly Chamberlin's *Summer Friends*.

DISCUSSION QUESTIONS

1. When the reader first meets Delphine, she appears to lead a simpler, less fraught, and perhaps less self-focused life than Maggie, and yet before long the reader sees that in actuality Delphine is more self-conscious and more aware of and troubled by issues such as social and financial status than her old friend. Talk about the differences between the inner and outer, or social, selves of the women. How does each woman meet or defy the reader's initial expectations?

2. At several points in the novel, Maggie and Delphine talk about the expectations their parents set for them, the expectations they assumed their parents set for them, and the lingering effects of their upbringings. For example, to a large extent Maggie has repeated her mother's style of parenting with her daughters, a style she thinks of as the opposite of "helicopter parenting." To a large extent, Delphine denies her mother's somewhat stern style of parenting by "spoiling" her youngest niece. Maggie is sure that her parents are proud of her social achievements. Delphine has come to doubt that her parents have any respect for the sacrifices she's made for the family. Talk about to what extent it's possible for an adult child to truly and irrevocably liberate herself from needing or wanting a parent's love and approval.

3. At various moments throughout the novel, both Maggie and Delphine realize that since their reunion they have each been making assumptions about and even passing judgment upon the other's life, something that as children and then young adults they had never

done. At one point Delphine notes that many, if not all, children have an ability to accept—almost not even to perceive—differences that might strike an adult as formidable obstacles to a relationship. In the context of the book as well as in the context of your own lives, talk about how along with a maturing of intelligence and a ripening of rational judgment the passing of time can also bring a narrowing of creativity, imagination, and liberality and of how it can sometimes even lead to a person's making unfair, even discriminatory decisions. Can such a decay of kindness and acceptance be reversed?

4. Do you think there is any value in Delphine's "relationship of convenience" with Harry Stringfellow? If so, where does that value lie? Do you think Mr. and Mrs. Crandall's silence about the unusual relationship is a sign of respect or disrespect for their daughter? The same question could be asked about Jemima's silence or refusal to voice an opinion.

5. The three women with whom Delphine has a personal relationship—her sister, Jackie; her neighbor Jemima; and, of course, Maggie—are each quite different and serve quite different purposes in Delphine's life. Talk about the value of each unique relationship, as well as about each relationship's possible flaws.

6. Maggie repeatedly claims that she has never had one great passion or one great love of her life. Do you think that most people are led to expect a central, defining relationship with a person, a career, or a physical place? And if so, is this a damaging romantic fantasy or is a defining passion a healthy goal toward which to work?

7. Today it's common for people to move away from the place where they were born and raised, and as a result, families can be scattered far and wide and communication becomes less face-to-face and more orchestrated by intermediary channels. The Crandalls, however, are an example of a family that has chosen to remain within close proximity of each other. Do you think Delphine made the right choice to return to Ogunquit after college? At one point she mentions that her homecoming was entirely undistinguished; she was treated as if nothing about her could possibly have changed. Should she have remained in Boston for a few more years before returning home? Should she have never gone home at all? And did she believe she ever really had a choice?

8. Maggie's family moved often, her grandparents lived across the country, and Mrs. Weldon had a penchant for extreme and frequent redecoration of their home. Interestingly, the adult Maggie lives in the town next to the one in which her parents finally settled and for years has been seeking some sort of "real" connection with others—whether through a church community, or with Delphine, or, finally, with her husband. What do you think is the source of Maggie's intense loneliness?

9. Delphine believes that change for the sake of change is fine for the young, who have plenty of time to correct and recover from their mistakes. Maggie thinks that Delphine's opinion is a smart one but isn't so sure she feels like being smart at this moment in her life. Discuss when and in what circumstances it's healthier or wiser to accept what is, rather than leave it behind for something other. Alternately, discuss when it is health-

ier or wiser to move on—and how it's ever possible to know the difference.

10. Delphine comes to realize that for a long time she equated selflessness with maturity. When do you think she began to take self-sacrifice too far, so that it eventually became not a sign of maturity but one of weakness?

11. Maggie claims that she's never really had to sacrifice herself for the sake of others, except perhaps to some extent when her children were small. Given, for example, her devotion to her friendship with Delphine, do you think Maggie is underestimating her capacity for sacrifice?

12. While watching the journalist Robert Evans on television one evening, Maggie and Delphine discuss the notion of work and its meaning. Talk about your own thoughts on the relative merits of work performed for the good of the wider world and work performed for the good of one's immediate world. Is one inherently more valuable than the other? In our society at large, or in your more local community, is one kind of work considered—rightly or wrongly—to be more valuable? Where does a person's social responsibility begin and end?

13. Delphine firmly believes that when revisiting one's past, perhaps especially one's romantic past, there is a danger of rekindling a generalized longing, restlessness, and dissatisfaction in one's present life, the result of which can only cause harm. Given your own experiences, do you agree with her?

14. In the epilogue, Delphine is grateful for Maggie, the person who "lighted the flame within" her. Share a personal story of someone who greatly changed and deeply affected your life in a positive way. Does that person—alive or dead, present or absent—continue to play a supportive role in your life?

15. Where would you like to see Maggie and Delphine ten, even twenty years in the future?

Holiday House / New York

Acknowledgments:
I would like to thank Ms. Roxanne Adonolfi and the faculty and students from Joyce Kilmer Elementary School and Stockton Elementary School; Ms. Harriet Fromme; my son, John Ryan; Adrianne Kalfopoulou; the band Smash Palace; and my husband, Stephen Butler, for all their exuberant support and outstanding inspiration.

Printed and Bound in October 2016 at Maple Press, York, PA, USA.
www.holidayhouse.com
13 15 17 19 20 18 16 14 12

Library of Congress Cataloging-in-Publication Data

DiSalvo, DyAnne.
The sloppy copy slipup / by DyAnne DiSalvo.–1st ed.
p. cm.
Summary: Fourth-grader Brian Higman worries about how his teacher Miss Fromme–nicknamed The General–will react when he fails to hand in a writing assignment, but he ends up being able to tell his story, after all.
ISBN 0-8234-1947-9
[1. Storytelling–Fiction. 2. Authorship–Fiction. 3. Schools–Fiction. 4. Humorous stories.] I. Title.

PZ7.D6224Slo 2005
[Fic]–dc22
2004060777

ISBN-13: 978-0-8234-1947-0 (hardcover)
ISBN-13: 978-0-8234-2189-3 (paperback)

HOLIDAY HOUSE is registered in the U.S. Patent and Trademark Office.

For my charming
and lovely nieces,
Madeleine and Rachel

BIG HIG'S DISASTROUS NEWSLETTER

as keyboarded on my computer by Brian Higm

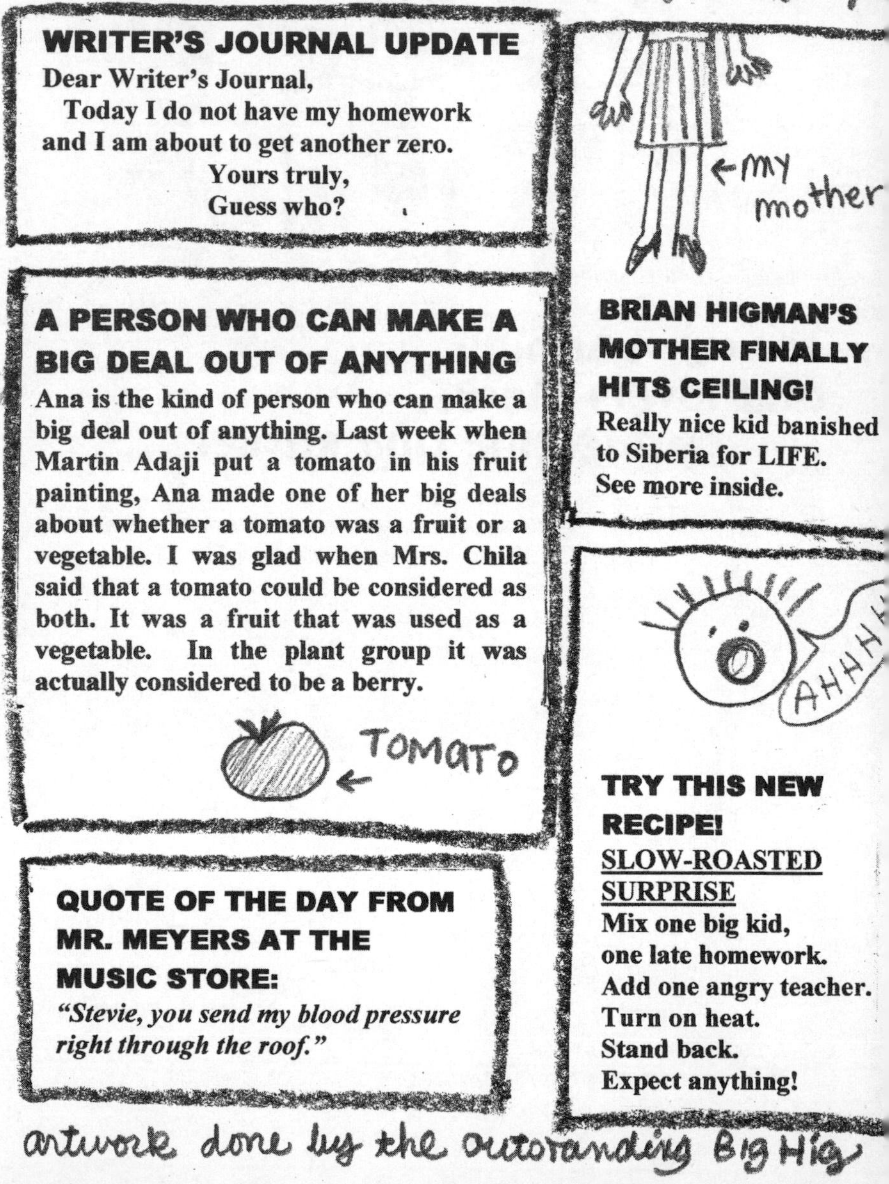

WRITER'S JOURNAL UPDATE

Dear Writer's Journal,

Today I do not have my homework and I am about to get another zero.

Yours truly,
Guess who?

A PERSON WHO CAN MAKE A BIG DEAL OUT OF ANYTHING

Ana is the kind of person who can make a big deal out of anything. Last week when Martin Adaji put a tomato in his fruit painting, Ana made one of her big deals about whether a tomato was a fruit or a vegetable. I was glad when Mrs. Chila said that a tomato could be considered as both. It was a fruit that was used as a vegetable. In the plant group it was actually considered to be a berry.

QUOTE OF THE DAY FROM MR. MEYERS AT THE MUSIC STORE:

"Stevie, you send my blood pressure right through the roof."

BRIAN HIGMAN'S MOTHER FINALLY HITS CEILING!

Really nice kid banished to Siberia for LIFE.

See more inside.

TRY THIS NEW RECIPE!

<u>SLOW-ROASTED SURPRISE</u>

Mix one big kid,
one late homework.
Add one angry teacher.
Turn on heat.
Stand back.
Expect anything!

artwork done by the outstanding Big Hig

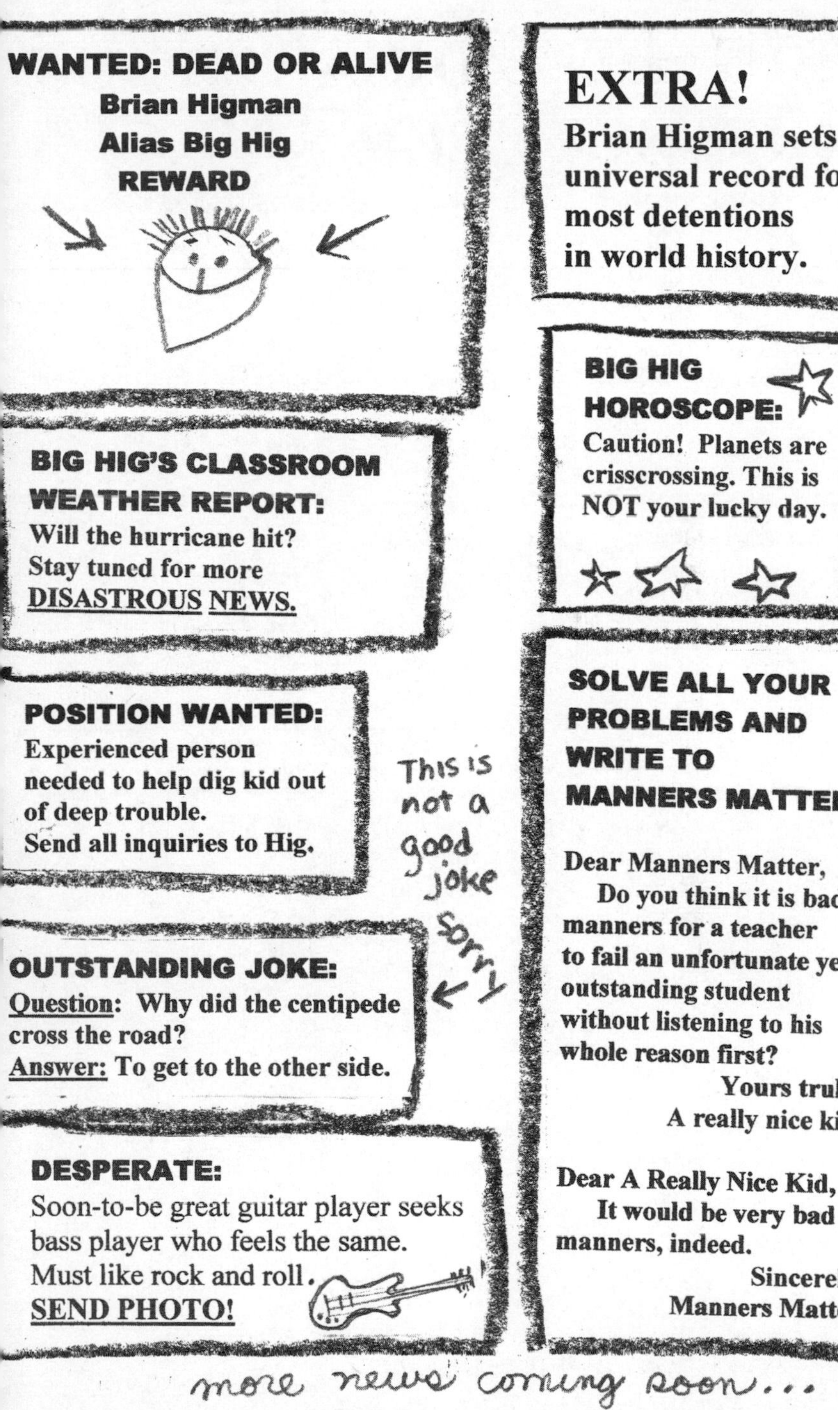

WANTED: DEAD OR ALIVE

Brian Higman

Alias Big Hig

REWARD

BIG HIG'S CLASSROOM WEATHER REPORT:

Will the hurricane hit?
Stay tuned for more
DISASTROUS NEWS.

POSITION WANTED:

Experienced person needed to help dig kid out of deep trouble.
Send all inquiries to Hig.

OUTSTANDING JOKE:

Question: Why did the centipede cross the road?
Answer: To get to the other side.

DESPERATE:

Soon-to-be great guitar player seeks bass player who feels the same.
Must like rock and roll.
SEND PHOTO!

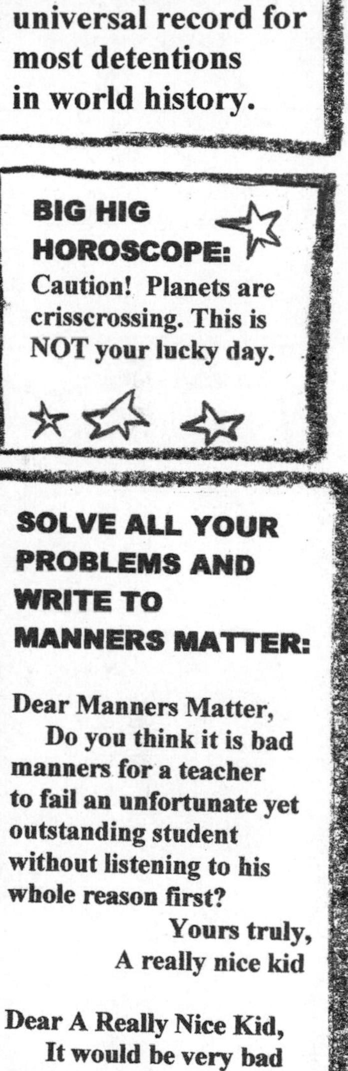

EXTRA!

Brian Higman sets universal record for most detentions in world history.

BIG HIG HOROSCOPE:

Caution! Planets are crisscrossing. This is NOT your lucky day.

SOLVE ALL YOUR PROBLEMS AND WRITE TO MANNERS MATTER:

Dear Manners Matter,
Do you think it is bad manners for a teacher to fail an unfortunate yet outstanding student without listening to his whole reason first?

Yours truly,
A really nice kid

Dear A Really Nice Kid,
It would be very bad manners, indeed.

Sincerely,
Manners Matter

contents

Chapter One
An Outstanding Zero

It was Monday morning. The entire kindergarten through fifth-grade classes at Franklin Elementary had just sat down after reciting the Pledge of Allegiance.

I, Big Hig, was fielding through my backpack, pretending to search for the written assignment I knew I didn't have.

"The word of the day is *outstanding,*" my ex-best friend, Ana Newburg, announced over the loudspeaker. Why is Ana my ex-best friend? That's a whole other story I'll get to later.

"O-u-t-s-t-a-n-d-i-n-g." Ana spelled the word slowly. "It is an adjective meaning exceptional or terrific. For lunch we will be having *outstanding* macaroni and cheese with *outstanding* fresh fruit and your choice of *outstanding* juice or milk. Thank you. Have an *outstanding* day."

Ana held her mouth too close to the microphone and made the loudspeaker screech. "AHHHHH!" Robby Zao fell against his desk and covered his ears. Josh Mendez closed his eyes and made a sour face. I was grateful for any distraction. It was only a matter of time before my teacher, Miss Fromme, began to collect Monday morning's assignment—the first draft—better known to her class as *the sloppy copy.*

After we hand in our sloppy copy it comes back with a mess of corrections and suggestions from Miss Fromme. Like: *Brian, more description for this opening sentence, please.* Or: *Brian, please remember to use your five senses when you write.* Uh! The next rewrite checks for grammar and spelling. *Brian, you do not need all these commas, thank you.* Which finally brings us to the final copy, if we end up living that long.

I personally do not mind writing. The problem is that I never have anything exciting to write about. Thinking up an idea is the hardest part for me. Anything I ever think about writing is either too long, too short, or too boring.

For example, why do the kids call me Big Hig? Simple. I am the biggest kid in our class and my name is Brian Higman. End of story.

And how about my family? Well, let's see. I have a mother named Florence. My pop's name is George. My older brother is Denny. My younger brother is Stevie. And I have a dog named Patches.

I guess I could try to write something about them. But that's where the long and boring part comes in.

Once I tried to write about a fishing trip we all went on. It was the day my pop decided we needed to spend some family time together. The sun was shining like pizza. My mother got two fishing poles from the basement and sponged off the cobwebs. Denny and I wrapped five peanut butter and jelly sandwiches in tin-foil. Stevie was in charge of packing the snacks. Pop piled everything, including us, into our Subaru station wagon and off we went. Mom turned up the radio while Denny played an air guitar in the backseat. Stevie counted and re-counted the number of cookies he had in his bag. "One plus two is three. Three plus one is four." I was relieved to know that my little brother did not have any ideas to supply us with any of his so-called entertainment.

When we got to the lake, we unpacked our stuff into the little boat we rented. Well no sooner did Pop finally ripple our canoe to what promised to be a good spot for fishing, when Stevie began to feel sorry for the minnows we were about to use for live bait. He patted his life jacket. "Don't worry, fishies," Stevie said in his superhero voice, "I'll save you." Then he picked up the pail of minnows and emptied the entire bucket into the water, yelling, "Free the fishies! Free the fishies!" You can believe me or not, but this really happened. Who wants to hear a story like that? I didn't think it was very good.

So instead of handing it in to Miss Fromme, I gave her a blank piece of paper. That was the first time I got a red zero.

Miss Fromme says that it is good practice to be aware of the ordinary things that happen in your life and learn to write them down.

Dear Writer's Journal,
Today I do not have my homework again and I am about to get another zero.

Yours truly,
guess who?

I was busy thinking of unexciting and ordinary things like journal writing and family fishing trips, when Miss Fromme motioned for the first table to stand. She pressed her lips together in a line. My stomach did a quick flip.

"First table," Miss Fromme said. "Ladies and Gentlemen! Less talk and more attention. This way, please." The kids at the first table made one messy line toward the front of the room. I watched as a pile of written assignments began to stack up on Miss Fromme's desk.

I could tell right away that Miss Fromme was not in a good mood. She did not even say thank you whenever another paper was added to the bunch. "Next table, please," said Miss Fromme.

I swallowed too much air at once and let out a little burp. It was all over for me. One more table and I'd be up there, too.

Ana Newburg walked into the classroom. She was all whoop-de-do from her loudspeaker announcement. She shook her bangs and rushed to her seat where she pulled out her sloppy copy. Ana held it up as if Miss Fromme had already given her an A+.

"Big deal," Robby Zao whispered to her from table three. He chomped on his pencil like a rabbit.

I opened my journal and wrote:

Ana is the kind of person who can make a big deal out of anything. Last week in art class, when Martin Adaji put a tomato in his fruit painting, Ana made one of her big deals about whether a tomato was a fruit or a vegetable. I was glad when Mrs. Chila said that a tomato could be considered as both. It was a fruit that was used as a vegetable. In the plant group it was actually considered to be a berry.

I put my pencil down.

Right now, the last thing I needed was for Ana Newburg to make some kind of big deal about me. After all, I had a very good reason for not having my written assignment. In fact, I had planned to do it all weekend. Only my weekend did not work out as I had planned. Now all I had to do was convince Miss Fromme to give me another chance.

Chapter Two
Don't Mess With the Facts

I sat in my seat and waited for my table to be called. I stared at my blank piece of paper. I could almost imagine the way it would look with the words written neatly on the page. It would have been chock-full of information—just like a newspaper.

The one thing I did know about was newspapers. Besides being the top salesperson at Robins Appliance Store, my pop was also the founder and publisher of *The Franklin Newsletter*.

The Franklin, as it is commonly known in our house, is the town's monthly newsletter. It keeps Franklin neighbors up-to-date on block parties, leaf cleanups, town meetings, horoscopes, weather reports, and other bits of local news that fill up a two-page leaflet. Don't Mess with the Facts is Pop's running motto.

My brother Denny says he's heard Pop recite his motto so many times that he doesn't even hear it anymore. Personally, I think Denny's bad hearing has less to do with my pop's motto and more to do with the so-called entertainment my little brother, Stevie, provides during the course of the day.

"Stevie, you send my blood pressure right through the roof."

I wrote that in my journal, too. That's a direct quote from Mr. Myers who owns the music store in town. And that goes double for me.

"Next table, please," Miss Fromme said. "The rest of the class please open your writers' notebooks and begin to journal your morning."

This is it, I told myself. I stood up. A long, loud bell rang. We were having an *outstanding* fire drill.

"Line leader up front, quickly," Miss Fromme said. "Quickly, quickly. Class, no talking or there will be no recess."

Kala Patel rushed to her position.

Saved by the bell! I love fire drills.

I stepped in line with the rest of my class and followed Kala into the great outdoors. We all went silently down the stairs and out to the back of the school yard.

"How come I never get to be the line leader?" Josh Mendez whispered to me. Josh had both hands stuck inside the pockets of his denim jacket. His glasses were crooked, and he smelled like lemon-scented laundry detergent.

"You were the line leader last month," I whispered back.

"I forgot," said Josh.

"I'm going to report you," Kala warned us.

The last thing I needed was for any more trouble. The autumn day was crisp and breezy. The trees looked like they were waving hello. I blew out a sigh of relief. At least in the school yard, I was temporarily saved. I relaxed a little and began to enjoy it. My mind took a break and started to wander.

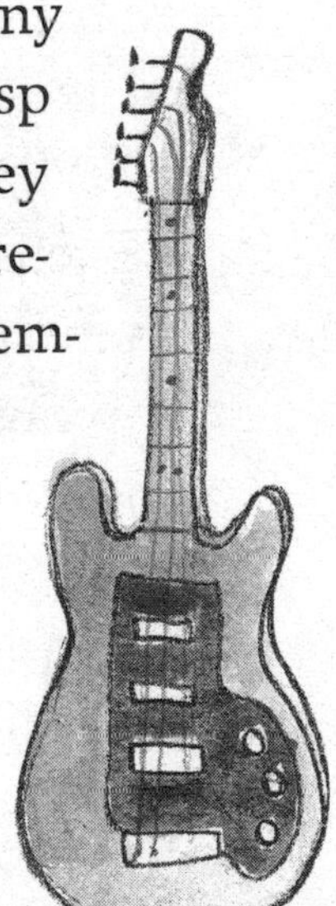

Did I happen to mention that I am in the market to buy my first guitar? Well, I am. I've had my eye on a really cool electric guitar that has been in Mr. Myers's music store for about two weeks. It's secondhand, but it's as good as new. Whenever I am in there, which is usually a lot, Mr. Myers lets me check it out.

I always go out of my way never to touch anything or ask Mr. Myers too many questions while I'm in there. Mr. Myers is the nervous type. And my little brother, Stevie, makes him nervous. Mostly I try to go into the music store by myself, but usually I am keeping an eye on Stevie for my mother.

Stevie touches everything and asks about a million questions at the same time. He also insists on singing one of his so-called entertainment songs as he whizzes up and down the aisles.

"Phone, phone on the range," Stevie sings. "Excuse me, Mr. Myers, what kind of instrument is this? Does it come in green? Green is my favorite color. What's yours? Can I try out these drums?"

"Settle down, Stevie," I say just like Pop tells him.

But Stevie doesn't listen to me.

When I told Denny about the guitar I was going to buy, he said, "You mean the red-and-black Stratocaster that's in the window?"

At the time I was helping him tape up a rock-and-roll poster of this jamming new band called The Edge. Denny's room had sheet music and CDs stacked in neat rows along the fringe of his rug. He was the rhythm guitar player in his band, Questions No Answers, which, by the way, practiced every Saturday afternoon in the basement of my house.

Denny stepped back and looked at his poster.

"I think that's the same guitar that Harry wants to buy," he said.

Harry Harrington, the *neighborhood-famous* lead guitar player in Denny's band? The one who was also in his first year of high school just like Denny?

"He can't buy it!" I said. "That's the guitar I've been saving up for."

Denny shrugged. He tightened the little rubber band on the ponytail he had just started to grow.

"Talk to Harry about it," he said. "Maybe you can work something out."

Talk to Harry? "No way," I told him.

And that's when I decided to go to Myers's Music first thing Saturday morning to buy it.

I stamped my sneakers on the school-yard ground as I thought about what happened next. No wonder I didn't have the time to write my sloppy copy. The whole weekend was one big family emergency. I had a perfectly solid reason for not getting around to writing it.

"How much longer do we have to be out standing in this *outstanding* school yard?" Robby Zao said, resting his chin on my shoulder. "There isn't even a fire."

Robby was right. There was no fire. Except for the one that was burning inside my brain. The bad news was that we would not be in this

outstanding school yard forever. Sooner or later we were going back inside, and I'd have to face Miss Fromme.

"All *outstanding* students return to class," Mr. Zifferman, the principal, said through his megaphone.

Miss Fromme raised her hand in a motion for her class to follow. The one thought that kept following me around was Stevie. Stevie who follows me into my room whenever I want to be alone. Stevie who tries to follow me on his Big Wheel whenever I take a bike ride. Stevie who wants to do everything that I do and then tells my mother all about it.

"Guess what, Flo?" Stevie says. "Brian took me to the music store again."

That really gets me boiling. Stevie chums up to my mother like there's no tomorrow. He even calls her Flo, which is short for Florence, and my mother allows it.

"After all, he *is* the baby of the family," my mother says.

"Baby my foot," I say. Stevie is nearly five years old and he's never even been to school.

One day Stevie asked Flo if he could stay at home with her instead of going to kindergarten.

And just like that, my mother said yes. I mean, nobody ever told me that I didn't have to go to school.

"Stevie will learn at home," my mother says. "He'll be all set by the time first grade rolls around."

Right. But who has to mind Stevie when my mother needs help? Me. And guess who'd rather be minding a bunch of monkeys on a desert island, lost forever somewhere in the middle of the Pacific Ocean, instead of watching Stevie? Me.

The more I thought about Stevie the angrier I got. Here I was, with my life in my hands, and it was all Stevie's fault. If it weren't for Stevie, I would have had my sloppy copy already written and ready to hand in to Miss Fromme just like everybody else.

Back in the classroom Miss Fromme had settled into her seat like a war pilot ready for takeoff. She hunched her back and held on to her desk. The kids at my table took one look at her and stood up without being asked. I shuffled my feet from side to side. I could already imagine the writing on my tombstone:

Maybe one day the fact would be that I would take over *The Franklin* and write my head off. But here were the facts today:

Number one: Miss Fromme was waiting for me to give her my written assignment.

Number two: I didn't have it.

Number three: I would not be seeing the light of day for the rest of the week if I didn't say something fast.

Chapter Three
Face-to-Face with General Fromme

I stepped up to Miss Fromme's desk to give her my blank piece of paper. Well, it wasn't a completely blank piece of paper. I had already written my name on top. That should count for something.

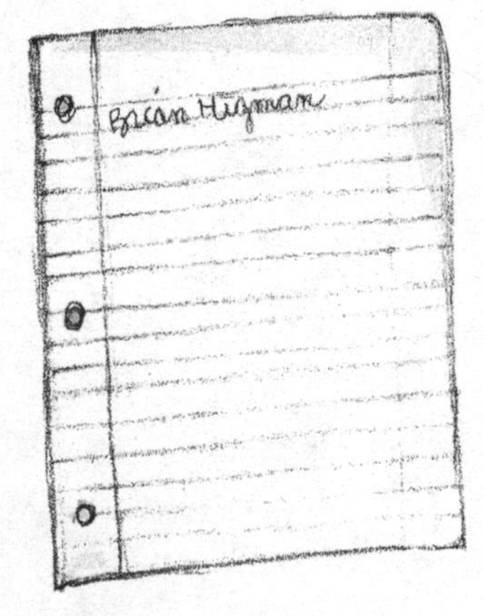

The closer I got, the braver I became. I'd tell Miss Fromme exactly what happened. At first she would probably get a little angry, but then she would probably understand. She'd probably give me a little extra homework. And I'd probably do the same thing if I was her.

I smiled to myself. Everything would be fine.

So I did what any kid like me would do—I ran for the bathroom pass. I slipped my paper onto Miss Fromme's desk before it was even my turn.

I knew it was a dumb excuse to leave the room in such a hurry, but I needed more time to think. As I walked down the hall, I thought about Ana. Didn't I have enough problems already?

It never really bothered me that Ana was a girl. Our parents were friends, and we got along. I liked baseball. She liked baseball. I had a dog. She had a dog. We both liked rock and roll.

Then all of a sudden, things started to change. Ana didn't want to play baseball anymore. Me neither. We wanted to start a band instead. We bugged Denny to teach us how to play the guitar. Ana wanted to learn the bass. Robby Zao was taking drum lessons. Josh Mendez said he wanted to sing. Everything was going great.

But then Ana joined the orchestra. She took up the cello. Nadine Ali became her new best friend. Ana didn't come over on Saturdays anymore when Denny's band practiced.

"You can't just quit the band," I told her.

"What band?" said Ana. "You don't even have a guitar yet."

This was true. I didn't have a guitar yet. But all that was about to change. In the meantime maybe I will just put a personal ad in *The Franklin*:

Desperate:

Soon-to-be great guitar player seeks bass player who feels the same.

Must like rock and roll.

SEND PHOTO!

On the way back from the bathroom, I could hear Miss Fromme reciting one of her favorite mottos: "Write about what you know. Or research what you don't."

I slinked into the classroom and put the bathroom pass back on the hook.

"Excuse me, Mr. Higman," Miss Fromme said. "You left me a piece of paper with your name written on it."

Miss Fromme folded her arms. She tapped her foot like she was in a hurry.

"Miss Fromme," I said. "I can explain."

"This is not the first time, Mr. Higman," she said.

Miss Fromme was right. It was the second time.

I knew that if I came home with another zero in English, I would be seeing a lot more than red on my mother's face. I think you'd call it fury. My mother didn't fool around with things like this. The last time she grounded me I had no TV or PlayStation for a week. This time could only be worse.

The newspaper headline would read:

BRIAN HIGMAN'S Mother
finally HITS CEILING
Really nice kid banished to
SIBERIA for LIFE.

Miss Fromme lifted her reading glasses as if a cloud of smoke had just fogged her lenses. She stared at me with her red marker ready on top of my blank piece of paper. Well, not totally blank.

I was cooked . . . No! Baked. . . . No! Burnt to a crisp. I could see it in *The Franklin:*

Try This New Recipe!
Slow Roasted Surprise

Mix one big kid,
One late homework,
Add one angry teacher.
Turn on heat.
Stand back.
Expect anything!

"It was all my little brother's fault," I blurted out.

Miss Fromme narrowed her eyes.

Miss Fromme. Just the name gives me the same chill as fingernails on a blackboard. In my family her name comes with a reputation.

The only wish that Denny ever had for me was, "I hope you don't get 'The General.' "

"The General," as Miss Fromme was respectfully known throughout the entire Franklin Elementary School, was not a teacher to mess with.

"Don't let her fool you when she folds her hands and tilts her head," Denny warned me early on. "That mean's she's setting the trap."

Miss Fromme folded her hands and tilted her head.

"Go ahead, Brian," she said to me. "You have my full attention."

"Thank you, Miss Fromme," I said, nearly saluting her.

I raised my chin and began to tell her what had happened.

"It was Saturday. I was all set for the beginning of a great weekend. I planned to do my

homework after lunch, and I had the whole morning to myself.

"I looked over at the bed next to mine. Stevie was still asleep. He had all the sheets bunched up to his neck. Our dog, Patches, was snoring on a pillow next to him. Stevie and Patches—now that was a match! We were never allowed to have a dog in our house until the day that Patches arrived. And I do mean *arrived*, which by the way is another whole other story.

"One afternoon I was in the living room drawing these really cool planes with a new felt-tipped pen I got. My mother was nearby on her piano, trying to figure out a song she wanted to learn. It was raining outside like you wouldn't believe, when all of a sudden there was this sound.

" 'Hooooooooow.'

"It was the kind of sound you couldn't put your finger on.

" 'Stop your howling,' Pop said to Stevie. 'A man can't work with a noise like that.'

"Stevie looked out from under the kitchen table. He was counting the collection of banana stickers he had stuck underneath.

" 'That's not me, Pop,' Stevie said.

" 'Hoooooow wow!'

"The noise was beginning to bug me, too.

"My mother pushed aside her piano bench and wove a pencil through her hair.

" 'That noise must be coming from the washing machine,' she said. 'I think it's time for a new one.' My mother went to check the washer, but it was spinning fine.

"Meanwhile, I could hear my brother Denny in the basement singing through his microphone. It sounded more like an 'ooooooo' than a 'hoooow wow!' Shaver banged his crash cymbal and kick-drum pedal while the crystals on our chandelier shook each time Ace Randall hit a bass note. 'Twang, Twang, EEEEEEEEEE.' The neighborhood-famous Harry Harrington raised the volume on his electric guitar.

" 'Hooooow wow! Woooooooo! Yoooow!' The noise was getting out of hand. I decided it was time to investigate."

I leaned against the white board and noticed that Miss Fromme was beginning to tilt her head the other way.

"And remember," I heard my brother's voice telling me. "If Miss Fromme tilts her head the other way, it means you need to use more descriptive language."

"So I got up from my soft, comfortable green couch with the red-and-gold flowered pillows and decided it was time to investigate," I said it again only this time better. **"The annoying sound was coming from somewhere. It made the lamp shade shake like jelly."** Hey! I thought. That simile was good.

Miss Fromme listened. She did not look impressed.

ALERT! RED ZERO CLOSING
IN ON ALL SIDES.
RUN FOR YOUR LIFE
IF YOU CAN!

Chapter Four
Fleas Not Lice

Position Wanted:
Experienced person needed
to help dig kid out of deep trouble.

That's how the classified ad in The Franklin *was going to read when I got around to writing it.*

"Sorry, Miss Fromme," I said, trying not to lose my train of thought. "I think I lost my train of thought."

Miss Fromme glared at Robby Zao who was laughing in his seat.

"Mr. Zao," Miss Fromme said firmly. "Is your writer's journal opened and ready? Or do you want extra homework?" Then The General turned to me. "Brian, please take your seat and see me after lunch."

"Miss Fromme?" Josh Mendez said in a whisper, as he barely raised his hand. "I'm supposed to go to the nurse's office and take my antibiotic now. I had strep throat all weekend."

Miss Fromme did not look happy. Thanks to my undone but soon-to-be, I'm sure, finished sloppy copy and a school fire drill, Miss Fromme's morning class time was quickly slipping away. She took the note from Josh's mother.

"Brian," Miss Fromme said. "Please accompany Josh to the nurse."

"But, Miss Fromme," I said. I held out my hands. I couldn't believe I was actually speaking. "I was just about to include some very important and descriptive information about the neighborhood-famous Harry Harrington."

Miss Fromme put both hands on her hips. "That won't be necessary, Brian," she said. "Class, let's get to our journals."

On the way to the nurse, Josh jiggled my sleeve. "You can tell me about Harry Harrington," he said. "I hate taking medicine. I need the distraction."

"Well," I said, "Harry Harrington is not

Miss Frommes' Class
READ TO WRITE

only neighborhood-famous because of his amazing guitar playing but also because of his two beautiful older sisters."

"I saw them once in a car," said Josh.

I nodded my head. "Harry told my mother that his parents paid more attention to his sisters than they ever did to him. He said it made him feel about as worthwhile as a flea."

"I had lice once," Josh said as he scratched his head.

"Fleas are different," I told him. "Fleas are something that my mother seems to have a soft touch for. She told Harry Harrington that he was more than welcome to 'come by the house anytime.' Harry took my mother at her word and started showing up for dinner nearly every single day. Once he even cooked us his recipe for chicken à la mode. Which, by the way, was not half bad."

"Chicken à la mode?" said Josh. He rubbed his belly. "I never heard of that before. But I wish I had some now."

We made a turn past the "Who's Who in School" bulletin board. Ana's face was plastered alongside the poem she wrote on leaves.

LEAVES
by Ana Newburg Miss Fromme

Falling, falling from the trees,
Gold and red and orange leaves.
Children jump in raked-up piles,
Dogs come sniffing with a smile.
Squirrels take some for their nest.
I like autumn. It's the best.

"Anyway," I went on. I shrugged off the poem. "It was so annoying having Harry Harrington around my house all the time. When I wanted to use the video game, he was already playing it. If I called my mother to tell her I'd be late or something, Harry Harrington would answer the phone. 'Higman residence,' he'd say as if he actually lived there."

Josh shook his head. "A flea," he said. "They're hard to get rid of."

"Exactly." I nodded. I was glad he was listening. "But then bad news turned into good news. Denny lent me his old acoustic guitar when I told him I wanted to learn. And now he and Harry both take the time to teach me chords. G, C, D, A."

I showed Josh the tips of my fingers. "I'm already getting calluses," I said. "That shows I'm really practicing."

Josh and I walked into the nurse's office. Mrs. Dunn checked Josh's name off a list, then opened the door of the small refrigerator she kept next to one of the sickbeds. I positioned myself for a little rest.

"Don't lie on that," Mrs. Dunn told me.

"I'm planning on getting sick later," I told her. "Maybe I should just stay now."

My mind was swirling with so much stuff. I began to wish that I had a piece of paper with me. I had this urge to write it all down. That's when I knew I was really not well.

Mrs. Dunn filled a teaspoon with gross pink stuff. "This is the part I hate," Josh said. "Quick, tell me the rest." But Josh swallowed his medicine so fast there wasn't even time for a joke. Okay, so maybe now Josh was feeling a little bit better, but as soon as we left the nurse's office to walk back down the hall, I began to feel sick all over.

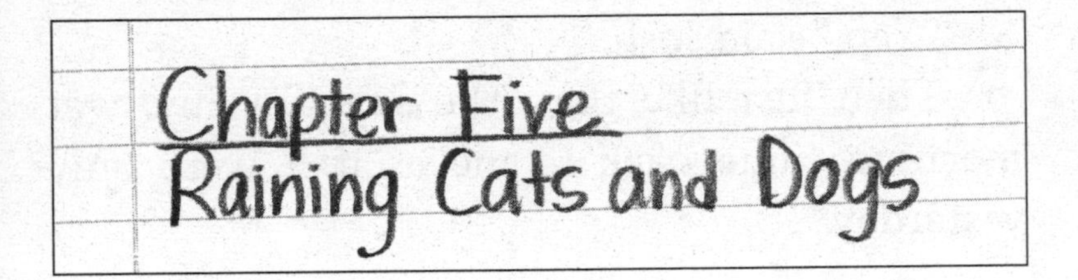

In my head, I wrote The Franklin *horoscope tip:*

Caution! Planets are crisscrossing. This is NOT your lucky day.

I squeaked my sneakers down the hall. "I'm really in trouble," I said to Josh.

"No kidding," he said. "Wait until you get home."

Josh wiped a pink smudge onto his sleeve. "But getting back to that howling noise. The one you were telling us about in class. . . ."

The howling noise?

"Oh, right," I said. "You mean the *hoow-wooooow* that was coming from somewhere?"

"Yep," said Josh.

Then just like that, the soggy, rainy, wet morning came back to me as if it were only yesterday. . . .

"I left my plane drawings on the floor and got up from the couch to investigate the howling noise. I was just about to check inside one of the hall closets, when Stevie made one of his so-called beeline dashes from under the table and yanked the front door open.

" 'It's a dog,' said Stevie, bending over and practically dragging it into the house.

" 'How did he get here?' I wondered out loud.

" 'It's raining cats and dogs outside,' Stevie said. 'That's how he got here.'

" 'Raining cats and dogs,' my mother repeated over and over as she dried the mutt with a bathroom towel.

" 'That sounds like a newspaper headline,' said Pop.

" 'Look at his spots,' I said. 'They look like black and brown patches.'

" 'That's his name,' said Stevie. 'Patches.'

" 'It can't be his name,' I said. 'It's not our dog.'

" 'I'll run an ad,' Pop said. 'LOST DOG FOUND. WHITE WITH BROWN AND BLACK SPOTS.'

" 'Patches,' said Stevie.

" 'Right,' said Pop. 'And if no one turns up, we'll say he's ours and call it a day. Now how about some lunch?'

"Anyway, after running the ad for a couple of weeks, no one showed up, and that's how Patches arrived."

"Ha! Ha!" Josh laughed as we opened the classroom door. "That was a funny story."

Miss Fromme turned to look at us. She sipped some water.

"Okay, boys, now take your seats. We're on page thirty-eight in our math books," she said.

Nadine Ali raised her hand. The tiny gold bells on her bracelet jingled.

"Miss Fromme," she said. "I was just wondering about one little part in Brian's story. Was the *hooooow-wow* howling coming from a ghost or the wind?"

"It was a dog," said Josh. "That's how they ended up taking their dog, Patches, in and keeping her."

I folded my arms. So did Miss Fromme.

I had a quick flashback. I remembered Denny staring hard into my face like a comrade preparing me for battle.

"And if The General folds her arms, it means she's ready for war," he said.

"It seems like you have a captive audience," Miss Fromme said to me. She closed her pencil on page 38 and looked at her watch for the millionth time. "You have two minutes to finish."

I stood up straight. I thought about my options. Go into battle, or go home with a zero.

"Well," I began. I started to remember. **"It was Saturday. . . .**

"I slowly inched out of my bedroom, leaving Stevie and Patches to whatever sweet dreams a boy and a dog could have. I didn't want to wake them up. I was on a mission and it was a secret.

"I was about to dig up the peanut butter jar that I had buried in the backyard near my pop's garage. The peanut butter jar had all

the money I needed in it to buy the guitar I wanted.

"I shoveled out the jar with one of my mother's gardening tools and brushed off the dirt. I held up the jar to look inside. Everything was still in there. I walked up the back porch steps and smelled coffee already brewing from the kitchen. Pop was up and reading the Saturday morning edition of the newspaper.

" 'Got plans?' he asked, looking over his paper. He dripped a teaspoon of honey onto his toast and paid close attention to the peanut butter jar I was holding in my hand.

" 'See this?' I said. I unscrewed the top and took out the sock that I had stuffed with money. Actually, there were two socks. One sock had the money. The other sock had more socks stuffed inside. That was my decoy. Just in case anybody ever found the jar and tried to steal it.

"Pop watched me pour about a pound of cornflakes into an ice-cream bowl. He looked at the crumbs of dirt that circled the jar around the table.

" 'Yep,' he said. 'I see it.'

"I held up the sock. 'I saved enough money in here to get myself an electric guitar. Denny said I could borrow his amplifier whenever he wasn't using it. I'm starting a band.'

"I could see right away that Pop was impressed.

" 'I admire a boy with gumption,' he said.

"Translation: a kid like me who could take it upon himself to have the courage to do something *outstanding*.

"All of a sudden I began to hear a stirring at the top of the stairs. The house was waking up. Steps padded closer to the landing. Milk dribbled down my chin. A flurry of paws clicked their way toward the back steps leading into the kitchen. It was Patches. That meant that Stevie was not far behind. I imagined my brother wide-awake and full of so-called entertainment.

" 'Peanut sat on a railroad track. . . . Toot! Toot! Peanut butter!'

"Oh no! Pretty soon my mother would be asking, 'Brian, honey, I need your help to keep an eye on Stevie while I give a piano lesson.'

"No way! I didn't want to take Stevie with me while I picked up my new guitar. This was going to be a moment in time that I wanted to remember forever! In a good way, I mean.

" 'Got to go, Pop,' I said in a rush.

" 'What's your hurry?' Pop asked me. 'How about some company?'

"I grabbed my sock and gave him a hug. Me and

Pop. Wow! What a morning! What could be better than that?"

Miss Fromme took a deep breath. "Two minutes are up," she said.

"Phew." I waved my hand like a fan in my face. "It's getting hot in here."

Ana tilted her head to one side and sat back like Miss Fromme.

"Can we hear the rest?" Robby asked, turning his seat toward the white board. "It sounds like something's going to happen."

"Something *is* going to happen," I told Miss Fromme. I slinked back to my chair. "It's not an excuse. It's a reason with gumption."

A reason with gumption, I thought to myself. I'll have to write that down in my journal. Maybe I should start a vocabulary section in *The Franklin*.

STEW: To cook by boiling slowly: To worry, as in to stew in one's own juices.

That was me. I was slowly boiling, and Miss Fromme looked like she was just about to raise the heat. She got up from her chair, pushed in her seat, and began to walk toward my desk.

Chapter Six
Fried to a Crisp

If I ever write an entertainment section for The Franklin, *I might not include a crossword puzzle. I do not like fitting words into boxes that meet across and down with a joining letter in between.*

I am more the word-jumble type. The word I am thinking of now is:

LEHP!

I watched Miss Fromme slowly making her way toward me. All of a sudden the loudspeaker crackled.

"Please excuse the *outstanding* interruption," Mrs. Confrontini, the school secretary, said. "Will the *outstanding* Brian Higman please report to the office."

Oh no. I wasn't even in trouble yet and I was already in trouble.

I looked at Ana. Even she looked nervous.

Miss Fromme leaned over to open the window. "Robby, please accompany Brian to the office," she said without even looking.

Out in the hallway Robby said, "Whoa! Are you just lucky, Big Hig? Or are you really in trouble?"

"I don't know," I said to Robby. "But I'm going to find out soon."

"Speaking of finding out," said Robby. "Are we starting the band or not? Did you get the guitar? What's going on?"

It was a good question. But it was not a question that I was ready to answer. I was still thinking about me and Pop on Saturday morning as we walked toward Myers's Music.

"It was just like one of those mornings you'd see in the movies," I told Robby, even though he didn't ask. **"The sun was out, the sky was blue, and the birds were singing a tune. . . .**

"I liked spending time with Pop alone. It was a rare occasion when Pop had a Saturday off from work. Being a salesperson was not an easy job. Especially on Saturdays. Pop said it was like the whole world was out buying refrigerators and ovens on Saturdays.

"We crossed the street and I hummed a little tune. Me and Pop on our way to the music store. That was something to sing about. But just as we turned onto Station Avenue, I looked down the block and saw someone familiar. It was Harry Harrington. Where was *he* going at this time of day? He was coming our way. He was heading toward Myers's Music. . . ."

There was a brown paper bag on Mrs. Confrontini's desk. It had my name written on it with crayon. It was my lunch.

"Hello, Brian," Mrs. Confrontini said. "It's

nice to see you again. Your mother dropped this by for you."

I tried to smile for Mrs. Confrontini.

"And by the way," she said, "I finally had the chance to meet that little brother of yours. The one that you were looking for the other day? I hear he'll be coming to school next year."

"Was he wearing two hats?" I asked.

Mrs. Confrontini laughed. "Yes, he was," she said.

I knew it. Stevie had stood in front of Mrs.

Confrontini's desk still wearing the raccoon cap with the earflaps snapped and the sailor hat on top.

"Since when does your brother wear two hats?" Robby asked me on our way back to class.

"Since two days ago," I said.

Miss Fromme glanced over and waved us in.

I crumpled my lunch bag inside my desk, opened my book, and got to work. Who cared about a zero any-way?

I'd start a "Manners" page for *The Franklin* and settle things once and for all.

Dear Manners Matter,

Do you think it is bad manners for a teacher to fail an unfortunate yet <u>outstanding</u> student without listening to his whole reason first?

Yours truly,
A Really Nice Kid

Dear A Really Nice Kid,

It would be very bad manners, indeed.

Sincerely,
Manners Matter

Kids all over the world would thank me.

I raised my hand. Miss Fromme shook her head. There would be no more interruptions for the rest of the morning.

We went through a lesson on identifying clouds. Cumulus clouds were puffy and piled up. Stratus clouds could be flat or layered or both. Cirrus clouds were curly.

We also had the pleasure of taking a pop math quiz on two- and three-digit division.

It was nearly lunchtime by the time Miss Fromme looked up and said, "Somehow, we have gotten through everything. Brian, I am still interested in hearing how your story ends."

What's this? I thought. The General is giving me another chance? The rest of my life could still be saved.

"You were telling us something about a guitar?" Miss Fromme said.

"You missed a lot," Robby Zao informed everyone. "Big Hig and his pop were just about to buy the guitar he saved up for when the neighborhood-famous Harry Harrington showed up at the same time."

Miss Fromme lifted her eyebrows and smiled like she was worried. "Go ahead, Brian," she said.

"Me, Pop, and Harry stopped right in front of the music store.

" 'What are you doing here?' I said to Harry.

"Harry smiled and shook hands with Pop. Harry's flannel shirt hung loose around his shoulders. I wanted a shirt like that.

" 'I was just on my way to your house,' said Harry.

" 'A likely story,' I said to myself.

"I reached into the pocket of my jeans and took out the blue-speckled Fender pick that Denny had given me. It was a medium.

Denny told me, 'A good guitar player is always ready to play.' That was me. And in about five minutes I'd have the guitar to go with it.

" 'Morning, George,' Mr. Myers said to my pop. 'Morning, fellows,' he said to us. Mr. Myers bobbed his head from side to side like a toy on the dashboard of a car.

" 'Where's that little brother of yours?' Mr. Myers asked me. He chuckled and gave Pop a wink.

"Pop stood smiling with his hands folded and his head shaking. He looked like he was praying for Stevie and understanding Mr. Myers at the same time.

" 'That little guy is really something,' Mr. Myers said, as he unlocked the front door. 'Just give me a minute inside.'

"We all waited while Mr. Myers got settled.

"I looked at Harry. He wasn't talking and neither was I.

"I cupped my hands around my face and pressed my nose against the window. There it was. The red-and-black Stratocaster. A glimmer of sun hit it just right, and it shined like a million bucks.

"Mr. Myers was taking his sweet ol' time.

He was turning on the lights, turning back the CLOSED sign to OPEN.

" 'Come on, come on,' I said to myself. I kept my sneaker close to the door, so I'd be the first one inside.

" 'Brian's here to buy a guitar,' Pop said all of a sudden to Harry.

"Harry shuffled a few pieces of gravel to one side.

" 'Want some help picking it out?' he asked me.

" 'No thanks,' I said just like that. 'I've got my guitar all picked out, and I have the money right here.'

"That's when I pulled out my sock. Only when I pulled out my sock, another sock fell out, and another and another.

"I had taken the decoy by mistake! My dreams were ruined.

" 'I have to go home,' I said to Pop. 'I'll be right back.'

"I took off running like an Olympic racer, darting around people and jumping curbs. 'See you,' said Harry as he gave me a wave. And when I turned the corner I saw him walk into Myers's Music."

OPEN

The lunch bell rang and nobody moved. Well, nobody except me. I was starving after a morning like this.

"What a flea!" Josh mumbled.

"Brian," Miss Fromme said, "I have been very patient with you this morning. I think you will agree to that. But the fact of the matter remains. You do not have your written assignment. Please see me after lunch."

I could feel my eyes beginning to glaze.

"Does this mean I'm getting a zero?" I asked. I might as well know now before I tried to eat anything. The sloppy copy loomed in the distance like a threatening weather report.

WiLL the Hurricane Hit?
<u>the Franklin</u> reported.
Stay tuned for more
<u>DISASTrous</u> <u>NEWS</u>.

"After lunch, Mr. Higman," Miss Fromme said firmly. Then she pointed the way toward the cafeteria as if I might have forgotten.

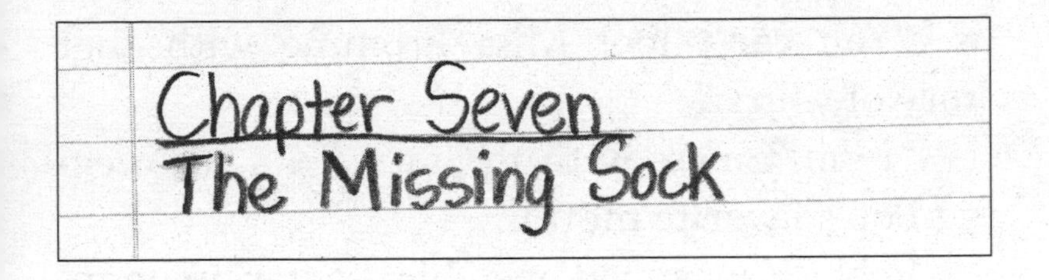

→WANTED DEAD OR ALIVE ←
Brian Higman
Alias: BIG HIG
REWARD

"You're in deep trouble now," Ana said to me in the cafeteria as she walked past my table with her lunch tray and sat down right behind us. "You can't fool Miss Fromme with that story of yours."

"I don't mess with the facts," I said, reciting Pop's favorite motto.

Robby Zao ripped open his vegetarian wrap.

"She's right," Josh said. "Miss Fromme will never believe you."

I was about to take a bite of my ham and cheese when I noticed a pink piece of paper inside my sandwich. I pulled it out. It was a note from my mother.

Hi Honey ♡
Family meeting after School! Try not to be late. Stevie has a surprise. Love,
xox Mom

I wiped the mustard off it and stuck it into my pocket.

"Why does your mother leave notes in your sandwich?" Josh asked me.

"My mother is not normal," I said.

Nadine Ali opened her chips. "I think your mother is fun," she said. "Remember the time we had a cookout in your backyard and it started to rain?"

Ana was listening. She pointed a carrot

stick toward our table. "I was at that cookout," she said.

"Ha! Ha!" Robby laughed. "We all got stuck eating soggy hot dogs and hamburgers inside your garage when the backyard drain clogged up."

"Remember?" said Josh. "And the backyard puddle got bigger and bigger until the tips of our sneakers were wet?"

I pictured the moment in my head. Me with my baked beans rolling off the side of my plate as we all pushed further inside the garage. We watched as my mother shuffled dinner plates onto this huge puddle like a deck of cards, while the rain cleaned the dishes for her.

"I think it was a good idea," said Nadine.

"I agree," said Ana.

In front of the cafeteria, Mrs. Wagner, the P.E. teacher, turned up the volume on Beethoven's Fifth Symphony. This was her signal for us to begin cleaning up our trays.

I, Big Hig, personally did not mind when Mrs. Wagner played her weekly tunes of classical music. Every week she had a new theme. All the composers had weird names. Last week it was Bach. The week before that it was Vivaldi.

Mrs. Wagner told us she got the idea from a circus trainer who tamed wild beasts.

"Okay, *outstanding* students," Mrs. Wagner said. "Let's get ready to go outside."

In the school yard, the kids from Miss Fromme's class were starting to crowd around me.

"Did you get the guitar?" asked Tyrone.

"What happened?" Chris C. wanted to know.

"I think Harry bought it," Jacelle said. Ana and Nadine and Martin Adaji moved closer to me like ants to a crumb.

I clawed my fingers through the chain-link fence. I was as angry as a wet hen just thinking about it.

"It was all downhill from there!"

"I left Pop at the music store, ran home, sprung the back door open, looked on the kitchen table, and saw that my sock was gone. The peanut butter jar was right where I had left it. So was the ice-cream bowl with half a pound of cereal still inside.

" 'Where's my money?' I shouted.

"I checked underneath the table to see if Stevie was playing 'bank.' He wasn't.

" 'Anybody home?' I yelled. No answer. Not even Patches came running.

" 'Looks like the troops have gone,' said Pop. The screen door closed behind him.

" 'Pop!' I said. 'My money is gone.'

"Pop rested his thumbs inside his pockets. I was glad he had followed me home. 'That money's got to be here somewhere,' he said.

"I rushed upstairs to check out Stevie's so-called hiding places, while Pop searched the whole downstairs. I looked inside the spaghetti pot that Stevie kept under a blanket. I crammed my way through his secret shoe pile. I scavenged through his hat collection. No luck.

" 'Any luck?' I called out to Pop.

" 'Not yet,' he said. 'Check with Denny.'

"I squeaked the door open to Denny's room.

" 'Denny! Denny!' I tapped his pillow. 'My money is gone. My sock is missing. It was on the kitchen table. Did you see it?'

"Denny rolled over and squinted his eyes.

" 'What time is it?' asked Denny.

" 'Great, just great,' I said to myself as I closed the door to Denny's room. Denny didn't know where my money was. He didn't even know it was nearly noon.

"I went downstairs and found Pop in the kitchen.

" 'It's not upstairs,' I said to Pop. 'I looked all over. It's gone.'

"Just then, Pop pitched his thumb toward a pink note on the refrigerator:

Went to library.
Stevie and Patches
with me.
Love,
Mom xox

"Pop opened the kitchen cabinet and grabbed two granola bars.

" 'Come on,' he said. 'Let's go.'

Mrs. Wagner blew the school-yard whistle. "All *outstanding* boys and girls please line up for class," she bellowed through the megaphone.

"What happened next, Big Hig?" Josh asked.

"No talking, please," Mrs. Wagner said.

Josh shrugged his shoulders and lined up with the rest of the *outstanding* students of Franklin Elementary. At least my mother had packed me an *outstanding* lunch. I needed the strength. After all, I was just about to come face-to-face once again with the *outstanding* General Fromme.

NOW HEAR THIS!
REPORT TO BATTLE STATIONS!
THE SHIP IS GOING DOWN!

Chapter Eight
An Illuminating Mess

Outstanding Joke:

Question: Why did the centipede cross the road?
Answer: To get to the other side.

I was not in a funny or original mood.

When we settled back into the classroom, Josh Mendez asked an *outstanding* question.

"Miss Fromme, isn't Brian's story like a *verbal* sloppy copy?"

If I would have had braces, you would have been able to see them flashing a smile in the afternoon sun. Josh was right! I meant to give Miss Fromme a *verbal* sloppy copy all along! It was an experiment.

Miss Fromme thought about it for a moment.

"You could say that, Josh," Miss Fromme said.

Could this be true? Was Miss Fromme actually going to set me free and believe my bonafide story? A rush of relief swept over me. I was no longer a captive! Blue skies were on their way.

Suddenly Miss Fromme arched her eyebrows. You could even say that she looked kind of sorry for what she was about to say next.

"However," said Miss Fromme. "That was not the assignment. The assignment was a *written* sloppy copy, and in all fairness to everyone, Brian did not do that."

"But his money was stolen!" said Fareed.

"He was just about to go and get Stevie," Joelle hollered.

"Harry Harrington, that flea!" said Zachary.

"Excuse me," Miss Fromme said. "But would this entire class like to stay in for recess tomorrow? Brian, may I see you for a moment?"

I buried my head in my hands. I felt the comfort of what an ostrich must feel like when it hides its head in the sand.

There was a knock on the classroom door. I looked up. It was our principal, Mr. Zifferman.

"Good afternoon, Miss Fromme," Mr. Zifferman said. "Good afternoon, *outstanding* students."

He lifted his shoulders and squeezed his eyes like a baby who just got tickled.

"I would like to introduce you to our new student teacher, Mr. Minty. Mr. Minty comes to Franklin Elementary fresh from State University," Mr. Zifferman said.

". . . Freddy, the Freshman, the freshest kid in town . . ."

Oh no! One of Stevie's so-called entertainment songs was stuck inside my brain.

"Do you mind if we stay and observe for a while?" Mr. Zifferman asked.

"Not at all," said Miss Fromme. "Brian Higman was just about to finish a story."

"Is that right, Brian?" asked Mr. Minty.

"I'm kind of at the end," I said, hoping to change the *outstanding* Mr. Minty's mind.

All of a sudden I understood the difference between my life and the life of an ostrich. An ostrich would never have to speak in front of a principal or a new student teacher. I sideswiped a look at Robby Zao. He was shaking his head up and down like a bird that was trying to talk.

"That's all right," Mr. Zifferman told me. "Just make believe we're not even here."

I raised my eyes. I had to do it.

"Well," I said without even blinking. **"I was just about to go to the library with my pop to see if my mother knew where my missing sock with the money was."**

Miss Fromme cleared her throat.

"Go on," said Mr. Zifferman.

"I had a sneaky suspicion that my little brother, Stevie, could be at the bottom of the missing money.

"When I got to the library, Patches was tied to the bench outside. He wagged his tail when he saw me coming.

" 'Good boy, Patches,' I said. And I gave him a pat.

"Inside, Stevie had made himself perfectly comfortable on the floor of the young-readers' section. He was taking the leftover clothespins that Mrs. Saha, the librarian, hadn't used to hang up her decorations and was attaching them to his shirt.

" 'Look! I'm a porcupine,' Stevie said, standing up when he saw me.

"The clothespins were sticking out in crazy directions.

" 'Stevie,' I said. 'I have something really important to ask you.'

"By now my face was covered in sweat. I was panting.

" 'What's wrong?' my mother asked. She brushed my hair back with her hand.

" 'Mom!' I said. 'Did you see my sock? I left it on the table. It had my money inside. I was going to buy my guitar this morning, but somebody took my money.'

" 'You're going to buy a guitar?' asked my mother.

" 'I saw the sock,' said Stevie.

"I turned around. 'I knew it!' I yelled.

"Stevie saw the look on my face. It was the same look that I had the time he took my favorite shirt and used it to dress up a snowman.

"That's when Stevie threw his sailor hat on the floor and made one of his so-called beeline dashes, crashing his way past Mrs. Saha and charging out the door.

TREE WARS
BIRDS

" 'Better go after him,' Pop told me.

" 'And come right back,' said my mother."

I stopped talking. It felt like a good time to take a break.

"Thank you, Brian," Mr. Zifferman said. "Later on, you can stop by my office and tell me the rest."

Miss Fromme cheerfully showed them both to the door.

I let out a breath that could have blown any stratus, cirrus, or cumulus clouds straight across the sky.

Josh Mendez raised his hand.

"No more questions," Miss Fromme said.

"But Stevie ran away," I said. "I tried to catch him, but I'm not a fast runner."

I sat back down as soon as I said it. I had crossed the war line. General Fromme did not like calling out. Ana Newburg raised her hand.

"Miss Fromme," she said. "Brian's story gave me a connection."

A connection? I thought. Wasn't that another one of Miss Fromme's famous mottos for writing? Make the connections whenever you can.

"When Brian told us about his little brother, it reminded me of my little sister, Bella," said Ana. "Every time we bring Bella to the supermarket, she takes cans off the shelves and puts them in our wagon. I could write a story about that."

Wait a minute. Was Ana trying to help me? I gave her a smile just in case she was. And then I took another chance.

"My brother was lost," I said to Miss Fromme. My arms began to wave and spin like a carnival entertainer. "We couldn't find him anywhere."

Miss Fromme was not smiling.

Her face looked flushed. She smacked down her book.

The battlefield is getting smaller. Enemy tanks are moving in. We need more troops! Quick! To the foxhole!

"It's practically the end," I said without thinking. I was wishing I had a white flag to wave.

"It *is* the end," Miss Fromme said. Her patience was gone. Her limit had been tested. "You will not be taking up any more of my class time," she said. "See me after school, Mr. Higman."

The ruling was in. I, Big Hig, would not be seeing the light of day for a good solid week. But that didn't seem to bother Miss Fromme. She went right on with her lessons.

"Writers' journals open and ready," Miss Fromme said for the second time today. "Kayla, what did you write about yesterday? And how did you illuminate the moment?"

"I wrote about the expression on my grandmother's face as my mother lit the candles on her birthday cake," she said.

"Very nice," Miss Fromme said. "How about you, Martin?"

Martin Adaji pointed his finger. "I saw a squirrel. His tail was fluffy and bent like a comma. That's all I wrote," said Martin.

"Good simile," said

Miss Fromme. "Boys and girls, you have twenty minutes to illuminate a moment. If you can't think of anything, look inside your journals for your seed ideas. Ready? Begin."

Miss Fromme set the timer and we all got to work.

I spiraled to a clean page and found my pencil. Before I wrote, I pictured the whole thing in my mind.

I left the library running after Stevie, following his trail of clothespins. "Hooooooow woooow," Patches was howling near the library bench.

"You can't leave that dog here," Mrs. Saha said. "He'll upset the whole neighborhood."

"Take Patches with you," my mother called after me. "And come right back with Stevie."

I looked for Stevie down the block.

"There he is," I shouted to Pop. "I'll get him."

It wasn't hard to see my brother. Stevie was the only kid running down the block wearing a raccoon hat with clothespins falling off him. He made a quick getaway into somebody's backyard.

Where was he going? I got to the driveway and stopped.

"Hello, Brian," Mrs. Confrontini said. "Are you enjoying your weekend so far?"

Mrs. Confrontini, the school secretary, was watering the flowers on her porch. I never even knew she lived there. "Hello," I said. Not sure what to say next.

Patches sniffed the edge of her lawn.

I scribbled down what happened next.

"Are you looking for something?" Mrs. Confrontini asked me.

Mrs. Confrontini did not have radar. My feet were stepping from side to side. My shirt was hanging out of my pants and one of my sneakers was untied.

"I'm looking for my little brother," I said. "You haven't met him yet."

This was before she had the pleasure of meeting Stevie today when he brought my lunch to school with my mother.

"What does he look like?" asked Mrs. Confrontini.

I shook my head at what I was about to say.

"He's about this big," I said, holding my hand up to here.

"Yes?" said Mrs. Confrontini.

"And he has on a raccoon hat with earflaps that snap underneath," I said.

"Yes," said Mrs. Confrontini.

". . . And clothespins sticking out of his shirt."

Mrs. Confrontini tapped her watering can. "I did see a boy who looked like that," she said. "I think he went in there."

Riiiiiiiiiing! The buzzer went off on Miss Fromme's desk.

"Time's up," she said. She clicked off the timer.

And the rest of the day was a blank.

When the three o'clock bell rang, I was startled out of my social studies book. "Ponce de León," I said as Miss Fromme mentioned something about discovering Florida.

The class stood up and began to gather their books and backpacks and jackets from the hall closet. Some of them made sure they had copied down their homework assignment for tomorrow. Others, like me, simply slid their social studies books into their desks and waited to see Miss Fromme. Josh and Robby huddled around.

"We're still starting the band, right, Big Hig?" Robby asked me.

"It's just a matter of time," I said.

Miss Fromme began to erase the board.

"Good luck," said Josh. "Things can't get much worse."

I rubbed my head. "You wish," I said. It was the story of my life.

Chapter Nine
The Last Chance

EXTRA!

Brian Higman sets universal record for most detentions in world history.

When the classroom was empty, Miss Fromme made some space on her desk. She pushed aside some books and folders and papers and then waited for me to step forward.

"I'm really sorry, Miss Fromme," I said.

I kicked the leg on her desk by mistake.

"You had a busy weekend, Brian," Miss Fromme said. She almost sounded nice.

I tried to remember what Denny had told me to do if Miss Fromme ever sounded nice. I scoured my brain. He never said anything. I was on my own.

caution: ALL transmitters are about to BLOW. THIS IS NOT A TEST.

"Miss Fromme," I said. "I'm not trying to fool you. Everything I told you is true."

Miss Fromme opened her top desk drawer. She took out a box of crackers and placed three on a napkin for me.

"Here," she said. Then she pushed up her chair. "Why don't you tell me the rest."

"I looked for Stevie all over Mrs. Confrontini's yard. I looked behind the concrete birdbath and inside the garden shed. I looked under some bushes and got little green pieces of fern stuck in my hair. But I couldn't find him.

"Patches began to pull on his leash and bark in a different direction. He must have picked up Stevie's scent.

" 'Good boy, Patches,' I said, letting him take the lead.

"Patches led me three houses down from

WHO
WHAT
WHERE
WHEN
WHY
HOW
FIVE SENSES
SMELL
SOUND

Mrs. Confrontini's house right to where Harry Harrington lived. That's when I saw Stevie.

"He was sitting on the front steps with Harry's two beautiful older sisters. One beautiful sister was helping Stevie untangle a couple of twigs that got twisted in his T-shirt. The other beautiful sister was straightening out his raccoon hat. I had never exactly met Harry Harrington's two beautiful older sisters. And this did not seem like the best time to introduce myself.

" 'He's so cute,' the first beautiful sister said to me. 'Is he your brother?'

" 'We're thinking of keeping him,' the other beautiful sister said.

"I was just about to say, 'Take him,' when I realized they might want to trade in Harry for Stevie.

" 'He's mine,' I said, raising my voice.

"Stevie got up. He bent his knees and jumped off the porch.

" 'Geronimo!' Stevie yelled. 'You'll never catch me while I'm still alive!'

"What was my mother teaching him at home? I rushed a quick good-bye to the sisters and took off after my brother.

"I held on to Patches's leash as we chased Stevie home.

"Denny's band was already rehearsing. The bass kick on the drum thumped like a heartbeat from inside my house. I could hear my brother's voice singing deep and low. Harry Harrington wailed out two lead notes.

"I stopped dead. The band was rehearsing. Harry was back from Myers's Music. Did he buy my guitar? I had to see. I pushed the basement window open. I couldn't tell. I stretched my neck. I thought I saw it.

" 'Hoooow wooooow!' Patches pulled away from the leash and began to bark up the maple tree.

" 'Stevie,' I mumbled. I ran to the tree and shook my fist.

" 'Where is my money?' I yelled to him.

"My brother had climbed up the maple again. There he was curled up on a branch. Stevie threw some leaves on my head.

" 'I'm not coming down,' he told me.

Miss Fromme stopped me right at the good part. I waited for the final blow.

"First of all," Miss Fromme said. "I can tell

you right now that this will never happen again."

"Never, Miss Fromme," I said.

"And second of all," Miss Fromme went on. "I would like to tell you, Brian, that everything you told the class this morning *and* this afternoon is exactly the kind of story that you could be writing down on paper."

I knew it had been a long day for me, but that didn't make any sense.

"Brian," she said. And she patted her desk. "I want you to write down the rest of your story."

"You mean I'm getting a second chance?"

"Write like you're talking to me," said Miss Fromme. "Remember, this is your sloppy copy."

I took out a blank piece of paper. I wanted to get this off my chest. I also had to get home for the family meeting.

Brian Higman *Miss Fromme*

I was frantically shaking my fist up a tree when Ace Randall, the bass player in Questions No Answers, asked, "What are you doing?"

Her long brown hair was dyed blue on one side. She flipped it back.

"Stevie's up there," I said.

My brother Denny had stepped outside the basement and stood around the tree with the rest of the band.

Denny looked up. Stevie threw more leaves.

"Is this about your sock?" Denny asked me, brushing leaves off his shirt.

"It doesn't matter anymore," I said. "Harry already bought the guitar."

Harry Harrington made a face.

"Dude," said Harry. "Your pop saved the day. No way was I going to get into a family argument and buy that Stratocaster. He said that guitar was already yours."

In one fat second I loved my pop more than anything else in the world.

I didn't feel so bad about Harry either.

When my parents came back from the library, Pop got Stevie out of the tree.

"That was a plumb dandy mess you got yourself into," Pop told Stevie as he edged him down a ladder.

Stevie ran into my mother's arms. "Flo!" he cried. "I was stuck."

In the kitchen my parents sat us all down at the table.

"One of you will be punished," Pop said. "Which one will it be?"

All I could think of was, Great, punish Stevie. If it wasn't for him none of this would've happened. I would've already had my guitar. I would've had my homework done. I wouldn't be in this stupid kitchen. It was all Stevie's fault.

Stevie was sitting on the kitchen chair. His feet didn't even touch the floor.

"Punish me," I said to Pop. "I was the one who was supposed to bring him back to the library. I'm sorry I lost my temper."

Pop squinted an eye at me and patted my back.

"That's right, Brian," Pop said. "Bringing back Stevie was your responsibility. And just for recognizing that fact, you will not be punished this time. Sometimes a person can learn his lesson by having the gumption to admit it."

"Wow, thanks," I said. And I hugged him tight. I even gave Stevie a little rub, though I washed my hands right after.

Mom held the peanut butter jar in her hand. "Let's get this straight once and for all," my mother said. I looked up at the ceiling my mother was about to hit.

"Stevie, did you take Brian's sock?" she asked.

My little brother was sniffling into a napkin.

"No," said Stevie. "I didn't."

"It just didn't disappear," said my mother.

Pop took out his wallet and gave me twenty dollars. "In the meantime," he said, "how about we take a walk back to Myers's Music and put down a deposit on that guitar before anybody else decides to buy it."

My pop was a genius.

"I'm finished, Miss Fromme." I handed Miss Fromme my sloppy copy. I looked in my notebook to double-check that I had written down all my homework assignments.

"Thank you, Brian," said Miss Fromme. "I'll look forward to reading it."

RAH! RAH! The Loser ties in OVERTIME!

"And, Brian," Miss Fromme called as I was nearly free out the door. "There will be no more chances."

Chapter Ten
The Outstanding and Exuberant Brian Higman

I walked home from school in a fog. The sloppy copy was done. That was a load off my mind. But I still had the weight of the missing money on my brain.

When I finally arrived home from school, I opened the door to find everyone waiting for me in the living room for the family meeting. My mother was sitting on her piano bench with Stevie and Patches nearby.

Stevie was wearing only one hat this afternoon. It was the sailor hat. He was also wearing a pair of blue mittens with one of my mother's aprons tied around his neck like a cape. Pop and Denny were sitting on the couch alongside Harry Harrington and Darleen and Cynthia, Harry's two beautiful sisters.

"What's going on?" I asked. I dumped my backpack on the rug.

Stevie held out his arms like a game-show host.

"Hooow! Wow!" Stevie said. He crawled on his hands and knees with his mittens. *"Ruff! Ruff!"* Stevie panted and sniffed around.

Patches wagged his tail.

"When does it end?" I asked my mother.

Stevie kept barking and acting like a dog. He shook his head. He licked at the air. He pretended to dig for a bone under the rug.

"Ta! Da!" said Stevie as he clapped his mittens and pulled out the missing sock!

"My sock!" I said. "I can't believe it." I pulled it away, and Patches jumped up. He tried to wrestle the sock from my hand.

"He's the robber!" Stevie yelled, pointing a mitten at Patches. Then Stevie took a so-called flying leap off two pillows and yanked the sock from his paws.

So that was it? The mystery was solved.

I took my seat at the family meeting and listened to the story from Stevie.

It seemed that today, while I was in class,

Stevie had gone into the backyard to look for worms. Spying on worms was one of Stevie's so-called science experiments. While he was carefully laying the slimy serpents back into the dirt, he noticed Patches sniffing around near Pop's garage. This was not unusual. Patches is a big sniffer. But then Patches began to dig something up.

Guess what it was! You guessed it. My sock. Patches had buried it and Stevie had caught him returning to the scene of the crime.

Well, I never would have suspected that a

dog could be a robber. I am not even sure if you can call a dog a robber. All I know is that Patches was the one who took it. Patches was the first one down the back kitchen steps the morning I left with Pop to buy my guitar. He must have smelled my sock. Liked it. Chewed it around. Then decided to keep it for himself.

What a dog!

The next morning I couldn't wait to get to school. I placed my peanut butter jar complete with money and sock on top of my desk where I knew it would be safe. Stevie would watch it for me.

I finished my cereal and put my bowl inside the dishwasher. I checked my backpack to make sure that I had all my homework.

My mother checked my forehead.

Stevie and Patches came shuffling down the stairs.

"Bye, Brian," Stevie said. I gave him a wave.

"See you later, Flo," I said to my mother as I whistled out the door.

Did I happen to mention that Ana Newburg was no longer my ex-best friend? I walked right up to her in the school yard this morning and said, "Ana, today I am going to buy my guitar.

"Fact number one," I said. "We think you'd make an outstanding bass player. Fact number two: We want to start a band with gumption. Fact number three: . . ."

Fact number three? The *gumption* threw me off.

"Big Hig doesn't mess with the facts," Robby told her.

"We're calling ourselves The Pitt," said Josh. "Since we'll be practicing in Big Hig's basement."

Ana rubbed the tips of her fingers. I'll bet she had calluses just like mine.

"Okay," said Ana. "I'll be in the band. But I'm not quitting the cello. And Nadine is still my friend."

Nadine Ali shook the charms on her bracelet. "Maybe I can play tambourine?" she asked.

My life was beginning to take a new turn.

I had an idea for a letter I would write to *The Franklin:*

Dear Franklin Newsletter,

As a neighborhood reader, I would like to compliment you on your creative paper, The Franklin Newsletter, Someday, when I finally take over, and write my head off, I will tell you how it saved my life.

It has been a pleasure doing business with you.

Yours truly,

Brian Higman

Mr. Zifferman was happy to see me. I was happy to see him.

It was my turn to be the loudspeaker announcer. I told him the rest of my story and then took a seat next to Mrs. Confrontini. When the Pledge of Allegiance was over, Mr. Zifferman handed me a piece of paper.

"All set?" he asked.

"All set," I said.

The loudspeaker crackled.

"The word of the day is *exuberant,*" I read,

making sure that I did not hold my mouth too close to the microphone. "E-x-u-b-e-r-a-n-t. It is an adjective that means enthusiastic or lively. Today there will be no *exuberant* fire drills," I said. "We will be having *exuberant* chicken nuggets and an *exuberant* recess outside with the *exuberant* Mrs. Wagner after lunch."

Mrs. Confrontini turned off the switch.

"By the way," she said. "I'm glad that everything worked out with you and your missing sock. That story you were telling Mr. Zifferman sounded quite *exuberant.*"

I was just about to tell Mrs. Confrontini that it was *not* a story, but then I realized it really was.

"It's historical nonfiction," I said.

In the classroom Miss Fromme handed back the sloppy copies from yesterday—including mine. Of course, there were a mess of suggestions and corrections, but I, Big Hig, did not really mind. I planned on keeping my five senses ready and alert for action. Sight, sound, smell, taste, and touch. My pad and pencil were in my top pocket. A true writer is always prepared to write. That was my new motto.

Chapter Eleven
A Happy Ending

After school, on the way back from Myers's Music, I carried my red-and-black Stratocaster in the new guitar case that Denny and Harry were able to get me for a bargain price. Even my pop had left work early to be a part of the *outstanding, exuberant,* and monumental occasion.

I guess you could say it was a family event.

My mother and Patches had showed up, too. Along with Darleen and Cynthia who held Stevie's hands while we were in the store.

"Twinkle, twinkle, little guitar," Stevie sang.

"It's a beauty," Mr. Myers said. He counted out my money and tucked it into the register.

When I got home I played my guitar until it was time for supper. My mother whipped up my personal favorite–spaghetti and meatballs.

"This is delicious," said Darleen.

"Mrs. Higman, may I have the recipe?" Cynthia asked.

Harry Harrington's two beautiful older sisters also said they'd be happy to stop by tomorrow to keep an eye on Stevie, if that was okay with my mother.

"Yes," I said. "That would be great. You're welcome to come by the house anytime."

As you can imagine, everybody went crazy when they heard about my guitar.

"You did it, Big Hig," said Robby Zao. "We're starting a band."

"Nice work, Hig," said Josh. He grabbed my hand and shook it.

The brand new day seemed destined to be bright.

Ana was the first one to put her homework into the homework bin on Miss Fromme's desk. Robby came back with Josh after accompanying him to the nurse. And Miss Fromme was standing in front of the white board, ready to set her timer.

"Okay, class," Miss Fromme said. "Fifteen minutes to write about a topic. Remember to visualize before you write and use your senses. Look through your journals for seed ideas if you need inspiration."

I flipped through my writer's notebook to see if I had any ideas.

Fishing trip with family . . . another zero . . . tomatoes are not only vegetables . . . a boy with gumption . . .

"Writers ready?"

"Miss Fromme," I said. I raised my hand.

I was just about to ask her if I could share a very descriptive and illuminated story about how our band, The Pitt, was going to enter the Franklin Elementary School Talent Show this spring.

But then I decided not to. Instead, I took out my sharpened pencil, smoothed open a clean page of paper, and wrote:

Brian Higman   Miss Fromme

It all started yesterday when my little brother, Stevie, had a so-called idea...

THE PITT

Miss Fromme

Chapter Twelve
Big Hig's "FACTS" for Writing

Big Hig's "FACTS" for Writing

1. Pay attention to the ordinary things that happen in your life and teach yourself to write them down.

2. Write about what you know OR research what you don't.

3. Organize your story with a beginning, a middle, and an end.

4. Think of the setting and the characters

5. Visualize the scene in your head.

6. Choose outstanding and descriptive word

7. Illuminate the moment including the five senses.

8. Don't be afraid to write with your voice.

9. Take a break if you get stuck.

10. DON'T GIVE UP!!!

BIG HIG'S DISASTROUS NEWSLETTER

as keyboarded on my computer by Brian Higm

WRITER'S JOURNAL UPDATE

Dear Writer's Journal,

Today I do not have my homework and I am about to get another zero.

Yours truly,
Guess who?

A PERSON WHO CAN MAKE A BIG DEAL OUT OF ANYTHING

Ana is the kind of person who can make a big deal out of anything. Last week when Martin Adaji put a tomato in his fruit painting, Ana made one of her big deals about whether a tomato was a fruit or a vegetable. I was glad when Mrs. Chila said that a tomato could be considered as both. It was a fruit that was used as a vegetable. In the plant group it was actually considered to be a berry.

CAUTION:

Planets are crisscrossing.

This is **NOT** your lucky day.

← my mother

BRIAN HIGMAN'S MOTHER FINALLY HITS CEILING!

Really nice kid banished to Siberia for LIFE. See more inside.

TRY THIS NEW RECIPE!

SLOW-ROASTED SURPRISE

Mix one big kid,
one late homework.
Add one angry teacher.
Turn on heat.
Stand back.
Expect anything!

artwork done by the outstanding Big Hig